Several Possible Conclusions

Also by Randall Miller

The Ability to Reason
Random Samples

About the cover

The cover is an *AI* generated illustration prompted only by the words, *'Several Possible Conclusions.'*

This was a suggestion from Collin Miller.

Graphic design work by Brett Grimes Design
www.brettgrimes.com

Several Possible Conclusions

Randall Miller

Kingdom For A Horse
Co-Authored by
Collin Miller

Several Possible Conclusions

First Edition
ISBN- 979-8-9854997-6-6

Dedication

This work is dedicated to my son Collin Miller who encourages me to pursue writing as both a passion and a personal journey.

Also to the authors of the many books I have read throughout my life which have inspired me to think outside of my own place in the world.

Rod Serling, L.P. Davies, Isaac Asimov, Arthur C. Clarke and L. Frank Baum come to mind.

Table of Contents

Kingdom for a Horse

Security Breach

The silent alarms went off first. The only visible sign of this which might be apparent on the faces of security personnel within view of the office staff or public would be a slight intensity of purpose. The training which they had received kept them from displaying emotion. These men and women were the best of the best. They were like coiled springs keeping the powerful force of their kinetic energy at bay… until needed.

The building alarms went off next. There was more than one tone used for these alarms. Each tone was dedicated to a specific alert. Everyone who worked in this building received frequent training on how to react when hearing an alarm. Different tones called for different actions. The tone sounding at the moment indicated to all who were in the building that they were not alone. There was an intruder, or possibly a group of intruders, which had gained entrance to the building and shattered the sanctity of their workplace.

Within seconds the building was in lockdown and the employees were evacuating to their assigned safe zones. Additional security personnel seemed to materialize out of thin air. Every stairwell, every elevator, every access point for entry or exit within the building was suddenly under the watch of these highly specialized security guards. The employees safely tucked away in the safe zones would never know that their security team had also dispatched snipers to the rooftop of the building. This all happened within the span of ninety seconds.

One thing was certain. This was *not* a drill. Despite every safeguard, despite every precaution, *someone* had gained access to the building. The information was confirmed quickly and passed on to senior management. The man and woman who occupied the two offices at the crown of the building were now in their own specially designed safe zone.

It was not unlike the war room at the White House. They were now receiving timely reports of all security personnel activities.

Although both the man, Albus and the woman, Regina knew the gravity of the current situation they found themselves in, neither would allow emotion to dictate their actions. This scenario had never actually happened before now. The rote actions of both the office personnel and the security team spoke to the ritual of training they engaged in frequently.

The elephant in the room was fear but none would acknowledge its' presence. The security team went about their business quickly yet thoroughly. It had only been minutes since the alarm sounded when images began to appear on the screens in the senior staff safe room. The images showed a person running through a corridor somewhere in the bowels of the building. This person seemed to know *exactly* where they were going. It was difficult to discern if it was a man or a woman. The security team did not discriminate. An intruder was an intruder and they must be neutralized, possibly without harm.

The screens were refreshing rapidly as more images were being displayed. As the intruder was running in each of the images the screens continued to refresh. Suddenly an image was frozen on the screen. The man and woman watched as the image was enhanced again and again until it was clear enough to make out the features hiding behind a ball cap, an eye patch and a COVID mask. The intruder suddenly turned toward the camera, pulled down the mask and mouthed some words before running off. The man and woman who were watching, Albus and Regina, reacted in unison at what they saw.

"JONI!!!"

Before leaving their safe place the couple was apprised of the situation to the extent that security had now determined. It was a good thing that they had managed to capture an image as she was leaving the building but there was a greater concern for them to consider. How did she gain access and how was it that she was able to elude the security precautions in place to detect and prevent entry? These questions demanded answers. It went without saying that a *former* employee, as she was, with top level security clearance as she had *had*, would most likely be able to defeat the systems in place. This was precisely why upgraded security measures had been installed. This could mean only one thing. There was still someone in place loyal to this person who had sought to bring down the company. That person needed to be found. At all costs.

A new tone was sounded throughout the building. It was an all-clear. Return to stations. Within minutes the employees in this building, nearly a hundred strong, were back at work.

As though nothing had ever happened.

Bad bishop

Albus touched Regina lightly on her shoulder to gain her attention. Regina turned to see concern etched into her husband's face. He seemed to reflect for a moment before he asked, "Were you able to make out what she said?"

"Yes."

"Was it what I think she said?" Albus was speaking with trepidation.

Regina nodded her head and responded icily, "She was speaking *to* us you know. *Only to us*."

Albus answered with a look that spoke volumes.

"For a person who doesn't talk much, she said a lot." Regina paused, then they both spoke in unison, saying the two words Joni mouthed that chilled them to the bone.

"Not safe."

Openings

The building which housed *NRG* Dynamics was an imposing structure. All glass and steel, it rose from the ground at an unusual angle defying gravity much the same as its products defied conventional power systems. This was a building whose tenants were forward-thinking and whose mission it seemed was to challenge the laws of science to discover what's-- *NEXT*.

Lana Taylor walked at a swift pace on the curving path which lead up to the building's grand façade. 'Follow the yellow brick road' she thought to herself as she noticed that there was a slight tinge of yellow to the walkway. There were no steps at this business campus, only curving, graduated walkways. All were welcome here. No roadblocks to prevent entry. That's not to say that there was an absence of security. The opposite was true. This was possibly *the* most highly secured building in the area but it was a *kinetic* security, hidden below the surface, a powerful force in reserve yet always ready to strike.

Lana was on her first big assignment for the tech magazine for which she worked. She had graduated with a journalism degree but her first love had always been mechanical engineering. Although she had fallen short of credits and gone a different direction with her education her heart remained firmly with the fascination she had for how things are designed and built. More so actually in how problems are *solved* to *allow* for things to work.

Lana had fought hard for this assignment, for this opportunity to interview one of the greatest scientific minds of her time, Albus King. This man was the Chief Operating Partner of Operations on record of *NRG* Dynamics but as is the case with many a self-made billionaire, the road to his success involved the efforts, and failures, of a great many others. That was the story which Lana hoped to tell.

Lana glanced at the tenant monument directory but did not stop. She was unfamiliar with both "LUCID" and "FM Robotics" but she gave herself a silent reminder to ask the question. Were these two companies *just* tenants? Or did they play some role in the future of *NRG* Dynamics?

Prior to entering the building Lana stopped to turn and take in a panoramic view of not only the business campus but the area surrounding it as well. The choice of location for the home of *NRG* Dynamics was to her a mystery. This was a business campus that had the look and feel of "The Getty," an opulent and expansive structure perched on the side of a mountain. It was the pure essence of The Getty albeit if it had been constructed in some future time. At odds with The Getty was the fact that this place was on the outlying slopes of the Santa Monica mountains. Big city meets the desert. How or why this building held a Los Angeles address was yet another mystery to unravel. At street level Lana saw only mountains to the west and desert to the east. Surprisingly, the sparse sands of Death Valley was actually equidistant to the bustling downtown activity of Los Angeles. This would not be the first anomaly which she would encounter.

Lana took a big breath, expelled it slowly then went inside the vestibule to pass through security. She sensed an incredible calm inside the building which helped her to feel at ease. Minutes later, after a thrilling elevator ride which shot her up to the highest floor in mere seconds, she was standing in the spaceship-like office of the man who had made all of this happen, Albus King.

Part One
The Interview

"You're on time."

"Yes, I appreciate that you are a busy man and I have no intention of wasting your time."

Albus had only thrown that statement out to gauge if this woman had been aware of the security breach. With any luck everything would have appeared normal upon her arrival.

"I appreciate that but my comment was more general in that most visitors see our LA address and *assume* that we are located near the city proper. We are not. Once they realize their mistake..."

"I used my GPS for navigation."

Albus snickered, "As do we all but... some folks," he paused before adding, "just don't *trust* it."

Lana laughed. "For me, it's more *appreciation* for the technology than *trust*."

Albus smiled. "I'm guessing that you are amongst the ranks of people who are still a bit unsure about where *AI* technology may take us in the not-too-distant future."

Lana was quick to reply, "And you're *not*?"

"Ms. Taylor," Albus began.

"Lana, please if you don't mind, Mr. King."

"Fine. Lana. And please, call me Alan."

"*Alan?* I thought your name was--"

"It is—. 'Albus.' Quite a bit of baggage to lug around, don't you think? I like 'Alan' better."

"Thank you, 'Alan'." Lana made a point of enunciating the name. "I appreciate that. I'm sorry. What was your comment in regard to *AI*?"

"*AI*." Alan said this as a statement rather than a question as though he may have just lost his place in a book he was reading. "Oh *that*! Yes. *AI*. *Artificial* Intelligence. Those two words fit together for me like 'jumbo shrimp.' A bit of a paradox. *AI*. Do I *embrace* it? Yes I do. But the better question is, does it scare the *shit* out of me? Yes. *Absolutely* it does."

"Well it would seem that we are off to a good start as I feel the same."

The two shook hands for the first time. Alan proffered a seat in front of his expansive desk which Lana readily accepted. To her surprise Alan chose to sit in the seat next to hers rather than the grand chair behind his desk which Lana took to be a warm and welcoming gesture. Not to mention that it would make her job of conducting the interview much easier as the proximity to him allowed her to read his body language and gauge his facial expressions better. Her original concerns about this man being guarded in his conversation were beginning to fade.

"Anagram."

"I'm sorry, what's that?" asked Lana.

"Our two names are an example of an anagram. Move the letters about and you get one or the other."

"Hmm, you're right. Interesting. You don't miss much do you?"

"Lana," Alan began, "I try not to miss *anything*."

"Fair enough. I will do my best to keep up."

Alan smiled. "You needn't feel that way, Lana. This is not a contest. You have my full attention," he paused, "*and* my respect. Where shall we begin?"

Lana understood that this was her moment, her greatest opportunity for an interview that could possibly *define* her career. It would be relatively easy, and great reading as well, to tell the story of *NRG* Dynamics as it is *now*, a mover and shaker in the energy business, privately owned and situated on a sprawling business campus *almost* in the middle of the desert! It would be topical to share how this company is owned and operated not just by Alan but rather by the complementing *team* of Alan *and* his wife, Regina. The quote, "behind every great man there is a great woman" came to mind.

This company, *NRG* Dynamics, had become an "embarrassment of riches" run by two amazing people, madly in love, who seemingly did not want or need the fame and fortune associated with their success. One thing that Lana had learned is that every dream, *every kingdom*, comes at a price. That was what she wanted. The *real* story, the story *behind* the story, the story that few actually knew and even fewer discussed. She felt that it was a story that Alan was probably burning inside to tell but his sense of propriety kept him from sharing. Lana believed that perhaps he has just been waiting for the right moment, and the right *person*, whom to tell. There was an energy in the air that suggested that the two may have telepathically agreed that that moment was *now*.

Lana, in her heart of hearts, believed that the best writers did not exchange "simple" words with "big words" just for the sake of making a piece appear more intellectual. It was her choice then to tell Alan's story almost verbatim as he spoke. Lana would even begin her article with Alan's epithetical comment, "The story of this company, and all those involved, can best be described as a '*chess match.*' With *real people*."

Opening Handshake

Twin sons of different mothers. In college the two boys were inseparable. The best of friends yet polar opposites but hey-- opposites attract, right?

Thaddeus Rex, (his real name, it graced his birth certificate), was jokingly nicknamed *"T-Rex"* by his group of party animal friends. Thad was the loud and boisterous one, always with a beer in hand (or something stronger).

Albus (his real name, although he preferred to be called Alan), was the quiet one, the token wallflower at every party, not much of a drinker, thirsty only for knowledge.

Although quite different socially, both boys were possessed of brilliant intellect. The major difference between the two was that Alan applied himself and Thad tended to chase a good time instead of a degree. Fortunately for Thad, laziness aside, he was both smart *and* lucky. At some point in time a professor (on a whim) had put the unlikely pair together on a project. While disaster may have been the anticipated result, the alchemy of the two actually caused the word "genius" to be tossed about. This was the beginning of their friendship and in time the impetus of the battle for the kingdom they would build together.

The two young men had a business startup while still in their senior year of college. It was an LLC known as "Chessmen Bros." The *"chessmen"* in the name referred to their penchant for playing what they laughingly called "full contact chess." Although evenly matched in their competitive spirit, there were grand disputes between the two but these were brotherly fights, not the disputes of angry men. Alan was the one who played strictly by the rules, always following the straight and narrow path. Thad, however, looked for every angle to *circumvent* the obstacles in his way. Rules and regulations were mere inconveniences. He never *admitted* to cheating, which was at some level *his* way of *not* being dishonest.

The *"bros."* part of their company name spoke to their kinship. Twin sons of different mothers to be sure. Despite their battles they were kindred spirits. While in college they always had the other's back, and every problem could be resolved over a few beers, (always fewer for Alan than for Thad). As time went on the disparity between the two began to grow. Even *before* the two would graduate and leave behind the microcosm of their college life for their "hello world" moment their friendship would be tested.

"You can be the moon and still be jealous of the stars." Gary Allan

This was a quote which Alan often felt matched what he would call the 'indignation' that he would get from Thad. Indignation, or perhaps it was just plain jealousy. Whatever label you might give it, it was a trait displayed by Thad that would spark controversy between the two for years to come. The first time this covetous nature reared its ugly head was when Alan invited his new girlfriend, Regina, to meet up with him one evening. An evening when Alan and Thad were already out together having a beer. And a good time.

A good time until Regina showed up. And then did not leave. *Ever.*

Thad felt like Alan's girlfriend was intruding on "their time." Thad's feelings in this regard would only grow stronger over the next few years. This jealousy driven animosity of his is precisely what opened the door for an opportunistic young lady named Quinn. She was known by her friends as *"Queenie"* due to her controlling personality and tendency to act like a prima donna. She was the *modern* definition of a diva to be sure.

On one particular evening when eventually Regina *did* leave, her absence gave Thad the golden opportunity he had been waiting for to share a secret he had been keeping from Alan. The secret involved a unique discovery he had made and he was quite eager to share how it could positively affect their future. This conversation was the genesis of their first business venture. It was in fact the catalyst for the business plan which lead to their "Chessmen Bros." start up.

Thad's enthusiasm about his discovery garnered Alan's full attention. He watched as Thad eagerly, almost *wildly*, jotted down the nature of his discovery on a cocktail napkin. He flipped the napkin over to sketch a few of his dream ideas which he believed to be possible with the development of his discovery.

Alan had done his best to control his skepticism as he began to think that this might be just another of Thad's crazy ideas of which there had been many. He was about to take a stab at popping Thad's balloon when an eavesdropping girl sitting at a nearby table heard Thad's raised and excited voice talking about an amazing "discovery." This girl heard opportunity knocking and she was eager to answer.

Quinn walked up to the table and placed her arm around Alan's shoulder. She met Thad's eyes with her own and said, "Sounds like a pretty good idea you got there but this one *here,*" jostling Alan a bit, "just isn't getting it, is he?"

"Can I *help* you?" Regina was back and she was in cat-fighting mode. She had only left to grab a beer and already some bitch was hanging all over her boyfriend.

Quinn responded without making eye contact. "Nope. I'm good. You fellas need anything from our server here?"

The scene is set. Strong *confident* female meets strong *abrasive* female. This should go well.

"I am *not* the *server*. That is my boyfriend, Alan." Regina pointed. "I will thank you to *remove* yourself from him." Regina had quite the strong tongue when necessary.

"Oh, *my bad*. Alan, it is my pleasure to meet you. My name is Quinn but—" she winked at Thad. "My *friends* call me *"Queenie"*."

A better name for her would be "trouble" thought Regina.

Alan, always a gallant gentleman, sought to make reparations and the proper introductions. "This is my buddy and soon to be business partner, Thad." Queenie shook hands with Thad. "And this is my girlfriend, and sometimes second mother, Regina." Alan laughed at his joke as did Thad. There was an icy staring contest being waged by the two girls as both kept their hands to themselves.

"Just curious, is *Regina* pronounced with a long "i" like *vagina?*" laughed Queenie, looking for support from the boys.

Regina was quick on her feet. "Well, everyone just calls me *"Reggie"* so I guess we won't need to hear *that* little comedic nugget of yours again, *will we*?" Regina had enough bottled rage riding behind that comment to stop a train.

Queenie was, however, immune to sarcasm and tugged on Thad's arm when she said, "Hey young man, I think we could be friends! What have you got on your napkin there?"

Everything that came after was a result of that singular moment in time with that one simple question. Queenie's unwelcome curiosity was at first only a splinter in Thad's, and Alan's, side. It grew over time. From splinter to dagger to sword, each more threatening than the last.

The Interview

"So *Queenie*, sorry, Quinn, was a thorn in your side from day one?" Lana poses a question.

"Putting it mildly yes. The events that lead to where we are today involve moves made mostly by the people who were empowered to make them. I observed every move and a fair share of the time these moves even met with my approval. It was the dark undertone of the moves for which I had little to no perspective. I have often been accused of being 'overly trusting' in my dealings with employees and friends."

"Don't be too hard on yourself. That accusation could be made of most of us."

"Yeah? Thanks for that but I think you understand my point. Quinn wanted "in" from the start. When she heard Thad sharing his ideas, the excitement in his voice, the plausibility of his dreams, well I guess that got her blood pumping. She saw dollar signs right away. She saw Thad as her meal ticket. To her credit she knew that Thad and I were committed partners in that venture. *Necessary* partners at that as neither of us could have built this company alone. There were *two* kings to conquer, not just one. She would use her womanly wiles on Thad—"

Alan cut himself short and laughed heartily at his comment. "Now *there's* something I never thought I would hear myself say!"

Lana laughed along with him before commenting, "Unfortunately true."

Alan nodded his head in agreement as he continued, "To win me over she would need to take a different route. She understood that we needed the best and brightest people to get us where we wanted to go. Once again, to her credit, she was one *hell* of a recruiter. We asked for the best and brightest and she delivered in spades. They were so, *so* bright. Thad and I were too immersed in our work at the time to even *begin* to see their dark side."

"The brightest lights are the ones which will blind you."

"Who said that?"

"I did. Just now."

Alan looked at Lana with reverence. "That, young lady, is a very profound statement. I thought it might have been a famous quote. I have a thing for quotes. I sure wish I could have had you whispering something like that in my ear a few years ago when all of this was going down. I was sorely in need of rational thinking at that time."

"Thank you for such a kind compliment however you did have Regina at your side, did you not?"

"Oh yes, Regina was my rock. Always has been, but—"

"But, what?"

"Well, Thad was my partner *too* and I felt like I owed it to him to keep an open ear to what he had to say."

"Even when he may have just been repeating what Quinn was telling him?"

Alan cast his eyes down for a moment before responding. He came back with, "Sadly, yes."

Lana had another question ready but chose instead to give Alan a moment as it looked as though he had something else he wished to share. Her patience paid off as he suddenly looked up and raised his hand in a "one more thing" gesture.

"By the way, if you don't mind."

"Go ahead, please. This interview is all about what *you* have to say." Lana was quick on her feet even when sitting.

"Thank you, it's just that I missed sharing something earlier."

Lana nodded to show her interest.

"Yes, well when Regina made the comment to Quinn that 'everybody calls me Reggie'..."

"Yes?"

"Well that is not entirely true. Or really even partly true."

"Oh-."

"Yes, *nobody* calls her "Reggie," or at least not many, that's for sure. I can probably count on one hand the number of people who feel comfortable in using that nickname."

"Really."

"Oh yes. Most of the employees simply refer to her as Ms. King," Alan held up a finger to indicate that there was more, "even though she *implores* them to call her Regina."

"Why *is* that do you think?"

"Respect. Plain and simple. Respect."

"Really."

Lana used one word replies whenever she wanted to hear more from her interviewee.

"Yes, well when you meet her you will see for yourself. Regina is the type of person who *commands* respect. Not verbally, and certainly not on purpose. It's just the way she carries herself. Her persona. She *exudes* control. While Quinn "practices" being the *boss*, Regina, well "leadership" is as natural for her as breathing. This place, this *company*, would not be what it is today without her."

The *true* story behind the *reported* story was beginning to take shape for Lana. This interview was going quite well. She felt it was time for her to dig in a bit more. To begin to understand who the other players were and what actions they had taken to help shape the company. She posed the question, were the four principals, Alan, Thad, Regina and Quinn involved at all with the hiring of the employees? This was the *ideal* question to ask as it turns out that the four of them each had a part in hand-selecting their team(s). It seemed that from day one "loyalty" was a keyword each was looking for in the resumes of their prospective employees.

Alan stated that he was unsure exactly of which people Quinn had brought in and which ones could be attributed to Regina (which spoke volumes), although as the story continued on those choices began to become more obvious. Alan began to tell the story.

"It started with Burton and Barry who had both been hired as interns. For a startup company with big dreams and little money Quinn used this intern hook masterfully to bring in bigger fish than we could at first afford. Wendell and Wilson were brought in at the same time. It was apparent at their orientation that there was already a clear divide in our company. We didn't see it but seemingly people from the outside picked up on it quickly. Burton and Barry sided with Quinn from day one while Wendell and Wilson, *of course*, saw Regina as the one to follow. Strange how that seemed to happen so early on in the process but there you go."

"May I stop you there?"

"Certainly. Do you have a question?"

"Yes, yes I do. You added "of course" when speaking of Wendell and Wilson. Just curious what that might have implied."

"Oh--, that. Sorry, I thought that you knew."

"Knew, what?"

"That Wendell is Regina's half-brother. Let me tell you something. Genius *runs* in her family. At an *Olympic* pace I might add."

"Half-brother. Is it a leap for me to think that this might have been an issue for Quinn? Perhaps even a leverage tool?"

"Not at all. We felt the same way so we kept it close to the vest. He has a different last name than her maiden name anyway so there was no obvious way for Quinn to make that leap. More than anything we needed Wendell on our team. That kid, not sure why I call him that since we *are* the same age, is brilliant. And as an engineer he possesses what I consider to be an incredibly unique skill."

"Oh really, and what is that?"

Alan leaned forward, eager to share. "He has an innate ability to explain even the most complex things in the simplest of terms. In other words, he could explain the DNA molecule to you and you would actually walk away understanding how the damn thing actually works."

"I'm sorry but I find that almost more amazing than everything else that you do here." Lana laughed to show that she was exaggerating her point.

"Trust me on that. If you meet him ask him something challenging. You will find his answer to be truly remarkable."

"Alright then, I might ask him why some people cut me off when driving just to get one car closer to a red light."

"Let's be fair, nobody knows why people do crazy stuff like that. He can only explain things that make sense." Alan laughed as did Lana.

"What about Wilson? Is he related as well?"

"To Regina? No. Long story, not related to Regina but he *is* Wendell's brother."

"Oh, well that's interesting."

"To say the least. Wilson was always a point of contention for Quinn, Regina and myself."

"Why is that if I may ask?"

"Simple answer. *True* answer. An acceptable answer for anyone, anyone that is not *ignorant*."

There was definite emphasis placed on the word “ignorant.” Lana hazarded a question.

“Quinn?”

“Yes. Quinn. You see Wilson is on the autistic spectrum.” Alan watched for a reaction from Lana and was pleased when he did not see one. He believed that he had good instincts about people and Lana was living up to his initial impression. “Wilson is classified as an ‘idiot savant,’ something which Quinn in all her ignorance struggled with mightily.”

“I’m curious. Is that wrong? I don’t wish to be insensitive.”

“Not at all. Clearly she had no idea what idiot savant means.”

“May I interrupt you just for a moment? I wish to be clear that *I* know what it means.”

“Well, let me ask you then. What do you *think* it means?”

“It means that,” Lana was careful with her words. This was obviously a sensitive subject for Alan and she wished to show no disrespect. “Let me start over. An idiot savant is an individual who has an exceptional aptitude in a particular field but may experience impairment in other things, like social functioning for example.”

“That is exactly correct. I applaud you for knowing that. Something tells me that if you did *not* know that you would have asked.”

“Well yes, certainly.”

Alan chuckled at what he was about to say. “Allow me to introduce to you Quinn, the black queen, whose initial response to this was, ‘why would a tech company hire an idiot’? No lie. That was her comment. Regina told me that that was the closest time she had ever come to striking another human being because at that moment she saw Quinn as less than human.”

“Wow, that’s--.” Lana was at a loss for words.

“Lana, I feel like I may have overshared just now. You may keep the gist of the interaction but please do not use the language. That was a private conversation. I hope you understand.”

Lana was nodding her head as she replied, “I do. I really do. And it seems to explain so much about Quinn’s *other* actions. Am I right about that?”

"I would say that you hit the nail on the head."

"Is there—" Lana paused, wanting to get this right. "Is there anything else which you would feel comfortable in sharing in regard to Wilson?"

Alan smiled. "Um, yes. Yes there is. That kid," Alan shook his head and rolled his eyes, "that kid is on an entirely different level when it comes to engineering and technology, science itself really."

Lana raised her eyebrows at this clearly effected by his comments.

Alan was quick to add, "Let me put it this way. With this amazing discovery that we had before us, Thad saw the *vision* of where we could go with it. Wilson, well Wilson saw the *path* to get us there. His name should be used with the same reverence as that of Stephen Hawking."

Lana gulped involuntarily. "Um, wow."

"Yep. Wow is the only word for it. But, as you know, his autism is for him like the wheelchair is for Hawking. It is the machine which allows him to function as he does and yet it is also the boundary which restricts him."

Lana waited, sensing there was more to be shared. She was correct.

"Wendell is a saint. He is Wilson's guardian angel. There is an unfathomable symbiosis between the two that has launched this company into another realm. Wendell is always there for Wilson but if asked both will tell you that Wilson, as the older brother, takes care of Wendell."

Alan was a bit teary-eyed as he added, "It's a beautiful thing."

Alan wiped his eyes and then was back to it, all business as he continued with the history of how the group of employees were brought on board.

"Warren, Wallace and Walter were hired shortly after Wendell and Wilson. The five of them bonded quickly so it was a given that the three new hires would find allegiance with Regina as well. Giving credit where credit is due, Queenie always had a commanding presence about her but one shouldn't sell Regina short. She had that rarest of skills, the ability to inspire loyalty. The employees loyal to Regina would defend her to their death which in a few unfortunate circumstances makes that statement *fact* rather than conjecture."

Alan paused, waiting for a follow up question from Lana. When it didn't come, he continued on.

"The company was growing quickly at that point in time and the company org chart was still a bucket full of water with employees bobbing for apples. As the company began to expand the individuals with graduate degrees and those poached from other companies for their expertise began to land where they fit best in the organization. This was always a company in flux, an organization filled with worker bees fighting amongst themselves to defend their queen. The real challenge was one of allegiance. Keep one indelible fact in mind. As there were *two* kings in this hierarchy there were also two *queens*. Since the time of the written word in recorded history there has been one undeniable truth; 'a house divided against itself cannot stand.'"

Upon hearing this last part Lana considered using *that* line as her title.

Addressing the Troops

It seemed to Alan as though a full team of eager professionals had been assembled and the time had come to put them on track with a singular goal. He had asked Regina to bring the group together for their first "all company" meeting. Alan initially had trouble with referring to it as such as it was *not* all-inclusive. There were other employees who handled mail, answered phones, took care of billing, etc. that worked at the company. Didn't they too have a stake in the company's future? Perhaps yes but Alan had to reconcile that *this* meeting was about what made this company *unique,* which was something they needed to keep safeguarded.

Alan had also asked that an organization chart be drawn up. He planned to share this *at* the meeting so everyone would know their place in the company. Job descriptions were revised in accordance with the org chart so all would understand how their responsibilities fit in line with those of others. Last but not least Alan, hopefully with Thad's support, intended to unveil the company's mission statement. Thad's commitment to the brand at that time, however, *already* seemed to be a concern.

Alan entered the conference room. Although he had made it a point to be early he could see that all attendees had already made their way into the room as well. That was a good sign. He went to the coffee station and pondered pouring himself a cup. He could use a strong cup of coffee; of that he was certain but—one of the first things he had learned about public speaking was to steer clear of hot liquids. They went right through you. Nothing worse than "having to go" when you knew you "had to stay." Alan had an important presentation to make. He smartly chose a bottled water instead.

"Wise choice."

"What's that? Oh yes, the water, just going to sip on it." Alan twisted the cap off and took only a sip. Regina smiled. Alan was *so* predictable at times.

"Will you need my support?"

"Every minute of every day. You know that." Alan gave Regina a peck on her cheek.

Regina retorted. "Thank you for that but *not* what I meant."

"I know what you meant. Thad should be up there with me delivering the message. We'll see if he steps up."

"You mean if "Queenie" *allows* him to."

"Don't--" Alan was shaking his head, clearly irked by Regina's comment. "Don't call her *that*. Her name is *Quinn*. Besides, Thad is a grown-up. He can make his *own* decisions."

"Tell *that* to his puppet master." Regina could not keep the smirk from showing on her face.

"Thad needs to know his place," Alan fired back. "And it's *not* at her feet."

Regina nearly spit out the drink she just took. Alan could be fiery at times. It took a lot to get him there but today's event was important. They were setting the stage for their future, for the rise of a new entity in the energy industry. Regina had no doubt in her mind that they were about to make history.

"Anything else troubling you? Better to get it pushed out of the way before you take the stage." Of course there was no stage. That was just a metaphor for the task he was facing.

"Troubling me? As a matter of fact there is," responded Alan.

"And what is that? What am I missing?"

"Well the whole idea of today's meeting is to bring us together. As one group."

"Okaaaay...," Regina drew out the word as if to say, 'and that means what?'

"I don't see a unified group."

"Of course not. It's a large room. People naturally tend to form little clusters within the larger group of those individuals that they know better or are more familiar with; you know that."

"Yes, Regina, I know how social interactions work. What I am *not* seeing is small clusters of friends interacting with one another before a meeting. What I *am* seeing, or what I *think* I'm seeing, is two factions finding their home turf before a battle."

"Don't be ridiculous. You're reading too much into it." Regina offered a brush-off hand wave gesture to support her statement.

"You say that you like you *think* you mean it." Alan looked her dead in the eyes.

"Well I *don't* if that makes you feel any better."

"You know, sometimes," Alan said plaintively, "it might be appropriate to bullshit me. Just a little." He used his fingers to indicate a pinch to illustrate his point.

"Noted. Hey, pay attention! Your factions are seated. You better get up there killer, before Thad steals your thunder!" They both laughed at that knowing that Thad would sooner be drinking a beer than delivering a co-owner's speech on the future of their company.

Alan walked to the front of the room, introduced himself and then welcomed the group to their first "all company" meeting. It was unnerving to see so many faces whose names he did not know let alone their background or place in the company. That would be resolved to some extent today. Each member of the group had been advised that the plan was to go around the room and allow each person to stand up, state their name, their title and to share what skill or expertise they brought to the table. Alan had wanted to attach a theme to the meeting. He thought *'We're All Cogs in The Wheel'* sounded pretty snazzy. Regina shot it down summarily stating that it was demeaning and missed the point entirely. She of course was right. Again.

Out of the corner of his eye Alan caught sight of Quinn nudging Thad to get up and join him "on stage." Quinn always wanted her piece of the pie, even if she had to share it with someone else. Alan introduced Thad as his equal business partner and then gave a short tutorial on how the two met and soon after formed the "Chessman Bros." company.

Thad completely surprised both Alan *and* Regina by taking his place "center stage" and then eloquently sharing that there is an evolution to all things in life. Alan stepped aside to let Thad take the spotlight as he went on to compare the "Chessman Bros." company to the chrysalis of a butterfly safely ensconced within its cocoon.

Alan looked to Regina at the back of the room and mouthed the words, *"What the fuck?!"*

Quinn caught sight of that interplay and muttered a response to Alan under her breath, *"Dick!"*

Thad wasn't done. Quinn had spent hours the previous night preparing Thad for this part of the presentation which no one had expected him to make. He absolutely *was* stealing Alan's thunder. Alan's problem was that he was not a "credit hound," never had been. As he was an owner of this company it was not much of a concern but if he worked somewhere else as an employee he would have found himself passed over for promotions time after time by those individuals who excelled at taking the credit rather than doing the work.

Thad concluded his portion of the opening statement by declaring how *excited* he was to share this beautiful new butterfly's name with the group. That was the moment when the company name *NRG* Dynamics was christened and introduced to the world. Regina stood at the back of the room fuming over the insolence displayed by Thad. Of course he was just following "boss's orders." Quinn was ultimately to blame for this display of one upmanship. Regina glanced in her direction. The smug look on her face confirmed Regina's opinion. Regina muttered under *her* breath, *"Bitch."*

The next portion of the meeting was dedicated to sharing the prime mover that had escalated the growth of the company, the discovery of the *"Regalis"* crystal. It seemed quite odd to both Regina and Alan that Thad had decided to sit this part of the meeting out. After all it was *his* discovery of the crystal, and *his* vision of its potential which had jumpstarted the company in the first place. Although this was certainly not Alan's area of expertise he knew enough to offer a layman's version of what the *Regalis* crystal was and how it could potentially change the energy industry. *Forever*.

Regina had determined that this was all part of Quinn's evil little plan. She probably had multiple reasons for having Alan give the tutorial about the crystal. First and most important was the element of *blame*. Everyone in this room would remember that it was Alan, not Thad, who had promised all the amazing things this chunk of crystallized rock could do for the company and for these peoples' lives. If it *didn't* work out like he said she would be the first one to point a finger.

Also, Quinn preferred to keep her employees in the dark as much as possible. The less they knew about things the better. *For her.* To say that Quinn was "controlling" was to say that the earth was round. While there may be some detractors to that statement it was certainly the popular one to make.

Last but certainly not least for Quinn was the issue of the *name* of the thing. *Regalis* sounded too close to Regina. Alan and Thad both maintained that it was *not* named after *her* but Quinn could not get past the coincidence.

There was rousing applause at the conclusion of Alan's dissertation of the *Regalis* crystal. This could not only be the biggest thing since the invention of the electric light bulb. It might actually *replace* it.

The time had come now for the members of the group to become the presenters, for each of them to step up and asseverate the part they would play in the future of the company.

The Interview

"I'm sorry, *what* did you just say?"

Alan looked up as if to find the answer to Lana's question posted somewhere on the ceiling.

"What?"

"That last word, *what* was that last word you just used?"

Alan thought for a moment and then said, "You mean *'asseverate'*?"

"Yeah, 'ass-whatever you just said'."

"My apologies, I thought you might be familiar with the word. It means "to declare or state solemnly or emphatically." You know like to attest or avow. Or to declare."

"Well if it's all the same to you I am going to use one of those easier words."

"What do they teach in school these days?"

"No "ass" words I can tell you that!" Lana laughed out loud. "Please. Continue. I apologize for the interruption."

"Sure, no worries. Where was I?"

"The group was about to take their turns standing up to introduce themselves. In other words, doing the "ass" thing."

"Point made. I encouraged Regina and Quinn to go up together to get the ball rolling..."

No surprise, Quinn went first.

Pieces on the board

"Hello everyone, I am Quinn Rex, the Senior Vice-President of Finance. *Everything* we develop *and* how we pay for it goes through *me*." The group was silent. No one was quite sure how to react to that statement. "And, in case you were wondering about my last name 'Rex,' I am Thad's *wife, not* his sister!"

Quinn apparently thought that was quite funny. Some people clapped. Regina made a mental note to herself that now she knew what 'a smattering of applause' sounded like. Regina started to open her mouth to speak but not before Quinn was to shout out, "Call me *Queenie*! All my *friends* do!"

'Which is why I don't' thought Regina to herself. Regina looked at Quinn questioningly as if to ask, 'are you done?' All she received was a dismissive wave. *Whatever.*

It was now Regina's turn to speak.

"Hello everyone and thank you all for taking time out of your busy day to join us for this meeting."

'It was a mandatory meeting, dumbass,' thought Quinn.

Regina continued, "This is a turning point for this company both in name and in direction. My name is Regina King, Alan's wife. For those of you who took Latin in high school, my first name translates to "queen"." Regina glanced at Quinn (Queenie). There could be no better dig at Quinn than for Regina to present herself as the king's "queen." What a moment.

"My role here at the company is described as SVP of Operations which basically means that I am responsible for overseeing *all* aspects of the company." Her actual title also included the key words 'Business Development' but she frequently left them off because she did not wish to come across as being plethoric. Also Regina would have liked to have stated that she not only had more "words" in her title than Quinn, she actually had more *responsibilities* as well but *that* would have been *petty*.

Regina then opened the floor for the team to introduce themselves to the group. Alan listened now with rapt attention as the officers, managers and engineers of the company each said their piece. He tried to commit each name and face to memory. They were the backbone of the business. Hopefully, they understood the importance of their individual positions within the company. While some of them may have considered Alan's job to be "cushy," he actually put in more hours each week than any one of them. But that's what owners and entrepreneurs do. And they never complain.

Alan's earlier comment about there being two *factions* rather than a unified group was now being played out as those loyal to Quinn spoke *first*. Those loyal to Regina did the honorable thing and waited for their "turn" to speak.

A tall black man stood up. He was easily 6' 4". Most of his life he had had to field the question, 'do you play basketball?' He was bitter about the truth, that the answer was always 'no,' and even more bothered that he had to endure the follow up comment. 'You should you know, since you're so tall.' What a pain in the ass.

"Hello all, I am Kenneth Knight, Director of Engineering," he paused as he touched the shoulder of the woman seated next to him, "and this is my lovely wife Felicia Knight who is the Director of Accounting." Kenneth knew that he would pay dearly for this indiscretion later that evening but it was worth it. It was worth not hearing her spout her maiden name. He was not a fan of women clinging to their maiden name and he was particularly bothered by how her name evoked attention.

Felicia's maiden name was Black. And she was by ethnicity "black." No need to make a joke of it. Felicia "Black" Knight. Not funny or clever really but there was one in every crowd that saw it the other way. The other part of mentioning her name was that she was a member of the Black family. "The" Black family. One need only think of iconic family names like Rockefeller and Kennedy to understand the significance.

The Black family had a presence in Atlanta where generations of family members had over time built a fortune in ethnic-specific media. Felicia came from wealth but like her other family members she relied more on herself than on 'family money' to make it in the world. Kenneth was both jealous and resentful of who she *was* and what she *possessed*. One could say that for all his towering height he was a small man.

Shorter in stature than Kenneth but a gentleman with perfect posture was the man who proceeded to announced himself next. "Hello. My name is Cardell Rookwood. I am the Vice President of Finance. I report to *Queenie*."

Alan and Regina exchanged a quick glance. It was a quite unnecessary but rather telling example of loyalty to *his* "queen." Regina made a determination at that very moment that she would keep an eye on *Mr.* Rookwood.

The next man that stood up had a name that did not fit his physique. He stood about 5' 2" and weighed maybe 130 pounds soaking wet. His voice came out more nasally and high-pitched than he would have liked. He had been called a nerd most of his life. He never escaped the damage of the ridicule. There was a chip on his shoulder that weighed him down daily. He actually walked with a stoop which did little to help with his height-challenge issues. He might have been passed by for the position he held in the company were it not for his prior work at a competing firm. Truth be told he was ill-qualified but evidently competency in his position was secondary. Quinn's plans called for him to be a "loyal" turncoat, specifically to the degree of the sharing of proprietary information he would have gained from his previous employer. Whether or not he was on board with such behavior was immaterial to Quinn.

"Um, hi, I mean hello. I'm Jon. I work in the engineering area. Thank you."

Quinn sighed. Was it *really* necessary for her to complete her employees sentences?

"What Mr. Hightower did not share with you is that he is the *VP* of Engineering. He comes to us from a competitor. His allegiance is to—" She *almost* said it. She almost said to "*me*." Quinn caught herself just in time and managed to say, "to *our* company."

For whatever reason, maybe she was just impatient, Quinn decided then to just point to each remaining member of her team and introduce them by first name only. Backhanded praise, one of her specialties.

"Please allow me to introduce to you *my* Project Engineers, Burton, Barry, Bennett, Bryson and Brandon. Burton is of course my *Lead* Engineer."

There is yet another exchanged glance between Alan and Regina. *"My"* Project Engineers? *"My"* Lead Engineer? Perhaps it was just semantics but with Quinn probably not.

Alan whispered to Regina, "*Lead* Engineer? When did that happen? Shouldn't that title have been assigned to Wendell? And what the hell is she doing sticking her finger in the engineering side of things?"

"It's news to *me*. Looks like Quinn has been quite busy *not* minding her own business."

Quinn continued, "*My* Staff Accountants, Berkeley and Brady."

The group clapped after each introduction. Regina was thinking to herself, 'Am I the only one who thinks this is weird?'

"And finally, *my* Security *Manager*, Benjamin." Hesitant clapping on this last one. Odd that she should put emphasis on the "manager" title.

Alan leaned over to Regina and whispered, "Did you happen to notice that all their names begin with *"B"*?"

"Yep," replied Regina. "I call them her 'Queen B's'."

Alan laughed out loud followed by an uncomfortable snort like a pig. All eyes turned in his direction. *That* was embarrassing. Alan held up his hand, "Sorry, I-uh, choked on something."

Quinn shot Alan an icy stare. He was rebuffed and thought to himself, she probably practices that look in the mirror.

It was time now for Regina's team to introduce themselves.

"Hi everyone! I think just about everyone here knows me. I am Brock Rampart, your VP of Operations. I work closely with Ms. King." He gave a bow to Regina. 'That's how you do it' she wanted to shout out to Quinn.

"Hello to all, I am Richard Castle, VP of Procurement. I prefer to be called Richard because I don't wanna be a 'Dick'."

A few people laughed but not everybody got the joke. It may have been a tad inappropriate. Of course who should follow him but the *HR* guy.

"Good morning to you all and welcome. My door is always open to you. My name is Anthony Templar. I am your Director of Human Resources. Thank you."

The woman who stood up next brought quiet to the room. She was an exotic beauty with perfect skin tone and luxurious hair. To her credit she was unassuming and did not seem to notice the attention she garnered with men.

"Please don't laugh at my name. It sounds silly but my parents intended it to be a statement of grace. I am the Director of Marketing for the company. My name is Noble Gesture. I look forward to working with you all. Thank you."

No one laughed at her name. They were too much in awe of her beauty. *'Why isn't she a model?'* thought everyone there, *especially* the women.

The next two men were quite similar in their approach to all things. Nothing fancy. Just get it done.

"Abbot Clarke, Director of Risk Management." He stood up, said his piece then sat back down.

"Jonah Priestas, Director of Legal Affairs." He did the same. Up, then down, no ceremony.

It was time now for Regina's group of middle management gents to announce themselves but they were not taking the initiative. Regina pointed at them, *any* of them, to stand up and start talking. They looked back at her questioningly, apparently wanting the same treatment that Quinn had given her team. *Fine.* Regina walked to the front of the room.

"Please welcome Warren, Wendell, Whittaker, and Wilson. These gentlemen are *our* Project Engineers." There was clapping. Regina paused. As she continued she made a point of enunciating the word "our."

"This is William, *our* Human Resources Manager, Wyatt, *our* Field Operations Manager, Wallace, *our* Plant Operations Manager and someone each of you met *before* beginning your employment with us, Walter, *our* Recruiting Specialist."

Everyone clapped at the conclusion of the introductions.

Regina tried out a joke. "Walter, you might have worked yourself out of a job here. This is one fine looking team! Do you have any plans for the future?" Regina laughed as did only a few others. It was a bad joke that captured only a modicum of nervous laughter. When Walter sat down he had a troubled look on his face. *Had she actually meant that?*

Alan walked rapidly to the front of the room to relieve Regina from her awkward moment. He thanked everyone again for attending and encouraged them to stop by his office anytime if only to just say "hi." The group clapped again as they were uncertain of what they *should* do. As the attendees slowly made their way out of the room Alan walked up to Regina and tapped her on the shoulder.

"Hey, what about the twins? I didn't see *them* get introduced."

"They were here the whole time. At the back of the room but they *refused* to be introduced." Regina put her hand on Alan's cheek to turn his head to face her. She lowered her voice then as she said, "They are, how do I say this in a nice way, um, *different*."

Alan said, "How do I say *this* in a nice way? They're freaking *creepy* if you ask me."

"Keep your voice down!" scolded Regina.

"I might be going out on a limb here honey, but I think they may already know that about themselves."

"Stop, you're being patronizing. It's not a good look for you."

"What are their names again?"

"Toni and Joni."

"Which one is the *girl*?"

Regina punched him in the arm. "Stop it! Now you're just being mean!"

"It's a fair question."

"I already told you. *Both* of the twins are girls."

"Call me crazy but neither of them looks like a *girl* and they sure as hell *don't* look like *twins*."

"Well news flash, nobody asked you for your opinion. They *are* girls, or so I'm told. And they're *fraternal* twins, not identical. Aside from all that I'm sure they are nice people."

"Nice, huh?" Alan shook his head and said the last part under his breath. "Nice, and *creepy*."

As the two parted it suddenly occurred to Alan that while all of Quinn's team of "Queen B's" had names beginning with *"B,"* Regina's team all had names beginning with the letter *"W."* He went over the names in his head once again and yes, that *was* the case.

Was that significant in some way? Or just a mere coincidence? He might never know.

Queen's Pawn

There was a buzz about the office now. The information shared about the *"Regalis"* crystal seemed to be taking on a life of its own. Its properties and potential had been shared with the group as plainly and genuinely as possible. It was through no fault of Alan's explanation. It might have been worse had Thad been the one to present the crystal to the group. After all it was *his* discovery. He would have been far more passionate in his telling of the finding and its incredible possibilities. And *challenges* which Alan had neglected to mention. What it all came down to was simple human nature. Human nature and the most dangerous element in nature although you won't find it on the periodic table of elements.

It is the element of *Greed.*

Wendell was the first to move with Wilson in tow. Both were Project Engineers with exciting new ideas brewing in their heads regarding the crystal that they were excited to share. The two made a beeline for the offices of Abbot Clarke and Jonah Priestas. Those two men seemed the most likely candidates for being able to answer the questions that would arise when developing their ideas. When birthing a grand new idea, those individuals which one takes into their confidence is all important. Wendell and Wilson chose well.

Down the hall a similar scenario was playing out involving Burton and Barry. They too were Project Engineers with ideas burning in their heads. Their ideas, however, were less directed at the development of new products or applications. They were laser-focused on the potential wealth that the crystal could bring to them. Their thoughts were more *marketing directed* than product development driven, which simply meant that they were putting the cart before the horse.

The two went first to Jon Hightower. He was, however, quick to brush off their ideas and suggest that they stay in their lane. 'We are in the *engineering* field, not in *sales*.' Jon did not take them seriously although he would later regret that decision.

Not to be deterred, the two then knocked on the office door of Cardell Rookwood who *eagerly* welcomed them in. Barry took the lead in sharing what they had in mind. Cardell smiled and chuckled to himself thinking that the best description of this moment was that this young man was "gushing with ideas." Every so often Burton would interject with an errant thought but Barry seemed to be the one running the show. Later on Cardell would admonish himself with the simple thought that it's the *quiet ones* you have to watch. Barry was a hot flame which would burn out quickly.

The meeting was not without merit however as financing would surely be needed to bring these two boys' ambitions to fruition. Cardell was in his senior years so everyone to him in this building was a "boy" or "girl." His seniority, not his age, was of utmost importance to him. These two boys were either clever or had just found their way into his office by dumb luck. Cardell held the reins to the finance department in this company and his loyalty to Queenie meant that he always had her ear. He chose to put some credence to their suggestions.

'Don't share these ideas with *anyone* else, are we clear on that?' he had said to them.

'Yes, "crystal" clear,' Barry had said with a laugh. Cardell held eye contact with them for several seconds before dismissing them. He felt he could trust them. What he unfortunately did *not* know is that they had gone *first* to Jon Hightower to share these ideas.

Details.

The Interview

Alan stopped talking, waiting for Lana to notice. She did just then, turning her head to Alan to say, "I'm so sorry. I got lost in thought for a moment."

Alan laughed. "No worries. We all do it. Something I can help you with?"

"As a matter of fact," stated Lana. "I am intrigued, *and* curious, about this wooden nameplate you have on your desk."

"Yes? What about it?"

"Well, it doesn't have your name *or* your title. It is actually a quote. From Mark Twain, is that right?"

"Yes, that is correct."

"So--, what is the story behind why that is on your desk in favor of your name and title?"

Alan leaned back in his chair for a moment before responding. He smiled as he said, "You're really good at this. I want you to know that. I could have easily rambled on just sharing history as I recall it but you—" He leaned forward and in almost a whisper said, "You want the *whole story*, don't you?"

"To the extent that you are comfortable, and willing, to share. Yes." Lana was deliberate and succinct in her reply.

Alan made a steeple with his hands and brought them to his face looking up to the ceiling as though searching for an answer. He then brought his hands down to the arms of the chair and made level eye contact with his interviewer.

"Very well then, we shall suspend the interview proper for a few minutes and I shall take you on a brief field trip. You're not just writing an article, Lana. I can see that now. You're writing *the story*. And to do that you need to know more about the characters *in* the story. The best place to start is with the main characters, do you agree?"

"Absolutely. Yes."

"Please read *aloud* the quote that you see there."

Lana nodded her head and then read slowly, showing great respect for the words as they were written, "*The more you tell the truth, the less you have to remember*."

Alan watched her closely, gauging her reaction. He was pleased that she was seeming to take this as seriously as did he. "You know, this is Mark Twain at his best. But--, he wasn't just attempting to turn a clever phrase. He was sharing an unvarnished truth. I live this statement every day. Do you want to know my character? It is engraved right there on that wooden plaque."

Lana was clearly impressed but also curious. "You mentioned a field trip? How does that factor in with what you just shared?"

"I did, didn't I?" Alan said as he rose from his chair. "In college Thad and I were big on quotes. We used them in every paper and every presentation. It was an easy way to set the stage for an explanation by sharing a worthy "example" if you will of a similar perspective. Not to mention the fact that we probably also scored a few brownie points for content research by tracking down said quotes."

Alan began walking towards the door to his office. He beckoned for Lana to follow.

"When Thad and I sat across a table from each other talking about the future of our would-be company, we challenged each other to find a quote that would best fit how we might govern our actions. Mine as you saw was to be a leader, not a boss. To be honest, truthful and transparent in my beliefs. And to share clear and attainable expectations of those individuals who had chosen to work with us. More than anything I wanted to be able to look in the mirror each day and respect the man that looked back at me."

Lana touched Alan on the shoulder which caused him to stop. "I think you have done *exactly* that." She waved her arm about in a grand gesture and added, "You should be quite proud of all that you have done."

Alan looked about him, seeing more than just the office space. In his mind's eye he saw his journey like a river over time forging ahead with a direction in mind but so often being forced to twist and turn due to obstacles along the way. He turned to Lana and said, "There *have* been casualties. I'm not proud of *that*."

"You don't exist in a vacuum." Lana offered.

Alan chuckled. "You know what? I might just put that quote on my desk to remind myself of that. While I might be the *leader* of the group, the followers are not *robots*. They do have freewill. They make their own choices and have their own voices. I can only prescribe a path to follow."

"'You can lead a horse to water but you can't make him drink.' Not sure who said that but I think it applies."

Alan grinned and said, "Nice quote. Good context. I think Thad would *really* like you."

"Will I have an opportunity to meet him?"

"Well, he no longer works *here* as you know but perhaps yes. Let's see how the rest of our time together goes. If nothing else at least you will have a sense of what he is all about. Please follow me to Thad's old office."

Arriving at Thad's office Lana was immediately taken aback. She was uncertain what it might look like but this was certainly *not* what she expected to see.

"Thad was a big game hunter?" Lana pointed to the menagerie of animal heads gracing the walls.

"No. No he was not."

"Then why--?"

Alan took a moment to take a fresh look at an office he had visited a million times before but at some point in time had stopped actually "seeing." It was ostentatious to say the least. The most obvious artifacts that caught the eye were the mounted heads of antelope, moose, elk, and caribou. There were mounted rifles as well seeming to indicate that each was the weapon of choice used to bring down the animal. The walls were dark wood panel, something which was at odds with the steel and glass of the building proper.

The furniture was overstuffed and covered with animal skin. Leopard, zebra and something exotic Lana did not recognize, all forced to coexist in the same space. A faux fireplace was the centerpiece of a library wall filled with tomes of great scholars. Although these books were real they were just serving as props. Thad had never been much of a reader. This library scheme was all for effect. Quinn was big on first impressions.

Alan had not answered so Lana asked her question again. "If Thad was not a big game hunter why all the dead animals?"

This time Alan was quick to reply. "I certainly have *my* opinion but I think you would have to ask Quinn that question to get to the real answer."

"Okay, that's fair, I guess. But why is there nothing here relating to the discovery of the *Regalis* crystal? Wouldn't *that* be considered Thad's shining moment, the pinnacle of his achievement with this company?"

Alan pondered this question for a moment before responding with what had come to mind in the first place. "I think it is because deep down Thad is both pragmatic and realistic—with himself. He would not glorify the discovery of the *Regalis* crystal for one simple reason."

"And what is that?"

"*That* is the fact that Thad did *not* discover the *Regalis* crystal."

"He didn't? But I thought you said—"

"I won't argue semantics with you. The truth is he didn't discover the crystal *itself*. The crystal has been out there possibly for *centuries*. It is easily found, yet hidden in plain sight if you will, which is why our competitors are having such difficulty finding it. They are energetically looking for something *new*, not harvesting something *old* which they have already seen."

"Oh, well then, what *did* he discover? If you are able to share."

Alan had a good laugh about the clandestine nature of Lana's question.

"It's fine. No government secrets will be shared by what I have to say. It's really very simple. What Thad "discovered" was the *potential* of the crystal. He spent countless days and weeks and long weekends working with it, asking it to share its secrets with him. What he had was just a *hunch* and a dogged determination to find out if he was right. If you want to know who Thad is don't look at this office or even most of what's in it. Thad didn't drag all this *crap* in here. *Quinn* did. She designed this office in the image that she wanted others to see him. But I know the *real* Thad. And so did he. He might have gotten lost a few too many times on his unintended journey of debauchery but in his defense he *did* have a rather untrustworthy guide."

"Quinn?"

"Yes, Quinn. Look closely at Thad's desk. What I will tell you is that there is only *one thing* there that speaks to Thad's *true* character."

Lana perused the desk for a couple of minutes before her eyes settled on a wooden nameplate similar to the one she had seen on Alan's desk.

"The quote?"

"Yes, the quote."

Lana walked over to the desk then and bent down to read the quote which was engraved on the nameplate. It was a quote by Louis Pasteur, the man who is credited with "discovering" the process of pasteurization.

Lana read aloud, *"Chance favours the prepared mind."*

In truth, pasteurization was a byproduct of Pasteur's discovery. As he was arguably the world's preeminent microbiologist, he is widely credited with the germ theory of disease. Pasteur lived in a time when beer and wine were critical to the economy of his home country France. It was not uncommon for these products to spoil, possibly becoming even dangerous to drink. There was a widely held notion that the cause of spoilage was "spontaneous generation," the growth of living organisms from nonliving matter. Most scientists at the time believed that heat killed life and there were those who sought to prove the theory. What Pasteur did was to identify the fact that it was the air which carried the microorganisms and that the exposure to air is what led to contamination.

Alan read the quote aloud and then stated, "Just as surely as I live by the meaning of my quote every day so did Thad. He was never looking to create the next big thing. He was only hoping to be *prepared* enough to *"see it"* if given the *chance*. The *Regalis* crystal is a perfect example of that. When he walked into this office he didn't see the things hanging on the walls. He saw this quote and reminded himself of his mission. Let me tell you something. I get more credit than I deserve with the success of this company and that's only because of the attention the press has given to Thad's antics away from work. The truth is that that guy had an unwavering desire to find "it." *Whatever* "it" might turn out to be."

"And he found *'it'*."

"He sure as hell did. And it's about to change the world."

"How?"

"In ways you never dreamed imaginable. Come on, let me introduce you to Regina."

Alan and Lana walked through a busy office area filled with cubicles on their way to Regina's office. At first Lana was surprised that none of the employees looked up from their work to hazard a glance at who might be passing by. Then she realized that considering the nature of the highly secretive work, which was done in this office, these people were encouraged to mind their own business.

Arriving at Regina's office Lana is quick to notice that there is a glass antechamber with an empty desk. Always in search of a missing piece to the puzzle, she asks what has happened to Regina's executive assistant. The journalist in her has asked that question knowing that the worst thing that could happen would be a rebuke stating that this is none of her business. She is surprised by Alan's ready and seemingly genuine answer.

"That desk has never been occupied as Regina has never had need of an executive assistant. You must understand that this is an incredibly intelligent, organized and capable woman. She knows what she needs and knows what she wants. She is an immovable force. With a heart of gold. And just between you and me, once you get to know her she is, in "engineer speak," quite malleable."

"I don't know that I have ever heard a woman described that way."

Alan smiled. "She is my queen. She may have a tough exterior but what's inside is just a friendly ball of goo."

"Nor have I heard a woman described *that* way."

"What can I say, I'm a man in love lacking the right words to express my love so I'm filled with gibberish."

"Noted. How about I leave that part out of my article."

"Much appreciated." Alan winked and then followed Lana into the office.

"Regina, please pardon the interruption. May I present to you Ms. Lana Taylor. She is the journalist doing the piece on our company for that tech magazine."

"Yes, yes. Please, please, do come in and make yourself comfortable." Regina offered a chair.

"Actually honey," said Alan, "we were just doing a brief tour of senior staff offices so we won't be staying."

"Oh, okay." Regina smiled at Alan. "I hope she knows that I am available to her at any time."

"Well I think she does now. Thank you for that. If you don't mind, I would like to share with Lana here the quote which you have chosen to display on your desk."

"Oh, certainly, please."

Lana walked up to the desk and leaned over to gain a closer look. This particular quote surprised her. Not the quote itself so much as the man who made it, none other than former president *John F. Kennedy.*

Lana read the quote softly to herself, *"I'm interested in two things. I'm interested in truth and I'm interested in fairness."*

Lana stood up. Both Regina and Alan were looking at her, possibly for a reaction? All she could say was "wow" in lower case.

Alan was nodding his head in agreement. It was clear to Lana now that it was Regina who kept this company on track. That it was primarily *her* strength, *her* grit, *her* wherewithal that kept this ship from sinking. As they say, behind every great man...

It was time to move on. Regina encouraged Lana to return to her office at any time. She was eager to be a part of the story being told. In her view this was more of a free marketing preview of their company than a history lesson. Lana followed Alan as he made his way down the hall.

"You may have noticed that the four offices of the senior staff members are situated at the four corners of the building. This *was* by design."

"Interesting."

"Yes. It was Quinn who engineered that."

"Really?"

"Yes. Quinn absolutely *hated* this location. She is more of a 'city gal' I guess you could say. Her office has the best view of Los Angeles."

"Does she still maintain an office here? I thought she had…" Lana did not finish.

"No, of course not. Her termination is final. We are still waiting for her to schedule a time to come collect her 'things'."

"Oh, speaking of things," began Lana. "I failed to take a look around at Regina's office, you know, to see how it is decorated."

"Trust me, you didn't miss anything. Her office is not unlike the engine tucked away under the hood of your car. Nothing to see other than working parts. Her time spent here at the office is always focused on work, *just* work."

"No hobbies?"

"Work *is* her hobby. Here you go, this is Quinn's office. Sorry, I forgot. I will need to call Security to have it unlocked. One moment please."

Alan stepped away to make the call. In the meantime Lana peered through the window at the executive assistant's desk outside of Quinn's office. It was similar to Regina's office except this area *had* been occupied. By someone. '*That* is creepy.' Lana thought to herself. It looked as though the desk had just been *abandoned*. Like in a science fiction movie where all life has suddenly just vanished. A half-filled coffee cup was on the desk along with a host of paperwork still in process. Incomplete. Suspended in time.

Lana motioned for Alan's attention, pointed at the desk and asked, "What happened to--?"

His answer was swift, and odd. "We don't know."

Lana was puzzled by his response. Why did he use the pronoun "we" instead of "I"?

A member of the security team arrived just then with a "key" to Quinn's office. The key was actually a coded magnetic card which he swiped across a small rectangular box with a glowing red light. The red light strobed before turning to green and then the lock disengaged.

"Would you like for me to go in first?" the security man asked Alan.

"Do you think that is necessary?"

"Just a precaution."

"No that's fine, just stay close if you will." He added, "Just a precaution."

Lana asked Alan, "Would it be alright if I was to have a look around?"

Alan responded, "Sure, I don't see any harm in that, let's just not touch anything, shall we? Knowing Quinn, every little thing has an *exact* place and I don't need to hear her clamoring about how we *messed* with her *stuff*. And as you can see, there is *plenty* of it."

"Okay, sure." Lana entered the office, stealing a glance first at Quinn's desk. Something caught her eye. Something *missing*. "Alan?"

"Yes?"

Lana pointed at Quinn's desk. "Does Quinn not have a quote on her desk? I don't see one."

Alan laughed. The security man who had remained in the room but was supposed to be invisible to his employer but could not help himself. He laughed also and rolled his eyes at Lana's question.

"But of course. Quinn could not possibly allow herself to be *left out* of an "executive" action. Which this was *not*. It was just something that Thad and I chose to do but since Regina did it as well *obviously* Quinn *had* to be a part of it. She *insisted* that we should see each other as "equal partners," even though she was never really in a position to pose the idea or even to suggest such a thing."

Lana commented, "If it's there, I don't see it," indicating with her hand that no such object was situated on the desk.

"You won't find it there. Quinn was the type of person who *always* had to do things one better than everyone else if you know what I mean." Lana nodded her head in the affirmative.

"Take a look around and do some self-discovery. When you find it you will know it. Her quote, as you might imagine, is *the* most telling."

"Alrighty then," said Lana as she began to roam about the large office, not touching anything. The office furniture imparted an instant message to any visitor. This was the office of someone of great importance. A mover and a shaker in the company. Someone of means. The furniture was not cheap and there was more of it than was necessary. 'Excess,'

Lana thought to herself. 'This woman is all about excess.' In appearance anyway.

The art package was eclectic. Lana did not recognize any of the pieces but as she would never consider herself much of an art aficionado that was not surprising. Lana determined that all of this work was done by local artists, commissioned most likely by Quinn herself. Unlike Thad's office Lana was relieved to see that there were no dead animal heads peering down at her from the walls.

Lana appreciated the elegance of the Waterford crystal whiskey decanter and glasses set on a brass bar cart. In times past this was known as a 'drinks trolley.' Oracle tower lamps were spaced about nicely affording the office an interesting glow. A banker's trust desk lamp provided ample light for Quinn when working at her desk. Her desk, Lana noticed, in comparison to her assistant's, was immaculate. Either Quinn was the type that concluded every business day with a tidy workspace or she delegated *everything*. Lana figured that the latter assumption must be the most accurate.

Lana had wandered about the office, taking in the décor and furnishings. At this point in time it would be easy to conclude that Quinn was a high-power work executive, an individual of means who could both afford and had come to expect the very best of life. But not so fast. This is where the charade began to fade. As Lana ventured over to the more personal areas, the bookshelves in the office, what she found was actually more in line with a teenage girl's bedroom. It caught Lana quite off guard. She thought she actually heard Alan chuckle behind her when she arrived at that moment.

Lining the shelves were photos of Quinn at every stage of her life doing one very important thing. *Winning.* Behind each photo was the trophy depicted *in* the photo. There were ribbons too. Quinn had excelled in everything she had ever attempted it seemed. From cheerleading to tennis to horseback riding her triumphs were readily apparent. These two bookshelves, one on either side of the large window behind Quinn's desk were nothing less than a shrine. To *herself*.

That is when Lana finally discovered the quote. Had she been asked earlier where this quote might be in the office if not on the desk Lana would likely have said to look for a poster-sized frame on the most prominent wall. She would have been wrong.

On an expanse of wall much too large for the small size of the frame was the quote. It was hand-written on a cocktail napkin. Lana's first impression was probably exactly what Quinn was shooting for. *Wow.* A glimpse of greatness caught *in the moment*. Like seeing the handwritten lyrics to a Beatles song. Historic. Significant. But unfortunately in this instance, *staged.*

Only the last word of that sequence applied to the framed cocktail napkin. Lana felt that she knew enough about Quinn now to make the determination that it was so *like* her to present her quote in such a fashion. Giving *herself* the credit for the content of the statement when all she had done was to look it up on her cell phone. Pitiful. For all that she achieved in life sadly, the real Quinn was a small person. Not in stature but in character.

Lana read the quote to herself thinking 'well at least she credited the true author.'

"Anything worth having is worth fighting for." *Susan Elizabeth Phillips*

After reading Quinn's quote, Alan who had been watching her closely commented, "It really says it all, doesn't it?"

"Yes," replied Lana, her eyes fixed to the quote. "And no. I believe she may have taken the writer's words a bit out of context..."

Alan shrugged. "Quinn lives her life 'out of context'."

Lana frowned. Something was... *off*. Just a little. It was— ah, the frame itself. It was off kilter, tilted just a tad to the left. Lana reached out with both hands to correct the problem. As she sought to make the frame level it struck her as odd that the frame seemed to be *resisting* her efforts. She gave a bit more umph to her actions. That is when she saw the string affixed to the corner of the frame. As she gently forced the frame into place she watched out of the corner of her eye as whatever it was the string was tied to was now suddenly *pulled loose*.

Unbeknownst to Lana this action of hers had triggered silent alarms. Throughout the building, security and senior staff reacted to pulsing phones. Alan, the security man standing next to him and Regina all opened their phones at the same time to see that the building was experiencing a "code red." Lana cocked her head to the side, perplexed by the placement of the string which was in fact fishing line. Behind her, in unison, she heard Alan and the security man shout, *"No!!"* in what sounded like slowed-down moaning voices.

Then came the explosion.

Leave my shit alone!

A large chunk of the wall blew out. Lana instinctively ducked and covered her face and head to protect herself from flying debris even as she was being thrown to the floor from the force of the blast. During the actual explosion, with her peripheral vision, Lana had seen a helmet emerge automatically from the slim backpack hidden under the jacket of the security man. The helmet advanced in graduated steps until it was covering his head at which time it locked into place.

Was that kind of thing even possible? Didn't that only happen in movies? This couldn't *actually* be happening. This was too much like science fiction.

Smoke now filled the air so Lana did not see the security man as he was moving towards her to offer protection. Alan had started to move towards her as well with his arms up to shield himself from any further blast. Upon receiving the alert Regina had rushed from her office. The alert not only signaled an intruder but also where that intruder might be.

Just as Regina arrives at Quinn's office the phone on the desk begins to ring. Alan is reaching for the phone in the same moment that Regina is screaming, "Don't answer that!"

Too late. Alan has already picked up.

Fortunately, Regina's worst fears are allayed. She expected something terrible to happen like she had seen in spy thrillers, that perhaps the phone might blow up in Alan's ear. It did not. He placed the receiver against his ear and despite the ringing in his ears from the shock waves of the explosion he heard an all too familiar voice.

"I figured it would be *you*."

"Quinn?"

"Leave my shit alone." Click.

Alan stood dumbfounded, staring first at the phone that was now issuing a dial tone and then at Regina. They shared the same fear. A shocked Lana was being checked out by the security man whose helmet, by design, had just as quickly retracted into his backpack. Like it had never been in existence. Alan and Regina made eye contact sharing the same sentiment. This Shakespearean tragedy they had been plunged into was not over yet.

The Interview

Alan and Lana are in the Regalis Café which is aptly named as the *Regalis* crystal is what feeds the lifeblood of the building in which it exists. The two are recovering from the effects of the explosion in Quinn's office. Alan is reticent to scold Lana even though he had admonished her to "not touch *anything*."

Two coffee-inspired drinks were being delivered to them at their table. Lana reflected upon the fact that it seemed no one just drank coffee anymore. There had to be a jumble of flavor profile names associated with your drink to make it sound interesting. Lana's drink of choice was an iced mocha latte while Alan was drinking a Café Americano which was pretty close to just drinking coffee. So much for Lana's theory although the days of saying "pour me a cup of Joe" truly were gone.

Alan took a careful sip from his cup and then shook his head trying to clear the ringing from his ears. Of course that did not work.

"I am so sorry about this, I—"

"No need for you to apologize. You told me not to touch—"

Alan held up his hand in effect stopping Lana in midsentence. "Please, it's not your fault. Perhaps this is good that this happened knowing as we do now that no one was harmed. This should give you some idea of how real this landmine of eggshells has been that we have been walking upon. There is just *so much* at stake."

"I understand," said Lana but she was not yet sure that she fully understood the scope of what motivated people to do the things they had done. She looked out the window at the endless vista of desert and mountain. There were two perspectives at play here she thought to herself. There was the beauty of the contrasting colors of burnt sienna land rolling along for miles before greeting a brilliant blue and cloudless sky at the horizon. And then there was the everyday life and death battles of the inhabitants of this land, always alert for their natural predators.

"Beautiful, isn't it?" asked Alan.

"That seems like an oxymoron. A place called *"Death Valley"* being considered *"beautiful."*

"I won't argue that point if you will agree that there *is* beauty to be found in chaos."

"Fractals."

"What's that?" Alan was caught off guard by such a comment.

"Fractals. Chaotic similarities. In my opinion. I did a thesis on the subject."

"That sounds fascinating. I would love to read it."

"Alan, once again, just my opinion but I think you have actually *lived* it."

Alan laughed. "That just may well be true. Should we get back to the interview? I'm afraid that we are being held captive here in the café until we receive an all-clear from security."

"I have no problem with that at all." Lana looked back out of the floor to ceiling windows of the café to the desert spread out before them. There was a garden area just outside the café with picnic tables for employees to eat their lunch under the shade of a grove of trees. Lana gave some thought to walking out there but she determined that she would see it some other time. Which she did. And it didn't end well.

"You know, it really *is* beautiful."

Alan smiled, appreciating her comment. He took another sip of his coffee drink. It was not as lip scorching hot as it was moments ago.

Another oxymoron? he asked himself. Sipping hot coffee inside the confines of an air-conditioned building that was just on the edge of a desert with the waves of triple digit heat suggesting ice cold water should be the beverage of choice.

"Worried about the explosion?"

"I'm sorry," said Alan, realizing now that he had been lost in thought. "No, no, that will all be resolved in time. I was just um, admiring the view. But it does lead me to something that I would like to say before I share with you how, um 'everything went down' as they say."

Lana laughed. "Okay, that works for me. I have blocked out my entire day for this so I am unconcerned with time although I do appreciate that you may need to leave this interview at any moment so I am respectful of that."

"Yes, thank you, I know that you are. Before we get back into, um, all that happened, I want to shed a bit of light on the motivations of these people. Yes there is the potential for wealth but let's not forget other great motivators like power, and prestige. We spoke about Louis Pasteur earlier. He was a man motivated by the desire to make great strides in science and to do good things for the human race. Did you know that he was also the scientist who developed both the rabies and anthrax vaccines?"

"I did not. That is incredible."

"Yes. I mention this because at that time, in the late 1800's, his contemporaries shared his quest for answers to diseases with such high mortality rates."

"As they should."

"Yes. As they should but--, think about Quinn's office for a moment and put some thought to how the introduction of "prizes" to a conquest can suddenly alter the purpose of the mission."

"I'm not sure I understand what you are driving at," said Lana. She then considered the trophies and ribbons which adorned the walls and shelves.

"Pasteur died in 1895." Alan paused for a moment knowing that date meant nothing to Lana. He was about to add context. "The globally coveted Nobel Peace Prize was first awarded six years *after* his death. One can only imagine how different both the quest, and the assignment of credit might have been with such a prestigious prize to be won." He paused again adding effect to his next comment. "People *kill* for that level of notoriety now. *Literally*."

The look on Lana's face spoke volumes. She fully understood both his words and his message. People associated with the *Regalis* crystal *had* been killed, some even in this building. The story she was ultimately to write would not just be about a struggling young tech company with an amazing discovery to drive its growth. This story was really about people. About their goals, their dreams, and their failures. And the motivation of some... to have it all.

What happened here could be seen as a series of chess moves, some made blindly in haste, some thinking six moves ahead. Some were made for self-protection, others for self-gain. There were limitations in any game, only so many ways to move and only a handful of players one could trust. In some instances it was all or nothing. Kill or be killed.

Setting the board

There was a great amount of activity in the months following the all-company meeting and the sharing of the discovery of the *Regalis* crystal. Just like in drawing sides for a pickup game of basketball the players in this game were choosing sides and being chosen by their superiors for what they could bring to the table.

Wendell and Wilson had an obvious alliance from the beginning and had now collected the support of Warren and Walter. Following in the way of Burton and Barry were Bryson and Brandon. This group seemed to grow in size quicker than their counterpart, possibly because Quinn may have been secretly nudging them along from the outside. Bennett and Benjamin were soon to follow.

It is important to note that while Brady and Berkeley were also counted amongst this group these two were definitely *not* all in. Regina picked up on this right away. She made a point of keeping in touch with them, quite discreetly, to have an insider's view of what they may have been plotting. With Regina, trust is always *earned*, never *given*.

Noble Gesture was eager to make a name for herself in marketing but foremost within *this* company. The thought of "backing the wrong horse" was not a concept that had ever crossed her mind. She immediately put herself out there offering to help all who were asking. Kenneth Knight was the first to step up, stating that he was "in need" of her services. He was a married man and an officer of the company. Noble made a judgement error in believing that those two things must make him trustworthy. *Big mistake.* Knight was a womanizer who frequently allowed other parts of his body to make decisions for him. Noble Gesture was a beautiful woman who now had a target on her back and Kenneth Knight was on the hunt.

It is not known if the *"Double U's"* as they came to be known were aware of the actions of the *"Queen B's"* as they moved to form a clique but it is interesting to note that they began to form a block of their own. Whittaker had approached Wendell and the two soon became close. They either did not notice, or did not care, that Joni seemed to be lurking about both of them at work and at *"Last Chance Gas"* which was a nearby watering hole where many of the employees would gather after work.

William had made fast friends with Whittaker and was now welcomed into Wendell's clique. The *"Double U's"* were now a well-defined group. They were company minded men whose allegiance were to the founding fathers of their company.

Late one afternoon Brady approaches the group while they were sharing a break and engaging in casual conversation. Brady is of course one of the *"Queen B's"* and seen as an outcast by this group. Walter has stepped in to intervene and remind Brady of his place. However, Wendell can find the good in anyone and is eager to include Brady in their discussion. While the group is initially uncomfortable with the appearance of Brady, Wendell sees no harm in the interaction. This simple act of kindness will pay huge dividends later.

En passant

The first episode of the two factions of the *"B's"* and *"W's" clashing* came when Barry accused Walter of stealing project work from his workstation. The opposite was actually true but Walter had not wanted to be disruptive nor cause ill will amongst his coworkers. He would quickly discover how low some people would stoop to cover their tracks and move up in the company. Toni and Joni, quick to support Barry, were *somehow* able to provide "proof" of Walter's indiscretions. It seemed so out of character to those around him who called him a friend however something like this simply could not stand. Quinn pressed upper management to agree that it was important to set an example.

Walter was summarily let go.

Score one hit for Barry.

The Interview

"Walter's dismissal lit the fuse. He was a *"Double U."* His firing at the "hands" of Barry shall we say, one of the *"Queen B's,"* was all it took. This was an escalation of ambitions, emotions, passions, and the stressors of competitive interactions. Use any metaphor that you wish. A kettle about to boil over, a pressure cooker about to explode, they all work. Or you can call it what I call it."

"And what is that?" inquired Lana.

"I refer to it simply as a prelude to a bar fight. Sadly," Alan put his head down and said, "it was *much* more than that."

"Is this the night that Kenneth Knight--?"

"Yes. That was just--, just terrible. If Quinn is to be believed, everything started innocently enough, and that *she*, the incredible Ms. Queenie, actually tried to keep things under control. I think you know me well enough by now to know that I put no credence to her statements. Quinn has zero background in engineering of any kind yet she rose to the level of senior vice president in a company whose *sole focus* is engineering. We are only now graduating to the level of manufacturing *products*. You have to give her credit though for the quote unquote *engineering* she displayed on that night when, and this is just *my* opinion, she sought to wipe out half of the company. The half that was devoted to *our* company mission. And of course to Regina and to me."

"How did that all go down? If you will pardon the expression."

If Alan took issue with the framing of her question he elected not to comment. Instead he continued on with, "Quinn said that she thought it would be helpful to get the "boys" together to, *her words* mind you, not mine, *"mourn the loss"* of Walter. Keep in mind that Walter did not *die*, he was just *let go*. Terminated. *Wrongful* termination if you ask me but by then it was too late. The deed had been done. Walter had been welcomed into the group of friends that I guess you could say Wendell had formed. This group of friends, call them the *"Double U's"* if you like..."

Alan drifted off for a moment, perhaps reviewing the names once again in his mind to establish that yes, all of their names actually did begin with "W."

He looked up into the patient eyes of Lana.

"Sorry. Long story short, that group had *already* made plans to gather at the bar down the street—"

"*Last Chance Gas*?"

"Yes, that is the place. Anyway, they were planning to you know, grab a beer and, how about this, to "lament the termination" of their buddy Walter."

"I prefer your terminology. So how does a bar fight spring from that?"

"It was the inclusion of Quinn's "followers." You know, I get it, they all work together, they were Walter's friends as well but... *Barry*? Why bring *him*? And Toni and Joni? What possible reason would there be to include *them*? Unless of course you wanted the whole thing to turn into one big clusterfuck, which it did. The worst of it was the fact that officers of the company were there. We are an inclusive group but that was *not* a company sanctioned event." Alan paused for emphasis then said, "My opinion was that that was just pouring gas on an open flame. Quinn's specialty."

Lana posed the question, "*Which* officers? If you don't mind me asking."

"We should keep the reporting of this piece as accurate as possible but please be aware that I am relying on my memory regarding this incident and *I* wasn't there. I suggest that you do some follow up to corroborate my list."

"Certainly."

"Very well then. I believe that the officers of the company there that night was Quinn for sure. And Thad was there. Noble Gesture was there and, of *course*, Kenneth Knight."

"May I stop you there? Why do you say "of course" when linking Noble and Knight? He was married to Felicia Black if I have that right."

"Kenneth used his marriage as a key to open doors for himself for business opportunities, vacation luxuries, that sort of thing. A devoted husband he was *not*. He was nothing but a predator, always on the prowl, and he had his sights in the short-term set on Noble. To be fair, she had done everything imaginable to *discourage* his advances. He was however a man lost in lust and blind to reason. How cold would it be of me to say that at the end of the day he got his just deserts?"

"I'm sure you have your reasons but I promise to keep that sentiment between us."

"Thank you."

"Is that all?"

"Pardon?"

"Is that all of the officers in attendance?"

"Um, no. Abbot was there as well. Abbot Clarke, our illustrious Director of Risk Management. Why he was there I'm sure bears the fruit of an entire story of its own. *I* certainly have no idea and if there is one thing that he did *not* do on that night was to manage risk. Who knows *what* was going through his head? I am certainly at a loss."

Alan shrugged and let his arms fall helplessly to his sides as the story unfolded.

Positional sacrifice

Wendell and Wallace arrived first at the bar known as "*Last Chance Gas*." This bar had begun its days as a legitimate gas station. The original gas pumps still stood as proud sentinels to watch over the place. In years past the original gas station was the last vestige of hope for a fill up of fuel before venturing on to the unforgiving stretch of road into Death Valley. Of course so much had changed since then. Cars were now able to travel farther and more efficiently. Other gas stations had popped up along the highway as well.

More than just a novelty, there was a panache afforded to one of the dinosaurs of the past. *"Last Chance Gas"* didn't miss a trick. From their themed cocktails to a faux gift shop with *"Last Chance Gas"* branded glassware and apparel this bar made the most of their notoriety which served to keep the place packed on most evenings. They opened for lunch on the weekends so parents could bring their kids. These youngsters would not dare enter the place without first announcing their presence by jumping a few times on the hoses outside near the gas pumps which were designed to ring a bell as a car drove over them.

William and Whittaker were the next to join the group followed soon after by Walter who was being accompanied by Warren. The two had started at the company at the same time. Their desks were side by side and they seemed to have a lot in common. It only made sense that they would have developed such a close bond. Walter, although bitter about what had happened, was a positive guy and not one to dwell on the past. He was eager to move on and put this behind him. Possibly more than anyone else he was looking forward to just having a good time. On the plus side he could drink as much as he wanted to as he did not have the burden of having to get up the next morning and go to work.

Wilson was not in attendance. By his own choice. Social gatherings were a challenge for him. Besides that he had never had a drop of alcohol in his life. Wendell, being the dutiful brother, made sure that Wilson accepted the ride home from work which was offered by Regina.

The evening at the bar started as would any other with a group of friends. Handshakes and hugs, who is buying whose beer and the like. No one wanted to bring up Walter's termination except of course Walter. He wanted the elephant in the room to be accounted for and then sent on its way so he could actually enjoy himself. The boys, the *"Double U's,"* appreciated his desire to put *them* at ease. Walter deserved the popularity which he had earned during his brief tenure at *NRG* Dynamics.

A few of the guys participated in a game of darts while the others drifted over to the pool table. Quarters were placed on the top rails to determine each player's challenge and place in line.

Only a half later, Noble Gesture of all people appeared on the scene eager to join in on the fun. She was genuinely welcomed. She also had the eye of every man (and woman) in the bar. Some of them wondered if she had ever been on the cover of Sports Illustrated. The Swimsuit edition of course. They didn't think that just because she was beautiful. Truth be told she looked awfully damn familiar to more than a few of the men.

Two more women arrived at the bar but went unnoticed. Also they did nothing to announce themselves. They were the equivalent of "coolers" at a Vegas casino. They had the uncanny ability to virtually spoil any party. They walked in like bodyguards, with Quinn following safely just behind. In seconds, the first two women did what they do best. *Disappear.* They just faded into the background. Their time here was official duty on behalf of Quinn. If they were to have a beverage it would be only water. Whether they had been brought along to *keep* the peace or *disrupt* it was still up for debate.

Quinn's mission at the bar had little to do with Walter's termination. That much became clear after the fact. His position at the company was of minimal significance to her. Quinn's primary concern was why her *'overtly glamorous'* Director of Marketing was choosing to spend her time in an employee dive bar *and* why her *'overtly amorous'* Director of Engineering, a *married man* mind you, had followed the other with something moving excitedly between his legs which was definitely *not* a tail.

Kenneth's hunt is successful. He has managed to track down Noble. Why she has chosen to place herself amongst a bunch of loser employees is beyond him so he moves to extricate her. She is at first pleasant enough to him saying politely "no thank you" to his offers to buy her a drink. Noble is actually quite attracted to Kenneth but she wants no part of an illicit affair nor does she wish to break up a marriage. She has spent several years remaking herself into the professional she is today. A man like Kenneth Knight, as handsome and accomplished as he was, simply was not worth what she stood to lose in the process.

Kenneth Knight however has had little to no experience in taking "no" for an answer when it comes to women. Take Felicia Black for example who was now of course Felicia Black *Knight*. What a catch she was. Not only was Felicia young and vibrant and strikingly attractive she was also *rich*. In Atlanta, her family name, "Black" was *synonymous* with wealth. Felicia, however, had been raised to be grounded and to possess a strong moral conscience. One would never know that she was a woman of means. She had worked hard for everything she had achieved and it was all well-earned. Quinn's opinion of Felicia was easily read on her face. She both respected *and* despised her. There was a rumor that Quinn had only hired Kenneth to be able to attract Felicia to the company. Keep your friends close and your enemies closer.

As Noble took a small sip of cocktail she felt a rather large hand press gently on her back. "C'mon pretty lady, let's go for a drive. I know a place where you would feel right at home. This place is for the "dailies"."

Noble scrunched up her face at that comment. The "dailies" was a slang term that Kenneth used to describe lower-level employees who did not have the luxury to come and go as they please during their workday. For some odd reason this was of great value to Kenneth. The fact that he knew which of the local hotels offered the best day rates might have offered some explanation.

Noble did the polite thing and responded by saying she had just arrived and wanted to spend some time getting to know everyone. She used the word "no" several times as earnestly as possible. Quinn walked up to the two of them just as Noble was nearing the point of pushing Kenneth forcefully away and saying, "I said NO!"

Kenneth was already drunk by now so the word "no" definitely does not compute. A romp with Noble was what he wanted and everything and everybody else had become merely a distraction at this point. Using subtle hand signals Quinn directed Toni and Joni to come to Noble's aid.

Kenneth felt a sudden *powerful* tug on each arm. He looked to his right and then to his left to see Toni and Joni on either side, clearly surprised by the strength they were exhibiting. He moved to pull away from them and quickly realized that that was just *not happening*.

Before this unfortunate scenario could play out and resolve itself Barry had walked up to place himself directly in front of Walter with a beer in his hand and a smartass look on his face. He looked at first to be alone but soon Burton, Bryson, Brandon, Bennett and Benjamin were in tow. If he was there to pick a fight he had come to the right place. All of the other guys, the *"Double U's,"* were several beers in before these *"Queen B's"* had shown up. Their sense of self-control was on the slightly fuzzy side.

Missing in action were Brady and Berkeley, whose reasons for not being there that night were considered to be lame excuses by the group. Their allegiance to the *"Queen B's"* would now be firmly in question.

Barry was an asshole and eager to display his claim to the title. He stepped up to Walter and poked him in the chest. "What the fuck are *you* doing here? This place looking for a bartender? I heard you were looking for a job. LOL." Barry had a swagger about him. The swagger of knowing that he had backup if things got real.

Walter did not take the bait. He was always the bigger man. "Nope, but no hard feelings. How about I buy *you* a beer?"

"How about you suck my dick instead?" Strange choice of words as Barry was actually the one *being* a dick. Some would say that he was just being *himself*. The guys surrounding him laughed on cue. Suddenly Walter felt uncomfortable and very unsafe. And at risk. Could this get violent?

Development

In another section of the small bar Quinn was taking control. "You." She was pointing at Noble. "You need to leave. This is not the sort of place with someone of your--, shall we say, um, *background*, should be seen."

"What the *hell* is that supposed to mean?" Noble was immediately angered by Quinn's cutting remarks. "We're not at work. You're not the boss of me here."

"Oh *really*?" Quinn turned to Toni and Joni and said, "Get them *both* out of here." She pointed at both Noble and Kenneth. Quinn glared at Noble when she added, "And I don't give a damn *how* you do it."

The look on Noble's face said it all. She had made a major misstep with Quinn just now and she would pay for it dearly. Better to go with the flow at this point and stop making waves. As they began to head toward the door Thad suddenly showed up. With Abbot. *What the hell?*

Kenneth saw Thad and Abbot, which gave him confidence. He tried to remove himself from the iron restraints of Toni and Joni. As if his wish was their command he noticed that Toni and Joni had released their grip. Kenneth now had a decision to make.

Closed

Walter had no sooner asked himself if the situation could turn violent than Barry took a swing at him. A good old American sucker punch. What cowards and bullies did to show how tough they were. Walter ducked artfully and the punch went wide. The loud reaction to that swing by Barry's "boys" now has the attention of the other clientele in the bar. The female bartender has her phone in hand and is calling 911. Experience has taught her how quickly domestic situations escalate when alcohol is in the mix.

No one other than Quinn and Kenneth had seen Thad come in but now suddenly he too would be in the mix wanting to be the peacemaker. Quinn steps quickly in front of Thad, places a hand on his shoulder and says commandingly, "This is not your fight. This is not *anybody's* fight if I can help it." Quinn looks around the bar searching for her personal muscle, Toni and Joni.

The unrestrained Kenneth has now joined the quarrel between Barry and Walter. His size alone dictates that whoever is not on his side will come up the loser. Kenneth, stumbling drunk now, is berating Walter with slurred and garbled speech but only his size and anger comes off as intimidating. Noble wants to help and tries to pull Kenneth from the fray. Momentarily forgetting his amorous "feelings" for her he nonchalantly slaps her away. Like swatting a fly.

Not wanting to look weak or hiding behind Quinn, Thad reasserts his position. The tension between Barry and Walter has now gotten out of control. The power titles attached to Thad and Quinn have no rule in this place. The situation is overheating and the voices are now raised in anger. Abbot, whose work role is Director of Risk Management, feels it incumbent upon him to offer his aid so he rushes forward. This is a slight distraction for Walter who looks his way. Barry sees his opportunity and takes it. Another sucker punch. This time however, it lands and Walter drops like a sack of potatoes. Whatever it was that Abbot thought he could bring to the situation is no longer of any concern.

The punch and the fallen soldier is clearly not enough for Barry. In his own inebriated haze he jumps on Walter and proceeds to pound away at him with closed fists seemingly wanting to do as much damage as possible. Walter is now both unconscious and defenseless. Abbot grabs Barry's arms in an effort to pull him free of the wounded Walter but it is to no avail.

Kenneth in his drunken drawl declares, "Leave 'em alone! Let 'em fight it out!"

Of course this is not much of a fight now. It is more of a beating. So many of the people in the bar are paralyzed with shock, wanting to help but fearful to get involved. Abbot is in a state of panic. He ignores Kenneth's directive and determines he will manage this risk his own way. He grabs a cue stick from the pool table and with both hands gripping the stick tightly he straddles Barry and then goes over his head with the stick and then under his neck. He pulls the stick backward with all his might effectively choking Barry. He is expecting his action to put an end to this fight quickly.

Kenneth isn't having it. He rushes over to pull Abbot away from Barry. Before he can get there the cue stick snaps in half. The force of Abbot's tugging combined with the fractured pieces of broken stick dig deeply into Barry's neck, gouging his throat as Abbot falls backward. Blood is spurting freely from the open wound as Kenneth descends on a now startled Abbot.

Kenneth is a large and powerful man. He lifts Abbot off of Barry with little effort and throws him into the dart wall. Abbott crumples to the floor with several winged darts falling from the boards and raining down upon him. Walter has regained consciousness and is now screaming at the sight of Barry's blood gushing on him from the open wound on his neck. Pieces from the broken end of one half of the cue stick is still impaled in Barry's throat causing even more damage as he flails about. Bloody foam is now gurgling up through his mouth as well. Abbot's efforts to stop a bar fight were evolving rapidly into involuntary manslaughter.

Kenneth is enraged and with the effects of alcohol racing through his bloodstream he feels empowered as well. He reaches down and picks up the other half of the broken cue stick, now wielding it above his head like a murderous weapon.

"Abbot! You little piece of shit! You want me to rip *your* throat open like you done to Barry?!"

Abbot is scared to death. He is backed up to the wall with no way out. He has Barry's blood on his hands and Kenneth Knight's scale of justice hovering overhead. He begins to scream.

Warren is standing closest to Kenneth and Abbot. There is no doubt in his mind that Kenneth is going to end Abbot's life. He is going to kill him brutally in front of everyone in the bar. Warren knows he must act. If he's smart he will have saved *two* lives.

Earlier when Barry had approached Walter he had a bottle of tequila in one hand and his unfounded accusations in the other. The tequila bottle was now on the floor within easy reach. Warren grabbed for it and yelled for Kenneth to drop the cue stick. Instead of being dropped it came swinging in Warren's direction. He was prepared for that move and ducked easily then came up swinging on his own. The bottle made a solid *thunk* sound as it connected with the side of Kenneth's head. He watched in horror as Kenneth's face turned slightly towards him and then his eyes rolled back into his head. A huge expulsion of hot breath rushed over Warren's face as Kenneth tumbled to the floor.

Just then the bottle shattered in his hand. Glass and tequila showered over Kenneth. Warren had fully expected the bottle to shatter upon contact with Kenneth's head like it did in the movies but it had not. This was another engineering puzzle to solve.

Warren is panicked now as he begins to see blood seeping from a large gash in the side of Kenneth's head. He is suddenly cold, going into shock, fearful that he has just killed a man.

Noble is rushing to Warren's side to offer comfort but Quinn stops her.

"Don't be stupid. As our quote unquote "spokesperson" of the company can't you see that you want no part of this? The press will come to you for answers to this melee especially if they know that you were in the thick of it. *Go!* Get the hell out of here before things get worse!"

Noble knew that Quinn fed on chaos so there would be no cooler head in a situation like this than hers so she took the advice and headed promptly for the door. It pained her to leave any of her coworkers in need but there wasn't much she could do for them. The sound of sirens growing nearer told her that help was on the way. Noble stopped at the doorway when she caught sight of Thad looking her way. She began to ask herself if maybe she should go back in. A stern glance from Quinn told her "NO" so she left and headed directly for her car.

Quinn turned to Warren, grabbing him by the shoulders, shaking him to get his attention.

"Are you fucking *crazy?!* What the fuck is *wrong* with you?! You just *killed* him! You just *murdered* Kenneth Knight!" Quinn had no idea at this point in time if that was true but it was beside the point. She wanted Warren out of the picture and this was one sure way to make that happen. "Do you have *any idea* what they will *do* to you?" Quinn also had no clue who "they" might be but the expression served a purpose. She saw the fear in his innocent eyes. He was just a kid who had for all the right reasons just done a very childish bad thing in an adult world. "Get the fuck out of here! *NOW!*"

Warren *ran* out of the bar. The sirens hastened his exit even more. He had no idea where he would go other than as far away from *here* as possible. He was not heard from again.

Kenneth was a hard man to keep down. He was up now and mobile although quite unsteady on his feet. The bleeding on his head appeared to have subsided but the possibility of a concussion seemed obvious. His drive for *fight* now seemed to have given way to his drive for *sex*. Seeing Noble leave the bar was all it took to get Kenneth moving in that same direction.

Quinn picked up on this and immediately leaned in towards Toni to whisper something into her ear with urgency. "You two take "the car" and follow him to make sure that *he* doesn't follow *her*. Got it?"

Toni nodded her head yes. "The car" referred to a nondescript and untraceable vehicle which Toni and Joni used for doing Quinn's bidding. The car itself was an old Ford Crown Victoria, a large car with a powerful V8 engine. This particular car had done service for a time as a 1998 Police Interceptor model. It was a heavy vehicle that could push just about any other vehicle off the road if necessary. More than a few times that *had* been necessary.

"One more thing."

Toni looked at Quinn giving her *their* full attention. Quinn then cupped her hand around her mouth before adding emphasis to every word, *"Teach that man a lesson."*

Quinn drew back and then pinched Toni on the cheek indicating her confidence in her abilities to complete her task. Toni smiled. This was not something which she did often. Quinn had learned early on that you need tell *only one* of the twins and *somehow* the other knew. As if to confirm this truth Joni smiled as well.

Spin

As the two left the bar Quinn was already on to another task. She had retrieved her cell phone from her purse and was now lifting it to her ear. She was calling Alan's *work* phone. Quinn knew full well that if she called

Alan's cell he would answer immediately, he always did, but in this moment she did not wish to speak *with* Alan. She wanted only to speak *to* Alan. Quinn needed only a moment to get into character for what she had to say. The curtain came up for her and she was "on."

"Alan, by the time you hear this message I'm sure that you will have heard of the many unfortunate circumstances that transpired last evening at that horrible place where the employees meet after work. I am already taking steps to minimize the damage which may have been done to *our* company's reputation. God only knows what was going through these peoples' minds. I'm sure that alcohol played a big part. I got there as soon as I could and did my best to mitigate the circumstances. Surely there will be some terminations in order. I will *certainly* do my part. I would like to meet with you personally to discuss *Wendell's* role in this, this—" Quinn hesitated for proper effect before adding, "—incident. Thank you."

Quinn cut her phone off and dumped it back into her purse. The police and paramedics had arrived, which meant that it was time for her to leave. She worked her way out of the bar and headed expediently to her car. The call to Alan's work phone was by design. Quinn had a plan and it required a bit of a waiting period to assure that the full measure of what had transpired this evening would weigh heavily upon Alan's shoulders. She knew him well. He would act in accordance with the counsel he was given, namely hers. What she hadn't planned on was someone else speaking with him *first*. A rare but unfortunate oversight on her part.

When making her call to Alan, Quinn had brushed past Wallace on her way to the door. She ignored his presence. Another oversight. He heard only a snippet of what he believed to be a conversation with Alan but it was enough to prompt him to place a call to his superior, Brock Rampart. On Rampart's voicemail, he gave a brief but accurate accounting of the events of the evening. This was an incredibly important phone call which would soon be of substantial benefit to both of them.

Rampart had all calls forwarded to his cell when not in the office so he actually listened to Wallace's message only minutes after it was sent. He forwarded the message to Alan's work phone and added an additional comment, "You will come to know your *true* friends by act and deed. I believe that Wallace can be trusted."

Off the board

Noble noticed the headlights coming up behind her. She was only a few miles from her apartment when they appeared. The car behind her with those headlights was coming on with increasing speed. They were only pinpoints of light a few moments ago. On any normal evening she would have had music playing and might have been singing along however tonight's events had her in a very somber mood. She just wanted to get home and hopefully find some peace.

The headlights were distinctive in several ways and therefore easy to spot. For one, they had a blue tinge to the light. These were probably an indicator that it was an expensive vehicle. Secondly, the lights were not constant. They were weaving back and forth behind her, at times blinding her in the rear-view mirror in one moment and then the side mirror the next. Noble worried that the driver in the car behind might be impaired in some way, possibly drunk. This made her decide not to go directly to her apartment. She instead took a few side roads which *she* knew well but might not be recognizable, especially at night, to someone unfamiliar with the area. Noble increased her speed as well.

Suddenly a second set of headlights appeared, visible to Noble only when the first car swerved back or forth. Moments later the second set of headlights had overtaken the first set. Noble was worried at first but then she noticed that their speed seemed to be decreasing. She took a quick right turn but did not see them follow. Noble dared to breathe a sigh of relief. She continued to drive on with her eyes darting back to the rear-view mirror for any sign of the first vehicle she believed had been following her. Her worst fear was that it was Kenneth.

As she continued to drive the threat behind her seemed to have been only a misapprehension on her part. Just then something caught her eye.

It may have only been a trick of the light but she thought she saw two beams of blue light for a brief moment pointing infinitely up into the night sky before disappearing completely. She was not wrong. The other set of headlights continued on.

Aftermath

Jonah Priestas was waiting outside Alan's door when he arrived for the day. He was the Director of Legal Affairs for the company. The events of the previous evening had been shared with him by a deputy sheriff who had knocked on the door to his residence just before midnight. Jonah had a full account now of everything the sheriff's office knew. The discovery of one "Kenneth Knight," deceased, who had apparently been driving while in an intoxicated state, had run his car off the road into a retention pond, would not be shared for several days.

Jonah entered the office directly behind Alan and took a seat in one of the chairs situated in front of Alan's desk. Alan set his laptop and padfolio on the desk. It appeared that whatever workload this day would present to him was going to have to wait. Jonah would not be here in his office at this hour if what he had to share was not of incredible importance.

Alan walked over to a bult-in wall bar. The cooler below was stocked only with bottled waters, both mountain spring and sparkling. There was a bottle of scotch and a bottle of bourbon on a glass shelf above. Both were gifts from vendors. Both were untouched. Alan had arrived at the bar for what the Keurig, standing *next* to the scotch, had to offer, fresh hot coffee.

"Jonah, care for a cup?"

"Please. Whatever you're having is fine for me."

"I like the Seattle's Best dark roast. You good with that?"

"That sounds perfect. No cream. I want to enjoy the coffee."

"Very well, two coffees black. So, what brings you in---"

The phone on Alan's desk was alerting him to an internal call. Alan moved over to his desk handing Jonah his coffee on the way. Alan's cup was just now brewing. He looked at the name of the caller and rolled his eyes. He picked up the phone.

"Yes, Margaret?"

"Good morning Mr. King. I am calling on behalf of Ms. Rex."

'Yes of course you are,' thought Alan. Why *else* would you be calling.

"Margaret I apologize, this is not a good time. May I reach out to her later?"

"Well sir, she has said that it is an *urgent* matter."

Alan laughed and surprised himself by saying out loud what he was actually thinking. "*Everything* is an urgent matter with Quinn."

"Did you not listen to my voicemail?" This was Quinn in the background speaking in a demanding tone.

"Pardon me sir, but Ms. Rex is inquiring if you have listened to the voicemail she left you this morning."

"Last night," corrected Quinn. "I left that voicemail *last night*."

"My apologies, sir. The voicemail was left last evening."

"Margaret."

"Sir?"

"I heard Quinn's request clearly. I am currently tied up with something that is *quite* urgent. I will reach out to her as soon as I possibly can. Please thank her for me for her patience."

"Yes sir, I will, thank you." Before the phone made it to the cradle Alan heard Quinn once again in the background saying, "That bastard will think twice once he's heard---"

Alan and Jonah's eyes met. The mood had been quite serious with the unexpected arrival of Jonah at Alan's office first thing in the morning. Still—the two burst out in laughter at what they had just heard.

Alan commented as he walked over to retrieve his coffee. "It would appear that I have provoked the ire of Ms. Rex."

"Is that a first for you?" asked Jonah. This was a genuine sarcastic *and* rhetorical question.

Alan chuckled. "I usually get at least a sip of coffee in me before the fireworks start." He came back to his desk and chose to sit not behind it but rather in the other chair in front of it facing Jonah. "To what do I owe the pleasure and/or concern for your visit?"

Jonah nodded his head. “I know you’re busy. I won’t waste your time. After hearing what I have to say you will no doubt appreciate the urgency I have given this matter.”

“Jonah, you know you have my trust. If you think it is urgent, I promise to give you my full attention.”

“Thank you, sir.”

“Alan.”

“Sir?”

“Please, I’m not big on the proper English stuff or etiquette or whatever. Just call me Alan so I will have some idea that you are speaking with me.”

Jonah was at first put off and then realized this was a common thing with Alan. Lose the formality and get to the point.

“Yes, Alan,” Jonah made eye contact, “of course. So, where to start? How about this? I am 100% sure that I know what Ms. Rex---”

“Quinn.”

“Pardon? Oh yes, yes of course, Quinn. I am 100% certain of what Quinn wishes to speak with you about regarding the events of last evening.”

“You have me at a loss here. What happened last evening?” Alan was showing great concern.

“Perhaps,” began Jonah, “you should listen to your voicemails. I say that *plural* because I am guessing that there may be several. For the sake of full disclosure I would advise that you ask both Ms. King, sorry, Regina and Thad to join us.”

“Seriously?”

“Yes. Seriously.”

“That bad?”

“No sir, worse. *Much* worse.”

Alan’s face changed to one of grave concern. “Sit tight, please. Let me grab Regina and Thad.”

Alan left his office. Jonah sipped at his coffee in his absence. He found himself checking his watch after several minutes wondering what was taking Alan so long. It was a good ten minutes before he returned with only Regina in tow.

Alan said as he was walking into the office, "It seems we have quite a few missing personnel this morning. I can only hope that you may be able to shed some light on that situation."

"May I ask who?"

"Certainly." Regina had taken command as she wont to do. "Thad is not answering his phone nor has anyone seen him yet today. Ditto for Kenneth. *And* Abbot. Wendell called off today, which explains why Wilson is not here. Also missing in action are," she counted off on her fingers as she said their names, "Barry, Benjamin, Bennett, Brandon, Bryson, Burton, Wallace, Walter, Warren, Whittaker, and William. What the hell *is* this, senior cut day?"

"Is that everyone?" asked Jonah.

"Toni and Joni are not here but not so sure that we can count them. I never know *where* the hell they are or *what* the fuck they are doing. Pardon my French."

"Oui."

"Clever. With the exception of Brady and Berkeley we are missing nearly the whole damn company. What the *hell* is going on?" Regina remained standing with arms folded. This posture meant that she was all business and wanted answers. Now.

"I will tell you what I know and if you could please allow me to get through it all before asking questions. That will help me to keep it all straight and not leave anything out."

"Fair enough. Go ahead Jonah, we're listening..."

In measured speech Jonah relayed to both Alan and Regina the extent of the events of the previous evening. In the aftermath apparently both Barry and Abbot had been hospitalized. Warren and Kenneth have not been heard from. Both Thad and Felicia are considered missing in action as well.

Jonah could only share what the sheriff's department had shared with him although he did add that he and Abbot were close. The two had discovered after they started their employment at *NRG* Dynamics that their families both attended the same church on Sundays. Alan had found that comment strange. He didn't realize that church on Sunday was still a thing.

"So you're religious," prompted Alan.

Johan was caught off guard. "Um, yes I guess so. We—"

"Stop right there please." Alan held up his hand. "I have *no* idea why I asked you that question. It has no bearing on our discussion and sounds disparaging to your faith which please believe me is not intended to be so. Please continue with the issue at hand. I'm sorry for the, um, just go on please if you could."

Alan could feel the cold reprimand of Regina's stare on his back as Jonah graciously offered forgiveness by ignoring the transgression and moving forward with his rundown of the previous night's events. It is at this time that Jonah suggests that they listen to the voicemails parked on Alan's phone, particularly the one from Quinn.

Alan, the COO and part owner of the company, Regina, his wife and SVP of Operations and Jonah, their Director of Legal Affairs all heard the very same thing in Quinn's speech. Treachery, greed, lies and deception. As they listened each arrived at the same conclusion at almost the same time. Synchronicity.

The decision was made to remove Quinn from the employment roster of *NRG* Dynamics. The absence of Thad was unfortunate but not a factor in their decision. The paperwork would be drawn up and they set a time just before the lunch hour to bring Quinn before them for the news of her termination to be shared.

Gambit

Noble Gesture had been front of mind for Quinn all morning. Her interactions with Kenneth were problematic. She *had* to go. Quinn had an inkling of an idea but it needed work. First on the docket for her was to face off with Alan and put the tragic events of last night fully on his plate. Quinn had Wendell in mind as the proxy instigator. She had learned recently through Toni and Joni, the "snoop sisters" that there were undisclosed familial ties between Wendell and Regina. She was about to blow that up. With any luck Wendell would be the scapegoat for the bar fight as well as a soon unemployed pawn in her masterful game.

Wendell *first*, and *then* Noble but, Quinn reminded herself, things don't always go as planned.

"Queenie?"

"Yes, Margaret."

"There is someone here to see you."

"Now is not a good time. Send them away. Who is it?"

The person standing at Quinn's executive assistant's desk in the antechamber is attempting to put Quinn's response in the proper order in her brain. Quinn not wishing to see her was *not* unexpected.

"It is the Director of Marketing, Noble—"

"I *know* who the Director of Marketing is in our company. What is it that she wants?"

"I don't know, she just requested to see you."

"Ask her what she wants." There was too long of a pause before Quinn added, "Please."

Quinn could hear a brief whispered discussion between the two women before Margaret came back on the line to say, "She says it is personal."

Another pause, this time followed by the statement, 'Send her in,' which was said with obvious reluctance. Noble entered Quinn's office confidently. This was her first time to visit this office and she was eager to look around the space to see what touches Quinn had brought to the space. The moment, however, did not allow for window shopping. Quinn was giving her a hard stare and any motion to break that stare would instantly give *her* the upper hand. Noble had no way of knowing that her first visit to Quinn's office would also be her last.

"What personal matter do you have to discuss with me? I'm rather busy. Please have a seat."

It was rather off-putting the way Quinn was speaking out of order. Was she doing this on purpose? Noble had intended to get right to the point but somehow without even knowing the purpose of her visit Quinn was beating her to the punch. Noble had no desire to go toe to toe with

Quinn. Word had already spread that "Queenie" was a rather formidable opponent. All she wanted to do at this meeting was to right a wrong and move on.

Noble Gesture sat down in the chair offered. She immediately recognized the fact that it was a straight hardback chair which offered no comfort. It had no padding and was overly tall causing her legs to dangle just a bit. Quinn had mastered the art of making one feel uncomfortable.

"Well?" asked Quinn with a strong level of impatience.

"I thought perhaps we could discuss something which concerns me."

"Perhaps if I was in Marketing I would have the same amount of free time you seem to have but I'm not. And I don't. Get to the point." The gruffness in Quinn's voice rattled Noble causing her to lose her nerve.

"I-I, I want to speak with you about Barry. And, and Burton."

"What *about* them? They're just *engineers*. Pray tell, how does *their* business come to *your* attention?"

"Well, as Director of Marketing I oversee all marketing efforts for the company."

"It's good to see that you have a keen sense of the obvious. I wrote your job description by the way so I know what you were hired to do. My question to you is what business is it of yours what those two employees are doing with their time?"

Noble took a moment to compose herself. It would be much too easy to succumb to Quinn's taunts and overbearing presence. She needed to get control of herself if she was going to have any chance at making her point with Quinn and walking out of this office with her dignity intact. Noble decided that the time for a cordial conversation had already come and gone. If it was ever there at all. She determined that she would switch to attack mode.

"Your two *'wannabe'* marketing boys are attempting to mount a social media campaign to *prematurely* get the word out about the *"Regalis"* crystal." The surprised look on Quinn's face gave Noble the confidence she needed to continue. "Not only are their efforts ill-advised but they are also unauthorized. My opinion is that they need to keep their noses out of things that do not pertain to them."

"I see." Noble finally had Quinn's attention. "Tell me if you would when these two "boys" as you called them, proposed their "campaign", as you call it, to *you*. By the way, one of them is in the hospital no thanks to you."

"*What?!* I—"

"Just answer the question. When did they approach you?"

"That's just it. They didn't come to see *me* with these crazy ideas of theirs."

"They didn't."

"No, they went directly to Cardell."

Quinn was watching Noble's face for any sign of dishonesty. She already was quite aware of what the two "boys" had done and to whom they had spoken. Leaving out the fact that they had gone *first* to Hightower made her want to distrust Noble's statement. Unless of course she didn't *know* that part which *was* in the realm of possibility.

"Let's see if we can resolve this," said Quinn as she picked up the phone and choosing not to put the conversation on speaker.

"Mr. Rookwood, our illustrious Director of Marketing is in my office sharing her concern about two of our "employees" putting together some type of social media campaign without her---," Quinn pointed at Noble and apparently searching for a word, "authorization. What can you tell me about this?"

Quinn listened attentively, nodding her head frequently but not speaking out. Quinn had been leaning back in her chair to listen, now she sat up straight to end the call.

"Cardell, you are such a dear. Thank you for taking them under your wing and showing them that this company can appreciate creativity," she lowered her eyes now at Noble, "*regardless* of where, or *whom* it comes from. You take care now. Bye, bye."

When Quinn hung up the phone Noble had a strange feeling that there had actually been no call at all, that perhaps that whole thing just now was just an act to put her at ease and then send her away. The feeling was too strong to ignore. Quinn's body language had been all wrong. She was never one to listen if there was an opportunity for her to do the talking. Noble steeled herself for what was sure to be a bloody battle between the two.

"So, from what I understand, what you consider to be impudent acts from these boys are more on par with the selling of Girl Scout cookies. I don't pretend to know all about what they have put together but I don't really care either. And, let me add, *neither* should *you.*"

Noble started to get up. Everything that needed to be said had been said. Or so she thought. Why then did Quinn tack on that last comment?

"If you know what's good for you..."

Noble would always have that nagging feeling that maybe she had only *thought* she heard Quinn make that comment. The comment which ignited a firestorm in her. It was certainly water under the bridge considering what came next.

"*What* did you just say?!"

"Don't you *dare* raise your voice to me, young--." Quinn had stopped in midsentence. She too had been standing and shouting angrily. Suddenly she was calm and sat back down taking a different tack. "Sorry, I was about to say young "lady," but you're no lady, *are* you, princess?"

Noble was dumbfounded. *What* had just happened? What had she *missed?* Whatever it was Quinn had completely shifted gears and now had the look of a woman *very* much in control.

"Perhaps we should consider this little talk of ours to be your exit interview. What are your thoughts about *that*?" Quinn was quite smug in her delivery of that comment.

"I don't understand," began Noble searching for words. "What do you mean?"

"Here, let me put it in 'laymen's terms' for you. Your services here are no longer required. We have decided to "let you go." Your position has been eliminated. Not *really* but for the purposes of explaining to you what I "mean" we'll go with that. Here's another one, and this one's a gem. Don't let the door hit you in the ass on your way out." Quinn had a nice laugh after that one. Noble was totally perplexed at the direction this meeting had taken.

"Noble Gesture. How does someone even *get* a name like that anyway?"

Noble opened her mouth to speak but Quinn shushed her. "That was a rhetorical question dear. I don't care to hear what you have to say nor do I care to see your mouth open any more than I already have. Your employment with this company has ended. There is no need for you to return to your former office to collect your, um, *things*. I will have everything sent to you."

Noble was not leaving. She would stand her ground. She would seek out Regina. She would go to Alan if she had to, there was no way that Quinn was getting the better of her.

"I'm not going *anywhere*. And there's not a *damn thing* you can do to change my mind!"

"Is that a fact?" Quinn said with a guileful sloth to her words. "Or is that your *opinion?* You know what they say about "opinions," they're like assholes, we all have them and most of them *stink*." Quinn laughed in a haughty fashion. "You do have spunk, princess; I'll say that much. Too bad it's all over your face. You shouldn't wear it like makeup, you know. Not the same. Not the same at all. I'm sorry, did I lose you? Here, this will help to put us on the same page. *Literally*."

Quinn pulled open a file drawer, rummaged about a bit for effect and then pulled out a magazine. The cover featured a young, attractive and alluring girl, wearing little more than a tierra and a veil with the "aftermath of sex" *splashed* upon her face. Her legs were spread leaving nothing to the imagination of the "reader." The girl on the cover, although a little younger, was the same woman who was now sitting across from Queenie.

"Noble Gesture. I always thought that sounded like a porn name. Am I right? Is this what authorizes you to make marketing decisions about social media?"

Noble was caught off guard but still had her wits about her. "It was a means to an end. I only did it to get through college. Not all of us come from money."

"Yeah? Well not all of us come *for* money either." Quinn laughed, thinking that was quite clever. "I didn't have a silver spoon in my mouth but you won't find me on the cover of some slut magazine. Tell me something, do you have access to these photos? Digitally I mean because these could be the *hallmark* of our social media campaign. Barry and Burton will get *schooled* on this one, right?"

"What the fuck is *wrong* with you?!" Noble was shaking, tears making their way down her face in streams.

Quinn ignored her, opening the magazine to find the spread dedicated to the young woman whose career was on trial. "Would you just look at this!" Quinn had found the gatefold page, what men that purchased magazines of this sort would call a "centerfold." "Well, I'm certainly no fashion model but if I'm not mistaken, this particular pose right here, with legs spread, that is *quite* a "noble gesture," wouldn't you say?"

"You *fucking* bitch! *Give me that!*" Noble was out of her seat, stretching herself across the desk scrambling for the magazine.

Just then the office door opened and Margaret entered, reacting to the shouting she had heard. "Is everything okay?"

Quinn looked up at Margaret and immediately calculated in her mind what this must look like to her executive assistant. The scene fit her needs perfectly. "Oh yes, Miss *"Gesture"* was *just* leaving. *Permanently.* Please notify Joni in Security that we may have a disgruntled former employee to deal with, won't you?"

Noble looked at Margaret plaintively. She would not make eye contact. Noble looked back to Quinn and of course found no support there. Margaret mouthed the word, "sorry" as Noble walked past her.

Noble was seething as she left Quinn's office. As far as Noble was concerned this was *not* how this should end but she had no idea what she could do. She left the building as quickly as she could. That comment about Joni had frightened her. There were rumors flying about regarding the twins, Toni and Joni. It *wasn't* good. They were like the evil villains in a horror movie.

"Margaret, be a dear and get Mr. Templar on the phone for me please."

"Yes, *Quee--*, Ms. Rex. Right away." There was a time for informalities and a time for professional courtesies. Margaret had no desire to tangle with Quinn. She was like a rattlesnake and at the moment she was making her dangerous intentions loud and clear. She had already struck once and may be coiling to strike again.

"Mr. Templar, thank you for taking my call." Quinn was being her most gracious self for this conversation. "How are things in the HR world? Don't tell me, you know I wouldn't understand any of what you had to say. Nor would I care. Listen, I have no idea why she chose my shoulder to cry on but it seems that Miss Noble Gesture, our Director of Marketing has tendered her resignation to me. I of course *pleaded* with her to stay but she appears to have ambitions elsewhere. In the, um, "entertainment" industry I believe. Let me know if I can be of any assistance to you. I'm afraid that she caught me at a bad time. I have a desk full of things to do. Gotta go. Take care Anthony."

Quinn hung up before the Director of Human Resources could get a word in. Another specialty of hers. It was *his* job to clean up whatever mess was left behind. She had one more call to make.

"Hello, Cardell dear? This is Queenie and yes, that was me earlier. Sorry, something came up and I wasn't able to talk. Listen, do me a favor and let your boys know that their work behind the scenes is being appreciated. Too bad about what went down with Barry. I had plans for that kid. Anyway, that's all I have to say. Anything for me? No? Okay, we're all good then. Oh wait, I almost forgot to share with you that Noble Gesture has left our employ. No reason given. You know, she always seemed a bit *flighty* to me. Anyway, take care. Talk soon."

Quinn hung up. Cardell knew her well enough to not even bother to say goodbye. The dial tone would always beat him to it.

Quinn had considered making lunch plans but the phone call from Alan she had been expecting took her mind off of lunch. As it turns out this was *not* the phone call from Alan she had been expecting. Quinn's world was about to be shoved off its axis.

Nature vs Nurture

The story behind the twins Toni and Joni sounded almost like a plot for a TV movie. Twin girls separated at birth, put up for adoption but when finding no success eventually went the way of foster homes until they were in their late teens. Both had seen their share of trouble on the streets even though they were raised in two very different worlds.

Toni had the benefit of landing in primarily upper middle-class homes with couples who either could not conceive or were unwilling to commit the time necessary to raising a child. These couples gave of their time begrudgingly and almost as a way to prove to their neighbors and friends that they were in fact "good people." Toni carried two burdens throughout her life. One was the fact that she knew that she truly was not loved by the people who cared for her. The other was the gnawing feeling that something almost greater than herself was missing in her life. She blamed everyone she came in contact with for shielding her from this wonderful thing that was forever just out of reach.

Toni and Joni were twins but fraternal, not identical. Toni was raised to *look* like a girl and *act* like a girl. Both things seemed quite foreign to her. She was always in a state of rebellion. She lashed out at others who would dare to complement her appearance and would then later lash out at herself, even to the level of disfigurement, to change what she knew to be wrong.

Joni was not a lost soul like Toni. Somehow she knew from day one that she would find what was missing in her life. She was not graced with the attractive features which Toni possessed. Her appearance would never turn a head. This was not something that gave her a moment's pause. Joni was out to find her way in life. Everything and everyone around her was just another step along her way.

The two girls were separated non-identical twins in different cities being raised in different environments by different people. Joni was comfortable in her own skin. Toni was always fighting with herself to appear more like the image she saw of her "other self" in her mind. As the two lived their separate lives little did they know that they were chasing the impossible, trying to make themselves into the *other* twin.

When fate finally brought the two together they became one. Not literally of course but they were of one mind about everything. The two were ruthless and unforgiving carrying a lifetime of bitter memories with them as the baggage for their journey.

Quinn had a knack for recruiting. When she met the twins she looked past their tortured souls and their denial of common social interaction. She did not see two badly flawed humans like others did. She saw instead two warrior princesses who wore their scars proudly and fought for their convictions to the end. Hiring two people for a job which required only one person did not deter Quinn in the least. She simply created a new job title to justify her action. Was it worth it? Absolutely. The loyalty she would gain from these two was priceless.

The Queen is dead, Long Live the Queen

As predictable as Alan, Regina and Jonah believed Quinn to be, they knew also of her incredible chameleon-like quality to change herself to fit the situation no matter how dire. When called upon for a meeting prior to lunch, in Templar's office no less, Quinn sensed the danger inherent with the request. Anthony Templar was the Director of Human Resources. He was someone she had spent a fair amount of time with, in order to bring on board the "talent" she wanted to have on her team. His inclusion in this meeting could mean only one thing. Somehow she had been beaten at her own game. To her surprise, Jonah, not Anthony or even Regina, lead the proceedings.

Quinn believed that *she* knew what was coming. What *they* didn't know was that terminating her was the same as cutting off the head of the hydra. She would soon be replaced by two others. Of *her* choosing.

Everything had felt wrong during the executive level termination of Quinn Rex. The calm and professional manner in which Quinn conducted herself projected an unsettled tension on the faces of all in attendance. The shared looks of Alan, Regina, Jonah and Anthony spoke volumes. Whether coining an old phrase or mixing metaphors the collective result was that they had just done the exact opposite of putting the lid on Pandora's Box. They had instead just opened a whole new can of worms.

Hallway skirmish

After Quinn left Alan's office, Regina and Anthony followed suit. Jonah and Alan had a brief conversation before Jonah left as well. As he was heading back to his own office he was to learn how quickly news can travel, especially when it is something which *could*, and eventually *would* directly affect the livelihood of a number of people. Several of those affected people suddenly appeared in the hallway to challenge Jonah about Quinn's abrupt departure.

Bennett was the first person to step in front of Jonah to press for an answer to what had just happened with Quinn in Alan's office. Jonah hardly felt that Bennett, as a Project Engineer was in a position to have such information shared with him at this level. He was, however, startled by the suddenness of his appearance. Jonah backed off just a bit to allow himself more personal space between the two.

Bennett was now joined by Benjamin who was posing the same question. Benjamin was the company's Security Manager so he was (perhaps) a bit further up the corporate chain but still not someone whom Jonah would choose to take into his confidence. This causes Priestas to now take another step back.

"Is there a problem?" Regina has shown up out of nowhere and is showing no fear in the presence of these somewhat disgruntled employees. As she says this she senses another person has arrived to stand at her side showing solidarity. It is Wallace, her trusted Plant Operations Manager. Although she made no outward expression Regina was appreciative of the support. There would be no mutiny on Regina's watch.

Cardell Rookwood, VP of Finance and an ardent supporter of Quinn Rex has chosen an inopportune moment to want his own questions answered. Wallace attempts to block his path but Rookwood forcibly moves him out of the way so that he may look Jonah Priestas directly in the face. Bennett and Benjamin feel emboldened by his move. Regina is nonplussed.

Wyatt has now entered the picture wanting to show his support as well.

In an uncharacteristic move, Bryson muscles his way past William and Wyatt to make it clear to all where his alliance lies. Perhaps he feels empowered by the apparition of Joni whose shadowed presence seems to move about the building like a ghost.

Bryson is about to step up for once in his life, to be the de facto spokesperson for his group when he feels a hand on his arm and a whispered voice in his ear.

"Don't do it. Nobody wants to hear what you have to say. Not here. And not now. A little bit of advice for you, watch your back. This ain't child's play."

There is little explanation for why William did what he did other than the fact that something about Bryson just rubbed William the wrong way. After speaking his piece, William stepped back knowing that he had effectively shut Bryson down. Soon he would take him out of the game altogether.

During the interaction between Bryson and William, Regina had gained control of the situation and sent everyone on their way. The two found themselves now standing alone with Regina eyeing them with a commanding glare.

"Gentlemen, do you need assistance in finding your way back to your workstations?"

"No ma'am." Both young men left with tails between their legs. It was best not to challenge Regina. Getting the best of Quinn was solid proof of that.

The Interview

"She's not done, is she? Quinn I mean."

"Oh no, we have definitely not heard the last of her although she is running out of ammunition so to speak. At this point in time, Joni is her lone warrior."

"One against the whole company."

"Yes, and unfortunately, we are the ones with the disadvantage."

"How so?"

"Quinn had every intention of taking control of this company and she was willing to result to just about anything to achieve her goal. In a manner of speaking she allowed Toni and Joni to plant "land mines" throughout this building. Not *real* land mines mind you but harmful enough in their own way to inflict serious damage. You experienced one of her little "gifts" in Quinn's former office today."

"Joni is playing for keeps."

"Joni is—a problem. Let's move on with the story, shall we?"

Team Building

It started with a well-intentioned idea proposed by Wendell although truth be told his original idea included only an afternoon in a banquet room at a local hotel with a motivational speaker. Wendell saw this as a bit of a team-building exercise to heal the wounds suffered as a result of the barfight at the "*Last Chance Gas*." It was actually Burton, who later chose not to even participate in the event, that put up the idea of a *Survival Trek*. Trust falls and walking on hot coals are passe he said. Get out in the wilderness if you really want to test yourself. Just for a couple of days. Survival of the fittest kinda stuff but you help your brother out if he is in duress. That 'help your brother out' stuff is what sealed the deal. That one little phrase made it all sound so homogenous as though they were *all* in this *together*.

Burton had gone quickly to Cardell Rookwood with the idea. After all, as VP of Finance he was the one who held the purse-strings. This adventure would not be cheap. Wendell was never one to squander company money. Burton did not hold that opinion. Nor apparently did Cardell who was able to schmooze the approval of his boss (at the time of the request), Queenie Rex. The funds allowed were generous and well-suited for the needs of the adventurers. These funds were placed in an account at REI where the men going on the trip could shop at their leisure for the necessary essentials. The only gripe came from Burton who muttered that they should have been given *cash* rather than have to sign for everything. This may have been the motivation for him sitting this one out. Even Cardell, who was a Burton "fan" thought that was a silly notion.

The Interview

"May I stop you for a moment? I have a question."

"Certainly," replied Alan. "And if you don't mind, I will need to use the restroom. That coffee went right through me."

Lana laughed at this and said, "Same for me."

"The question first. What would you like to know?"

Lana smiled her thank you for Alan being willing to handle this bit of business before the other.

"How many were on the trip? And do you recall their names?"

"Certainly. Let's see, there was Wendell and, how about this? I will read off the names to you and you keep count."

"That sounds fine with me. I am currently at one with Wendell."

Alan laughed. "Good to know that I haven't lost you! Okay, let me think here for a minute so I don't miss anybody. Oh wait! I have a *much* better idea. I have a picture of the group right here in my office."

Alan jumped up and walked briskly to the credenza behind his desk. He knew exactly where to go to locate the picture. He brought it back with him and stood beside Lana for the two to view the photograph together while he pointed at each person and shared their names.

"I will go left to right."

"Okay great, this picture is super helpful for me to get a feel for who each of them is as a person. Could you maybe throw in your own observations about each as you point them out?"

"Certainly. We'll start with the one on the end here. That's Bryson. Very timid, not the type that I would have expected to have gone on this little adventure. He did not make it past the first day. Next is Brandon. As you can see, he is a tall lanky fellow. Got along well with everyone but perhaps a bit too willing to follow orders without question. He was his own worst enemy."

Lana looked up to Alan who added, "Just my opinion."

"Which is exactly what I'm looking for, go on."

"Next is Bennett here and that one's Benjamin there. They were bad eggs. Hand-chosen by Quinn so we *should* have seen a red flag. The next one is—"

"Wait! Can I guess on this one?"

"Certainly."

"That one is Cardell Rookwood."

"You are absolutely right. What made you think to guess that he is Cardell?"

"Everything about him, the way he holds himself, his stature, his posture, his—confidence."

"Yeah, well he certainly has that in spades."

"Well, he is, *was*, a VP so he has that "air" of being in charge about him."

"Fair enough, care to tackle the next one? Who do you think he is?" Alan narrowed his eyes to see if Lana would accept the challenge.

"Well, I'm not sure that is a fair question. I don't really know all of the names so—"

"This is a name you have heard. This *is* a fair question. Take a guess."

"Wendell?"

Alan laughed. "Nope, Wendell is that quite handsome young man just to the right of him. Sorry, what I did just there was to use your presumptive powers against you. That whole 'air of being in charge' thing due to their position in the company. Wendell looks that way because he is always at the top of his game. That man there, to his left, is Jonah Priestas, former Director of Legal Affairs. Jonah was a man of supreme confidence in his abilities as an attorney. As a matter of fact he was a trial lawyer for several years. That man was battle tested when it came to legal concerns. But—"

"But?" Lana prompted.

"But outside of his element he was a fish out of water. He was woefully unprepared for a jaunt in the wilderness. We'll get to his part of the trek here in a minute but he should *never* have been out there. And even though Cardell was imminently qualified *he* should not have been out there *either*."

"And why is that?"

"They were both senior officers. They had no business interacting with employees outside of work in that way. Call me old-fashioned but I just don't see it as an appropriate way to build relations. My opinion. Not everyone agrees with it. And like I said, on the physical side, Cardell was in fine shape and completely up to it while Jonah was a fish out of water gasping for breath from the moment he pulled on his backpack. Tragic."

"What--?"

"We'll get to that, let me just say this, a better way of describing this 'Survival Trek' would be to call it 'thinning of the herd' because that was the eventual effect."

Alan stood up. "I'm sorry but I *really* have to go." Seeing the sudden dismay on Lana's face he added quickly, "To the bathroom. I have to go to the *bathroom*. We're not done here."

Relief washed over Lana's face as she said quickly, "Can you just tell me about these other two?"

Alan had the sheepish look of a child embarrassed by his inability to "just hold it" like his mother would have said. As he was walking away, he shared, "The one next to Wendell is Wyatt. I don't know much about him other than he was too easily swayed by anyone he chose to call a friend. The person next to him is William. What I know about him is that he was a bit of an influencer. I believe that *he* is primarily responsible for the actions taken by Wyatt. And his own of course. I think that gives us nine. I will be *right* back."

Lana needed to use the restroom herself. She got up from her chair and went to return the picture frame to its rightful place when something caught her eye. Alan had his numbers wrong. There was a *tenth* person in the photo. Standing just behind and a bit to the right of Cardell was another face largely shadowed by the men standing just in front. Lana looked closer and an immediate thought came to mind. She guessed instinctively who this must be but she chose to wait for Alan's return. She wanted to hear *him* say it. On her way to the restroom Lana laid the picture frame down on her seat.

When the two resumed their conversation Lana was eager to share that she had guessed who the mystery person was in the photo.

Alan said, “Wait. What? Lemme see that.” Lana handed the frame to Alan. He held the picture up to his face examining it closely. He whispered, “Oh my god, that explains *so much*.”

“Wait,” said Lana. “You didn’t *know* she was on that trip?”

“No. No I did not. And I can see that you have already determined who this person is when you said ‘she’.”

“Well, let’s just say that the shadow on your face seems to match the shadow covering hers.”

“So you know then that it’s--?”

“Joni?”

“Yes. Joni. And to think that we have always mistakenly thought the devil to be a man...”

Part Two
Survival Trek

Day One

Take your pick if you choose to call this day one or day two. The reality was that the group had spent the bulk of their day on this 'survival trek' journey just getting to the place where their adventure in the wilderness would begin, the Mt. Whitney Portal. Cardell Rookwood, an avid climber (if *his* word is to be taken), had chosen the climb to the peak of Mt. Whitney as their Survival Trek. His reasons were that it was nearby, just a bit over 3 hours from their office and that it held the distinction of being the highest mountain in the contiguous United States with an elevation of 14,505 feet. Dating back to the Cretaceous period, this was a mountain of rock, granite to be precise. Cardell liked to make the joke that this journey was going to be 'like a walk in the park,' *Jurassic Park* that is, which was always followed by a bellow of laughter.

The group met up first in the town of Lone Pine, California before heading on to the Mt. Whitney Portal. Lone Pine is the way point after traveling out of the city. It was a common stopping point to grab a bite to eat and discuss the adventures to be had in the next two days. This was intended to be only a weekend jaunt. It serves to recall that Gilligan's Island began as a three-hour tour.

Bryson, Brandon, Bennett, Benjamin, Wendell, Wyatt and William *(and Joni)* had all managed to cram into Bryson's van. Adding in all the necessary gear made for a tight and uncomfortable journey. This, thankfully, *was* just a three-hour tour from the big city. Bryson drove because after all, it was *his* van. Joni, oddly by *her* choice, sat in the small space between the third-row bench seat and the back window with much of the gear. She never once complained. Neither Joni nor her sister Toni really ever had much to say. They were the type who listened intently and then took quick and decisive action.

Cardell Rookwood, the self-proclaimed 'man of the wilderness,' drove separately in his Porsche 911 Turbo. He had Jonah Priestas as his wingman. Jonah was not of course his first choice. His preference would have been Benjamin, Bennett, or even Joni. Jonah, however, was the proper choice for a number of reasons. For one he and Cardell were both senior officers of the company. Secondly, the two were at odds over the decision to terminate Quinn. If this was to be a trip to heal old wounds the two needed to start mending fences now, the sooner the better. Both of course were accustomed to the finer things in life. While Cardell would have enjoyed hearing of Jonah's discomfort from riding in the van it would be contrary to the purpose of the trip and he might have to answer for that. Needless to say, the two men in the Porsche arrived in Lone Pine well ahead of the rest of the group. Bryson drove at the speed designated by the signs along the road. Cardell tested the limits of his tachometer, redlining it most of the way on the twisting mountain roads.

Since they were so early to arrive Jonah suggested that they take a side trip to the Manzanar Historic Site. Thinking that this was perhaps something to do with an Indian tribe Cardell gave a thumbs up and logged it into his GPS. It was a bit of a surprise for him when they arrived. It was nothing less than a sobering feeling once it fully dawned on him just what they were seeing.

The Manzanar Historic Site north of Lone Pine is the site of one of ten American concentration camps where more than 120,000 Japanese Americans were incarcerated during World War II from March 1942 to November 1945. With over 10,000 inmates at its peak, it was actually one of the *smaller* internment camps. This site has been identified as the best preserved of the ten former camp sites. It is a desolate place with ever present dust and climate extremes. The rows of identical 20 foot by 25-foot buildings were poorly designed for shielding their occupants from the weather. Each "apartment" housed up to eight people.

Jonah would have liked to walk around a bit and learn more about the place and its history. Cardell however, a man who did not wish to recognize a reality other than one of his own making, summed up his thoughts by simply saying, "Let's go."

Fifteen minutes later when the entire group had joined up in the parking lot of a hardware store they discussed where the crew might grab lunch. Wendell suggested that they choose a restaurant where they could enjoy regional cuisine. He had in mind a place where there might be some historical photos of the town and their surroundings posted on the walls, possibly even inherent in the architecture. All agreed to the idea. Things turned out a bit differently.

Wendell and the "Double U's" went to the Mt. Whitney Restaurant where much of what Wendell had been hoping for was on display. The walls were covered with photos, posters and other paraphernalia of a different era. Apparently the town of Lone Pine had been used by Hollywood back in the day as the set for cowboy movies. More recently the outskirts of the town had doubled as Afghanistan for a major motion picture.

The "Queen B's" chose the Bonanza *Family* Restaurant or at least that's what the sign read on one side of the building. On the other side it read Bonanza *Mexican* Restaurant. The menu featured Mexican food. It was good but not what was expected.

Cardell and Jonah dined together but separate from the others at Margie's Merry Go Round Restaurant. The building and main dining room was circular, hence the name. The two were uncertain what to expect but it was certainly *not* Chinese food. They both enjoyed their meal even though both thought the cuisine seemed out of place in a remote western town.

Joni was comfortable being either with her sister or completely alone. This is why she chose to head off on her own. She had a cheeseburger, fries and a Coke at Carl's Jr.

Upon arrival at the Mt. Whitney Portal, the starting point for most individuals interested in making the trek to the top of the mountain, there was a noticeable sigh amongst the group as they ran into their first roadblock. The shortest and most popular route to climb Mt. Whitney is a 10.7-mile trail leading out from Whitney Portal which seemed the most obvious route to take. So much of the planning for this adventure had been done by Cardell as he was the designated "expert." He claimed to have already made the climb. He had not. Crestfallen looks passed over the faces of the group when it was shared that they might need to alter their course a bit and not follow the standard route. So, what was the problem? The Park Rangers were apparently asking folks to show their permit. Cardell stated that the permit thing was bullshit, that they were just being "difficult."

The truth of the matter is that a permit *is* required for such an event. This was primarily for the safety of the climber to alert the rescuers in advance where you might be in the unfortunate event that they need to come find you and transport you to safety.

The group was ready to call it a day and head back but Cardell had a simple solution that was guaranteed to change their minds. He claimed that "he knew the area" and that there were "other ways" to get there outside of the diligent watch of the Park Rangers. Several members of the group were uncomfortable with the idea of breaking the law and voiced their concerns. Cardell laughed and said, "They're just *Park Rangers*, they're not the *Police*. It's not a big deal." This happened at a truly opportune moment for Cardell as Jonah, the company's Director of Legal Affairs was outside of earshot. Being that he was subordinate to Cardell he might have kept quiet anyway.

They reparked their vehicles, this time in the furthest spots from the entry point as possible. The group unpacked their gear and without further ado headed off into the wilderness. To a casual observer they might just be heading out to the woods for a company picnic.

The group hiked for close to two hours before deciding to pitch their tents and bed down for the night. There was no sense of overexertion on the first day, which instilled in them a false sense of confidence. They built a fire and then settled down for a group chat to begin to repair the divide that had recently plagued them. Unfortunately, things went wrong right away.

The sun is setting and the moon is now visible just through the trees as the wood in the campfire crackles and spits. William likes to get a rise out of people so it is no surprise to anyone when he poses the question, "So, has anyone seen the movie *'Deliverance'*?"

Wyatt, self-elected wingman for William, is quick to respond. "Is that the one about the four guys who go canoeing and hunting in the back country somewhere and they meet some creepy hillbilly dudes?"

"Yeah, and one of the four guys gets man-raped by one of the hillbilly dudes and some weird kid plays a banjo?" This from Brandon.

"What does one thing have to do with the other?" Jonah preferred to have context when included in a conversation.

"I dunno, just the way I remember it I guess."

"Why would you even bring that up?" Bryson countered.

"No reason."

"Well that's not the kind of story I want to hear after what happened to me today at that restaurant."

"What happened, Bry?"

"Well this will sound stupid."

"I think that much is a given with you." This from William, the asshole of the group.

Bryson attempted to ignore him. "I bumped into some guy on my way to the bathroom. He was kinda gross lookin' if you know what I mean."

"Like one of them creepy hillbilly dudes?" Wyatt asked eagerly.

"Um, kinda, yeah. Anyway, he says to me what's your name? You look to be familiar."

"What did you say?"

"I said, hi my name is Bryson."

"Oh-kay, and what did *he* say?"

"He said no, what's your *first* name?"

"I said, 'that *is* my first name.' So then he says, well then, I don't know no "Bryson." What's your last name? So, I said Carl. Then he says to me, *'Bryson Carl'*? He looked sort of dumbfounded like when he repeated it. So then I say yes, that's it. Then he says, 'what kind of fool has two first names?' and I said, 'me I guess' and he thought that was some kind of funny."

William laughed heartily at this, always willing to have someone else as the butt of the joke.

"What happened next?" Cardell was curious.

"He looked straight at me and I tried to look straight back at him you know but one of his eyes kinda was going the wrong way. I don't know if I laughed or something but he looked mad and just walked away. It's got me all freaked out thinking he might show up somewhere wanting to teach me a thing or two and now you're talking about that *'Deliverance'* movie and here we are out in the woods..."

"Give it a rest Bryson and man up a bit, will ya? Joni is here to watch out for you." William always took the lead when there was need of a nasty comment.

"Fuck you," said Joni and disappeared into her tent.

"Did you *hear* that?! That's the most I've heard her say since the day I met her."

"Shit," said William. "I didn't even know she could *talk*."

"I gotta pee," said Bryson.

"Okay, watch out for hillbillies!"

"Shut up!"

Scare tactic

It is later in the evening, the sun has gone down, and there is a noticeable chill in the night air. Bryson has left the campfire (again) to relieve himself in the woods. He has had more than his share of the moonshine that someone in the group brought along. It wasn't at all what he had expected. This stuff was sweet tasting and went down smooth. Bryson makes his way out to his chosen spot. It is a mammoth sized tree which will keep him well hidden from the group as he does his business.

The fresh air is invigorating but he does not feel like the master of his domain. To be honest he is a man afraid of his own shadow. Bryson has found himself out of his depth both in the stress of the company he works for (a battle for power and dominance rages on daily) and the reality of a trek in the wilderness for which he was neither eager nor prepared. The potential for injury or worse, death in this forbidding territory has Bryson beside himself with apprehension. He is a meek young man who is easily spooked. To say he was "critically" on edge would not be an exaggeration.

The expelled sigh of relief from Bryson as he started to urinate covered the sound of William approaching. Bryson jerked, and peed on himself a bit, when he heard William speak.

"You didn't listen did you? When I told you that you needed to *always* watch your back?"

Bryson's face was white with fright as he sought to distinguish William's facial features in the darkness. He recognized the cruel little chuckle first.

"That little piece of advice will never be more true than it is right now." William got close enough to Bryson's face that he could feel the heat of his breath. "You know, anything could happen out here. *Anything*." William paused a moment to let the gravity of his words settle in before he added, "There's still time to get out before that "anything" happens. We don't need you here. And we don't need you at the company."

Bryson had lost his concentration on the job at hand and was steadily peeing on his pants and shoes. He saw that William had noticed this and looked back at him with beseeching eyes. Bryson's look was met with abject pity by William.

Bryson felt William's hand pressing into the small of his back pushing him into the bark of the tree. He then felt William put his lips to Bryson's ear and whisper, "You had better fucking 'get out of Dodge' before you embarrass yourself more than you already have..."

Bryson stood for a moment uncertain what to do. He had held his breath and now he was shaking. He turned around and William was gone, seeming to have disappeared into the night. The volume of the night sounds now turned up to "11". He looked down at his frightened penis still in hand and wished that he was somewhere else far, far, away from here.

Day Two

The next morning found the group one person short from the day before. Bryson was missing. All of the items he had packed for the journey were gone as well so his departure was not at first considered alarming, only unfortunate.

William offered the first opinion, "I think he's fine, he probably just chickened out. I found him in the woods last night crying his eyes out, scared by the whole deal." This was a lie but it felt like the truth to William as he said it and it sounded a bit like the truth to the rest of the group as *they* heard it. "Hopefully he will think to come back to pick us up when we return."

The others nodded their heads, their thoughts now mindful of the fact that Bryson had been their transportation. William grimaced. This was not something which he had taken into consideration. Unlike the others, he had every reason to believe that they would not see Bryson again. At the parking lot or at work. William pulled out his phone and found the Uber app. The minivan that Bryson drove had received more than its share of jabs from him and the group but truly it had been the perfect vehicle for ferrying the group and all of their gear to their survival trek departure point. William checked to see if a similar vehicle would be available. There was thankfully. He would wait to book upon their return when they would discover that Bryson had left them behind. William would be the first to point the finger.

The Interview

"I have a question."

"Please, ask."

"Who hired William? He is one of the "Double U's" as you call them but his actions seem out of character with the rest of that group."

"You are quite astute, Lana. On the trip back in the Uber van, Wendell asked William that very question."

"Oh really? And?"

"And his answer will not surprise you. He said that he had met a woman at a one-day seminar. By pure coincidence they sat together to hear the speaker during the last portion of the event. They walked out to the cocktail hour together and shared a casual drink. Before she left this woman had offered him a job."

"I am assuming this woman was Quinn."

"Your assumption would be correct."

"The pieces of this puzzle are really beginning to come together for me."

Alan smiled and nodded his head then suddenly became very serious.

"Is there something wrong?" inquired Lana.

"Wrong? No, nothing is wrong. I was just thinking that I am leaving something out. Something important to the story. This is a 'meanwhile back at the ranch' sort of thing."

"I'm afraid you lost me there."

"Oh sorry, what I mean is that there was activity here at the company while this group was away on their survival trek that is important to the cohesiveness of the story you intend to tell. It is an aside from the team building exercise but no less important to how everything eventually played out."

"Well alright then, I am eager to hear it."

"Alright," began Alan. "It is quite simple, really. This movement of funds for the survival trek got Regina thinking about the fluidity of our income. Burton inadvertently helped to jar us into considering how our cash reserves were being handled. Perhaps Cardell Rookwood was more than he appeared. Regina suggested that I should start to "shadow" Cardell a bit, keep an eye on his movements and what he was doing. I asked her, 'Why me?' and her reply offended me a bit if I am being honest."

"Why is that?"

"Well," Alan continued, "she said that Cardell would not be put off by me or suspect anything as I was not seen as an "imposing" or "intimidating" figurehead in the company."

"And?" posed Lana.

"And—I said, well, why not you? Regina I mean."

"Sure."

"You know what she said?""

"I think I could guess."

Alan nodded his head and said, "And you'd probably be spot on. *She's* the imposing figurehead. *She's* the intimidating one."

"And how do you feel about that?" Lana being the concerned psychologist.

"Well obviously she's right. I mean, *I'm* scared of her and I'm married to her. In the long run it turned out that she was right. Cardell allowed me to get too close and I started to see that things weren't right. Not only that but I started to learn how to find out 'where the bones were buried' if you know what I mean by that reference."

"I do." Lana confirmed.

"So at that point in time I brought Anthony Templar, our Director of Human Resources into my confidence regarding our concerns. He was instrumental in the review of everyone who had been hired, what we could learn of their background, and this is significant, who was directly or *indirectly* responsible for bringing them on board. It was like suddenly seeing the random placement of stars in the night sky come together to form a constellation when we painstakingly began to connect the dots. The dots are the stars in this instance to make the metaphor work."

"I was able to figure that part out, thank you." Lana shot Alan a cursory glance.

Alan nodded at this and then continued on with the telling of the main story.

Survival Trek

Joni had no knowledge of the negligible but real relationship between Quinn and William when Brandon approached her.

"Do me a favor?"

"Why?"

"You mean "what"."

"Why." Joni glared at Brandon. "Mean why."

Brandon was taken aback. It had taken him half the day to muster up the courage to approach Joni and here she had gotten the better of him with the first words he had spoken.

"Why? Because William is an asshole and needs to be taught a lesson."

"You teach?" inquired Joni, staring Brandon down as though he had offered to kill someone.

"Um, yeah, I mean, yes, I want to, you know, send him a message, so to speak."

"Message." Joni said this as though the word was foreign to her.

Brandon could see that he was losing her attention. He needed her help to invoke some sort of revenge on William for his treatment of Bryson. Brandon was certain that William was to blame for Bryson's hasty departure. He needed to do something to get Joni willing to help him. Suddenly he had a thought.

"William fucked Bryson over. I want to fuck William over back." He paused, wondering to himself if what he said made sense. He then added one more thing for effect. "For Bryson." Brandon wasn't sure why he found himself speaking in broken English like Joni. He hoped she would not notice and be offended.

Joni was not offended. She was instead—*interested.*

Joni reached down into her pack and began to rummage about searching for something. Brandon could see that she was clearly perturbed but he did not know why. She held up her pack, shook it and said, "*My* things."

Brandon nodded his head and answered with, "Yes."

Joni said with a snarl, "Someone touch."

Brandon backed up a step and quickly said, "Not me. I would never..."

Joni shut him down by muttering to herself, "Joni know. Big shit man."

Brandon was uncertain how to take her comment. Was she blowing this off like it was no big deal? '*Big shit*, man.' Or was she referring to someone in particular. 'Big shit *Man*.' He was fairly certain it was the latter. He even had a guess who it might be but would keep that to himself.

Joni then pulled a plastic baggie from her pack and held it up to the sunlight. She was examining it closely but Brandon could clearly see from where he was standing that it was only half full. Whatever was in there, some of it was missing, that was his takeaway. He waited, not wanting to say or do anything that might piss her off.

Joni turned to Brandon and said, "*You* ask. *I* give."

"Okay?" Brandon did not intend for that to come out as a question.

Joni peeled open the bag and motioned for Brandon to open and cup his hands. She poured a small portion of the contents of the bag into his hands. Joni said, "You no eat."

Brandon bent down to smell what was inside and was instantly repulsed. "This smells *awful*!"

Joni smiled. "Smell bad. Taste not bad. William eat. Get sick." Joni followed this last part with an even bigger smile, the evil kind. That smile scared the shit out of Brandon.

Brandon declared, "I don't want to kill him! Just scare him."

Joni got stone-faced as she replied, "William. Be scared. Very."

Since she didn't use the word "dead," Brandon decided he would go ahead and give this a try. What she gave him looked like jerky which he was fairly certain was exactly that but— this was jerky with some type of additive that would effectively cause food poisoning. Brandon had never had food poisoning so how would *he* know that this punishment did not fit the crime? The next step was to get in a position to feed some of this crap to William and then stand back and watch the fireworks.

The group was coming out of the forested area and still ascending. They could see their breath now as they were losing the relative warmth provided by the trees of the forest area. Their surroundings were soon to resemble more of a moon walk than a mountain hike. The colors around them had all turned to grayish white rock. The craggy mountainside had the effect of looking like a collection of stalactites reaching for the sun. For lack of a permit they were not following a well-defined path. Every step came with trouble underfoot as the various sizes and shapes of the rocks made for a treacherous walk.

Every member of the group was becoming winded so their pace was slowed. They stopped for a water break and to take in the view from their perch on the western face of Mt. Whitney. Brandon saw this as his opportunity to approach William.

"Want some jerky? A bite of protein to give you some energy?" Brandon had practiced his offer silently to himself for more than an hour. It came out just as he had intended.

William looked at Brandon with an irritating scowl and asked, "Is this any good?"

The question caught Brandon off guard. Was he asking if this meat was tainted somehow? Or was he simply asking if it was tasty? Brandon froze. This irritated William.

"Hello, McFly? Does it taste good or not?"

Brandon suddenly realized that the paranoia he was feeling was unfounded. He misread the question *and* the scowl. The question was super normal and hey, William scowled at *everyone*. He had *no* idea that he was Brandon's mark and another victim of Joni's unscrupulous ways.

"It smells terrible, not lyin' about that," said Brandon. He laughed at his diplomacy and his honest appraisal of the food product. Of course his comment was met with a frown. Taking a different tack, more of a challenge, Brandon said brazenly, "Here." He then placed three pieces on his forearm and then declared, "We'll play three card monte and see if you can pick out the bad one."

Brandon's ploy worked. "You're a dumbass!" snarled William and then snatched all three. He put one to his nose and drew back instantly. Brandon had not lied. The smell truly was terrible. William then held his nose while he popped the piece into his mouth. He worked it about, made a face and then gobbled up the next one.

'Who's the dumbass now?' Brandon thought to himself.

Out of the corner of his eye Brandon could see that Joni was watching intently as William consumed the tainted jerky. Her face was that of a child ready to blow out the candles of a birthday cake when William began chewing on the third piece of jerky. When Brandon saw Joni mouth the words, *'All three,'* is when the burden of having done something truly awful to another human being came over him. Joni on the other hand simply checked another box on her satanic to do list.

Wyatt had watched the interaction between William and Brandon with growing interest. He thought he saw Joni mouthing the word *"three"* but had no idea what that could mean. All he could be certain of was that something didn't seem right but as the group trudged on towards the summit he just could not put his finger on it. Wyatt would have the riddle solved for him only a few hours later when William made a strange face and then bent over to vomit. Heavily.

When William stopped and leaned over a cliff to vomit the looks of concern from each member of the group of the group was genuine. Except for Joni. She struggled. Her look of concern was forced and difficult to maintain. She seemed to know this and chose to step away from the group. Wyatt frowned as he saw Brandon rush over to her, panic rather than concern showing on his face. Wyatt had no idea what the two were saying to one another but one thing was certain, this was no accident, they were up to something.

After twenty minutes of involuntary retching, William assured everyone that he was okay to continue so they started moving further up the mountain. William's movements were jerky (no pun intended) and erratic. He was moving slowly and painfully. He had the will to keep going but his body was fighting him every step of the way.

Just at that moment he did a rather unexpected thing. He pulled his pants down in view of everyone and attempted to squat. What happened next was *horrible*. Like a clogged sewer pipe that was suddenly cleared waste just shot out from him. Diarrhea from hell. The redness on his face matched the burn he was feeling below. Everyone in the group had an involuntarily dry heave at the sight of it. Joni nonchalantly finished off her bottle of water.

The trek continues as the summit begins to seem like it is further and further away. It is the same perspective trick played by the desert as you travel towards a large object in the distance. It appears huge from far away but begins to diminish in size as you get closer. And then suddenly the object is there right in front of you. On a mountain there are other tricks at play. The thinning of the air makes forcing air in and out of the lungs difficult. There is the matter of the actual expense of energy to traverse the distance. And of course the fact that ascension meant climbing which meant added exertion. All of these things combined spoke to the fact that mountain climbing required preparation of which this group had done very little.

Wyatt is quite bothered by what Brandon has done but he has always been one to turn the other cheek. He has been surprised by how well he has done during this journey. His breathing is good, his energy is good and his mind is clear. He is actually enjoying the challenge. Wyatt looks around and lets his eyes follow the movements of each of the team members. Even though some are better than others they all seem to be struggling to some degree. The worst of the bunch of course is William.

That is when his eyes settle on Brandon. The one who had caused such duress for William. Something was not right with him. Not just mentally but physically. His movements were awkward and his breathing was wrong. Each step he took seemed forced and overly physical. That's when it dawned on him. Wyatt had read about this. Brandon was beginning to show signs of altitude sickness. This gives Wyatt an idea. For some reason he thinks of the Grinch and considers this to be a 'wonderful, awful idea'.

Two can play that game he tells himself. Wyatt determines that he will do the friendly thing and offer Brandon some advice on how to deal with this oncoming rush of altitude sickness. He will offer advice. The *wrong* advice.

Wyatt approaches Brandon and begins to explain to him the visible symptoms of altitude sickness that he is displaying. They have yet to reach the summit and Brandon is worried about not only making it there but making it back as well. This whole survival trek thing is turning out to be a horrible adventure.

'It's like getting rid of the hiccups,' Wyatt tells Brandon. 'Just do what I do and if I'm right I think you will start to feel better.' Wyatt left himself this *"out"* with the *"if I'm right"* comment. The opposite of that of course is *"if I'm wrong."* Wyatt could not be held to the standard of being an expert on altitude sickness. He will simply say that he was just trying to "help."

Wyatt tells Brandon, 'We'll race ahead of the group and that sudden amount of exertion should *expel* that "altitude demon" from your body.' 'Really?' asks Brandon. Wyatt replies, 'I think it's worth a shot.' The two of them take off running which is really more of a jog.

Wyatt is not the only one to have seen Brandon's odd behavior and recognized it as altitude sickness. This is a serious disorder and not to be taken lightly. When he sees the sudden burst of speed from Wyatt and Brandon as they break away from the pack Cardell yells out in an attempt to stop them. He is unsure whether or not they heard him. One thing is certain though and that is that they did not stop. Only bad things will happen if they continue on.

Within minutes both are winded but Wyatt encourages Brandon to fight the pain and keep going. Suddenly Brandon loses his footing and tumbles to the ground. He attempts to get back up but is weaving back and forth drunkenly. He puts his hands to head trying to force out the effects of a raging headache.

Brandon is now bent over and cramping badly with the dry heaves. Cardell catches up to them and is furious. "What the hell are you doing!? Are you trying to kill him?!" Cardell is directing his fury at Wyatt, something which he does not appreciate. Wyatt does not report to Cardell. Plus Cardell is a member of the *"Queenie"* tribe, something else he does not appreciate. That would of course change at some later point in time.

Cardell is still barking at him. "This is the *opposite* of what you should be doing if you experience the signs of altitude sickness! Don't you *know* that?!"

Wyatt wants to put this interaction to bed before the remainder of the group catches up to them. He decides to just play dumb. "Oh yeah? *My bad.* I guess I just got the two remedies switched around in my head. Exercise more or stop and rest."

Cardell replied, "I should have you *terminated* for this."

Wyatt had no reply but it did cross his mind that this is who and what Joni meant when she referred to 'Big shit man.' This is a guy who is too big for his skis. Wyatt determined that he would steer clear of Cardell for the remainder of the journey. The little voice inside his head told him he probably needed to either update his resume or find a way to climb the corporate ladder faster than this Cardell bastard.

The Hut

Making it to the summit was not the big victory each of them had envisioned when they set off on this trek. They were now a wounded group. All of them were suffering in one way or another. And none of them felt the warmth of camaraderie that this team building exercise was intended to invoke.

They were a broken bunch. Bryson was a deserter. All were unsure if they would ever see him again. William had food poisoning. He had lagged behind the group and made frequent stops as he had bad stuff coming out of both ends. Brandon was suffering from the effects of altitude sickness. No one had thought to bring along anything medicinal. No aspirin, no Tylenol, no Dramamine. They hadn't even brought Band-Aids. Ill-equipped for the journey to be sure. On the plus side they did have the most fashionable gear and the tastiest chef-inspired gourmet dehydrated entrees.

Still though, arriving at the Mt. Whitney summit was a blessing. It afforded everyone time to rest and collect their thoughts. It brought closure to a trek that seemed as though it would never end. The views from their vantage point on Mt. Whitney were incredible even if it was more like being on a strange planet than on a mountain in Southern California. Most of the group wandered about taking in the moment. Eventually the excitement of the achievement gave way to the cold that was seeping through opened garments. The full sun had a clever way of making you feel like you were basking in the heat of a summer day.

The group shuffled towards "The Hut," also known as the Mt. Whitney Summit Shelter. The group saw this as a palace, the first *real* shelter from the elements in days. A palace it was not. The 11 x 30 shelter was constructed of concrete-mortared granite harvested from the land on which it was built. The hut featured a roof of corrugated steel riveted to a steel truss frame. It consisted of three rooms with windows in each and had east-facing doors in both the north and south rooms. Iron shutters had been built into the structure to cover the windows and doors during extreme weather conditions. While not much to look at in a photograph it would become to the weary traveler a heavenly sanctuary.

Every member of the group has been struggling with the physical pain of the effects of using muscles not often needed. The exertion of the climb has been taxing their bodies and strained their lungs to take in and expel every breath. Their necks ache as they have been looking mostly down at the ground, at the loose rocks below their feet so as not to fall, missing out on the incredible vistas of endless miles of unspoiled earth spread out before them. They have been listening to the sound of their own breathing, the rapid beat of their heart pumping feverishly to keep pace with the demand, the all too frequent complaining of those around them, and the sound of total silence when they stopped for a break.

Now that the group was safely inside The Hut with nothing required of them, all they wanted to do was let exhaustion take them away for a much-needed nap. Wendell obviously had not received the memo. He was eager to expound upon what he knew of the mountain from what he had read prior to their leaving. As he started to speak, and in their opinion, *drone on* with his tales of historical data, they realized that they were too tired to listen but also too tired to complain.

Wendell shared with the group that 'The Hut' was originally, and "properly" known as 'The Smithsonian Institution Shelter' as it was members of that society who actually designed and built the structure in the years 1908-1909. There was common conjecture at the time from an unscientific deduction that this peak was the state's highest point. It was the need to prove or disprove this hypothesis which drew scientists to make the climb. Mount Whitney as it is now known was "discovered" in July of 1864 when a group of scientific Americans traveled as the California Geological Survey's Brewer Party. Once they confirmed the elevation of 14,505 feet as the state's highest point they named it in the honor of Josiah D. Whitney, the survey's Chief Geologist.

Only a few ears perked up when Wendell went on to say how fascinating it was that as long ago as 1896 scientists were showing concern about the planet by doing what we would refer to today as "climate change experiments". *In the year of 1881, a gentleman by the name of Samuel Langley would make the statement, "In no country is there a finer site for meteorological and atmospheric observations than Mount Whitney and its neighboring peaks." In 1896, the Swedish scientist Svante Arrhenius would draw upon Langley's measurement of interference of the infrared radiation by carbon dioxide in Earth's atmosphere to make the first calculation of how earth's climate and temperature would change from a future doubling of carbon dioxide levels. This scientist would claim the Nobel Prize for chemistry in 1903.

**Information found in Tulare county treasures.org*

As Wendell spoke he knew that only half of the group might actually be listening with interest. Most were just so beat down by the journey that they were hovering in and out of consciousness. There were two individuals, however, who were clearly not listening because they were engaged in talking to one another. Make that three. Joni was not actually engaged in the conversation that Bennett and Benjamin were having but Wendell could see that she was definitely eavesdropping. At some point the two young men also caught wind of this and got up to move outside to continue their discussion. To their surprise Joni got up and followed them out. If Wendell had any guess at all as to what they might be up to it would be 'no good.'

Just then Bennett said, "You going to leave out the part about Haley's Comet?"

Wendell pursed his lips and narrowed his brows. "What does the mountain have to do with Haley's Comet?" Most everyone on the group leaned forward. It seemed that what Wendell *didn't* know was of more interest than what he *did* know.

Bennett smiled at this, enjoying having the upper hand over Wendell. He shared his tidbit of trivia eagerly. “On May 23rd in the year of 1910 an adventurer, *just like us…*” Wendell frowned at the emphasis which Bennett placed on this last part which was *far* from the truth. He continued on. “…by the name of G.F. Marsh witnessed the passing of Haley’s Comet in the night sky from this same vantage point.”

“What was his name?” asked Wyatt, pulling the attention away from Bennett.

“I just *told* you. G.F. Marsh.”

“Yeah I know but what is the G.F.? George maybe?” Wyatt could get under Bennett’s skin with his stupid questions.

“Yeah sure, let’s go with George because really, who *fucking* cares?!”

Wyatt shot a dirty look back at Bennett and then slunk away muttering to himself, “Just asking a question.”

Wendell touched him on the shoulder and said, “Let’s go outside for a minute. I want your opinion on something.” Wyatt got up immediately, welcoming the exit from Bennett’s ire. Once outside Wyatt proclaimed, “Bennett is such an asshole.”

“And you my friend,” stated Wendell, “have a keen sense of the obvious.”

Wyatt smiled at this but then wondered if it was more of a backhanded compliment.

“Did you actually want my opinion on something? Or were you just saving me from an unpleasant situation?”

“Both, actually,” said Wendell. “Come take a look at this.” Wyatt followed behind Wendell who arrived at a point on the peak then stopped and pointed. Take a look at this USGS benchmark disc. Wyatt bent over and peered down at the disk reading to himself the numbers which were imprinted there. It read “14,494 ft.” as the stated elevation. Wyatt looked up at Wendell and said, “That’s not right.”

Wendell smiled in agreement and said, “As an engineer I am offended by their inaccuracy. This peak measures 14,505 feet.”

Wyatt nodded his head in agreement but then said, “There must be more to this.”

"Oh I'm sure there is," said Wendell. He would later do a bit of research to clear up the discrepancy for his own sake.

When Wendell and Wyatt returned to The Hut they found themselves entering a room of weary and disinterested travelers annoyed first by the singing of *"Waltzing Matilda"* and then by the monotone droning of Jonah sharing his bit of trivia. He is holding up his backpack and referring to it as "swag" stating the origin of the term to be one used in the song. The lyrics of the song describe the journey of a down on his luck "swagman" who turns to stealing sheep from a local squatter. The swagman term, originating in Australia, refers to a transient laborer, travelling by foot from farm to farm and carrying his meager belongings rolled up in a "swag."

No one really seemed to care. The room was quiet other than the wind finding its way through any unpatched area of wall. A sense of dread was felt by all because they knew that arriving at the top actually meant that they were only to the halfway point of their journey as they still had to make it back to the parking lot where they hoped they would find Bryson waiting in a warm van.

The longer they stayed in The Hut the more delayed was their departure. Eventually the sun touched the horizon and the decision was made that it would be too dangerous to head down at dusk and too difficult to find a place to camp for the night. It was an easy choice to make, spend the night in The Hut. Tomorrow morning they were all expected to be back in the office. That wasn't going to happen. Cardell stated to the group that as soon as he had cell service he would call in and report their change in plans. This gave everyone a pass which allowed them the peace of mind to relax and enjoy what they expected to be the least stressful link of their journey.

Day Three

The first light of dawn was merely peeking over the horizon when Cardell's brain alarm forced his eyes open. He got up and went outside to check to see if there was any life remaining in the small fire they had built. His intentions were to make coffee for the group. As each member of the group awakened the noise level and activity encouraged others to awaken. Soon they were all standing outside warming their hands around a cup of weak coffee and standing at the peak of the highest elevation in the contiguous United States. If this was a celebratory moment it was not evident in their faces.

The sun was now visible over the eastern horizon. The time had come for them to gather up their remaining strength and make the trek back to humanity. The group lineup was noticeably different as they began their descent from the summit. In the lead was Cardell, which was not surprising as he had taken the lead before, however on the way down he had Jonah by his side. Jonah was of the inaccurate opinion that descending would be *easier* than the ascension had been. In some ways this may have been true but he would soon discover how the journey *down* a mountain might be fraught with more peril than the climb.

Walking directly behind Cardell and Jonah was Wendell who kept glancing at the ground because it seemed that he had grown an extra shadow, possibly two. Staying uncomfortably close behind him were Bennett and Benjamin who had Joni following just as close behind them. It was as weird as it was ominous. Nothing good could come of this thought Wendell. He was guarding his every movement now worried about the actions one of them might take.

Bringing up the rear were the walking wounded, William and Brandon. Wyatt shuffled along just ahead of them allowing himself the opportunity to slow down and check on their wellbeing every so often.

Wendell was the first to notice the change of direction. Jonah was quick to chime in. He had noticed it as well.

"Cardell, this is not the way we came."

Cardell was at first perturbed with Wendell's comment but then chose to change his tact. "You are quite observant, Wendell." Cardell said this with just a tinge of sarcasm in his voice. "And yes, you are correct. If you recall, the route we took was an *alternative* route which allowed us to steer clear of Park Rangers who might stop us to view our permits. Which, you may *also* recall, we do *not* have. As we are returning *from* the mountain and not going *to* the mountain, the permit should no longer be of any concern. We are taking a more *direct* route back and as we are already overdue for our return it only seems prudent to shave off as much time as possible. The shortest distance between two points is a direct line. You're the engineer, is my math correct?"

Wendell did not take the bait and react to Cardell's smartass comments. He was soon to learn why the man had derision in his voice when he spoke to Wendell. It had not been as apparent as it was now. This team building exercise was failing at a high level. He was quickly losing faith in Cardell as a senior officer of the company.

"That makes good sense to me," said Jonah who was all about avoiding conflict.

Wendell nodded his head in agreement and on they went. One thing became clearly obvious to Wendell as they continued on and the landscape began to change around them. He had a strong sense of direction and paid attention to the topography around them. He was almost certain now that Cardell had been lying to them. If he had this figured out correctly in his head they were now travelling in the exact *opposite* direction of where they started. What could possibly be his motive for such an action?

Guitar Lake

When they at last arrived at a viewing point of Guitar Lake, Cardell was actually eager to share his deception. "You have my humble apologies but I know you will forgive me now that we are here and you can view this wonderful spectacle for yourself." Cardell gave Wendell a friendly shoulder punch. "You can thank me later." Incredibly, after possibly adding another full day to their trek for coming this way, Cardell *winked* after that comment.

"What is *that*? A *pond*?" This from Jonah who was admittedly *not* an outdoorsman.

Cardell was immediately flustered by Jonah's supposition. "*A pond?!* No you *dumbass*, it's a LAKE! Have you never seen a fucking lake before?!"

Jonah replied in kind, "Have *you* never seen a fucking *map*?! Because this *lake* wasn't on it, not the one I looked at anyway. Where the *hell* are we?"

Cardell chose to dismiss Jonah and his comments altogether as he addressed the group. "My friends, what you see before you is 'Guitar Lake'. Isn't it something?"

"Why do they call it Guitar Lake?" William asked weakly, still recovering from his bout of food poisoning.

"Isn't that obvious?" urged Cardell. "Look at it. It's in the shape of a guitar."

Unfortunately for Cardell they had come into the area with a bad angle of the lake. The only way for them to view the suggested guitar shape was to cover a few more football fields of rocky ground. Cardell lied again when he claimed that the coveted view was "on their way."

Eventually they were all able to take in the awe-inspiring view of the resplendent guitar-shaped lake. Unfortunately at this point in their journey, most of them felt that it did not play a tune they could dance to. A wave of displeasure was voiced by the group when they learned that the correct route to get back to their starting point meant turning around and heading back the way they came. Impossibly Cardell's popularity sunk below that of Joni's.

Later in the day sudden spontaneous cheers go up from the group as they find that they have come to the point where they are leaving behind the barren rocky portion of the mountain and entering the wooded region. This is a sign of progress. This is a sign that they are more than halfway home, home being of course a relative term. Although there was cheering and the palpable sense of uplifted spirits they were, in literal terms, not 'out of the woods' yet. There were dangers to be found everywhere in the wilderness. All too soon they would be offered proof of that fact.

Wendell senses something is not right. He slows down purposefully to be able to walk step for step with Bennett and Benjamin. This comes with the added risk of having Jodi shadow his every move as she is maintaining her pace of one step behind. Wendell stays alert and even though Bennett's movements are being made stealthily Wendell is quick to catch on to what has been happening since arriving in the forested area.

Bennett has been doing the unthinkable. With willful intent he has been leaving behind him a trail for wildlife to find and to follow. Bennett has actually been dropping remnants of food as well as bags of his own personal waste. The scents emanating from both would alert the sense of any hungry animal, most likely a bear, within range. There is *real* danger here as they *will* come calling. And while black bears typically steer clear of humans they are *wild* animals and when provoked in some way can exhibit a savage display of aggression.

Wendell challenges Bennett on his actions. His claims of just wanting to have a chance at seeing and taking a photo of a bear in the wild are suspect at best. Wendell must ask himself how far down the rabbit hole of greed Bennett might already have travelled.

"You're placing the entire group in danger," said Wendell. "This is a very stupid thing you are doing. If you don't put a stop to it immediately I'll—" Wendell paused, uncertain as to how much more he wanted to say.

"You'll what? *Fire me?* Ha! I don't work for *you*. You can't do *shit* to me!"

Just then Jodi approaches Benjamin. She cups her hand and whispers something in his ear. Benjamin looks up quickly making eye contact with Wendell. He then looks back to Jodi. "Is this legit?" he asks her. She nods her head assertively. Benjamin now beckons for Bennett to come stand beside him. He whispers something in *his* ear. A look of surprise crosses his face as he says, "Are you fucking kidding me right now?"

Benjamin points to Jodi and says, "Ask her."

Bennett glances at Jodi. He sees affirmation in her face which gives him the courage to confront Wendell. "So *"Golden Boy,"* is it true that you're Regina's *half-brother*?" He says this as though he is tasting something vile.

Wendell glares back at him with fire in his eyes. He ignores Jodi, not wishing to give her the satisfaction of knowing that the card she has played has had its desired effect.

Bennett was in his element now seeing that he may have drawn first blood. "That would explain a lot wouldn't it? Let me venture a guess. That mental mess of a human, *Wilson*, is *your* brother, right?" Wendell's entire body tensed up at that comment which told Bennett he had struck a nerve. Wendell was vulnerable now that his secret had been exposed. A wave of anger swept over him. Both hands made into fists wanting to do damage. Bennett saw this. He *so* wanted Wendell to take a swing at him right now. Wendell was taller and a bit stockier but Bennett was a *fighter*. He expected this skirmish would be over quick.

Wendell had amazing control of his emotions and his actions. He looked around. The group had come to a dead stop. This standoff between him and Bennett had now involved them all. Wendell weighed his odds. If this situation became violent who would rush to his aid? Jonah? No, Jonah was useless. Just a frightened fish out of water. William or Wyatt? William was too weak and Wyatt too timid. Cardell? Not likely, he was a strong *Queenie* supporter as was Bennett, Benjamin and of course Jodi. *Particularly* Jodi.

Wendell frowned. Jodi was the wild card. Whatever Bennett had started Jodi was sure to finish. He had come to believe that she might be capable of just about *anything*. That supposition was not something he wished to test in the middle of nowhere. He compromised by making a veiled threat.

"When we return, my familial ties to Regina will of course no longer be a secret. Neither will the negligent actions you have taken during this group trip. We will see what *she* has to say about all of this and oh, by the way, in case you forgot, she *can* fire you." Wendell poked at Bennett's chest for emphasis. Bennett's eyes went wide with fury at such an indiscretion. In Wendell's opinion, Bennett was effectively done as an employee of *NRG* Dynamics. He figured that any additional dangerous acts he might perpetrate in view of the group would only serve to help seal his fate.

"Oh yeah?!" Bennett screamed. "Want to see how frightened I am?" Bennett has been the one responsible for carrying much of their food stores. With a single motion he pulled his backpack off, reached inside, grabbed all that he could and threw it up into the air. Although they were traversing a wooded area now they were still at elevation which means some of the food goes tumbling down the side of the steep hill which will make it challenging to recover.

Jonah immediately panics as he sees the food for their return journey flying through the air. He screams out, "No!" and then vainly rushes to capture it. Jonah is both awkward and clumsy. His sudden lunge will cost him dearly. As he stumbles forward his foot is caught by a tree branch and he falls with all of his weight on his left leg which has engaged a rock outcropping. There is a jagged portion of rock occupying the space where his leg will land.

Rock. Paper. Scissors.

Rock. Pants. Leg.

Rock wins.

The fabric of Jonah's pants tears apart as does the soft flesh of his inner thigh. A great spurt of blood emerges rapidly coloring the rock a bright red. It turns a darker red as it mingles with the cool forest air.

Wendell is sure to have nightmares, never will he forget the look of sheer terror on Jonah's face as his leg was rented open up by the unyielding rock. He saw more than he was prepared to see. He saw the white of bone now exposed. This situation was now suddenly very real. And very serious.

Surprising to all were the lifesaving actions of Cardell Rookwood. It was a known fact that Jonah Priestas had engineered the termination of Quinn "Queenie" Rex. It was also a well-known fact that he was a dyed in the wool follower. Somehow he rose above that and rushed to Jonah's side. With great urgency he tore away strips of Jonah's pants and then fashioned a tourniquet to stem the flow of bleeding. Wendell watched this scene play out with consternation, an inner struggle playing out in his mind. These actions did not line up at all with what he knew of the relationship between Cardell and Quinn and the smoldering dislike for Jonah which Cardell seemed to keep burning inside him. It was completely out of character but it certainly seemed that for all intent and purpose Cardell appeared to be hell bent on saving Jonah's life. That would soon change.

The Interview

Lana was on the edge of her seat. "There has been no release of information regarding Jonah's condition, isn't that correct? What happened to him? And what happened as a result of all the food and waste which Bennett so haphazardly discarded?"

Alan nodded his head in acknowledgement of her questions. "I was about to get to that. But before I continue on let me say that Cardell was no saint. It may appear on the surface that he was a man among men but in truth he was the lowest of the low. Regina had begun to uncover so many layers of deception occurring within the company, things tying Rookwood to Bennett and to Benjamin, most certainly to Burton. You may think that those three *"B's"* as we call them were just *pawns* in this game but their actions were no less catastrophic than the actions of their superiors. All of this will be revealed as I tell the story. For now though, you are about to hear the rather gruesome and graphic details regarding Jonah's fall. Do you need a break or should I plow forward?"

"Oh, um, well," Lana leaned back for a moment thinking to herself and running some thoughts through her head. She leaned forward, posing a question. "Is it-- *bad*?"

Alan's face provided the answer with a grimace before he softly said, "Yes. Yes, it *is* bad. Very, *very* bad."

"Okay," said Lana. "If you will give me just a moment." She got up and left the room knowing now where to find the ladies room. After only a few minutes she returned looking composed and focused. "Alan. Please continue."

"Very well," said Alan. He then began to relate what happened after Jonah's serious injury and the open invitation for wild animals to find them which Bennett had so hastily gifted.

My Bad

Cardell has managed to staunch the flow of blood from Jonah's leg but the injury is quite serious. The need for medical attention is more than obvious. Cardell reaches into his pocket to check his phone. *WTF?!* He realizes that he has done a very stupid thing. He has left his phone *"ON"* this entire time with no way of keeping it charged. Whether or not cell service was available now was immaterial at this point. His phone was dead. A look of genuine frustration and dismay appears on his face as he considers the fact that if *he* has left *his* phone on—

"Everyone! Quick, check your phones! Does anyone have service?!"

Each member of the group did a search with their hands to locate their phones. The looks on their faces matched their statements, 'I got nothing' and 'My phone died.' They were not used to being disconnected from the world. This was a small thing. No phone service. But it could mean that Jonah would die as a result of their failure to plan. Cardell cursed himself. They should have planned to keep only one or two phones on and active at a time. This would all come back on him for this, he was sure of it. After all he was the most senior company member of this group. What was the old adage? 'If you fail to plan, you are planning to fail.'

Cardell had a sweet deal going on with his job right now and he didn't want to ruin it. He needed to do something that would redeem him in the eyes of the group. True he had taken quick action to render Jonah first-aid but if he was being honest with himself he knew he did that out of impulse. He would just as soon have been willing to watch Jonah bleed out. In some remote region of his brain it would have evened the score for what Jonah had done to Quinn.

For the time being, he needed to take action that would keep up the appearance of him doing all he could to save the life of a member of their group. Cardell's true opinion was that he did not expect Jonah to survive the journey back to the parking lot. And even if he did, they would certainly need to call for a Life-Flight helicopter. Thankfully, (Cardell is thinking of the expensive interior of his expensive Porsche being ruined by Jonah's blood), there would be no possible way of transporting Jonah in the tights confines of his sports car without causing more injury. Neither Bryson *nor* the van would be there. Of that he was certain. The outlook for Jonah was grim at best.

Cardell realized then that he was being inactive, lost in thought. He quickly put his phone away and took control. He sensed that he had just narrowly beat Wendell to the punch. He had the makings of a plan and the skill set to get it done. He started giving commands to the others. A few of them were dispatched to gather up the foods which Bennett had tossed away. It would be a bit treacherous but they really couldn't afford to leave these things behind. To the others he directed them to search and find two fallen branches roughly 8 feet in length. Cardell has determined that they will fashion a makeshift *"travois"* which they can use to better transport Jonah. He knows that he will have Wendell's full support on this, which is important now and will be important later as well when the events of their adventure are being shared with Regina.

Cardell and Wendell do most of the work building the simple machine. A travois is an A-shaped structure which may have originated with the American Indians. It features a platform stretched between two poles fashioned together at one end and then splayed out from there. The tip of the "A" portion of the structure will be the pulling point. The platform (sleeping bags) will be where Jonah will lie. The outer two points of the pole will drag along the ground. This simple machine is not ideal but with no wheels at hand this will prove to be the most efficient method of moving Jonah to safety.

Wendell is impressed with Cardell's ingenuity and with his engineering mind in full gear they make quick work of their creation. Moving Jonah onto the travois will be the most difficult thing many of them will ever face. The pain they were causing him was intense. The screaming was almost too much to take. Thankfully for all he passed out from the exertion and the loss of blood. William cursed himself for bringing up the mention of the movie *'Deliverance'* as they now seemed to be *living it*.

Cardell wonders to himself is it just him or have the animal sounds in the forest grown louder and more pronounced? He looks over to Wendell. The look on his face seems to say the same thing. Neither read this as a good sign. Both are thinking of the element of cause and effect. There are certainly consequences to every action. The trail of "breadcrumbs" left behind by Bennett (*the cause*) have yet to have an *effect*. Cardell and Wendell know that could change at any moment. Right now that was their greatest fear. They were basically waiting for the other shoe to drop.

Each member of the group has been taking turns being the one to pull the travois forward with Jonah onboard. It was slow-going as this was an exhausting and tiring effort. Due to the narrow path they must follow along the edge of the incline of the hill only two people at a time could be hooked up to the simple machine. Only Bennett and Benjamin complained of their call of duty. Jodi volunteered before being asked. Truth be told she might *not* have been asked such was the fear of interaction with her. Unlike the others, *by choice* she pulled the travois *alone*. No one was keeping score but if they had it would be no surprise that her effort gained the most ground. She was slight in stature but made up for that with sheer determination and will. Jodi's abilities could be likened unto that of a spider's web. It was a lesson learned too late by her quarry when they realized they had greatly misjudged the deception (and danger) hiding inherent within the fragile display.

So it is the half-hearted efforts of two fools which can be blamed, if blame is to be assessed, that lead to the events which follow. The travois is dependent upon a level surface in order to keep the weight of its load safe from shifting or possibly even tumbling out. Jonah has been tied securely to the structure so there is no chance of him tumbling out. There is a concern however of tipping in favor of the embankment to their right. Should he tip too far it would be his own weight which would carry the travois over the edge and skid down the embankment.

Failing to grasp the severity of the situation they were in, combined with their childish behavior (Bennett and Benjamin are punching one another back and forth in a mock fist fight), one of the poles of the travois trails over the edge of the narrow path. Jonah himself leans over at the wrong moment to view the danger he would face if he were to fall. His weight combined with the weight of the food items which the group had collected and tied around his body make for a heavy and rather unsteady load. The explanation for tying the food around Jonah on the travois was twofold. The device itself was better suited to the carrying of this burden plus by lightening the load which each member would carry, it would serve to give them a reserve of energy they would need when taking their turn tugging along the travois.

Each member of the group (with the exception of Bennett and Benjamin) watched in slow motion as one of the poles strayed further and further towards the edge and the threat of Jonah sliding over the edge went from possibility to reality. Gravity took control at that point by latching onto the weight of the passenger and greedily pulled Jonah over the edge of the embankment.

Bennett and Benjamin felt at first only a slight tug and then suddenly they were yanked off their feet and hit the ground hard. Both grasped anything they could hold onto to stop the slide down the hill that they too were now experiencing.

"Undo my pack!" yelled Bennett. Benjamin reached over and with some effort was finally able to free Bennett's backpack from the travois.

"Undo mine!" yells Benjamin. Bennett is in a better position to help Benjamin as he now has two hands free. Benjamin is quickly released from the tether. Now without the anchor weight of the two young men Jonah and the travois quickly begins to slide away from them.

It is of no surprise to Wendell that Bennett and Benjamin would attempt to save themselves first even though the inherent danger was not facing them. He yells to Cardell to help him stop the slide of the travois. Cardell's "attempt" to help is half-hearted at best and they both lose their grip. Wendell swore that he heard Jodi laugh as Jonah slid away as surely did his hope for a safe return. Incredibly one pole of the travois struck a tree on the descent which turned it around. That turn forced the other pole to come into contact with and then wedge itself into the junction of two other trees.

The first tree had served to slow the progress of the travois. The second (and third) tree had stopped it altogether. Jonah was now nestled in between two trees like a fallen hammock only twenty yards down the embankment. With the perplexity of the steepness of the hill it could just as easily have been twenty miles. The odds of Jonah's recovery had just multiplied exponentially. He sensed his predicament and began to wail. No one was looking her way but even if they had Jodi would have made no attempt to hide the smirk that crept along her face.

Wendell is the first to act. The screams from Jonah intensify the group. He is attempting to rally this team to do whatever it takes to pull Jonah and the travois back up the slope. They are all tired and drained from the events of the journey but Jonah's *life* was now at stake. They *must* pull together.

Wendell has his back turned when cause and effect suddenly catch up to another. He is engaged in an anxious discussion with other members of the group. They are laying out the options of how to safely and expediently recover their work associate. Joni has seen what has just happened and leaves the group. This is of no concern to Wendell, which unfortunately allows several precious seconds to elapse which might have made a world of difference.

Cardell is on his belly leaning over the edge. His outstretched arm is of no use to Jonah as he is twenty yards down the steep incline. It is a rote action being made out of abandoned hope. The rules suddenly change for Cardell as he sees a game changer enter the picture. It is a large and apparently hungry and agitated black bear heading in the direction of where Jonah has ended up. He is now in more peril than can be imagined.

Fortunately Cardell knows what to do. When in the presence of a grizzly bear one should play dead and pray the bear will lose interest in you. A black bear, however, is much different. They want nothing to do with people and are easily spooked. Making noise and waving one's arms about is the best policy to ward off a black bear's interest. Cardell's proclaimed knowledge of the wilderness will come into question later when it is discovered that he had advised Jonah to lie still and play dead. Doing the absolute *wrong* thing as well as being packed up with unsealed containers of food can only lead to a black bear encounter from which Jonah Priestas may not survive.

Cardell glances first in Wendell's direction before he shout/whispers down to Jonah.

"Jonah! Listen to me! There is a bear coming your way! Keep your mouth shut and keep absolutely still. Do you hear me?"

Jonah's eyes go wide with fear as he looks around wildly and finds the bear ambling his way. It is snuffling at the ground and at the air. It has obviously followed the scent, breadcrumbs if you will, which Bennett has been leaving behind. The bear has been tracking them and is now yards away from the space where a severely injured (and bloodied) man as well as a bounty of food is tied down to a makeshift travois. The bear is now in this space and has become the preeminent threat.

Jonah is terrified. This might explain why he at first chose to follow the advice given him by Cardell. Now he is asking himself *why* he trusts Cardell. Jonah and the bear have not yet made eye contact but that moment is about to happen. When Jonah's frightened eyes meet those of the surprised animal, instinct causes it to unleash an angry howl. The bear is hungry. It has been on the prowl for several hours and now it feels challenged. There is nothing anyone can say or do at this point to alter the situation and what happens next.

Wendell turns at the sound. His body is instantly cold at the urgency of the bear's howl. He sees Jonah whimpering yet quiet, in full view of the bear. He sees the bear eying Jonah oddly, possibly thinking that Jonah with his open wound must look like a half-eaten steak. What a *horrible* thought. Then Wendell looks to Cardell and clearly sees him making a shushing motion with his finger to his lips. That son of a bitch! Placing his own life at risk Wendell has a shout ready to come from his mouth in hopes of startling the bear when suddenly it happens. And it happened *so fast—*

The bear lunged at Jonah with jaws gaping open. It was unable to discern the difference between Jonah and the group's food packages. The bear attacked with incredible ferocity. The bites taken by the bear were huge and veracious. The daggers of teeth ripped away fabric, skin and bone with ease. The tardy shout from the group made no impact on the bear at first. It was in a mad rage of feeding. In seconds which seemed like hours, the bear fed upon the contents of the travois which included the body of Jonah Priestas. His screams only seemed to encourage the bear attack more. Eventually the mauling subsided and the bear was sated. It looked up to the group as if seeing them for the first time and appeared to be jolted by the sight of them. It ran down the hills and disappeared into the dense forest brush.

Wendell looked from the place where the bear had gone to what remained of Jonah. It was a bloody mess. Suddenly he clenched up then heaved and vomited. Wendell had just realized that Jonah was still *alive*.

Cardell was seemingly unaffected by the gruesome scene. Wyatt had kneeled down beside him. He too had seen how Cardell had mislead Jonah upon the bear's arrival. He looked Cardell in the eyes and said, "What have you *done*? You know what to do in the presence of a bear. And you know the difference between the handling of a grizzly bear and a black bear. What you told Jonah was *wrong*. And you *knew* it."

In Cardell's mind he went immediately to the earlier situation when Wyatt had scorned him by shirking his responsibility in the food poisoning incident. It was the least normal thing to say but Cardell said it anyway. "My bad. I must have got the two remedies switched around in my head." He said this looking fully at Wyatt. It was both a vengeful statement and a *re*vengeful statement if there was such a thing.

The group stood silently as they watched, and *listened*, to Jonah Priestas take his last gasps of life. Cardell mutters a silent devotion under his breath to Queenie upon the death of Jonah. *"For my queen."*

By sundown, the group had made it back to the remote parking area of the Mt. Whitney Portal where Cardell had left his Porsche. As he expected it sat alone with no van in sight. He offered to go get help as it was after all his vehicle. He had already left before it dawned on Wendell that it would be Cardell's version of events that the authorities would hear first. Although somewhat problematic he *hoped* that ultimately the truth would prevail.

The group waited, tired and beaten for help to arrive. Somehow they had managed to cover up Jonah's corpse securely and return him from the wilderness back to the world where his remains could be humanely put to rest. He left behind a wife and two children.

Although still living none of the remaining "survivors" left the survival trek truly unscathed.

Even Joni was effected. She—wanted more.

Part Three
Cross-Check

There was an unsettled calm in the offices of *NRG* Dynamics upon the return of the individuals who had been on the *Survival Trek*. Of course not *all* of the group had returned. There was a buzz going around about what may have happened to Jonah Priestas. All sorts of rumors had found their way to Regina's office. She did her level best to squelch them all. Another company meeting had been announced to touch upon these rumors and to share openly with the group the particulars of the outing.

This meeting was still several days away which led to speculation that perhaps Jonah had passed and there was the need of allowing time for family grieving and funeral arrangements. No one wanted this to be true but his absence was so obvious. Those who *had* returned were not talking. The only one who gave any indication that these rumors may hold validity was Joni whose coy looks kept them active.

The *Survival Trek* was by all accounts an unmitigated disaster. It was supposed to have been a team building exercise. In Regina's mind it had served only to demonstrate the great divide that existed within the company. If she had not known it before it was certainly obvious now. As obvious as black and white. There were two *"competing"* factions in the company; those who pledged their allegiance to her and Alan, and those who chose to follow Quinn and Thad. Regina balked at the usage of the word *competing* but unfortunately she was all too certain that it was spot on. She had yet to give full credence to the idea that Thad might actually have turned against his close friend Alan but she had to admit that it *was* possible. If anyone was capable of doing such a thing to a man it would be Quinn.

It is early, early on Thursday morning. Only a handful of people are in the office at this point in time. More will begin to arrive as the sun begins to make it presence known. Regina is waiting for Cardell Rookwood inside his office with the lights off. She is consumed with dark thoughts regarding the *Survival Trek*. The group that had gone on the journey left on Friday of last week. They had been due back in the office on Monday morning. That of course did not happen. They returned yesterday, which was Wednesday. They were on the mountain for nearly *five* days with only two to three days of rations. They had called themselves *"Trekkies,"* a simple play on words. Ten company employees had set out on this adventure. Not all of them had returned. Mystery surrounds two of them as one was still missing and the other was dead. The fact that Jonah's body was almost ripped in half was particularly disturbing.

Yesterday had been quite a busy day for Regina. She had met with each returning member of the group with the exception of Rookwood and Joni. She saved those meetings for today. Her first meeting had been with the one person she trusted the most, which was Wendell. She knew that she needed to maintain a certain amount of objectivity to what he shared because he could not have heard and seen all of the things that happened on the mountain. Still though his perspective would prove to be invaluable to her. As she considered his testimony, it dawned on her that he appeared to be the only one who did not seem to be "pointing fingers" at the others. Wendell was a man without guilt so the truth came easy for him.

Regina heard a beep which was the result of the use of a proximity card. Cardell Rookwood had arrived at his office assuming the door would be locked. Regina heard a grunt from Rookwood as he must have realized that he was unlocking an already unlocked door. Regina knew that this would surely bother him and cause him to be uneasy. Perfect.

Rookwood does not venture further into the office. Instead he flicks on the lights and scans the room. He appears at first to be startled to see Regina sitting in his desk chair but quickly regains his composure.

"Are you surprised to see me?" queries Regina.

"You? No. I am not surprised to see you. I would have been surprised to see Alan."

Regina ignores this bit of sarcasm. "You look none the worse for wear," Regina comments, matching Rookwood's sarcastic tone, "considering all that you have been through."

Cardell is uncomfortable with the situation. He would have liked to have taken his seat behind his desk and affected a position of authority. Regina was one step ahead of him by occupying that seat. She kept him standing and off balance.

"So, I am not surprised to see *you* but I *am* surprised that Joni would *allow* you access to my office." Rookwood says this with all the bravado which he can muster. If he is expecting to put Regina in a defensive posture he is mistaken. Like the skilled chess player she has become, she is thinking several moves ahead of him.

"I recognize the fact that Joni is the "Director" of Security but I do not need her approval to gain access to *your office* and or any *other* for that matter. You are forgetting that Joni reports to *me* now. As do you."

This last comment stung Rookwood. It was very direct and said without any qualms or hesitancy. Regina was everything everyone said about her. Alan might be the President of the company but Regina was clearly the one in charge. Rookwood is relying on his alliance with Quinn to see him though this bothersome hurdle.

Before Cardell can stand his ground and make a case for why Regina should leave his office and let him get on with his day she makes the statement, "You have five minutes to tell me your version of the story of what happened during the Survival Trek. *Your* version that does not subsequently end with your release from this company as an employee. *Your* version differs from *mine*. Let me be clear about that last part."

Cardell chuckles and parrots Regina, "My *release*? That's rich."

"You're burning daylight, Cardell. I'm not hearing a story being told. I am being more than fair by allowing you the opportunity to tell your version of the story and that doesn't seem to be happening, does it? Please bear in mind that in all fairness to you, I would prefer to have our Director of Legal Affairs be a part of this discussion today but he can't be here right now. Or *ever* for that matter. And why is that Cardell?"

Rookwood appears to be dumbstruck at Regina's offensive attack. He stutters trying to get something out.

"What's the matter Cardell? Cat got your tongue? Okay fine, I will say it *for* you. Our former Director of Legal Affairs can't be here with us today because he is *dead*. Mauled by a bear. His body nearly torn in half."

"You can't blame me for that! It was a wild animal! We had no way to defend ourselves."

"Well, it appears to me that it was common sense which was required for the situation and clearly you were *unarmed*."

Regina scolded herself after that comment. She was becoming emotional, which was not what this situation called for. She needed to calm herself and deal with this like she would any other problem. With a level tone and cold resolve.

Rookwood pulls his shoulders back and stands a little straighter determined that he will tell *his* version of the story and dodge this bullet. The problem is that he has lost his opportunity and Regina isn't having it. That bullet he is attempting to dodge has been fired from a cannon. He knows what is coming next and chooses to deflect it. That decision will end badly for him.

Regina is seated comfortably in Cardell Rookwood's chair while he is still standing awkwardly in front of the desk, his coat and briefcase still in hand. Cardell attempts to master the moment by mustering his courage and hitting Regina with everything he's got. It isn't much. Cardell says, "You can't fire me. Queenie will--"

Oh dear.

If there ever was a *"worst possible thing to say in this moment"* ---

Regina bristles at this and jumps up angrily from Cardell's desk chair knocking it to the floor. She has fire in her eyes as she leans forward, places her hands on Cardell's desk and says in a menacing tone, "Queenie will *what*?!"

Rookwood is now frozen in place. A deer in the headlights. After five seconds of uncomfortable silence, Regina commands, "Cardell, clean out this desk." Rookwood is blasted with the subtlety of Regina making the statement "*this* desk," not "*your* desk." If there was a positive force in this world to offset the negative charge of Queenie it was clearly Regina.

And-- she was still talking. "... gather up your things and leave the building. *Now.* Security will take your badge and keys on the way out."

As Regina is making her way around "the" desk, eager to leave Rookwood's office, Cardell makes an idiotic statement, "I think you're forgetting how well-connected I am."

Regina stops, looks at him confidently and replies, "I think *you're* forgetting how well-connected *I* am. I am *married to* the owner and president of the company. I am the Senior Vice President of Operations. I have the prerogative to *make* this decision as well as *execute* this decision. If you wish to challenge my authority, take me to court."

Regina left in a huff and did not look back. Had she done so she would have seen a broken man. For all his bluster Cardell Rookwood was as insecure as a child on his first day of school. He would not be heard from again. That was just fine with Regina.

The phrase *"and the news spread like wildfire"* was never more true than what happened after Cardell Rookwood's departure from his former office. When Rookwood passed through security for the last time at least one of the individuals he encountered was still faithful to Queenie. He dutifully sent a message to Toni who he knew to be in the building that day. This action was not in the interest of preserving the peace or the safety of the occupants in the building. He was starting a forest fire. And he *knew* it.

After hearing of the summarily firing of Cardell Rookwood, Toni immediately texted her sister Joni who forwarded her text on to Quinn. Moments later a text appeared on the screen of Toni's cell phone which simply read: *"Do bad things."* This prompted an evil smile from Toni. Toni is in need of a release from her anger. She puts her phone in her pocket and goes to work.

There are two objects on Whittaker's desk which tend to garner the attention of anyone passing by. To a casual observer the two objects are identical. To those in the know, which was just about everyone in the office now, there is a distinct difference. One of the objects is an actual rock purported to contain a *Regalis crystal* inside which was, no one would argue, kind of a big deal. One would of course have to *crack the rock open* to be certain.

The other "rock" on Whittaker's desk is an incredible 3-D printing which had taken hours for him to create. The math alone to achieve the copy was impressive. The *Regalis* rock is heavy, heavier than its appearance would suggest. This is one of the attributes of the *Regalis* crystal which gave more credence to Whittaker's claims that this rock did *indeed* hold a precious *Regalis crystal* inside. Whittaker was always joking about how *'one day, one day'* he would know for sure. That day seemed to have arrived.

In terms of weight the other rock was the obverse of the original. Weighing only a few ounces it defied explanation when first picked up by an unknowing individual. The joke had been played on just about everyone in the building. *'Which rock is heavier?'* The first one strained the arm when lifting, the other was light as a feather. Everyone was in on the joke so whenever there was a "newbie" to be found others gathered around to watch the reaction.

The area where Whittaker worked with the other Project Engineers was generally fairly quiet. Engineers tend to be rather focused when engaged on a project. When asked later none of them could recall just *when* Toni had appeared in the area. In fact none of the engineers even noticed her presence until *after* "the scream." And what a scream it was...

Whittaker's hands were laid flat on his desk as he prepared to use them as leverage to lift his body up from sitting for several hours. To say his hands were vulnerable at that moment would be an understatement. To say that Toni had a gift of fortuity would be a fact. She knew and understood the difference between the two *"rocks."* The godawful scream happened when she lifted the *real* rock, the impossibly heavy one, and then slammed it down with force onto the back of Whittaker's right hand.

Whittaker's scream cut through the calm of the engineering room and echoed off the windows to instill a cringing panic to everyone within the room. Chairs toppled over as the men in the room jumped up from their desks. All eyes, widened with surprise, were now turned to Whittaker who was still screaming at the top of his lungs. At first these were just screams, now there were words formed within the screams.

"My hand! My hand!"

The engineers saw Whittaker first, his face now bright red, one arm holding the other, and then they saw Toni. Her presence here was an anomaly. It was the single factor which disrupted the equation and these guys lived *solidly* in the world of logic and reason.

Wyatt was nearest to Whittaker when the incident happened. After Whittaker and Toni he was the first of the group to have a good look at Whittaker's destroyed hand. The force which Toni had used had caused the bones to splinter and the fingernails to crack. A minimal amount of blood was visible but that actually made it look worse. This was a deep bruise and the hand was continuing to swell. Discoloration has already begun with the hand presenting first as a dark red now changing to purple. Over the course of healing there would be a virtual rainbow of colors.

Whittaker was staring at Toni in obvious agony. Toni's hand still held the rock in place on Whittaker's hand, perhaps even now exerting force. The screaming has not abated. Finally she releases the pressure and allows the rock to tumble from her hand which settles on the desk eerily close to the 3-D printed version. Whittaker has stopped screaming. He is now shaking and breathing erratically looking as though he might pass out.

Toni begins to turn away then catches the eye of Wyatt. She gives him a hard cold stare and says, *"What?!"*

Wyatt asks simply, "Why?"

Toni gets right up in his face, her eyes burning anger into his and fires back, *"He touch me."*

Toni had said, *'He touch me,'* not he *"touched" me.* Wyatt wasn't even sure if that mattered but it was worth contemplating all the same. As Toni walked away in a manner showing that her job here was done, Wyatt could not help but to consider also that that was the first time he had *ever* heard her speak.

Toni's act was brutal. The consequence of the action meant that Whittaker might never have full use of that hand again. He denied ever *"touching"* her. Even if he had, the punishment did not fit the crime.

Unfortunately for others in the building Toni-- was not done.

A measure of the security detail were in Regina's camp which meant their first call was to Brock Rampart. He was on his way out of the building on his way to an appointment. Brock was not aware that Toni was able to intercept his messages. He had just entered the parking garage when he got the call and saw the running figure whom he knew to be Toni. Little did he know that he was soon to be in the path of a runaway train.

Richard Castle is the VP of Procurement. A *"crazy"* day in his world might mean that the shipment of a particular item could be delayed for a week. There would be a sudden flurry of activity to find the missing item locally. That was the extent of his crazy. Richard was stable and straight as an arrow. He was a company man and kept to himself. He had genuinely earned both his position in the company as well as his reputation as a man who could be counted on to do his part without fail. That being said, he did not hesitate when he heard Brock Rampart call out to him, *"Stop her!"*

Richard had just pulled into his assigned parking spot within the central parking garage. The garage was designed to accommodate the full workforce of the three companies residing on this business campus. Richard drove a gloss black 7 series *BMW.* Just before emerging from his car he had received a security alert of the highest order. As he heard Brock call out to him and he saw the person running he quickly made the connection and sprang into action. In his haste he left his car door wide open.

Richard was much closer to the individual running through the garage than was Brock. He was gaining ground and began to ask himself a rather important question. *What was he prepared to do if he actually caught up to this person?* At this point in time he had no idea of gender. He was assuming it was a man.

Just when Richard had determined that he would put an open field tackle on this guy as he had done many times in his days as college football player, the person suddenly stopped and turned toward him. Richard skidded to a stop almost falling forward. To his surprise he actually knew who this person was although the two had never spoken.

It was Toni, the Director of IT. *Ha!* He smirked at the thought of her title. As far as he was concerned, that girl couldn't even *spell* IT. Yep, he recognized her for sure but-- she looked *different.* She had, oh my god, the evil look of a *killer* etched upon her face.

Richard took a step back. That was when he noticed that her hand was *bleeding.* Moreover Toni was *holding something* in her bloodied hand. She lifted the object now with *both* hands. It was-- an *axe.*

What the fuck?!

Richard took another step back. Something kind of like a smile crossed Toni's face and then the tables turned. The *"pursued"* became the *"pursuer."* Toni advanced with the axe in hand as Richard turned to run.

Although the façade of the building which housed *NRG* Dynamics had been constructed recently giving the appearance of *"new,"* the actual bones of the building dated back several decades. Back to the days when a coiled fire hose and fire axe were housed in a large metal cabinet near a stairwell, accessible in a time of emergency by simply breaking the glass. Toni had done exactly that and now had a dangerous weapon at her disposal to aid her in an escape from the building.

In her flight Toni considered Brock Rampart a *concern.* This man she was chasing now, Richard Castle, was simply a *distraction.* Toni hefted the heavy axe and then swung the weapon with wild abandon. The moment she felt resistance, and heard the *scream*, she knew the weapon had found its mark. Richard went down fast, his body now writhing in pain. But-- there was a problem. Toni's efforts to pull the axe free were eluding her. She hadn't counted on losing the axe so soon. A change in plans was necessary as the axe was lodged firmly in Richard's back.

Toni looked about the garage for Brock. She had heard him yell but didn't see him, however, before she could work at retrieving the axe she heard the squealing of tires. Brock had jumped in Richard's car in an effort to gain an advantage over Toni. She saw the BMW coming her way and turned to run dodging in and out of cars parked at random.

Toni's cell buzzed. She glanced down and saw that it was Joni. She stopped dead not wanting to miss the call. *"Sister?"*

It was *not* Joni. Rampart had used technology to thwart Toni's run from justice. The call had actually come from *his* phone. The call had been made to distract her just long enough to---

"Oh shit!" exclaimed Brock.

The BMW was powerful. And *fast.* Brock had come up on Toni quicker than he had anticipated. He hit the brakes too late. He watched in horror as the BMW lifted Toni off the ground like a rag doll and threw her forward. Miraculously she got up but now she was occupying the space between the car and a concrete column. He felt his foot pressing down on the accelerator and his mind telling him it was the brake pedal. As if he were just a patron in a movie theater he looked on as the force of the car first impaled, then crushed Toni's small frame into the unforgiving concrete. Brock bore witness to the horrified look on her face for only a fraction of a second before the air bags deployed. He had had every intention of bringing Toni to justice but the loss of life was too high a price. Brock sat immobile in Richard's car for several minutes overwhelmed by the moment. No tears came. He wondered what that said about him as a person.

Regina was still several minutes away from learning of Toni's assault on both Wyatt and Castle as well as the horrific end to Toni's short life. Toni and Joni had both just turned thirty when hired by Quinn who had placed extra value on their youthful energy.

Regina was back in her office making phone calls. Her agenda this morning was to rid the company of the vermin left behind by Quinn. Cardell Rookwood had already been terminated. In Regina's mind Jon Hightower would be next. It is remarkable, she thinks to herself, that he answers his phone on the first ring and accepts her invitation to come to her office. Regina's expectation is that this meeting will be brief. Jon, however, has a bit of a surprise for her which may explain his eagerness to take her call.

Jon Hightower enters Regina's office and accepts her offer by a wave of her hand to take a seat but *something* is not right. Jon is a squeamish man who would eagerly search for any possible reason available to *miss* her call. The fact that he nearly skipped down the hallway to be in her presence has her radar up. *Way* up.

"Tell me Jon, in your own words, why I find your eagerness to meet with me so odd. Are you of the opinion that I have some good news to share?" Her eyes are unwavering, drilling into his soul as Jon attempts to answer in a confident manner. There is no way that he will ever find himself comfortable in her presence. For one he is the nervous type, always a bit fidgety and guilty even when such an action does not apply. Also, he knows that Regina is like an obsessed dentist, drilling down with her questions until she finds the root.

"Regina." *Bad start.* Jon clears his throat and straightens his posture. "Ms. King."

On any other day, in any other situation, Regina would have preferred to be addressed by her first name. But not now. And not today. And not by this jackass. Jon was their appointed VP of Engineering with a degree in frickin' Economics. Just another one of Quinn's clever ploys. In Regina's opinion Jon's tenure here at the company had been "borrowed time" since day one.

"Ms. King."

"You said that already. You have my full attention. Soon I will feel like you are wasting my time. Please. Speak." Regina's body language was less than friendly but Jon mustered his courage and began to share a few tidbits of information that were sure to deflect her, at least for the time being anyway, from seeing *him* as the primary target of concern.

"You and I have not been on the best of terms shall we say."

"An obvious statement of fact. Will there be something of more substance to follow?"

Jon was not swayed by her sarcasm. It was a trap. A landmine. He had stepped on these before and had the scars to prove it. But not *this* time.

This time he *did* have something of substance to bring to the table. Something of *value*. Something of *concern* which Regina would surely think was something that required immediate action.

Regina only half-listened to Jon Hightower's babble of gossip as he attempted to set the stage for the plot to follow. Her ears perked up as she heard the names of the players. Two names with seemingly no connection to one another. Until now.

There had been rumors of Quinn being unfaithful to Thad and in Regina's estimation these rumors were probably true. But not Thad. *Never* Thad. The unlikely suggestion that Thad, an owner and partner of the company, her husband's closest friend since college may be having an illicit affair was simply *unthinkable*. And with an *employee* of the company no less. Before making any move or decision Regina made a risk assessment. Hearing the names *Thad Rex* and *Felicia Black* put side by side in such context and the term "intimate relationship" added in for good measure made for only one tangible result. The risk factor regarding this "rumor" was to her of the highest order.

After hearing the "gossip" he had to share he could see in her eyes that she understood how possible it was that this was factual information. Jon smiled inside, careful not to show his true feelings. The outcome of this meeting was better than he could have hoped for. She had said only thing before motioning to the door for Jon to leave. She held a finger to her lips and said, "Not a word." Jon had stupidly made the silly hand gesture of zipping his mouth and locking it with a key. It didn't matter. She had already moved on, searching for Felicia Black's number on the company register. The target was off his back now and Regina had something to keep her busy for a while. While she may have wanted to terminate him when he walked into her office that action was off the table. At least for now.

So certain was Jon that he was clear of Regina's radar that he took the remainder of the day off to play a round of golf at the club. Out of sight, out of mind. Jon would learn later that not much got by Regina. She knew exactly where he went after leaving her office. It was not a stretch to claim that Jon Hightower was not the brightest bulb in the pack.

The Interview

"Lana."

"Yes?"

"I'm sure you have done your research regarding the company so please take no offense. If you will allow me to fill in some gaps regarding the direction of the company. I fear I will lose track of the story if I do not retell it chronologically."

"Oh, but of course. It is *your* story to tell."

"You are very gracious. Thank you." Alan gave her a nod.

"I do appreciate your concern for accuracy." Lana smiled.

"I will keep this brief. It's just that during all this turmoil it would be easy for your readers to think that the company was in a downward spiral when the very opposite was true. The company was having a bit of a renaissance moment one could say. It was mostly tied to the work which Wilson was producing. Some people referred to him as 'the boy in the bubble' as he is on the autism spectrum and seems to live in his own world never allowing any of the distractions of *our* world to deter him from his mission."

Lana leaned forward; her interest piqued. She had read of these inventions Alan was referring to but did not know the background of their origin. Wilson had produced a light panel like none other ever conceived. In Wilson's words it was 'like a window with sunshine.' What he meant by that was that the panel was "allowing light in" as an indirect source. All light sources need to be filtered or shaded in some manner to not cause damage to the human eye. This light panel was truly like an actual window which *allowed* light rather than *produced* light. It was enough light to fill a room yet remained always retina friendly. It was an incredible feat of engineering. The panel was of course powered solely by the *Regalis* crystal. Wilson claimed the panel would be a reliable light source "indefinitely." When asked if he actually meant "forever," Wilson was quick to respond saying, 'no, not forever, because "forever" is not quantifiable.'

Alan continued on.

"When Wendell brought Wilson into the company he was very clear on what our expectations of him should be. He told us that Wendell possessed an *inner vison*. If you will allow a bit of an odd analogy, Wilson was not harnessed to the restrictive prejudices of "what can't be done" simply due to the fact that other attempts had already tried and failed. He was all too willing to "take the reins" and gallop full speed towards his goal. Early on in his work it was actually necessary for Wendell to protect Wilson from the scorn of his peers."

"Scorn?"

"Yes. Driven mostly by our Lead Engineer, Burton. It was fake news to be honest and of course it was seated in jealousy. He would laugh and say things like "wish I could sit around all day and just fuck off at my desk." He was of course "throwing shade" at Wilson when in reality he was quite aware of Wilson's capabilities. The truth was that he wanted that spotlight for himself. And he would do anything to get it."

"Anything?"

"Anything."

"Like—what?"

"I will tell you."

Don't mess with Wilson

If there was one rule that everyone at the company knew it was don't mess with Wilson. Wilson was special but not in the way that many might think. He was not given any unique privileges or opportunities not afforded to others. No, Wilson was special because Wilson had a gift. He could *see* engineering design in his mind's eye. He could manipulate the images in 3D, perhaps even 4D, and troubleshoot complex problems faster than a computer. What he lacked was the simple understanding of consumer need. Fortunately, he had Wendell by his side. Wendell was a trusted family member and friend who was capable of providing Wilson the direction needed to set him on the right path for industry wide *disruptive* product development.

Not everyone of course felt that Wilson should be the chosen one. As Lead Engineer, Burton was chief among them and struggled with Wilson's success daily. His dislike and discomfort of Wilson's work brought out the worst in Burton. Which is what lead him to seek out Joni for some advice on how to turn the tables.

'I don't want to hurt the guy,' Burton had said. 'I just want to get the jump on him. You know, be one step ahead of him so that the credit for his next big project will rightfully be *mine*.' This was a language Joni understood and soon there was a plan for Burton to *find* Wilson's plans and make them his own. He would doctor up Wilson's current plans a bit, just enough to make them unsuccessful. The result would be Wilson would fail. Burton would succeed.

The plan was genius. Failsafe. Burton had Joni to thank for that. She had given him security clearance (which could not be tracked) as well as a time and date (3:30 pm on Sunday) when the fewest amount of employees would be in the building. Burton followed Joni's advice to the letter. With one exception. He took it upon himself to add a bit of drama to his actions. He wore an all-black Ninja like costume. There was absolutely no need of it. Burton blended in by virtue of the fact that he was *allowed* to be there. This getup would absolutely draw attention to him if he were to be seen by anyone. And of course he was.

Burton is haphazardly going through the drawers of Wilson's desk searching for anything that looked even remotely like a work project. Joni had provided him with keys to Wilson's desk and the login information for Wilson's computer. They were both banking on the simple thought that "autistic" Wilson would be incapable of explaining that his workstation had been violated and valuable work materials stolen. This was of course decidedly inaccurate. Autism was *not* the equivalent of ignorance which is what Burton had in spades.

Regina had heard a sound which made her suspicious. She had stopped by the office to pick up some things she planned to work on from home. She was just leaving, checking each level (it was a thing) before she left. As fate would have it, she was in the same place at the same time as *someone* in the Engineering room. *Someone* who had *no place* being there. How this someone had thwarted security and found their way in here she had no idea but this was the last place in the building where Regina could possibly tolerate an intruder.

Regina reached into her purse to pull out her phone to contact security. She found instead the gun she carried for her own safety. Before she could put it away the noises grew more pronounced. Anger driven by the sense of personal and business violation made her advance towards the sound with arms outstretched and gun firmly in both hands now. Regina took self-defense training classes and was proficient with a firearm. She had no fear of this someone. And she would not relinquish company materials without a fight.

The noises were coming from Wilson's workstation. She knew it could not be him. She had just spoken with him before leaving her office. He was at his apartment teaching himself how to make a spaghetti dinner.

Regina rounds the corner past a row of cubicles and now has a clear view of Wilson's workstation. There is someone dressed all in black rummaging about in Wilson's desk. Now this person is seated and has begun to type something on the keyboard. A familiar graphic lit up the screen confirming that this individual had just gained access into the mainframe. Everything that meant anything to this company was in there and now at risk.

"NO!" shouted Regina. She began moving rapidly towards the individual seated at Wilson's workstation. All Regina could think of at this point was that either Quinn or Joni (or both) had hired someone to gain access to Wilson's computer and steal invaluable company information. Wilson would of course be blamed. And why not. His handicap made him an easy target. This thought only enraged her more.

"Get the fuck away from there and put your hands where I can see them!"

Burton panicked. He had never seen this side of Regina. And she had a gun. He did not think she would use it plus at this point in time she had no idea he was actually somebody she knew. Somebody who worked for her. Ah, the outfit was a clever idea after all. Burton just wanted her to back down so he could get away. He needed to do *something*. He picked up the stapler and hurled it at her. Not really *at her* but in her direction. She did not take this well and fired her weapon. Her intent was only to wound the intruder. The bullet nicked his shoulder while the force of the impact turned him away from her. Regina rushed towards him.

The pain was like a firebrand searing his shoulder with burning pain. After the initial wave of heat passed, a deeper more lasting pain began to settle into his bones. Burton let out a yell. It did not sound like him. There was still no way for Regina to know the identity of this intruder. The all-black outfit made him anonymous *and* dangerous.

Burton saw that Regina was now advancing on him with the gun trained at his chest. What the fuck was she thinking?! Burton leaped at her with the thought of taking her down. His shoulder still hurt like hell but the fact that his identity was hidden gave him the courage to maybe take a few swings at her. Not really hurt her. Just give her a bit of tough love.

What happened next happened so fast that it was just a blur. Regina had stopped and built a stance. Burton, however, had kept advancing towards her now swinging his arms wildly at her. He is yelling "you fucking bitch!" which can't be the best way to find common ground. She is yelling something back at him but it doesn't matter. Burton does not stop and now has a savage looking dagger in hand. This has escalated quickly. It is her or him. Regina holds her ground. The gun goes off again. This time it seems incredibly loud. There is a cloud of gunpowder in the air and for a moment in time both individuals are uncertain as to what the consequence will be...

And then the intruder in black is lifted off the ground with the force of the close-range shot. He is falling backwards in slow motion and then (she will never understand why) Regina fires the gun again. Whatever chance for survival Burton had was lost in that moment.

The intruder in black is now just a discarded rag doll lying in an impossible position. There is a security detail, a team of four men rushing through the aisles of the Engineering Room to set up a perimeter. But the threat has passed and the damage is done. Regina ignores their commands to hold her position. They know who she is, she has no fear of them. Gingerly she lays her weapon down and approaches the intruder in black curious of his identity. She grasps the face covering, a balaclava, in her hand and begins to pull upward. Regina now has a clear image of his eyes and her body goes cold. Recognition floods her brain as she tugs the garment from Burton's head.

Regina takes the dagger, (a *found* item), from Burton's hand and tosses it back onto Wilson's desk. It was just a plastic toy but the thing looked so goddamned real. She begins to shake and then to cry. Regina is not done. She puts her face close to Burton's and whispers indignantly, "You bastard. What have you made me do?"

Dark Times

In the aftermath of Burton's death Regina's moral compass fell victim to her anger and guilt. As a result her mental health declined. She had taken a man's life and could not reconcile her actions. She could no longer look herself in the mirror. Regina had always been the bedrock of the company, the foundational support for others. She was the captain of the ship, navigating the waters of corporate competition. Now she was lost and open to conspiracy theories she once ignored.

Alan was at a loss to understand how to bring her back. Her current obsession with the blossoming relationship of Thad and Felicia Black was overwhelming her and affecting her judgement. Alan trusted Thad with his life. This storm cloud of suspicion which hung over Thad and Felicia threatened to rain on their marriage which had survived many a thunderstorm. But could it survive a hurricane?

During work hours Regina finds herself spending her time reaching out to Felicia Black. She has even visited her residence in hopes of speaking with her one on one. Regina has never been one to allow someone else to fight her battles. She has to know if this "relationship" rumor is true.

These actions which Regina is taking is now of great concern to Jon Hightower. In his mind it can lead to only one result, conflict resolution. In an uncharacteristic move of his own Jon tracks down Felicia to "warn" her of Regina's troubled state and to muddy the waters as to her motives. His story is rather convincing if a bit farfetched. He tells Felicia that Regina is attempting to bring down the company one figurehead at a time. While *completely* untrue, the story does have merit from the standpoint of the names of those who *have been* "taken down" already. Gone are Jonah Priestas, Noble Gesture, Toni Bishop, Richard Castle, Kenneth Knight, and Cardell Rookwood. The most surprising of course is that even the mighty Quinn has been taken down.

Jon allows the weight of that name to settle before he mentions Burton's name and artfully inserts the word "murdered" which they both know not to be true but it languishes in the air regardless.

Jon could see that Felicia is swayed but still unconvinced. He needs one more nudge to send her over the cliff. During his drive home an idea pops into his head. Anthony Templar could be that nudge. If he can show that Regina is gunning for Templar, the company's Director of Human Resources no less, how could Felicia *not* believe that Regina was changing sides and had now *replaced* Quinn as the black queen in this twisted chess game?

Jon Hightower may have had an evil spirit but definitely did not possess the intellect of an evil mastermind. The fact that he botched his attempt to remove Templar and make Regina the patsy would have been anyone's prediction. Too late he realized that he should have gone to Joni but now she was out of the picture. He had to come up with something on his own, which he did. It failed miserably.

The next day, at his office desk, Jon Hightower sat down and did his very best to forge Regina's handwriting on a notepad bearing his own name and title. His lack of skill had him pressing down firmly with the pen on the pad leaving a traceable indentation on the page below. The message read simply, "You're next." Jon would like to believe that this was an original idea but he probably saw it in a movie or read it in a mystery novel. He signed it R.K. and then leaned back to appraise his work. His shook his fist in the air at his accomplishment. He was pleased.

Were he to seek a second opinion he would have heard that it was a foolish and amateurish effort. And an easy trail to follow. But, since that didn't happen, he waited until he believed that he was the only person left on his floor, got up from his desk and then tiptoed down the hallway. Wearing a sign that reads, "I feel guilty about my actions" might have been slightly less obvious.

Hightower looks around to see if anyone is watching. Nope, only the security cameras which seem to hide in plain sight now. Jon slips the note underneath Templar's office door and then walk/runs back to his office giggling like a teenager who had just toilet-papered a house.

When Anthony Templar arrived for work the next morning and discovered the note he did something which Jon had not expected. He reported it to Security who then shared it with Rampart. This spelled bad news for Jon Hightower. If your plan is to take down a member of the senior staff it should not include making the formidable Brock Rampart aware of it.

Rampart now began to take an interest in Jon Hightower's daily activities. After finding the notepad with the indentation of the forgery left not so cleverly on his desk Brock determined that Jon was up to something and he was hoping to catch him in the act. He could not imagine to what length a fool like Hightower would go to achieve his goal.

The steps which Jon Hightower *would* take to spook Anthony Templar into thinking that Regina was gunning for him escalated quickly. Jon found himself in a dark place and the only light he could see was pointing him in the direction of acting out against Templar. All his life he had been bullied due to his small size, his tiny voice, and his lack of athleticism. Through no fault or action of his own Templar has become the antagonist. Jon had nothing of substance to blame Templar for but that does not impede him from the actions he is taking in his ill-fated mission.

Rabbit Hole

Jon Hightower peeked inside the rabbit hole the moment he slid the forged note under Anthony Templar's office door. He then began a journey further down the rabbit hole with threatening emails sent from what he believed to be "safe" computers at the library, random phone calls at all hours of the day and night and letters with no return address. The notes inside were "old school" villainy, cutouts of letters from magazines to spell out their threat.

Anthony Templar did not know the origin of this campaign but he assumed Brock Rampart did so he took it all in stride. He did as he was told and reported each incident directly to Rampart. Brock asked him to trust him that it would all be resolved soon and things would return to normal. That was in fact contrary to how Brock truly felt. He was of the opinion that Hightower's antics might soon turn violent. He was on constant alert, knowing that he must catch him in the act in order to put this situation to bed permanently.

Brock is sitting in his car listening to a podcast. He glances in the direction of Jon Hightower's condo every few minutes. This is not the first time that he has done a stakeout and then followed Jon to see what he might be up to but—something inside him told Brock that this just might be the last. As if to justify his thoughts Jon steps out of his condo, turns and locks his door. He looks around furtively before descending the stairwell to the parking lot. These nervous glances are a sign for Brock that Jon is up to no good. He turns off the podcast, puts his car in gear and waits for Jon to make the first move.

Jon turns left out of his condominium complex and is heading for the entrance ramp to the freeway. This is convenient for Brock as his car is facing that direction and he can ease in behind Jon's car without attracting attention. Jon's condo is in a lower income area which surprised Brock when he first sought it out. He didn't know Jon's salary nor his financial situation but surely he could have done better. Where Jon was headed now was where Anthony's home was and where Brock might have expected Jon to live as well. Brock had made a mental note to look into Jon's past but had not yet begun the task. His curiosity about Jon Hightower was nagging at him now like a bothersome tooth.

Brock had looked up Anthony's address on Google Maps for just such an eventuality. He knew exactly where Jon was headed so he was able to hang back just a bit. Jon was the nervous type so Brock made sure that the headlights of his car appeared only infrequently in Hightower's rearview mirror.

It was less than a twenty-minute drive from Jon's condo to Anthony's residence. Brock chuckled as he watched Jon douse his lights and roll up to the curb quietly. The man was in "stealth" mode. For several minutes nothing happened and Brock had to guard against impatience. Just as he began to think that Jon must have lost his nerve the car door opened and Jon emerged, dressed all in black. A "ninja rook" in full battle gear no less.

Brock is ready. He is armed with an LED flashlight registering 10,000 lumens which could penetrate the blackest night up to 1700 feet away. It is his only weapon. Shining this light in Jon's face will literally scare the shit out of him. Brock is actually looking forward to that moment. He gets out of his car as well and shuts the door softly. Jon is already making his way across the lawn and towards the house. This catches Brock off guard. He was expecting Jon to just leave something in the mailbox. He sets off on a trot to shorten the distance between himself and Jon. He has no idea at this point what Jon might have in mind.

It is nighttime so the darkness helps but Brock would prefer having somewhere to hide. There are no trees in Templar's front yard so no place for him to dash behind. Brock Rampart has an apt name. Like the definition of a "rampart," the wall of a castle, Brock is a formidable man. Like the linebacker he once was, he is a stout man so he might even be mistaken for a tree. The only improvement of his name would be to call him "Brick" instead of Brock. Which his fellow college football players did as that was his adopted nickname.

Brock is worried. Jon is heading towards the house but not in the direction of the front door. Also he has something in his hand which Brock is struggling to discern what it might be in this darkness. His worst fear would be that it is a gun but that would be quite unlike Jon. But—who knows how deep the rabbit hole was that Jon has climbed down into?

Whatever the object was it had some heft to it and Brock was beginning to get the sense that Jon's intention is to hand deliver it to Templar. *By air*. Just then a light switch is flipped and the front room of the house is illuminated. There are curtains but they allow light to filter through them and a figure passes by the window. Jon reacts to this and starts running full tilt towards the house. Brock's thoughts are confirmed as he sees Jon suddenly come to a stop and his arm arch back for a throw.

Brock instantly charges towards Jon but realizes that he may be too late. He calls out.

"JON!"

Jon is in the act of throwing. Hearing his name catches him in mid-throw. He is not much of an athlete so the throw was already badly off target. Brock's call to him unfortunately *corrected* the throw. The figure inside the house is now peeking out through the curtains and sees an object hurtling towards the window only seconds before it smashes its' way through. The figure which is Templar tries to avoid the object as best he can.

In the front yard of Templar's house Jon is off balance and has his arms stretched out to catch his fall. Brock is about to ruin his day as he comes at him like a freight train to make an open field tackle. It was the worst angle and position for Jon to find himself in as the full weight of Brock Rampart came down on his body. He heard the frail bones of his forearms snap as they pressed into the hard earth. A scream of shock and pain comes from Jon as Brock rolls on top of him. He passes out and his body begins to quiver.

Understanding that Jon is no longer a threat Brock bolts for the house. He has no time to hope that Templar is able to unlock and open the door. Brock instead makes his way carefully into the house through the large, now shattered picture frame window. His eyes locate the object which Jon had thrown. It is a black metal skull adorned with voodoo symbols.

"What the fuck?!" Brock says aloud.

Just as he begins to process the skull he realizes that there is greater damage done inside the house than the broken window. Templar had been able to dodge the incoming projectile but as he turned away his foot had caught the edge of a chair and he had fallen face first into a large glass-topped coffee table. Brock sucked in air at the sight of Templar's body sticking up out of the coffee table with a growing pool of blood spreading out below. What a horrible way to die.

Strange what the human mind conjures up when dealing with extreme trauma. Brock thinks to himself that he must be looking at an art project where the artist has depicted a man jumping into a pool but the water is actually glass.

It is wrong and unnecessary and Brock knows this but he has momentarily lost track of both his composure and his sense of self-control. He walks away from the gurgling sound of a man taking his last breaths through a severed airway. The heavy tempered glass of the table found his throat and had cut him deeply. Brock now intends to even the score.

Jon is wanting to get up from the ground but his brain is failing to make sense of the fact that his arms are broken and have become just floppy and useless appendages. He sees Brock coming towards him through bleary eyes. Surely he will help.

The kick to his ribs came hard and fast followed by several more less targeted blows to his body. Jon was coughing up blood by the time Brock mumbled some invectives at him and then headed towards his car. Anthony Templar was beyond saving now and Jon Hightower didn't deserve to live so Brock left without calling 911. It was a bit of a risk leaving the scene of such horror but it was one he felt he had to take. Brock was fairly certain that any neighbors who might have looked out their window would not be able to recall what car drove away after the second bout of screaming from the man who was later found scrunched up tightly into a fetal ball on Anthony Templar's front lawn.

The broken window encouraged the investigating officers who arrived later to enter the house (Brock had left the door open) and find the deceased man who face planted into the glass coffee table. Making sense of what happened, and *why*, would plague them for weeks.

The Interview

"Let's stop here for a moment. I am going to ask you for a bit of a favor."

"Oh?"

"Yes, it's regarding Brock. I shared everything with you just now for context with your story but, well, I see no reason for you to include his being there *at the scene*. I feel like he has suffered enough. And just so you know, if it helps in any way, he eventually *did* go to the police to share what he knew of the situation. He has served his share of public service hours in atonement for leaving the scene of a crime, etc."

Lana was pensive, considering what had just been shared, weighing her moral obligations against her journalistic values. A question needed to be answered before she would agree to Alan's terms. The question was probably more personal than professional.

"Did that incident--?" She paused and then finished with, "*change* him at all?"

"Hmm." Alan's body language suggested that he may have been keeping something inside that needed to be released. "*Change?!* I'll say. Put it this way. Brock was like an action figure in a video game. He had this hard exterior shell where everything just bounced off of him. After that event he was, um, *different*. It was like he had crawled *inside* of that shell for a while."

Lana kept her silence to allow Alan to continue. She could see that he had more to say. He did.

"Honestly, it was a tough time for me. Not only was Regina a bit of a mess, mentally you know, but now Brock was out of sorts as well. Regina has a very small community with whom she relies on and places her trust. In that community is me of course, then there is Wendell, Wilson, Brock and Thad. So much had happened that challenged her faith in the people around her. I'm talking about all the other employees here, which certainly includes Quinn and her minions. Jonah and others we have lost. Then Wendell was directly involved with the death of Jonah as he was *there*. That shook him up, which in turn affected Regina. Because of Quinn's greed and ambition Regina began to lose faith in Thad and then this thing with Brock. Next to Regina he may have been the strongest of us all. If you will afford me another odd analogy he was the "lighthouse" for the company. He was our rock that stood strong against the currents.

His light guided us in each day. Once he went down, well Regina, she began to lose hope."

"What happened next? There must be a missing piece to this puzzle of which I am unaware."

"That's true. That is *very* true."

Lana tried not to seem impatient but was now quite eager to learn what skeleton in the closet yet remained. "Would you care to elaborate?"

Alan smiled and then gave himself a moment to collect his thoughts before continuing.

"Certainly. In Regina's darkest moment and, no pun(s) intended, with our "lighthouse" having gone "dark," a new "beacon of light," shall we say, emerged on the horizon. This person was a *very* unlikely candidate for becoming Regina's most trusted foot soldier but she was already in a weakened state. In the heat of battle there are good decisions made and quite often there are bad decisions made as well. And then, well, sometimes there is the worst-case scenario where the *unthinkable* seems like a good idea."

"Please, do tell. Does the "unthinkable" have a name?"

"Yes. Yes, it does. *'It's'* name is Wyatt and he nearly brought this company to its knees."

Part Four
Material

'Perception is reality.' Although many others have stated the same in various ways, this is a quote made by strategist Lee Atwater which Thad Rex believes to this day to be true. Amidst the turmoil he had removed himself from the daily grind of the *NRG* Dynamics office and now believes that his perspective may be more accurate than the other senior officers in the company. It was a "forest for the trees" sort of thing. You can't see the totality of the situation when you're immersed in it.

Thad had kept his finger in the pie the entire time even though Regina felt wholeheartedly that he had just *checked out*. While it was true that he had fallen under the spell of "Queenie," and for all the wrong reasons, he has since been able to extricate himself from that smothering blanket of a presence. There was a guilty pleasure in the fact that he *knew* that he had escaped her wiles but *she* did not.

Thad truly hoped that someday soon he and Alan would recapture the friendship they had once known. Once that happened Thad could bask in the light of Alan's encouragement upon hearing of his partner's tremendous progress. That would *truly* mean something to him. Thad had always enjoyed the accolades given for his vision, for his ability to see possibilities that others did not see. But he was a social disaster. His interactions with others was uncomfortable at best. His insecurities could only be quelled by the abuse of alcohol. Because of his addiction, and it surely was that; his relations with both personal and professional acquaintances suffered dearly. But now he was a man on the mend. He was not quite ready yet to say, "Hello World." But soon. *Very* soon.

Felicia Black has become accustomed to being underestimated. She is female and she is black. She comes from a wealthy family. All her life Felicia has struggled to come to terms with the fact that in this world those were considered to be three strikes against her. If you added in her youth she was done before she ever had a chance to get started. If you want to take that extra step and get downright stupid, which many of her mockers had done, the family name "Black," by virtue of a reference to color, also was of no help. Why someone felt that saying, 'You're a *black* "Black",' was either clever or funny was beyond her. Felicia knew she was fortunate to have the family she had as their strength of character was second to none. Their advice always rang true, "Rise above those who would seek to take you down. Rise above and see how small they will become."

For Thad and Felicia to find each other should not be considered a happy accident. They were two souls *destined* to find one another. At some point in time there might even have been divine intervention. When the two met, both were married but neither was happy. They shared one immutable thing in common during that time. Both were married to their polar opposite, a controlling self-absorbed person whose ambition for more than their share in life was their motivation to get out of bed each morning.

When Thad and Felicia first met, Felicia was married to Kenneth Knight and Thad was newly separated from Quinn. Apart from the obvious they were too alike to not be attracted to one another. Truth be told they were both also too loyal to their mates to even assume that an attraction might be possible. Fast forward several months later and things were suddenly different. Felicia is now a widow and a "hush hush" divorce between Quinn and Thad is in the works.

It was actually Berkeley and Brady who brought the two together for their first clandestine meeting. The two staff accountants had seen through the veil of deception which Quinn had tried to pull over them. As they reported directly to Felicia they sought her out in confidence and quickly learned that she too was not in accordance with the moves that Quinn was making. What she discovered during this brief interaction with her youthful accountants were that they were trail-blazing young men of integrity and vision. They also had the ear of Thaddeus Rex, one of the owners of the company. They suggested that Felicia meet with Thad to disclose what she knew of Quinn's behind-the-scenes double dealings. This was first and foremost to be a business meeting. All of that changed, however, when they looked into each other's eyes and saw one another again for the first time.

At their second meeting, it was love at first sight.

Game changer

Thad has gone into hiding although the word "hiding' is too strong of a term. He is actually just working from home and not reporting to work. He knows that Regina has begun to doubt his allegiance to the company, which is quite concerning to him, but what can he do? His marriage to Quinn, "Queenie" as she wished to be called, was a sham. It had been since day one. Thad had finally come to terms with his *own* motivations in life. He looked up to Alan and wanted so badly to be held in the same esteem as he was by his peers. But that was not to be. Thad was instead the quintessential party boy, a label (and a burden) of which he felt he had carried unfairly for far too long. To Thad, living with Quinn was like wearing a heavy winter coat on a hot summer day. He was exhausted from the effort of trying to make it fit. The weight of it. The heat and pressure of it. The daily discomfort. *Everything.* But again, what could he do?

Thad's *"everything"* changed when Berkeley and Brady sought him out for a private discussion. This is when Thad learned of Quinn's infidelity. As well as the name of her lover. It was—*Wyatt?!*. So much suddenly made sense to him all at once as he began to recognize the moves which Wyatt was making had not been his *own*. Thad recognized that strategy all too well. It was *Quinn*. *She* was the puppet master making her moves through her surrogate, Wyatt. He had already been able to ingratiate himself with Quinn's "team" of losers. Now Thad was learning that Wyatt had managed to find favor with Regina which could, if gone unchecked, bring down the entire company.

Poor Regina, overwhelmed by the moment, and taken in by the charms of a con man. It was just so unfortunate. Unbeknownst to her she was now backing the *wrong* horse. Worse, she had her sights on removing *both* Thad and Felicia.

Berkely and Brady have come to see Thad to inform him that Wyatt sees Felicia as being *disloyal* to Quinn and now wants her out. This news weighs heavily on Thad as he realizes that they certainly do have their work cut out for them if they are going to be able to turn things around.

Joni does not express herself often. Or well for that matter. She is a very private individual. For most of the years of her life she had only herself and the incredible sense inside her that there was something or someone else out there. After what was an incredible journey of endless dead ends she finally found the other half of her soul. It was her twin sister Toni.

Toni was the only person with whom she could *confide*. She would later meet Quinn and discover that she now had another woman in the world with whom she could *communicate*. And *possibly* to trust. Still though, it was only Toni with whom she could share her secrets and her soul. But now Toni was dead and Joni was once again on her own. And alone.

In her hands was the only picture Joni had of her and Toni together. Wordlessly she was speaking to the image of her twin sister, telling her how Queenie had *betrayed* her. And how Quinn had *also* betrayed Thad by sleeping with Wyatt and making him now the heir apparent to the throne of the company.

Joni always knew that Queenie was a selfish money hungry bitch but now she was no better than a common whore. She was *unclean* now. Wyatt had her attention and Joni was on her own. To make matters worse, Wyatt now had *Regina's* attention as well. How could two women in such powerful positions be so *visionary* and yet so *blind?!*

Joni set the picture frame on the table and stood up with new vigor and conviction. They had killed her sister and probably wanted to kill her too. That was not going to happen. She was going to take Wyatt down, and anyone else who got in her way. The first step was to convince Regina that *Wyatt* was the bad guy in this big mess. The fact that everyone believed that Joni just took orders and did not have a mind of her own would work well in her favor. If she could cast dispersions on Wyatt's objective she could possibly change Regina's opinion of him. And she would be doing what she did so *very* well. Causing mayhem and disruption. It almost seemed too easy.

Joni touched the photo of her and her twin sister and said, "This for you sister. This for you."

Joni knew what she had to do. She left her small apartment, heading out for a visit to the residence of Alan and Regina King. She had a simple message to deliver. No matter *who* you are, you are *not* safe. While it was true that Benjamin had reached out to her for help in causing a disruption at the King's home, she wasn't doing this for *him*. Joni was doing this for Toni. God help anyone who got in her way. Benjamin, whatever the hell he was trying to do, was on his own. Joni worked alone.

The home of Alan and Regina King is a technological marvel. As one would expect. It is a "smart" home equipped with just about every interesting and helpful gadget anyone could imagine. The home and the property are worth millions but that was not always the case. When they first purchased the home and the surrounding acreage it was certainly not what it is today. The growth of their company in tandem with their own notoriety had in effect catapulted a sleepy area outside of the city to an affluent, in demand neighborhood.

The growth of the company had given the couple the resources required for turning a small Mission bungalow style house with exposed beams and a terra cotta roof into the expansive "smart" home it is today. Much of the architecture of the original home still remains with the improvements built around and upon it.

The road leading up to the area surrounding the property had only recently been paved within the last couple of years, paid for by the residents of the small community. The Kings, being the first to stake their claim, had the premier location with an incredible view of the desert in the distance. Their property line behind the house ended with a dramatic drop-off which was a product of decades of erosion. Below was a "wash," a shallow channel which follows the contour of the land, in effect allowing water to flow down and away from higher elevations. This can be a dangerous place to be as it is susceptible to flash flooding as well as becoming a protective corridor for wildlife to hide.

The Kings had both 'NO TRESPASSING' and 'CAUTION: DANGEROUS AREA' signs posted in conspicuous places. Neither should be necessary as this was private property but in the interest of safety...

Alan and Regina King are home for the evening. The majesty of the setting sun has already occurred and now the sky has turned to black with only a handful of stars making an appearance in the night sky. The couple are preparing for another late dinner. There is a wonderfully rich spaghetti sauce simmering in a pan on the stove.

Regina is making one of Alan's favorite dishes tonight, something he calls "Gina's Folly." This harkens back to a simpler time when they had just met and were getting to know one another. Regina's cooking skills back then could be considered more "willing" than "able." On one particular evening, in an effort to make spaghetti for the first time, 'Gina' as Alan called her back then, made something entirely different. Perhaps indescribable as spaghetti but—Alan absolutely loved it! It was a mistake to be sure but a good one. Alan dubbed it "Gina's Folly." It was now almost a special occasion each time she made it. The funny thing about it was that there was never a formal recipe to work from so it was different every time. But that was all just part of the fun.

The pasta and meatballs are set aside, already cooked and waiting to be blended into the mix. It is the sauce that is taking its good, sweet time. And that's just fine with Alan. The longer it simmers the richer the flavor. Regina suggests that this might be a good time to share a cup of coffee, enjoy some quiet time to relax and reflect. As much as both would enjoy such a thing, their conversation inevitably drifts to work issues. There is always so much to discuss. The future of their company is at stake as is the welfare of both themselves and their employees. This is not something either of them can take lightly.

Alan has excused himself to go to the bathroom. He pours another cup of the dark Colombian coffee for Regina before he leaves the room. Before taking her first sip she blows gently on the surface of the liquid to cool. Just then Regina hears a sound at the front door. A frown crosses her face. Her first thought is that it must be an animal. The two live in a veritable fortress now so an intrusion of any kind other than a small roaming animal would seem quite rare.

Regina gets up from the kitchen table and looks down the hallway. She can see light peeking out from under the doorway of the bathroom which means she can pinpoint Alan's location. The sound did not come from the hallway. Her frown now furrows into concern. A rush of adrenaline flows through her as a score of scenarios rush through her active mind. Regina is always only one blink away from full battle readiness. Just then a soft blue and green circle glows about their Amazon *Echo.* A look of perplexity crosses Regina's face.

"Alexa, do I have a notification?"

There is a cadence and a decorum to Alexa's speech pattern. This is by design. We want our interactive robots to be both warm and friendly. Regina's eyes go wide with anticipation as what she hears she *knows* to be wrong. Immediately and completely *wrong.*

"Amazon—"

Before the second word has been spoken Regina bolts for the door leading out to the garage. There is a keypad to the right of the door. Quickly she enters a special code which enables the door to open but then safely lock back into place on its own after she passes through.

Once inside the dark confines of the garage she does not turn on the overhead light but rather trusts her memory of where she is walking. She also does not engage the heavy primary garage door. Regina has already determined that it is neither an animal nor a "friendly" who is responsible for the sound at the front door. She is purposefully moving in stealth in an attempt to have the element of surprise in her favor. The fighting spirit in her has not yet allowed her rational "what the hell do you think you're doing" brain to catch up. It would tell her that what she is doing is a fool's errand and she is risking her own safety.

Regina finds the side door in the garage which leads outside. She is turning the knob when her thoughts shift to an image in her mind's eye of the inside of the house. Regina mouths the words, 'OH MY GOD' as she visualizes Alan leaving the bathroom and hearing Alexa speak in a voice which is *not* her own---

"Amazon package. Front door."

"No, Alan. *NO!*"

Regina is picturing Alan reaching for the handle of the front door. She screams silently as the picture screen inside her head goes white with the small but effective explosion which takes out the entirety of the front door with a force which would most likely kill anyone standing just inside.

"Damn you!!" Regina cries as she rushes through the side door. She is in full vengeful mode when rounding the corner of the garage at a mad dash. She sees a figure moving furtively away towards the far side of the house. Regina looks up, turning her neck back and forth as she is running and thinks to herself, 'There should be lights on overhead.' Just as quickly she realizes that whoever has planted the explosive device at their front door has also disengaged the outside security lights. Uncertain of Alan's fate Regina tells herself that she is on her own.

As she runs after the diminutive figure Regina hazards a glance at the front of the house. The damage speaks for itself. If Alan had attempted to open the door he is dead now. Regina feels an anger and an energy she has never known flow through her as she shortens the distance between herself and the furtive perpetrator.

As Regina is running at full gait she notices that she has two items in her hands which she must have grabbed while moving through the garage. One is a flashlight and the other is a golf club. The time was now upon her to let the purpose of the item in her right hand be known. Regina swung the golf club with all her might and struck the interloper in the back of the head. That person went down. *Hard.*

Regina also went down as the swing of the club has thrown her off balance. She heard a nasty crunch as she went down fearing that perhaps she had broken a bone.

Regina got up slowly, patting down her arms and legs. Nothing was amiss. There was no blood. There was no pain. What she heard must have come from the fall of the intruder. That person however was already back up and running towards the back edge of the property in a direct path for the "wash."

Regina was running again too but not at the pace she had been earlier. This was for two reasons. First, she knew there was nowhere for this person to go. Secondly, she was certain now that she knew the identity of this person. Knowing who she was dealing with *definitely* changed the game. The element of unpredictable danger was now in play.

Still though, Regina called out *her* name.

"JONI!!"

Joni stopped dead in her tracks and turned to stare viciously at Regina. Joni was always the proverbial animal trapped in a corner, more dangerous when cornered than when left alone.

A puzzled look crossed Regina's face as she looked closer at Joni. Something was *off*. It was hard to tell in the darkness just what it was but there was something not quite right about Joni's... *head*. Perhaps it had something to do with her fall earlier? After all the back yard of the King's house was mostly rock garden. Impacting the ground face first without injury was unlikely.

Regina still had the golf club gripped tightly in one hand and just remembered what she had in the other. A flashlight. A high intensity flashlight. Curious about what she was seeing Regina aimed the powerful beam of the flashlight directly at Joni's head and switched it on. The light lit up Joni's face. Simultaneously Joni elicited a primal scream.

It has been said that time slows down to accommodate the senses during times of high stress or duress. Perhaps this is true as Regina was able to see clearly what was causing Joni's head to appear misshapen. It was a pair of night vision goggles strapped onto her forehead and covering her eyes. It was evident now that the goggle apparatus had cracked as a result of her earlier fall. One of the lenses was shattered. The possibility of pieces being wedged into Joni's eye crossed Regina's mind. The scream, however, was a result of the sheer intensity of the light source of the flashlight traveling through the night vision goggles which were designed to greatly magnify available light. Wedges of sharp plastic in one eye, a burned-out retina in the other. Joni was toast.

Apparently Joni did not see things that way. Figuratively speaking. Factually she probably could not see at all but that did not seem to matter. She turned and ran. *Away* from Regina. And *towards* the wash. Regina yelled after her to *'Stop!'* The flashlight beam caught Joni in a moment of cartoon ecstasy with her body suspended in the air, her legs still pumping with no ground below. And then the moment of realization before the fall. Like Wile E. Coyote in a roadrunner scene, next comes the inevitable pull of gravity. And down she went. The only thing missing was that small puff of smoke at the end.

Regina approached the edge cautiously looking down into the abyss. Joni had just plummeted from the fat into the fire. Regina knew the fall would not kill her. The greater concern was that now Joni was in an environment which would seem to her like an alien planet. With limited eyesight and possible injuries from the strike of the golf club and the tumble into the wash Regina put the outlook for Joni's survival at bleak. She asked herself if this was redemption for the demise of Jonah Priestas.

As Regina was standing there staring out into the black nothingness of the night, the moment suddenly caught up with her.

"ALAN!!"

Regina just realized that she had been so caught up in the chase that she had forgotten the explosion and the welfare of her husband. She abandoned the golf club and turned to run. The flashlight she kept tightly in hand needing it to navigate back to the front of the house.

Once Regina had arrived at the front door, the area of the explosive blast, Regina began to *imagine* that she heard Alan calling to her. She laughed in spite of herself. It was *silly*. Here he was suddenly standing right in front of her and *he* was asking *her* is *she* was alright. *He* had been the one who had sustained the blast at the front door. She must be in shock. Imagining things that are not real to save herself from the truth. The truth of her husband's death. But then she feels his arms around her, comforting her, soothing her, holding her. It all seemed so *real*. She blinked several times to be certain that her eyes were open and she was not dreaming. He is standing there with her and he keeps saying something over and over again in a language which she would later describe as *'dreamspeak.'*

'Honey, are you okay? Honey, are you okay? Honey, are you okay? Honey, are you—'

"—okay?"

Alan's hands are gripping Regina's shoulders tightly, willing her to come back to him from her dreamlike trance. Her eyes blinked again and then her mind allowed her to believe that this moment *is* real and that Alan *is* alive. The sudden look of disbelief turning to joy told Alan that she was back. They hugged each other tighter than they ever had in their time together.

Regina pushed him away and said, "But *how?!* How are you not *dead*?!"

Alan laughed. "I'm not *dead* because I'm not *stupid*. I heard the same thing you did. *Joni's voice*. I could have yelled from the bathroom but that might have been too little too late. I trusted that you would hear her voice and move AWAY from the door. I had my phone with me. All I did was give it a simple voice command. 'Open the front door.' And then BOOM!"

"Open the front door. You just said that like you were cursing at Joni."

"Oh, trust me, I was! But what about you? *You chased after her?!* What the hell were you *thinking*? And just look at you! Did you hunt down and kill a mountain lion while you were out there?"

Regina laughed at this and then told the story of chasing Joni and her tumble over the edge of the property. Alan listened intently and smiled in all the right places. Then he said the one thing they both were thinking, "Joni is like a female version of Michael Myers. My gut tells me that she may well be coming back."

"Like a bad penny," said Regina.

"No," replied Alan and then uncharacteristically said, "like a fucking *terminator*. I won't feel safe until I see the goddamn red light go out in her eyes."

"Jesus, Alan."

"Yeah, you may want to give Him a call. We very well may need Him."

The night is not over. There was still much to be done. The first and most important thing to take care of was the damage done to the front of the house. The couple would have to spend the night in a nearby hotel. They would need to call a contractor to repair the entryway. Thankfully there had not been a fire. They must also alert the local police. Alan pulls his phone from his pocket to do just that. He looks over to Regina and says, "Before THIS happened," he is pointing at the front door, "do you even remember what we were talking about?"

It was of course a rhetorical question but he should have known better with Regina.

"Of course I do. We were talking about Thad not reporting to work at the office and what Quinn may have done to bring Felicia Black over to the dark side."

Alan smiled, then said, "Game. And match."

Alan called the police then and reported the incident. The person on the other end said they would send out a cruiser immediately. Regina heard Alan say, "No, that is not a concern," before he ended the call.

"What was that last bit about?"

"What?" asked Alan.

"That bit about you saying 'no, that is not a concern'."

"Oh. She asked if we felt that it was safe to go back inside and I said that is not a concern."

Regina looked at Alan with worry etched on her face. "Let's think for a moment. Should it be?"

"Should it be what?"

"A concern. Do you, do *we*, feel like it is safe to go back inside?"

Alan thought about her comment for a moment before replying confidently. "I think we both know that Joni works alone."

Regina heard those words. There was surety in them. He was stating a fact.

"Yes. Yes she does. Come on, we need to pack some things for the hotel stay before the police arrive." The two walked arm in arm into the house. Both were right about Joni. And both were wrong about the house being safe.

Regina and Alan go separate directions after heading back into the house. They went through the side garage door which Regina had used to exit the house. She made sure that both doors were once again locked firmly in place before they went their separate ways. Regina picked her way carefully over the debris from the blast and went on to the master bedroom seeking a hot shower to remove herself from the weight of what had just happened. Alan stayed in the kitchen attending to the stove now after realizing that the burner was still on under a pan of simmering spaghetti sauce.

Just then there was a sound behind him and out of the corner of his eye he saw a figure move from the opening leading to the dining area to the door leading to the garage. As Alan turned his head his eyes opened wide with surprise as he saw a man desperately touching numbers on the security keypad in hopes of landing upon the correct code to open the door.

Alan's brain said, *'Stay quiet.'*

Alan's mouth said, "What the *fuck?!*"

The man turned at the sound of Alan's voice. Alan at first did not recognize the man as his face presented at first as a caricature of "*PANIC*." The man was trapped. The door to the garage was locked. The man looked briefly to the opening to the dining area from where he had come seeing this now as his only possible exit. Alan saw this too and reacted by pressing a button near the light switch. This activated automatic doors which effectively shut off the kitchen from the outside world. This was now a "safe room" but, with this strange man stuck here with Alan, was it really?

The man had black grease paint smeared over most of his face with only his eyes showing to reveal what he might be thinking. These eyes showed an appreciation for the tactic which Alan had just employed.

What they didn't show was that he was thinking he had been beaten. There was now a new resolve being displayed. The look of *"PANIC"* had been replaced with cold, steely eyes and the onerous obligatory face of *"DANGER."*

Alan heard himself say, "Oh shit," and then the man charged at him.

Alan did the first thing that came to mind. He slung the contents of the simmering hot pan in the man's direction. The scream was one to die for. The man brought his hands to his face as the heat of the spaghetti sauce burned his skin.

Alan did not hesitate. He slapped at the wall button to inactivate the sealed doors and bolted for the hallway. *Damn it!* It didn't work that way! He still had to enter a code. In his haste he also had forgotten that the door to the dishwasher was down and blocking his path. He deftly attempted to step around it but that moment of indecision had cost him. The man tackled Alan from behind and they both went down hard. The door of the dishwasher broke away from the unit as Alan's face impacted the lower rack. A butter knife cut a gash into his forehead just missing his eye.

Alan felt the man roll off of him and step away. *Was he giving up his advantage?* Oh my god, no, he was reaching for the knives on the counter. Alan scrambled to his feet as the man came at him brandishing a French knife. He made several "fake" chopping motions at Alan before actually attempting to cut him. Amazingly Alan still had the spaghetti sauce pan still in hand. He instinctively reacted by gripping the pan tightly with both hands and swung mightily in the direction of the knife.

A loud clang erupted as the pan connected solidly with the knife. That sound was followed immediately by a cry of pain as the weight of the pan continued on its swing path to snap the man's wrist. Time took a pause for both men to stop and look down at the now useless appendage. It was already beginning to turn a nasty shade of purple. The man's eyes showed anguish, which changed quickly to fury. He was now an injured, trapped and desperate animal, no longer acting out of fear. For him it was kill or be killed. If Alan had been startled and frightened before, now he was *terrified*.

The man lunged at Alan. He did the only thing he could think to do. He quickly pulled open one of the two refrigerator doors. The timing was perfect. The force of the man making contact with the door bent the hinges and then allowed the door to hang open lazily. Alan then did what he thought to be almost comical. He began grabbing items from the refrigerator and throwing them at his attacker. He threw each item as though he was throwing a fastball. His intention now was to take this man *down.* Alan's life was in danger. *Regina's* life was in danger.

Alan didn't throw an apple or a head of lettuce. He threw glass jars of whatever he could find. Pickles, grape jelly, jalapenos, whatever. The man put up his one good hand in a vain attempt to ward off the blows. Bad move. One of the jars hit that hand full on. Both men heard an audible *'snap'*!

There was only one place left for the man to go. Directly to the left of the garage door were stairs leading down to the basement. The man had no idea if there might be an exit from the house by going that way but his mind called up an old phrase, 'any port in the storm.'

Alan had the upper hand now and he knew it. He also knew that nothing good could come from this man ending up in their basement. Who knew what he was capable of? Yes, he was trapped but if he was suicidal, in the basement he would have access to a way to not only kill himself but to kill them all. The gas furnace.

Alan tried to tackle the man but he backed up too quickly and Alan landed instead face first on the floor. The man however took the brunt of the action as his feet went out from under him. The mixture of spaghetti sauce, jalapenos, grape jelly, pickle juice and more, made for a sloppy, slippery mess. The man fell backward and hit the railing of the basement steps. The top of the railing caught him just under his waist. One section of the wooden railing held firm however while one section cracked, then splintered, yielding to the force put upon it. Alan watched in horror as the man went over the railing in a back flip. And then landed horribly.

Alan waited for a moment uncertain of what to do next. He could not see the man from where he was standing. And there was no sound at all coming from the stairway. Should he hazard a glance? Was the man yet lying in wait for him to do just that? That's what always happened in the movies.

Alan shuffled gingerly across the saucy food-laden kitchen floor. He then peered cautiously over the railing. What he saw made him gasp. The man was lying in an impossible pose with his head at the wrong angle to his body. His eyes were still open but dead, staring out at nothing.

Alan took a few steps down the stairway still keeping a safe distance. This close he could see without a doubt that the man was dead. Probably broke his neck with the bad landing. He had to be dead. There was no way anyone could hold a pose like that and still keep breathing.

Alan was patient. He counted out a full minute before deciding to sate his curiosity by wiping off some of the grease paint. Who was this man that had *invaded* his home? And had even tried to *kill* him?!

Alan went and grabbed a napkin from the table. After returning to the body he applied the napkin to the man's face. This seemed like too much of a coincidence for this man to be at their house on the same night as Joni. *Joni worked alone*; his brain argued. Alan so much wanted to *not* know that he *did* know the identity of this man. Let him be a random burglar. It would help him to believe that the plot to take his company down did not go as deep as Regina claimed. The man's eyes stared past him as he dabbed at the face with the napkin.

As the grease paint was being wiped away Alan now began to recognize the man. Anger welled up in him as he said under his breath, you *mother fucker*. Then he spit into the man's face.

Alan is suddenly feeling very claustrophobic. Even though he is in the kitchen of his own home this area of the house is currently serving as a barricaded safe room. And he is stuck in here with a dead body. Alan takes his steps carefully over the floor now strewn with food waste and broken glass. He keys in the code which will open the safe room doors. He is wondering if he will see Regina waiting impatiently on the other side.

Alan guessed right. Regina is standing there in the blast debris of the hallway wearing only a towel. And an attitude.

"What the hell are you *doing*?" she demands. Before Alan can utter a syllable she adds, "And what the *hell* are you doing with my *good pan*?!"

Alan hadn't realized that he was still clutching the spaghetti sauce pan tightly in hand. *Good* pan? He didn't know she had a *good* pan. Aren't they all the same? Not that it really matters now. He still would have grabbed that one to defend himself because—well, because it was there.

"I--."

"Look! It's all scratched! What have you done to it?!"

"It is? I--." Alan looked at the pan and saw only the remnants of a rich spaghetti sauce.

"The *bottom* of the pan, you fool!" Regina was now in fine form.

Alan turned the pan over and saw that there were several prominent scratches. This made sense to him now as he recalled that the pan had taken several hard strikes from the French knife. Alan was about to say he was sorry when—

"*My spaghetti sauce!* Alan, what the *hell*?!" Regina had that 'I love you dearly but I could just kill you right now' look on her face. 'Wait till she sees the kitchen,' Alan thinks to himself. And then of course she did.

"Alan! *What the* fuck *happened in here?!*" Oh no, Alan thought, she *never* used that word. The shit's about to hit the fan now for sure. "I was gone for fifteen minutes! Excuse *me* for wanting to take a hot shower!"

"Careful where you step," Alan said with genuine concern.

"You *think*?!" Regina fired back.

Alan had no words. He started to say, *'there was a man'* but that would not have come out right. Instead he stood silently while Regina surveyed the damage. He thought he heard her say, 'What the hell have you done to this place?!' but he was lost in thought going over the events in his head. It was too incredible to believe all that had just happened in such a short span of time.

While Alan was reflecting on the traumatic experience he had just survived Regina was picking her way through the kitchen. She was probably making comments as she went but Alan wasn't listening. The kitchen truly was a mess. Beginning with the floor, most of the condiments from the refrigerator and just about all of the spaghetti sauce was now a bizarre sidewalk art project. Broken glass, spaghetti, meatballs, pickles, banana pepper rings, jalapenos and globs of grape jelly gave a bas relief effect to the landscape of the floor. The door of the dishwasher was twisted badly and a portion of it was touching the floor. The lower dishwasher basket was bent with many of the prongs now folded into a waffle shape much like the design now indented on Alan's face. Alan took note of the fact that Regina was looking from his face to the dishwasher several times as she was mentally putting two and two together.

"Your forehead is bleeding. Is that from the dishwasher?"

Alan replied, "Yeah, there was a butter knife sticking up the wrong way..."

"You only have yourself to blame for that you know," scolded Regina. "How many times have I told you, sharp end down?"

"It was a *butter* knife for chrissakes! It doesn't *have* a sharp end!"

"Tell *that* to your bleeding forehead."

Alan threw up his hands in mock surrender. This battle was unwinnable. He stepped back and watched as Regina continued to move through the debris of their kitchen.

The door to the refrigerator was hanging at an odd angle. Regina tried but it would not close. Then her eye caught sight of the wooden railing to the basement stairway. Alan tried to focus so that he could be prepared for her questions. He was expecting perhaps, 'Oh my, what happened?' or 'The railing is broken and the room is a mess, are you okay?' Well, to put it simply, that's *not* what came out of Regina's mouth.

"How many times have I told you to fix the newel post? Now just look at it. Half of the spindles are broken. We will have to replace the whole thing. And of course there's my ruined pan as well—"

Alan looked at her sideways. This behavior was so off the map for her. *Why was she acting this way?* They had *both* just gone through a traumatic event. *Why?* And then it hit him. PTSD. Post Traumatic Stress Disorder. Most people know it from hearing of the effects it had on soldiers returning from war but it was a real thing that could affect anyone. It was completely impartial to whom it touched. Even the strongest of people could be affected. Like Regina. Alan needed to refrain from retaliation and offer care and concern instead. Plus, he somehow needed to prepare her for the sight of a dead body on the stairwell.

"Regina."

"What?!"

"I'm sorry about your pan."

She was giving him a hard stare. No words.

"And your sauce. And the meatballs."

Still nothing.

"And the kitchen."

Still nothing. She seemed to be waiting for him to finish.

"And the stairway railing, the newel post especially."

Regina finally spoke. "Alan, what happened in here?"

Alan was caught off guard by her sudden return to normalcy. She had asked the question calmly. Softly. The anger was gone for the moment and she seemed willing to listen. To understand. He decided that he would tell her the worst of it first to see how she would react. He was totally unprepared for how *that* went.

"Regina, I killed a man."

"Yeah? Well I did too and with a whole lot less mess." Regina was of course referring to when she had shot (and killed) an intruder at the office. The intruder had turned out to be Burton.

Alan was taken aback by her reply. At first he was going to unleash a tirade of derisive comments about how she should respect the sanctity of life but stopped himself. He knew this woman so well. She was not at all being herself in this moment. Perhaps he wasn't either. She had always been strong for *him*. This was his moment to be strong for *her*.

"I felt threatened. I felt like he was trying to kill *me*. So I fought back. With everything I had." Alan paused for a moment and added, "Including your good pan."

"It appears to me that you used the entire kitchen as a weapon."

Alan laughed. He couldn't help himself. It was a silly thing to say. In this context perhaps the *silliest* thing to say. He responded in course.

"Yes, I suppose I did." He looked about the kitchen and then back at Regina. She was looking deeply into his eyes searching for something. He continued, "If I had to do it all over again, I would have *saved* your pan." He paused then added, "*And* your sauce. And your pasta, and your meatballs."

Regina blinked and then some switch in her brain was suddenly clicked off.

"Oh Alan! Thank God you're alive!" Regina threw her arms around him and hugged him with all her strength. He hugged back knowing this would be a difficult road back from the mayhem and violence to the ordered and structured life they had led before.

After several moments of closeness Regina stepped back from Alan and asked, "Where's the body?"

He shrugged his head at first. The question was just so matter of fact. Then he answered, "He's over there," pointing at the stairwell.

"Should I look?" asked Regina.

"I think you need to," responded Alan.

"Okay," said Regina as if she was being *told* to take on this task. She walked up to the fractured stair railing and peered over. She gasped at the sight. Not at first at who it was but rather the violent posture in which the body lay. Once she was past the processing stage of the scene she was able to peer a bit closer at the face of the deceased. Alan somehow was not surprised by her comment as it began to dawn on her that this was one of their own.

Regina muttered, "I thought Joni worked alone."

Alan said without giving it any thought, "Same."

Regina walked around the railing now and ventured down a few steps for a closer look. The recognition was there in her subconscious mind but the name of this man had not yet come to her.

And then, just like that she said, "Oh my god, that's---"

The Interview

"That's-- *who*?!" demanded Lana. "Don't keep me in suspense like this. Who was the man?"

Alan sighed and said, "Benjamin. The man whom I killed was Benjamin."

Lana's hand went to her mouth. Clearly she was shocked. "But it was self-defense.."

Alan shook his head in agreement. "Yes of course it was but still, I *killed* a man. I have to live with that the rest of my life."

"I'm *so* sorry. I don't know what to say."

"There is nothing *to* say I'm afraid. Both Regina and I go to counseling once a week." Seeing the question forming on her lips Alan added, "Yes, I do think it's helping."

"Oh good." Lana was silent for a moment. Processing. "Please, if you would, help me to understand something."

"Certainly."

"Why would Joni do what she did for Benjamin? He had no hold over her that is apparent. As a matter of fact, didn't *he* report to *her*? Plus, you keep saying that she works alone."

Alan smiled. "You have that right. Joni Bishop's title was *Director* of Security. Benjamin's title was Security *Manager* and yes, he reported to Joni. I will tell you that Regina and I went through this same scenario. In retrospect it was like looking through the wrong end of a telescope. Everything became so small, so distant and so hard to define but—If you turn it the other way around, meaning that *Benjamin* was doing this for *Joni,* suddenly the images become primary in the frame and are much easier to see. It becomes obvious then that Joni was using Benjamin to get what she needed, something she could not do on her own."

"And what is that?"

"Joni wanted what everyone in this industry wants, the secret to how the Regalis crystal is *harvested*. Our computers at work, Regina's and mine, have already been scrubbed at Quinn's command looking for this secret formula. The next logical step was to check our home computers. That is something Joni could not do on her own."

"Why not? She was the Director of Security. Her sister was the Director of the IT department. Wouldn't she have had everything she needed to get that done?"

"One would think. The problem was that she had everything but the *knowledge* of how to get it done. That's why she needed Benjamin. You see most of Quinn's appointments were given their titles not by *qualification* but rather by *access*. By assigning those titles to Toni and Joni, who know virtually *nothing* about computers or security systems, Quinn was basically giving them full access to the IT department and the security apparatus of the entire building. Even my home."

"Holy shit." Lana's eyes went wide when she heard those words come from her mouth. "Oh gosh, I am so sorry. That was unprofessional of me."

Alan laughed. "Perhaps it was a bit unprofessional but it was certainly human. You are forgiven."

"Oh thank you. Obviously, I reacted that way because this is not just a power grab. This is a well thought out and structured attempt at a company takeover."

"Yes, that is absolutely true. Which is exactly why you are here. You "get it," and we need someone who "gets it" to tell our story."

"Thank you. This is the opportunity of a lifetime for me. And yet there's more, is that correct?"

"Oh yes, there *definitely* is more."

Part Five

A Triumvirate of Women

Felicia Black / Opposites attract

Thad has moved in with Felicia Black. The relationship between him and Felicia has continued to blossom however this move was prompted largely by the information shared with Thad by Berkeley. Apparently, Thad and Felicia were now on Brock Rampart's radar which is never a good thing. Berkeley had followed Brock's car one evening. It was more educated guess than hunch. He was not surprised when he observed Brock find a parking spot on the street in direct eyeline with Thad's apartment.

When Berkeley shared this with Thad he had seemed more concerned that Brock was aware of his new living arrangements than the actual stakeout. It was Felicia's idea for him to move in with her. They took the high road in this arrangement as their relationship was still in the early stages meaning that Thad would have his *own* bedroom. The move happened in a clandestine fashion so as not to alert Brock of the change. Thad, Felicia and Berkeley as well, had a chuckle over how many wasted hours Brock might spend outside Thad's apartment simply waiting for him to emerge.

Thad's exit from the lavish home he had shared with Quinn to a studio apartment had been quick and pain*ful*. He had much *more* stuff than he realized and soon had much *less* space than he needed. The apartment was more of a knee jerk reaction than a well-conceived plan. Thad had had enough of the whole situation and just needed to get *out*. The *house* he left behind was very nice but it was *not* a *home*. The apartment he moved into was a viable residence but was *not* a palace by any stretch of the imagination. For a man who was soon to be considered an industry giant, this was all quite a humbling experience.

And he wouldn't trade it for the world.

Quinn Rex / Passed Pawn

Thad's decision to move out of their house could not have been more timely for Quinn. She had several 'irons in the fire' as they say so he had just become a mere distraction for her. Quinn was undaunted by the fact that she had lost her title and position with the company. There was 'more than one way to skin a cat' she would often say much to the bother of those who felt the adage was revolting. Quinn had a gift for getting under everyone's skin.

Quinn, *'Queenie'* as *she* preferred to be called, was a collector of people. She collected them for what she thought they could do for her. Genuine relationships were of no value. This explained the sudden "attraction" she had for Wyatt. He was a timid little creature in her eyes and not worth the time she would need to spend to build up his character but—the herd was rapidly thinning at the company. It just so happened that he was in the right place at the right time to be the benefactor of Queenie's deft artistry of using and bending people to her will.

It was almost too perfect. Wyatt held the position of Field Operations Manager which could be considered a pivotal role for upward movement in management. Additionally his current position allowed for him to make his own schedule, to be in or out of the office as his workload would require. The essential element was that he was considered to be on Regina's "team." That perception would not change. Until it was too late.

Regina King / Promotion

A major announcement had just been made to the world. It was delivered by none other than Regina herself. One of the mega resort casinos in Las Vegas had committed to using *Regalis Crystal* generators to power their entire property. This was no small task as the property included two hotel towers with more than 4,000 rooms, over 500,000 square feet of rentable convention space, 200,000 square feet of casino space with slots and table games, 30 plus world class restaurants and lounge venues plus a championship golf course. This was a commitment on a very high level and a proof of concept that had the attention of power brokers around the world.

The company now had the attention of those individuals who would ensure its success. The company was poised for greatness but—was it ready? Behind the scenes the work that Regina and Alan had done to put together a well-structured workforce had taken a severe beating. So many losses of human capital in such a short period of time. Recovery from sourcing outside the company seemed risky after such a major announcement so Regina was forced to look *within* the company. This is when (magically it seemed) Wyatt's name was brought to her attention. With his particular skill set she saw in him a candidate for a newly created position and a much more powerful place in the company. *Almost* a twin to *her* position. Regina was eager to put this idea into motion however what she had misconstrued as "good fortune" was actually the devilish work of Queenie behind the scenes. The idea of turning one of Regina's own loyal team members against her was something she relished.

Wyatt was promoted without the consultation of Alan, a strike to both their professional and personal relationship. That damage, however, was now done. Regina was not known for making mistakes in character. This one, however, was a big one.

Quinn Rex / Foreign Affair

The moment Queenie had determined that Wyatt was her target, his life and several others would change dramatically. She made no attempt to hide her "affair" with Wyatt from Thad. Quinn gauged his reaction perfectly. Thad was hurt but not retaliatory. His way of *"I'll show her!"* was to just move out. She could have asked for nothing better. Whether or not he chose to seek a divorce or dissolution was completely up to him. If her developing plan worked as she hoped there would no longer *be* a need for Thad in her world. She had found his replacement in Wyatt. And although she found Wyatt to be a bit smarmy for her taste he was certainly a loyal subordinate. He did what he was told. At the company if not in her bed. All that she needed him to do was listen well and execute her plan. Both would prosper. She could find love elsewhere.

Felicia Black / Silent Partner

Thad has found a happiness he has never known before. After moving in with Felicia his entire world has changed from playing second fiddle to being a full-fledged partner. But this "partner thing" had nothing to do with his position in the company. This was all about his first true and genuine loving relationship which he had found with Felicia Black. He wanted to spend every waking minute he had with her. He wanted to experience every new day with her as though he were seeing everything again for the first time however *this* time, everything now seemed so beautiful and brand new.

Felicia was still employed and felt a tinge of guilt each day as she waved goodbye to Thad from her car in the driveway as she left for work. As happy as she was in the relationship she reluctantly had to admit to herself that *something* had to give. This obligation she felt to keep their feelings for each other hidden from the world was contrary to who she was as a person. There were already rumors circulating about that Quinn was cheating on Thad *and* that he had moved out. Although Felicia and Thad had not engaged in anything worthy of being called "cheating," perception was reality and people would think what people would think. Felicia decided that she would discuss with Thad that very evening the idea of coming out of the dark and into the light by sharing the truth of their newfound love with the world.

Thad could not have been more supportive of her wishes and they made their announcement the next morning. Felicia makes the mistake of calling off from work that day to allow for people to talk on their own. She and Thad would spend the day at her expansive condo enjoying their time together and sharing their love for one another. They stayed in bed all day oblivious to the repercussions that would come from the news they had shared.

Quinn Rex / Token

There is no correlation between Felicia's position in the company and Wyatt's but somehow Quinn has found a way to twist that notion into fake news and affect Regina's decision-making from afar. 'There are always wolves at the door,' Regina would comment later when deliberating her actions regarding the promotion of Wyatt to Junior VP of Field Operations. He would now have an equal level of power as Brock and by virtue of assignments, nearly the same power as Regina herself. Only Quinn, in her nasty way of typecasting people, would view Regina and Wyatt in the way that she did making the comment that there were now "two queens to rule the empire." She was taken at her word with those hearing the comment taking into account only the significant power which Wyatt had been granted. And while that was true Quinn was also sniping at Wyatt behind his back. Few knew that he was gay and that this notion of an "affair" between the two was by arrangement only. When she called him her "queen," it was actually derogatory in nature. It was Quinn being Quinn.

The promotion of Wyatt was a *huge* leap made at a time when the company could ill afford a mistake of such magnitude. Regina, however, was in a position to do just that. Those few individuals who might have been able to sway her errant decision were not in place at the time to see it happen. Alan was too busy with the successes the company was having with Wilson's industry disruptive *"Sunlight Wall Panels"* and the new *"Regalis Crystal"* power generators to check in with Regina. Brock's time was being "spent" *(wasted actually)* as Regina's watchdog outside Thad's empty studio apartment.

With Wyatt in place at the company Queenie now has time to set up the carefully placed dominoes of deception which will cause havoc once they begin to fall. Her first target will be none other than Felicia Black because *that* bitch took her man. It is a vengeful act even though she no longer has any need or desire for Thad. It was, she supposed, simply the principle of the matter.

Next in line would be one of the two kings. It was Thaddeus Rex who had to go, as he was the key to undermining the strength of the company structure. With Thad out of the picture and Wyatt in place, Quinn could start to peck away at the enviable bond between Alan and Regina.

Husband and wife, COO and SVP, king and queen. Causing a rift between those two would put the company at risk for a takeover. Then at that time, as the dominoes would begin to fall, Queenie would be there eagerly picking each of them up.

Things at the company were about to get *very* ugly. Very ugly indeed.

Regina King / Quandary

Regina is now moving at a furious pace to keep up with all the changes and challenges which have been placed before her. It would be fair to absolve her of the guilt she would feel for the obvious mistakes and poor decisions she made after the severe trauma which she has endured. But, one had to admit that she had made, and would continue to make, these decisions on her own. Regina being Regina would indeed own them all. *Including* the steps she had taken to remove Felicia. And Thad. Although Alan might never forgive her for that last one.

The Interview

"Would it be fair to say that the company at that time was precariously balanced on the head of a pin?"

Alan looked up to the ceiling and scrunched his face while musing. He said, "Lana, I believe that you may have spent too much time with me. You are starting to take on my odd analogies."

Lana chuckled at this.

"Don't get me wrong, I *do* see it that way although it would be more appropriate to say that we were balanced on the tip of a needle. Or a knife's edge. Almost *any* move could result in harm for us all." Alan said this last part with a face as grim as the memory he was about to share.

"What did you do?"

Alan laughed. *"Me?* I did *nothing* and take full credit for that. It wasn't Regina *either* for which she continues to apologize to this day."

Lana looks puzzled. "Then who?"

Alan smiled. "The answer to that is not only *"who"* but also *"what"*."

"I'm afraid I don't understand."

Alan responded with, "The *"who"* is Felicia Black. Excuse me, her name is now Felicia Black *Rex*. And the *"what"* is, what else? True love."

"Are you telling me that I am actually writing a *love story*?"

"That is *exactly* what I am telling you. Maybe one of the best."

"I'm honored. Please continue."

"The "catfight" (as many in the company chose to call it) was always between two strong personalities, Regina and Quinn. Who knew that a third woman of equal character would emerge to alter the course of the company which was being derailed by an outside source. This woman would in effect lose her personal battle but win the collective war."

Alan watched as Lana processed what he had just shared. He spoke slowly and concisely. He did not want her to miss one of the most important pieces of the puzzle. Alan continued with his recounting of critical events.

"The person I am speaking of was Felicia Black Knight. While she may have hoped to come on board with the company as any other employee and earn her stripes, her ambitious husband (now deceased) had thrown her under the bus on day one. The fact that he had married Atlanta "royalty" was of major importance to him. Not one to feel comfortable standing on his own merit, his marriage to a member of the well-known "Black" family from Atlanta gave Kenneth Knight instant credibility. He was, however, clearly a misfit. His work ethic and desire for personal gratification caught the ire of the Black family clan. Felicia's parents and grandparents, and even *great* grandparents had had a hand in forging the city that Atlanta is today. They were movers and shakers in community planning, owned their own business enterprises and even now were continuing to effect change. One of Felicia's brothers is running for the senate and her aunt is a well-known lobbyist in Washington, D.C."

Alan paused. Lana looked up from her copious note-taking and said, "Go on. I'm keeping up."

Alan nodded his approval and continued on.

"The unwritten golden rule in the Black family was that no one, whether connected by blood or by marriage, received a free ride. The

Lord helps those who help themselves or in other words, you made it on your own or you didn't make it all. What this meant for Felicia was that she had grown up strong, intelligent and independent. *And* humble. Not to mention tenacious. She would fight for what she believed in but always in a fair manner. If she were to lose she would accept the loss with humility and walk away with head held high. Now place Quinn Rex in the picture. In Felicia's opinion, Quinn was the antithesis of everything she believed in. The veiled moves being made by Quinn "Queenie" Rex had not escaped Felicia's attention. Once she recognized the damage that Quinn would inflict upon the company Felicia set about putting in place her own ways in which to counteract them."

"Is that it?" Lana asked.

"Nope," replied Alan. "She first had to convince Thad that there was a problem and that she was the one to fix it."

"Hmm, how did that go down?"

"I can only give you my best guess—"

White Queen / Black Knight

"Felicia, don't you see that I don't *care* what Quinn does anymore? She can't hurt me now. I have you in my life. We're together and that's all that matters to me."

Felicia looked at Thad with an alluring smile. She was standing in her bedroom, half in and half out of her night gown. She was heading for the bathroom to take her shower when Thad had started to plead with her to call off work and come back to bed.

"We could be like John and Yoko," Thad implored. "This will be our lost weekend."

"You never stop, do you?" Felicia scolded. "Well, it's *not* the weekend and *one of us* is expected to *show up* at work. I for one do not want to lose my job. You're a cofounder of the company so you get to lay in bed all day. I'm just a worker bee. I *have* to show up and actually *contribute.*"

Thad threw a pillow at her and said in a whining tone, "Stop painting me as a freeloader."

Felicia shot Thad a beguiling look which encouraged Thad to add, "And get your ass back to bed!"

"Careful what you wish for!" Felicia exclaimed as she allowed her emotions to get the better of her and flung herself at Thad still lying in the king-size bed. She was all in for this spontaneous morning lovemaking but once over she would be back on track with her preoccupation to stop Quinn from taking everything from Thad that he and Alan had worked so hard to build.

Their moment of ecstasy was interrupted by Felicia's cell phone. She had a specific ringtone for every caller and this one was quite distinctive.

"That's Regina! Why is she calling *me*?" Felicia rolled over and grabbed her phone from the nightstand. Upon viewing the screen she could see that she had somehow let time slip away. It was already midmorning. "Oh *shit*! I'm *late*! *Really* late!"

"Hand me the phone, *I'll* talk to her," Thad said with a devil may care lilt to his voice.

"That would be the *least* helpful thing you could do right now. Be quiet. I *have* to take this."

Felicia touched the screen on her phone to accept the call. "Hello Regina, I--."

"Why are you not here?" she demanded.

This angry tone and full-on assault of a question caught Felicia off guard. Her intention when answering the phone was to be self-deprecating with a silly apology for her tardiness. A white lie perhaps to cover her indiscretion. This bullish call from Regina pulled aggression out of her instead. The two were about to bang heads. This would not end well.

"When did *you* become my supervisor? I don't report to you. And when did you start taking attendance for that matter?" Felicia regretted her words the moment they came out of her mouth. She glanced at Thad. He was mouthing the words, *'Oh my god.'* Felicia had overstepped and she knew it.

"*Everyone* in this company reports to me," Regina fired back.

"Oh really, I think Alan might be surprised to hear that. The last time I checked he was *your* superior."

"Holy shit, Felicia! Cool your jets!"

"Was that *Thad* I just heard in the background?! You two playing hooky from school? Did I catch you at a bad time? Were you in the midst of your "morning grind"?"

Felicia had placed the phone on speaker. Both her and Thad were wide-eyed at what they were hearing. Both were speechless.

"What's the matter? Cat got your tongue?!" Regina paused for a moment before saying, "Listen, I didn't call to interrupt your little 'soiree' there that you're having this morning."

Felicia wrinkled her face at that term. She was so literal that any word used out of context bothered her. This bit of disquiet on her part allowed Regina to have the last word.

"The company is moving in a different direction now if you haven't noticed. Your services will no longer be required. I will have your things sent to you. No need for you to shower and pretty your face up to come into the office. And tell Thad he needn't bother to come in either. We have had his office repurposed for *Wyatt's* use. Wyatt is someone I can trust to be *here*. On time, and by my side."

"You don't know the whole story about me and Thad. And you certainly don't seem to know the truth about *Wyatt*. If you did, you wouldn't—"

"Don't tell me what I would or would not do. Wyatt has earned his place in this company. You may be a widow and far be it from me to cast dispersions on how you manage your personal lives but as for Thad, *he* is still married."

Much to Felicia's dismay Thad jumped into the conversation. "I will have you know *Ms.* King, that Quinn and I are separated."

"Oh is that right?"

"Yes, yes it is."

"And I suppose you feel that gives you carte blanche to do whatever the hell you want. Good old Thad, still the party boy."

Thad was surprised by her comeback. He was on the defensive now. "It is not public knowledge but we *are* getting a divorce."

"Is that right? Well good for you. I think we can all agree that that is long overdue. It doesn't change my message to you. You are either *married* or you're *not* married. There is no middle ground. This "separated" bullshit is the excuse you have given yourself to allow for cheating. I won't have liars and cheats in *my* company."

"It's not *your* company Regina." Thad fired back with open hostility.

"Says the man lying in bed with someone other than his wife. Not that I can blame you. Felicia is a big-time trade up from Quinn. Unfortunately for you Thad, she is out of your league. One morning she will wake up and ask herself what the hell am I doing here with *this* loser?!"

Felicia ended the call. She looked at Thad who said facetiously, "That went well."

Felicia ignored his comment and said, "We *have* to do something."

Thad replied with, "Can you believe she gave that twerp my office?!"

Felicia threw her hands up in a helpless gesture. "After all you just heard, *that's* your concern? Not, 'hey, I just got fired *and* just hung up on the Senior VP of Operations!?' Who by the way in case you forgot is married to your business partner!"

"No, it's just that, I mean, well it's *my* office."

"Which you haven't been to in weeks."

"That's not fair Felicia. You know my situation."

Felicia could hear the pain in Thad's voice. "I didn't want any of this." He immediately sought to explain himself. "Wait! That didn't come out right. I didn't mean "this, this," you know "us." I meant this whole mess with Quinn. I wish I had never met her and *you* know how I feel about "cheating"."

"Thad honey, you are loyal to a fault. And yes, I do know what you mean. I also know that right now, it's not "we" that has to do something. It is "I" who has to do something."

Thad looked earnestly into Felicia's eyes as he asked, "What are you going to do?"

"I am going to call someone whom I *know* Regina will listen to."

"Wendell?"

Felicia smiled. 'They're so cute when they're young,' she thought to herself. "No. Someone up the chain. Someone... higher."

"Higher?"

Felicia shook her head at Thad's inward struggle. She set him at ease quickly.

"I'm calling Alan."

"Oh."

As Thad said this it dawned on him that while Regina was inarguably the queen in their company there was no denying the simple fact that Alan was still the king and this was *his* kingdom. The fact that he and Regina shared the wealth equally was a beautiful thing. Their strength complemented one another. As a rule Alan leaned on Regina but the trauma she had experienced must have taken a toll on her. She was not herself. Felicia was quite intuitive in that she sensed this and felt the need to make clear to Alan that it was now *his* time to be strong for *her*. It wouldn't be easy but if he didn't bring her back now all could be lost.

The Interview

"So did she call?"

"Yes. Yes she did. She called me that instant. And she shared with me more than was necessary."

"What do you mean?"

"I mean that she told me everything."

"*Everything*?"

"Yes. Everything. She told me that Quinn and Thad had separated and were seeking a divorce. She told me about the "relationship" she had with Thad. She told me that she had invited Thad to come live with her. And *why*. She told me that he slept in his own bedroom and that they were careful to not allow this current "situation" to become "cheating" because they both knew that once the divorce was final that they were planning to get married. And let me tell you something. Those two 'were' and 'are' *madly* in love with one another."

"You don't hear *that* too often these days."

"No, unfortunately no you don't. But it's fair to say that we all have "needs." And well, the two of them, shall we say, succumbed to those "needs"."

"Succumbed. You don't hear *that* word often these days either."

Alan laughed. "Sorry, I guess I feel compelled to use "big words" when being in the company of a journalist."

"Well thank you," said Lana. "I just hope I know the meanings of all the words you choose."

"How are we doing so far?"

"So far so good. Did she say anything else?"

Alan seemed lost for a moment then said, "Oh yes. Yes she did. She related to me, in detail I might add, the conversation she had just had with Regina. That she had been terminated. Just like that. She included the fact that she and Alan were in *her* bed at the time. She told me that it was important to her that *I* knew that she had nothing to hide. And nothing to *gain* by sharing what she did with me. It was her love for Thad and her duty to choose the straight and narrow path, to do what was right for the company that prompted her call to me. I have nothing but love and respect for that woman. You might say that it was *her* sacrifice which ultimately saved the company."

Check

After Felicia had placed her call to Alan she felt two loving hands caress her shoulders.

"It is done." Thad whispered these words gently into Felicia's ear with what she believed to be joy in his voice.

"Thad honey," Felicia said plaintively, "I just lost my job."

"I know," he said, now placing his arms around her in a warm embrace, "but we still have each other. Isn't that enough?"

Felicia turned to face Thad, looking deeply into his eyes and replied, "Thad dear. I don't think you understand."

"Sure I do. I mean I don't think that you *have* to work but I know that you want to be independent. You'll find another job. With your skills. And your *name—*"

"Stop! That's exactly what I *don't* want. You mean the world to me but I can't just be the product of someone else's worth. That wasn't just a job to me. It was a statement of my worth. It was proof to the world, *to my family*, that I can make it on own."

Felicia is sitting up now having shrugged off Thad's advances. He was showing a pouty face but Felicia was not in a playful mood. "This isn't a game, Thad. You might feel differently if this was happening to you but you don't have to worry about that, do you? You are a cofounder, the king of your domain."

Thad was now worried that he had offended Felicia. He sidled up next to her and took his hands in hers and said, "Look, you're right. I admit that I don't know what it's like to lose a job that defines me—" *OH SHIT!* Wrong choice of words. This tender moment just went south and left of center. Felicia had a look on her face that frankly scared the crap out of Thad. What to do, what to do, what to do...

Thad's phone pinged. Saved by the bell. Instead of making eye contact and listening intently to Felicia's concerns Thad takes the cowardly route and reaches for his phone. There is a text from Berkeley that lights up the screen.

'If I know you, you're still in bed. Get up and get dressed NOW. Brock is on his way.'

Thad mutters, "What the hell" and texts back, *'Let him come. He can bust down the door at the apartment for all I care. I'm still at Felicia's.'*

'Hello! I know *where you are dumbass. That's why I'm warning you. Brock is on his way THERE! To Felicia's condo!!!'*

"SHIT!" Thad throws his phone down on the bed and yells louder, "SHIT! SHIT! SHIT!"

Felicia was not one to mangle or misuse the English language. She was also rather intolerant of curse words. Just as she was ready to scold Thad for his outburst, his phone pinged again. He looked at the screen and shouted, "FUCK!"

It was now Felicia's turn to let down her guard and express herself. This was rarefied air for her. "What the HELL is wrong?!"

Thad appeared frantic. He jumped up from the bed with phone in hand.

"Quick, get dressed! Something bad is going down."

"What?! What is happening?" Felicia has abandoned her personal concerns and has now turned her full attention to what has Thad so frazzled.

"Brock Rampart is on his way HERE."

"Okay, so he figured it out, you're staying with me. What's he going to do about it? He's not a hitman for goodness sake. Why be so worried about *HIM*?"

"Because" Thad said with one leg in his pants and one leg out, "he won't be coming alone."

"Oh. Who's with him? *Should* we be worried? Do you want me to call 911?" Felcia was always so pragmatic. Bless her heart.

"No. They can't help us. They can't help ME. That's who she's after now. ME. First you and now me. She's not done swinging her axe. More heads are about to roll."

"What are you talking about?" Felicia demanded. "WHO are you talking about?!"

"Regina. That's who. Regina is coming HERE. And Brock is w*ith* her! Nothing good can possibly come of this." Thad zipped up his pants and threw a shirt on. He then began to leave the room but stopped and turned when Felicia hit him with a question.

"What has you so worried? Regina can't fire you." She then paused and reflected for a moment before asking, "*Can* she?"

Thad put his hands on his face and rubbed vigorously then continued on by pulling his fingers through his hair. Felicia had *never* seen him so unsettled.

Thad responded, "I wouldn't put *anything* past Regina. Whoever said 'this is a man's world' hasn't met *you*. *Or* Quinn. *Or* Regina."

Felicia looked puzzled for a moment then said, "Is that *somehow* a compliment?"

Thad took a deep breath and tried to calm himself before saying, “Yep, it sure as hell is. *Women* run this world. Not men. We only *think* we do. The king might claim his domain over the kingdom but we all know it is the *queen* that has all the moves. And the power. Am I right?”

Felicia smiled. “You know what? Somewhere in that mixed bag of metaphors is a truth that I wouldn’t have thought you were willing to acknowledge.”

Thad smiled back. “You know what? You just peeled back a layer of the onion. But I’m not going to cry.”

“What does *that* mean?”

Thad seemed at peace suddenly with the situation at hand.

“It means that you know me better than you thought you did. And it means that *I* know me better than I thought I did.” Thad paused for a moment to allow his comment to make sense to Felicia. “Look, I know why they are coming here. I know what their mission is and I think you do too. Regina wants my head and you know what? I’m going to offer it up to her.”

Felicia looked stunned. Thad continued.

“Let’s be honest with ourselves, Felicia. I wasn’t happy there. And neither were you. Am I right?”

“Well—”

“I know I’m right. Felcia, this isn’t bad news that you received today.”

“It isn’t? It sure feels like it is.”

“Well, it’s not. I tell you what it is.”

“What?”

“It is a sign. A sign telling you that it is time for a fresh start.”

The doorbell rang. Thad laughed. “And that, is my sign that it is time for a fresh start for me as well.” Thad walked over to Felicia and placed his hands on her shoulders. “Felicia my love, they haven’t taken us *down*. They have lifted us *up*. Come on, let’s go greet our axe-wielding coworkers.”

Felicia nodded her head up and down and said, “You have a ‘shit-ton’ of positivity for a guy who’s about to lose everything.”

"Wherever did you learn these terrible words that are tumbling out of your mouth?!"

Both Felicia and Thad laughed at that and then Thad said, "Not to worry my dear. I'm not losing *anything*. You'll see."

Thad opened the door. Felicia and Thad burst out laughing. It was not who they expected. Berkeley and Brady looked at one another obviously not understanding what had these two laughing like they hadn't a care in the world. Thad, seeing their confusion urged them to come inside.

After giving each one a warm man hug he said, "I can't tell you enough what it means to me that you are both here to show me, and Felicia, your support. You have proven yourselves to be great friends. Trusted friends. I assure you that this has not gone unnoticed and I promise you that both Alan and Regina, whenever she gets her head on straight again, will know how invaluable you are to the company."

Berkeley spoke up first. "We want to help."

Brady added, "Yeah, whatever we can do."

Thad shook his head knowingly. "I knew I could count on you guys. The good news is that I think I know what is coming and ---"

"And?" Berkeley prompted.

"And I'm good with it."

The doorbell rang. "Oh, here they are now. I want you guys to watch their faces as I steal their thunder. They won't see this coming." And then he laughed.

Thad opened the door. Standing outside were Brock and Regina with two of the most serious looks two faces can muster. Thad said, "Oh look who's here!" Then he pointed first at Brock and then at Regina as he said, "It's 'Check.' And 'Mate'."

Brock and Regina had absolutely no idea how or why that comment could be funny but it sure seemed hilarious to Thad and Felicia. Berkeley and Brady were cracking up too. Berkeley even mimed the words 'check' and 'mate' causing the four of them to laugh even harder.

This was not the confrontation that Regina and Brock had expected.

The King is dead. Long live the Queen.

The Interview

Lana has just listened to Alan describe how Felicia had shared *everything* over the phone with him regarding her relationship with Thad as well as her termination by Regina, all of which might have ultimately saved the company.

"That is wonderful. But I still feel like there is something... *missing*."

"You are absolutely correct. What's missing is what happened next. With Wyatt. Regina had in mind that Wyatt would replace Thad yet still report to her. She had bought into all the fictitious lies which Quinn had generated about him. All to elevate his status in the eyes of one person. Regina. And it worked."

"She went behind your back to promote him."

Alan winced at that comment. "Let's not phrase it that way. I prefer to say that she chose not to consult me on that matter."

Lana knew when not to push. She accepted what Alan had said and then prompted him to take it further. *"And?"*

"And... then she told me all that Regina would need to hear to know of the conniving actions being taken by Quinn which would in effect reveal the true character of Wyatt. I might add that these revelations were like a smack in the face. Much like a dousing of ice-cold water with the hope being that this would snap Regina out of her "funk" as Felicia called it."

"Did it work?" Lana leaned forward, eager to hear the answer.

"Yes. Yes it did. A bit late but yes it did."

"What do you mean by a "bit late"?"

"It was bit late to save Thad. Regina was "all in" on his removal from the company as well. She had started referring to him as her 'Judas.' I would try to interject, to say that I trusted him with my life but nothing doing. Regina's mind was set and she even enlisted the brutish behavior of her pet pit bull to help get it done."

"Brock Rampart?"

"Ah," Alan smiled broadly, "I see you *have* been listening."

"What happened? What did they do?"

"Let's finish the deal with Wyatt first."

"Certainly. Please continue. Sorry to get ahead of the story."

Alan said, "No harm done. So, back to the conversation I had with Felicia. What she said next was what would take Wyatt completely out of the picture. Regina may have later cleaned up her own mess but make no mistake, let's give credit where credit is due, it was *Felicia* who took down Wyatt."

"Noted." stated Lana.

Alan gave her a wink and said, "Moving on then. Here is how those events transpired."

Alan proceeded to describe to Lana how all of the pieces fit together. How it all revolved about Quinn. How she was the *Alpha* and the *Omega* of the plot to take control of the company known to the public as *NRG* Dynamics.

"As it came to be revealed, all that Quinn had ever wanted out of her marriage was control of the company. The problem she was facing now was that since she had pushed Thad away, how would she get this done from a distance. There were two key factors which could not be ignored. One, she no longer held a key position in the company and two, limited resources made the task of executing her plan all the more demanding as a number of her minions were now gone, including her formidable sergeant at arms, Joni. Quinn of course was undaunted by these challenges. In her mind they were merely setbacks. In her mind deceit, deception and domination were merely solvable mathematical word problems."

"I see," commented Lana. "Go on."

"Thad was already on the outs with both Regina and Alan which would make her first ploy that much easier to pull off. Quinn wanted out of her marriage with Thad. Whether or not he wanted that as well was unknown to her but—if she could give *him* a reason to want out of the marriage, that would be another matter altogether. The idea came to her as she was searching for *someone* (an employee of the company) loyal to Regina whom she could "turn" to her side. That someone was, as you now know, Wyatt."

Alan paused. Lana had her head down and was writing. Alan began speaking again when he saw the wave of her hand motion for him to continue.

"Step one was to convince Thad that he wanted out of the marriage. This was accomplished simply by "confessing" to Thad that she was cheating on him with Wyatt. It was too much to ask of him to stay at the house with Quinn being an admitted adulterer. This was of course not true. Quinn had no feelings for Wyatt other than having him do her bidding at the company. Her reasons for inviting Wyatt to move in with her were twofold. One, she knew this would "force" Thad to leave. Secondly, she needed to be close to Wyatt to "infect" him with her disease of greed and deceit."

"What Quinn *hadn't* planned on were the rumors that went with Wyatt moving in with her. These rumors plagued her like bees buzzing around her head. Why? For the most trivial of concerns but nonetheless challenging. Wyatt is gay. He had not come out and shared this with the world for his own reasons but there were a few individuals in the company that knew his truth. Were Thad to learn of this it would make her claims of being unfaithful to him with Wyatt a bit more difficult to substantiate. Having him stay with her kept him away from those who might be inclined to gossip."

Lana was shaking her head and grinning at Quinn's foray into evildoing.

"So, Quinn's next step was to gain control of the company. She would be the puppet master to make this happen. Wyatt would be her puppet. Her pet name for him was "my queen." She rarely called him by his name. 'It's not because you are gay,' she would tell him but rather because you will soon rise to the same level as the queen in residence. Regina. Wyatt was not ignorant to Quinn's intolerance of his lifestyle choices but he was a willing adversary because the payoff in the long run was to be quite significant. The sacrifice was only in the here and now. He would have the rest of his life to enjoy the prosperity of his actions."

"Best laid plans..." Lana mumbled.

"Exactly," agreed Alan. "Anyway, Quinn delighted in watching the pieces of her plan drop into place. There were additional circumstances favorable to the outcome she desired. A hard slap on the face of infidelity by his partner opened Thad's eyes to the fact that there were other fish in the sea. It was of no concern to Quinn that Thad seemed to have become infatuated with Felicia Knight. If anything it helped. Thad had moved in with Felicia, which caused even more unrest in the social climate of the company."

"The other favorable circumstance was the effect that trauma was having on Regina. Suddenly she was at risk for mood swings, knee jerk reactions and poorly developed decisions. Quinn seized on this troubled time for Regina which in turn yielded the token promotion of Wyatt."

"This house of cards which Quinn had built came fluttering to the ground when Felicia placed that all-important call to me." Alan was pointing at himself with his thumb. Lana laughed at this as Alan was the only other person in the room. Alan continued, "That prompted me to reach out to Wendell with the idea of staging an intervention. This was a high risk undertaking for me because, let's face it, I know Regina all too well. She would be absolutely furious upon entering the conference room where this was to be held and seeing the assemblage of folks there even if it was with the best of intentions."

"Oh dear, I'm almost afraid to ask but—how did that go?"

"Well," Alan began with a dubious look on his face, "let's just say that Regina was a bit out of character that day. To be honest, she became quite verbal with me when she saw both Thad and Felicia in attendance but—I stayed strong and stood my ground. Having Wilson in the room gave us an unfair advantage as it forced Regina to keep her anger in check. You see an outburst from her could easily cause an episode from him. Wendell was there as well. Regina mimed 'Et tu Brute' to him but he of course just let that pass."

"Seated next to Thad were Berkeley and Brady. This came as a bit of a surprise to Regina at first but she would later learn that their friendship and allegiance to Thad and to *me* had been invaluable in keeping the corporate structure intact. Once Regina had settled and come to terms with the purpose and intention of the meeting, Brock Rampart was also brought into the room. The timing of his inclusion was essential to bringing both Regina and Brock back on board with the mission of the company."

While Alan would never have characterized things this way, truth be told, he could not have been more eloquent or compassionate in his handling of the intervention. It was a necessary risk having Wilson in the room. His autism would at times prompt him to say the wrong things at the most inappropriate times. However he was also known to say the most right things in the most opportune moments. This fortunately was one of those times.

"The time had come when everything that needed to have been said had been said. It was now time for Regina and Brock to process what they had heard and accept it as truth. What was called for was a quiet moment of reflection. Something else happened instead."

"Oh?" said Lana. "What was that?"

"This may surprise you. It *certainly* surprised *us*."

Lana leaned in, eager to hear what Alan had to say.

"Of all people, Wilson stood up and said, 'I have something to add to this conversation.'"

"*What?!* Really?"

"Yep."

"What did he say?"

"Well before I share what he said, first I think you should know that, to their collective credit no one in the room reacted vocally or with any type of body language."

"I'm sorry. I don't know what you mean."

Alan shrugged and said, "Maybe it's just me but I was worried that the people there might have reacted with the proverbial *"Oh no."*"

"But that didn't happen."

Alan smiled. "I am very happy to say that you are correct. That did *not* happen. In fact, they were all quite respectful. Once Wilson had the floor the room became very quiet. All eyes were suddenly on him. And then, bless his heart, he just froze. The attention was too much."

"Oh no!" exclaimed Lana. She then added, "And now *I'm* saying it."

Alan gave Lana a knowing smile and patted her on the knee. "Not to worry, dear Lana. A flush of humanity overcame Regina the moment she recognized Wilson's panic. She *instinctively* knew what to do. First she waved her hands about involving every person in the room with the simple message, 'nothing to see here.' They all got the message and diverted their attention away from Wilson."

Lana's mouth was open in anticipation of what would come next. Alan could not help but chuckle and show her the motion of using his thumb to close his mouth. Although slightly embarrassed she urged Alan to continue.

"Well, at that point Regina now had control of the situation. She said calmly to Wilson, 'I am interested in hearing what you have to add' to which Wilson said, 'Okay.' And just like that he was fine. He then proceeded to share an unreported piece of major news." Alan paused to let that sink in before he shared that, "All three tech companies that share this business campus, *NRG* Dynamics, LUCID and FM Robotics would be moving *exclusively* to *'Regalis Crystal'* generated power by the first of the month."

"Wow!"

"Yes, that was *big*. Everyone gasped upon hearing the news except Regina. She kept her composure and simply responded by saying, 'Wilson, that is *incredible*.'"

In a rather straightforward fashion, Wilson said, "I know." And then he sat back down.

The Interview

"Now *that* was a moment." stated Alan.

"I can imagine." said Lana. "What happened after?"

"Normalcy." Alan shook his head with determination. "Normalcy came after. We licked our wounds, counted our losses and then went back to work. Since that time, nearly every week one of those three companies is seeking a patent for a new "this" or "that" involving the use of the *'Regalis Crystal.'* That intervention brought Regina back but more importantly, it brought us *all* back."

Lana started to get up but stopped when Alan held up his hand and said, "Before you go."

"Yes?"

"Please allow me to offer you an interaction which was shared with me. This is not for print but definitely for context."

"Okay, what is it?" asked Lana.

"After Wyatt left the company our dear "Queenie" placed a "nastygram" call to Felicia."

"Oh! I would be delighted to hear that!"

"I thought you might. It was a short interaction because as you know neither of those two mince their words. It went something like this—"

"You took down 'my queen'."

"Oh, I took down a queen alright but I am not referring to Wyatt. Notwithstanding the poorly granted promotion he really is just a pawn in this game."

"Oh really? Then to whom are you referring?"

"You."

"Me?!"

"Yes, you."

"But why me? I must ask, what team are you on?"

"Not yours."

"And then she hung up the phone."

"A coupe de grace."

"Indeed."

Last Chance Gas

As Alan walks Lana through the lobby area it occurs to him that he has left out a critical piece of the story. He wants to share but it is rather personal. He determines that if he asks Lana to paraphrase the events she can include without oversharing.

"You know, I met Thad one night for a beer at the *Last Chance Gas*. I hadn't seen him in a while and well, frankly I missed him. Plus I wanted to let him know that I understood how much all of this had cost him. That I still cared about him. I thought he might need to cry on my shoulder and I was willing to offer him some help."

"You are a good friend, Alan. Did he accept your generosity?"

Alan chuckled. "No, but not for the reasons you might imagine. He was actually in very good spirits. On top of the world really which made absolutely *no sense* to me. I was worried that he might have gone off the deep end until—"

"Until, what?"

"Until he shared with me that he plays the game at a *very* high level. Wait until you hear this!"

"I'm all ears!!"

Two friends, a warm hug and a cold beer

"It's just so—"

"So what?" pressed Thad.

"Sad."

"Why do you feel that way? *I'm* not sad." Thad had a bit of a surprised look on his face.

"You're, you're *not*?!" Now Alan showed surprise.

"No. Why should I be?"

"Because you're giving it all up! Everything you worked for! Everything *we* worked for. You're just *giving it all up*. Quinn will take *everything*!! And for what? A wo-" Alan stopped himself.

"Go ahead. Say it. I'm giving it *all* up. For a *woman*. *Say* it." Thad gave Alan a hard yet friendly stare.

"No."

"Why won't you say it?"

"Because I won't mean it the way I would say it. Because I know better." Alan was shaking his head as if to shake off the demons crawling about wanting to get in. "On the surface? Sure, I see her as Yoko Ono breaking up the Beatles but—"

"But?" prompted Thad.

"But-- there is always truth behind the blame. Yoko didn't break up the Beatles any more than me claiming you're giving it all up for a woman. I *know* the truth. I should say I *think* I know the truth. We have become so distant over this last year. But if I know *you*," Alan paused, lowering his head, squinting his eyes and pointing a friendly accusatory finger, "like I *think* I know you, the truth makes everything worth the cost."

"Alan. You know me better than anyone, well *almost* anyone." Thad winked, thinking of his newfound love with Felicia Black Knight. Strike that. Felicia Black *Rex*. "And yes, it *is* worth the cost. It is worth *everything*."

"It's the part about Quinn taking it all that has blindsided me, making me react as I did. Tell me, if you will, what *do* you get out of this?"

Thad smiled the broadest smile that Alan had ever seen grace his face.

"Alan, for the first time in my life, I get to be happy. *Truly happy*." A tear ran down Thad's face as he spoke these words. Alan embraced him with the type of hug that only a true friend can offer.

"I love you brother. Seeing you happy makes all of this worth it for me too." Alan wiped his face as he was tearing up now as well.

"Felicia is truly the love of my life."

"That is *so* great to hear."

"Which makes Quinn—"

"I wasn't going to say it."

"The biggest *loser*."

"We will make the best of things like we always have. It won't be easy. Or pleasant. We will just-- *Wait*. What did you just say?"

"I said, 'Quinn is the biggest loser.'"

Thad let that sink in before continuing on.

"I may have claimed that I was blindly in quote unquote "love" at one time with Quinn but we both know that was a lie. It was always just a way for me to keep up. With *you*. But my eyes are wide open now and they have been for a *while*. She gets *nothing*, Alan. Remember, I am a chess player at heart and a *damn good one*. I saw what she was doing and I simply outplayed her. She was so caught up in *her* own moves that she didn't see *mine*."

"I can't believe this," says an exasperated Alan. "What are you saying?"

"I'm saying that she's done. She's out! She's gone, left like a dog with her tail between her legs. Alan, remember when we changed the name of the company? When we had the big reveal? Back when we, well *you*, announced our mission statement?"

Alan nodded his head.

"It was not more than a month or so after that when it hit me like a truck. The full force of what she was doing and how much I had--, sorry, how much *we* had to lose. Shortly after that, with Jonah's help I did it."

"Jonah?" Alan asked with exasperation. *"Jonah* helped you? But I thought you *hated* Jonah!"

"It was only a ruse, his idea to keep Quinn off our scent. She was always sniffing around in places she wasn't welcome. Additionally I made a few "professional moves" shall we say to put her in the frame of mind that she was *winning*, that she was gaining ground. By that time I believe that she was far too immersed in patting her own back to notice the knives that I was sticking in it."

Thad paused for a moment enjoying his turn of phrase.

"Alan, I changed the structure of our partnership agreement. And--" Thad smiled his most evil smile, "she *signed* it. It's all yours now, Alan. Yours and Regina's. The company, the patents, the intellectual property, *everything*. It's all yours. The Kings win."

Alan was in shock. Thad took Alan's hand in his own, shook it then gave him a warm hug. He whispered in Alan's ear, "You deserve it. You *both* do. You *and* Regina."

The two men, twin sons of different mothers, held the embrace longer than would seem appropriate but neither cared. This was a moment that would last forever in their hearts.

"Please tell Regina that I understand. That she *only* did what she did because she *had* to. For the sake of the company. For the sake of your marriage. She's a great person, Alan. I know I have never told you that but I always knew it from the first moment I met her. Please tell her for me that jealousy makes a man do ugly things. *Stupid*, ugly things. I'm not proud of myself *or* my behavior during that time. But Regina, *wow*. She never gave up in her battle to get me to see the truth, that Quinn was just *using* me. What *she* didn't know is that at some point I turned the tables and *I* was using *Quinn*. I could never be better than you Alan so I needed "props." And a circle of friends. And a party scene to keep me in the news. But the truth is, that was really never *me*. I just hope Regina can forgive me. And I hope that someday we can be friends."

Kingdom for a horse

"Hey! *Chess* player!"

Alan and Thad whirled around. The bar was busy and spaces were few. Personal space was not a thing so neither of the two had noticed that Regina was standing directly behind them. She had heard *everything*.

"So," Regina stated with her arms crossed and a motherly glare aimed directly at Thad, "it appears that you traded your *kingdom* for a *horse!*"

Thad could not help but laugh out loud at the clever metaphors she had just employed. The *"kingdom"* was of course his stake with *NRG* Dynamics, the company which he had helped to create. The *"horse"* was an homage to the moves which Felicia Black Knight had made in this real-life chess game. Said a different way, Felicia had been the *black knight*.

Regina held out her hand as a peace offering and said, "Well played, my friend. Well played."

Thad looked at her outstretched hand and shook his head. "Naw," he said, "family gotta *HUG*!" Thinking that two could play the metaphor game, Thad said, "Hey, I always knew you were the *good* queen!"

Regina laughed out loud and said, "I thought for sure you were going to say, 'the good *witch*'!" They both laughed as she gave Thad a big hug. Thad whispered in her ear, "Tell Rampart I said no hard feelings, alright?"

Regina chuckled. "You're assuming that man has lost a minute of sleep over *anything* I have ever asked him to do? Think again!"

They both laughed at that and just as the embrace had met its time allotment, Alan decided to jump in on the hug as well. It looked silly but they didn't seem to care. By this time Felicia had shown up as well but she kept her distance and gave them their moment. Sadly, this was the beginning of the end for the business partnership of Albus King and

Thaddeus Rex. Happily though, it was only the end of the *beginning* for two men finding new paths in their lives with their loving partners.

Game over_

Interview concluded

"Alan, I can't thank you enough for your time and all that you have shared with me today."

"Believe me Lana, the pleasure is all mine. If you tell our story as well as I think you will, we shall forever be in your debt."

Alan had walked with Lana from the conference room to the front doors of the *NRG* Dynamics building. The two shook hands. Lana surprised herself by giving Alan a hug which he surprised her by reciprocating warmly.

"Before you go—"

"Yes?" asked Lana.

"Would you like a quick tour of the business campus? I can give you a brief treatise on the "goings on" of our neighbors."

Lana laughed at Alan's phrasing and replied, "Sure. That would be quite nice actually."

Alan offered Lana his arm which she gracefully accepted and the two left the *NRG* Dynamics building arm in arm. The midday heat had brought a stillness to the air. A dry heat is how it was typically described. Lana always brought a bottled water with her to stay hydrated in such conditions. Although they would probably only be outside on the campus for 15 to 20 minutes the arid temperature could pull you down quickly if you were unprepared.

The two were walking side by side now. Alan was one of those individuals who talked with his hands so it was necessary for him to be unencumbered. They were heading for a building that looked like it had *landed* on earth from another planet. The design of the building required the viewer to consider that a portion of the structure was *floating* above the business campus. This was not true obviously but the effect was there all the same.

Lana was eager to reach this portion of the building as it was angled just so to provide the greatest degree of shade from the unforgiving sun. As they felt the cool change of temperature sweep over any exposed areas of skin Alan began to talk.

"Before I speak with you about the building whose shade we are stealing," Alan laughed, "I will tell you about the friendly folks at that building over there. That is FM Robotics."

"Okay, what do they do? Robotics I am assuming?"

Alan laughed. "You nailed it. Robotics it is but—" he paused, "this is robotics at an entirely different level."

"How so?"

"This is *AI* robotics. Robotics in containers that look like us, move like us, *talk* like us."

"Containers?"

"Doesn't sound very scientific does it? I don't know what else to call them. *Exoskeletons? Shells?* I sure as hell don't want to say *bodies*. That's a bit too *"Terminator"* for me if you know what I mean."

"Okay now you're scaring me. Are these not "good" robots?" Lana leaned forward which was also unconsciously leaning away from FM Robotics.

"Trust me, Lana. You will not find a better man than Frank Morgan. He is the "FM" in the name. It's just that this whole *AI* thing is such unexplored territory. And not all men have the same pedigree as Frank Morgan."

"Why do I feel like there is more there that you're not saying?"

"Well, Frank has a competitor who is, of his own choosing, becoming a nemesis. His name is Francisco Marconi."

"I believe that I have heard of him."

Alan leaned forward and made his next comments in almost a whisper. "A bit of free advice? Keep your eyes on the dichotomy of those two men. They are both reaching for the same star but... they will *not* be holding hands along the way. That could be your next big story. After this one of course." Alan said this as he pointed at the building of the company he helped to build, *NRG* Dynamics.

The two enjoyed a moment of calm. It was warm outside but not overly hot in the shade being provided by the futuristic building that housed the LUCID team. Alan now pointed at the LUCID building.

"This building is the home base for "LUCID" which is a company dedicated to the exploration of the realm of endless possibilities."

Lana nodded her head approvingly. "You should be their spokesman. Is that *their* tagline or *your* personal perspective?"

Alan smiled. "It is actually a little of both. I know the owner quite well. We attended college together but never shared classes. I did not have the opportunity to get to know him like I know Thad but still well enough that when our paths crossed *after* college we discussed the possibility of our two companies finding some common ground. This is the result of our discussion."

"So, what may I ask, do they do? LUCID. Laymen's terms if you please."

Alan stopped and looked up at the structure then turned and pointed at an art piece in front of the building. The sculpture was a grand sweeping statement of reaching to the sky and leaving the gravity of life behind.

"They do *that.* Not the art piece itself but the essence of the dream the artist must have had to bring it to life."

Alan could tell that Lana was more confused with his answer than she was prior to asking. He continued on, speaking with passion. "Our dreams have no boundaries. It is only when we awaken that we feel the weight of reality pressing down upon us. Tell me, is there a place in the world, the universe really, that you would give *anything* to visit but you *know* you will never have the opportunity *or* the means to get there?"

Lana opened her mouth to answer but Alan cut her off. It was a rhetorical question and he wasn't done. "Or is there something real, or imagined, that you have dreamed of doing but you know to be impossible? *That* is what they do."

Alan was looking at Lana eagerly anticipating a response. She was intrigued by what he had said but more so bewildered by his message. "*That* was laymen's terms? Just my opinion but I think they just might have a few challenges selling *that* to the consumer. Based on what you just said I would have *no* idea who their target customer might even be."

Alan laughed. "That's fair. And totally on me. I get quite excited when I talk about LUCID and their mission. *Too* excited it would seem. Let me tone down that message a bit so you will have a better appreciation for how and why they are about to change the future."

"Well now you have me excited! That is a bold statement. I'm all ears."

"Here, let's have a seat and I will tell you, *in laymen's terms*, what is *NEXT*."

"Okay!"

Alan and Lana sat on a park bench and she listened raptly while Alan explained what could soon be possible...

"Think about your dreams. The good ones. The *really* good ones. The ones that you think about all day. The ones you find so amazing that you can't wait to tell your friends and coworkers. The ones that you miss terribly as the memory begins to fade almost as quickly as you wipe the sleep from your eyes. These are the dreams that just seem so *real*. So *possible*. And yet, so many of them are truly *impossible*, aren't they? The places you go, the things that you do. They are either outside of your means to do them or are possibly only figments of your imagination and don't actually exist. In *our* world."

Alan had Lana's full attention now. She was on the edge of her seat literally waiting for what he would say next. And after all, that *was* what she was really waiting for wasn't it? What is *NEXT*?

Alan seemed quite pleased with himself. He had given the LUCID technology quite a resume. Now it was time to deliver on the hype.

"LUCID is working on technologies that will allow you to go anyplace in the world you want to go for a *fraction* of the cost of actual travel. Or anywhere you can *dream* of going... and have it seem absolutely *real*. It is called LUCID dreaming. You are awake and fully conscious-- while dreaming. The technology they are developing will reach deep into your mind to unlock your greatest desires and—"

Alan paused giving his next comment considerable thought.

"And? And *what!?*" prompted Lana.

Alan spoke softly, carefully. "The potential to relive your memories. Think about the possibility of being able to spend time once again with loved ones who have passed. And if I understand this correctly, they believe that ability to access all facets of the brain will enable the patient to not only relive the memories but to make new ones as well. To live the remainder of the time you may have missed with them. Years of lost time regained and experienced in only minutes."

Alan wiped his eyes, which had become teary during his explanation.

"Patient?"

"Pardon me?"

Lana leaned forward. "You used the word *"patient."* Why?"

"Oh that," said Alan. "Yes well it *is* a new technology and a new *procedure*. It is considered by the government agencies which oversee these things as "experimental." One of the downsides of new technology. A cross they have to bear. I'm sure they probably use some other term like "passenger," "traveler" or even "explorer." That word "patient" was mine. As for the actual experience, they will tell you that it is not dissimilar to what you might feel like after an hour-long massage. Some people leave feeling invigorated while others might feel drained emotionally and need some quiet rest."

"But it's not *harmful*?"

"No, no, it's not harmful at all." Alan, ever truthful, thought for a moment before adding, "That I am aware of."

This last comment more than any other, grabbed Lana's attention.

"Do you think that you might be willing to assist me in gaining an audience with your friend here at LUCID? For a possible story?"

"Yes, I think I can. Actually, I *know* I can and I *will*."

The two stood up, shook hands and then had another brief hug.

"Lana."

"Yes?"

"When you write your story, about *us*," Alan was pointing again to *NRG* Dynamics. "Do not allow yourself to fall into the trap of writing a fairy tale story of two kings of industry battling over the conquest of territory. It was never that black and white. That is *not* the story. The friendship which Thad and I have never wavered. It was never me against him or him against me no matter how it may have appeared on the surface. This story is truly about the two women behind the men."

Alan paused. "Sorry. I'm not comfortable with the word "behind." Let me put it this way. If Thad and I are considered to be the "Kings" of our industry then Regina and Quinn must surely be seen as the "Queens." As our equals and certainly at times yielding *more* power than we could. So this is really a story of the battle of two *queens*. And to oversimplify things, if the good guys wear white, then Regina is most obviously the white queen which in turn makes Quinn—"

"The black queen."

"Now that you understand who your protagonist is you can write your story. Good day, Lana."

"Good day, Alan. Today was, how can I say this—" With both hands Lana expressively acted out her head exploding. "Life-changing."

LUCID

After leaving the interview with Alan at *NRG* Dynamics, Lana Taylor heads directly across the business campus to the sweeping futuristic structure that is LUCID. There are no stairs to navigate on this campus however there are well defined inclines that will tax the leg muscles unaccustomed to such effort. Lana is starting to get winded. Just as she stops to catch her breath another person brushes by her in great haste nearly knocking her down.

"Hello! Excuse me!" Lana shouts out after the person, wanting her exasperation to be known.

"Fuck you." This was the reply. It sounded odd though as there was no emotion delivered with the words. It was flat, almost as though the person was saying 'you're welcome' to a 'thank you.' The person gave a half-turn of their head as they continued on.

Lana gasped. She *knew* this person. Correction. She knew *OF* this person. Under her breath, in an alarmed whisper, she said, "Joni! What the hell--?"

The receptionist looked up as she heard someone approaching. She immediately dialed Everett Marsh, the CEO of the company.

"Yes?"

"Senator McKinney is here."

"What the hell does *he* want?!"

"Sir, I'm sure I don't know. He is just now approaching the desk. Should I--?"

"No, that will not be necessary. I will be right down. And Blanche?"

"Yes sir?"

"My apologies for the bad behavior just then. The Senator seems to be able to pull out the worst in me."

"Understood, sir. He is not my favorite either." Everett chuckled at this as he ended the call.

The gentleman in the dark brown suit and perfectly shaped cowboy hat stepped up to the receptionist's desk to announce himself.

"Afternoon, ma'am, I am Senator Bob McKinney. I have some business here today." The senator said this with his thick Texas drawl assuming that the accent alone would make him sound charming. It did not.

"Yes, Senator, it is good to see you. *Again.*" Blanche placed emphasis on the last word because this was not the first time, or even the *tenth* time for that matter, that the two had spoken. The Senator was not her favorite person for one simple reason. He had little regard for his public.

"Oh yes, of course, I thought I recognized you."

"Did you?" Blanche fired back with a tinge of insolence in her voice.

"Tryin' to be polite, ma'am," the senator replied as though such a meager reply was all that was required of him. Everett Marsh arrived just then to save the senator, *and* the receptionist, from further discomfort.

"Good afternoon Senator. To what do I owe the displeasure of your unannounced visit?"

"Did *you* call him?" The senator asked Blanche as a rebuke. He did not wait for a reply but instead turned to Everett to comment, "You know, it's not always about *you*. How does a man end up with a silly name like 'Everett' anyway?"

It was a throwaway jab, a rhetorical insignificant comment to which Everett had a ready reply.

"All the clever names like "Bob" were already taken." The senator tried to hide a sneer as Everett continued with, "Why are you here?"

"I have an interview."

"Well, unfortunately all of our positions here require *skill* and *effort.*"

Blanche snorted when she attempted to suppress a laugh. The senator ignored her and said, "I am *conducting* an interview thank you. Ah, here she is now. Right on time." He turned to Blanche and said with a commanding tone in his voice, "Make "*Dream Suite A*" available for me will you?" No please, no thank you.

Just then Everett sees and recognizes the person (in his mind "trespassing") in his lobby who is here to interview with the senator. He grabs the senator by the arm and says with clenched teeth, "If you think for one minute that I would consider putting that, that "person" on my payroll, you had better think again."

The senator looks down at Everett's hand clutching his arm and then leveled a venomous gaze at him that spoke volumes. "*Your* payroll?!" The senator let that sink in before adding, "The last time I checked, your company has yet to achieve profitability so your survival at the moment is reliant upon *my payroll*, is it not?" The senator did not wait for an answer. He didn't need to. They both knew that his statement was *nearly* accurate. The funding came from the government by way of the Texas senator. The senator turned away from Everett to greet his prospect.

"Hello, you must be Joni. My pleasure to meet you." The senator held out his hand to shake. Joni did not take it. She instead just nodded her head. The senator dropped his hand to his side. This bit of impertinence could be overlooked. After all he was not interviewing Joni for a position which would require any level of social interaction. "Very well then, follow me." Joni followed dutifully behind as the senator made his way to a conference room where a group of individuals were hurriedly gathering up their things from an unfinished meeting. The senator had obvious "pull" in this building.

Everett Marsh was not accustomed to being taken down a peg in his own building. Before he could expend any time being annoyed over the interchange a quite attractive woman, smartly dressed and seemingly brimming with confidence, was making her way across the expansive lobby.

"Sir. Sir?"

"Wh--, what?" Everett pulled his eyes away from the woman to focus on Blanche who was holding a phone out to him. "I have a call for you and your, uh, jaw is hanging open."

Everett quickly put a hand to his face and then realized that Blanche was just putting him on. He gave her a "caught in the act" look and then offered a sheepish grin as he replied, "I have a call?"

"Yes. It is Mr. King. Alan. From next door."

"Oh yes, I will take that." Everett took the phone and said with a smile in his voice, "Hello Alan, it is good to hear from you. How may I be of service?"

Alan proceeded to explain that he had intended to call earlier but got caught up in other business. He then shared that a lovely young journalist would be making her way into his building to announce herself. Everett replied by saying that he believed that she had already arrived.

"Oh, she's there now then." Alan is speaking on the other end. "Well that's on me. I should have contacted you sooner. If you could just give her a minute and perhaps schedule an appointment for another time. She will explain her mission and I am absolutely certain you will want to be on board."

Everett nodded his head as he made eye contact with Lana and said, "Alan, your endorsement is all I need. I will speak with her now."

"That's great, Everett. That's just great. Hope all goes well."

"Thank you Alan. Hey, real quick, I have something to share that may be of interest to you."

"What's that?"

"Well, the senator is here—"

"That's *your* problem Ev, and of no interest to me." Alan chuckled aloud.

Everett said, "Ha-ha, very funny. I wasn't finished. He is here interviewing a person."

"A person." Alan repeated.

"Yes, a person whom you know."

"Okay, and who might *that* be?"

"How about I give you a hint? *She* is wearing an *eyepatch*."

There was total silence on the other end.

"You still with me? You know who I am referring to?"

"Yes, unfortunately I do. Brock calls her 'the pirate' now because of that thing. *Regina* is responsible for that by the way."

"I know. You told me the story."

Alan was quiet for a moment before asking, "What would the senator want with *her*?"

"Nothing good, Alan. Nothing good. Hey, I better go. This young lady is being very patient with me."

"Certainly. Give my regards to Ms. Taylor. And Everett?"

"Yes, Alan."

"Keep me informed of the "Joni" thing, won't you."

"You got it my friend. Let's grab a beer sometime."

"That sounds great. Yes, let's do it! And by the way, we've been saying that now for six months straight."

"I know! We're both just *so damn busy*!"

"Take care of yourself, Everett."

"You too, Alan." Everett handed the phone back to Blanche and turned to face Lana. "Hello, Ms. Taylor. I am pleased to make your acquaintance."

"Oh, thank you! It is so gracious of you to make time for me on such short notice."

"I am glad to do it. I understand that you have just spent the day with Alan King."

"Yes."

"He speaks highly of you and I think the world of him. How might we help one another?"

Lana was about two-thirds of the way through her brief explanation of her desire to write an article on what LUCID was all about when two people walked past on their way through the lobby to the exit doors.

"Was that *Senator* McKinney?!" Lana asked, clearly taken by surprise.

"Yes," replied Everett, "and please don't ask what he is doing here."

"And that was Joni *with* him?" Lana added.

"Unfortunately yes, and I have *no idea* what she is doing here."

"It can't be good."

"Oh, so you *know* her."

Now that "*Dream Suite A*" was unoccupied Everett motioned for Lana to follow him. He asked if she needed water or coffee. She said no. The two sat down to talk. He did his best to explain what his company was all about and how he hoped for his company to be disruptive in the travel segment. Much of what he said Lana felt she had heard before from Alan. This was all '*marketingspeak*' and didn't cut to the core of the inner workings of this futuristic business concept. Her job, after all, was not to rework marketing copy from a sales pamphlet but rather to dig and discover what the public never sees. After the time she had spent with Alan, Lana was convinced that this was her calling.

Everett had glanced at his watch more than a few times. Now he chose to express to Lana that as it was nearing the end of the workday perhaps they could schedule some time for more discussion between the two tomorrow. Lana realized then how caught up she had just been in learning what she could about *this* business venture. She nodded her head and replied, "I am so sorry, Mr. Marsh. You have been so gracious with your time. Where are my manners?"

Everett smiled and said, "I assure you, Lana, it was my pleasure to spend these moments with you. Does 9:45 am tomorrow morning work for you?"

"Sure!" Lana was a bit too eager to hear that she would be welcomed back so soon. "I mean, yes that would be fine with me."

"Good, good. I will be waiting for you in the lobby tomorrow morning and we will resume our discussion."

"Mr. Marsh?"

"Call me Everett, please."

"Certainly, will do. Thank you." Everett nodded and smiled. "Everett, might I ask why 9:45? I'm fine with it, it just sounds, I don't know, like an off time?" Lana held up her hands in a helpless gesture.

Everett smiled again and said, "If you're thinking that all I am going to offer you is fifteen minutes of conversation before my next meeting you are quite mistaken."

"No, I—"

Everett held up his hand to ward off her comment as he continued. "I have a business meeting, a presentation if you will, that my marketing team and I will be sharing with members of the Board of the National Association of Travel Agents. It will be quite an informative session and, might I add, a great starter piece for you. I will of course spend some time with you after the meeting as well."

"Oh! Well thank you! That is much more than I would have expected. I promise to be here promptly at 9:45."

"Great, I will see you then." Everett stood up to escort Lana from the room. Lana followed him out of the meeting room and they crossed the expansive lobby together. Lana looked up, only now seeing the collection of abstract '*Birds in Flight*' sculptures hanging above her. She stopped for a moment in awe of the grandeur of the art package.

"Pretty incredible isn't it?"

Lana nodded her head while still taking it all in.

"That art piece was designed specifically to complement the sweeping arc in front of the building."

"Quite impressive. The two seem to work perfectly together."

"Yes, well, that is probably due to the fact that both the artist and the architect of this building are one and the same."

That *was* impressive. Lana's eyes went wide but Everett missed her expression. Lana noticed then that he had glanced once again at his watch. She had overstayed her welcome. They were but a few steps from the front door of the building now.

"Please forgive my impudence. May I indulge you for *one more* question? A *simple* question to be sure."

Everett smiled his best impatient smile. "Why certainly. What is it?"

"Thank you so much. I just know that this will float around in my head all evening if I don't ask now." Lana looked at Everett and inquired, "Am I right to assume that LUCID is *both* the business name as well as an anagram?"

Everett flashed a bright smile, this time wide with gleaming white teeth. Lana took this to mean that she had just asked the "right" question. She had stumbled upon the one "little" thing that he was truly proud of as an accomplishment.

"Lana, it may surprise you to learn that that question is rarely asked of me. I am, however, *always* eager to share as it originated from yours truly."

"Which does not surprise me."

Everett bowed, which seemed rather odd to Lana, as he said, "Thank you for that compliment. It speaks to your character."

A pensive look fell upon Lana's face as she thought to herself, 'That is the *second* time today someone has said that to me. First Alan and now

Everett. Perhaps they know something about me that I don't!' A broad smile accompanied that thought.

Everett was continuing on unabated. "The word "lucid" in simple English means something that is expressed clearly, easy to understand. In literary terms it means bright or luminous. In psychological terms it means something a bit deeper. It is described as an experience of the dreamer who is not only dreaming but is *aware* of his dreaming and *consciously able* to control events. That word in and of itself speaks clearly of our mission here. I was able to take it one step further by discovering the hidden meaning in each of the letters which make up the word."

The buildup to the climax was so powerful that Lana hoped that she would not be disappointed with the payoff. She was not. It was instead, she thought to herself, a flash of brilliance. Everett spoke softly as he related that LUCID meant "**L**everaging **U**ndiscovered **C**apabilities **I**n **D**reams."

Lana's brain hurt with all the things she had stuffed into it today but she couldn't be happier. Not only did she have the incredible story of *NRG* Dynamics to write but she now had what appeared to be an equally amazing story about the company and concept, which was LUCID.

As she strode across the business campus on her way to her car Lana felt that strange feeling that someone was watching. And there was. Someone with a sneer on her face and an eye patch over one eye. Arriving at her car, Lana dumped her bag on the passenger side and got into the car. As she settled herself into a comfortable seating position she moved the rearview mirror with her right hand to where she could see her face. She smiled genuinely at the refection peering back at her as she said, "Lana, you have a bright future ahead of you!"

Lana turned the key then and the engine growled to life. As she was leaving the parking garage Lana was confused for a moment about which direction to turn. She chose one and drove on. As it happened, she was *right* about which way to turn but unfortunately *wrong* about the prediction for her future. Had she bothered to look, she might have seen Joni standing in her vacated parking spot. A bad omen to be sure.

Part One

Sweet Dreams

The next morning

As promised, Lana is right on time.

Also as promised Everett is waiting for her in the lobby. He says 'I took the liberty' while handing her a steaming hot cup of Seattle's Best coffee. Black.

"Oh thank you so much!" declared Lana. "I didn't have time for a cup this morning. I stayed up late last night working on my first draft of the *Regalis* crystal piece."

Everett stopped in mid-stride. Lana nearly plowed into him.

"If this is a bad time..."

"What?" Lana is puzzled. "Oh wait, you mean a bad time for me to be here?"

"Yes," Everett said, "if you have other obligations..."

Lana laughed. "Thank you for your concern but please no, let's not reschedule. I'm here and "rarin' to go" as they say. Besides, I'm a big girl and I am fully capable of walking and chewing gum at the same time."

"You are also fully capable of a mouthful of euphemisms as well I see."

Lana laughed a nervous laugh to which Everett gave her a wink then took her by the arm to guide her in the direction of the marketing presentation which was to begin promptly at 10 am. Lana fell in step quickly. She held off on attempting to take a sip of coffee. There would be plenty of time for that in just a few minutes.

As the two walked down the corridor to the presentation room Lana was struck by how few people they passed in such a large structure. And the few people which they did encounter all seemed to be wearing white lab coats and surgical masks. 'Should I find that odd?' she asked herself. Or is that business as usual in a place like this? She made a mental note to pose that question at a later time.

Once inside the presentation room Lana's eyes were drawn to the title emblazoned on the screen.

Take Your Dream Vacation... And Never Leave Home!

A man in the room had seen it as well and had a comment.

"Well that's not exactly true, is it?"

"No, I guess it is not," replied Everett but thinking to himself, what *is* true is that 'there is one in every crowd' like the old saying goes. This gentleman was a Midwestern fellow who had never been out West. He ran a travel agency from the comfort of his own home, which was in effect a double wide trailer, but the success of his business spoke for itself. There were a lot of small companies these days hiding behind an impressive web page. Forgoing the brick-and-mortar route saved them a bunch of money. Everett had his own opinions, which he smartly kept to himself, about businesses which operated in this fashion. For the benefit of the other travel agent professionals in the room Everett offered an honest answer.

"I will speak with our marketing team to see if that tagline 'Take Your Dream Vacation and Never Leave Home' can be tidied up a bit. You do get the gist of the message though, yes?"

Everett had done a masterful job of showing grace to the oddball question and then turning the tables on the gentleman to highlight his ignorance. Everett had very little patience for ignorance. The other most maddening thing was that this was the *first* slide of the PowerPoint presentation. There were *29* more to go.

"Oh, sure, sure," said the Midwestern gentleman, "I get it alright. Just trying to be helpful."

Everett nodded his head in appreciation of the reply. Then the gentleman added a comment that grated on Everett's nerves. "I have a rather discerning clientele you know."

"I'm sure you do," stated Everett. "Where might I ask do you call home?"

"O-H!" shouted the man. The room was uncomfortably quiet. The man looked from face to face of the other attendees. None of them seemed to know that his statement was supposed to prompt a call back from them.

Everett knew. "I-O," he said.

"Thank you!" shouted the man. "Go Bucks!"

Everett let that battle cry hang out there on its own for a moment before continuing on. 'Read the room' he felt like saying to the man from Ohio. The other people in the room were from a variety of places, some from New England states, some from California, one from Europe and one from Australia. Everett's next comment came with the fervent hope that there would be no more interruptions during the presentation.

"Each of you have been provided with a notepad and pen. Please feel free to jot down any questions, *or comments*, you may have *during* the presentation, and we will address them *after* the presentation."

Lana suppressed a laugh as she took note of the fact that Everett had put this man from Ohio in his place. She was a bit torn in her feelings towards Everett. She *really* wanted to like him. He was polite, intelligent, attractive, engaging—she could go on, but he was also a bit arrogant and a tad condescending. Those two tiny little things nagged at her as she turned her attention back to the presentation.

The slide presentation was ingenious and well-crafted for the intended audience. To their credit, the travel agent professionals in this room, including the man from Ohio, seemed to understand that what Everett was extending to them was a peace offering. An unnecessary invitation to a party from which they could just have as easily been excluded. After all, their customers could contact LUCID directly, on their own, should they wish to use their services. Everett, however, was a savvy operator and he recognized that explaining how LUCID works to his future clients was his greatest challenge. Planting LUCID in the travel segment delivered instant customer familiarity and credibility.

This was a gift really for the travel agents. It was another product for them to sell. A product which was not burdened with the hardship of extended travel. This was something which would appeal to most of their clients. *IF* they could afford it.

The remainder of the presentation went smoothly. Everett had these folks enthralled. Lana too was immersed in the moment as well however she had some other things on her mind which caused her attention to stray. While Everett was certainly a fabulous speaker and you couldn't find a more passionate and educated person to "sell" this product, *where* were the marketing folks? Wasn't it *their* job to make the marketing pitch? Lana added that question to the others scribbled down on her mental list.

The presentation was over, the question-and-answer session had concluded and the attendees had started to file out of the room. Lana had stood up as well and found herself following the Midwesterner from Ohio. Each attendee was shaking Everett's hand and commenting on what they had seen and heard in the past hour. Lana scrunched her face involuntarily thinking of what might transpire between Everett and this man. What she was envisioning was not pretty.

Both men surprised her. The man from Ohio shook Everett's hand firmly while apologizing sincerely for being disruptive. Everett was his best self as he placed his left hand on the man's shoulder, accepted his apology graciously and then said that his comments were taken as intended (helpful) and that he really would discuss possible phrasing options with the LUCID marketing team. The Ohio man walked away with a smile and a vested obligation to sell LUCID as best as he could to his clients.

Lana watched Everett as he watched the Ohio man walk away. She smiled and said, "That was a genuinely nice thing you did right there."

"Perception is everything, is it not, Ms. Taylor?"

Everett walked out of the room and was several paces down the hall before he realized that she was not following him. "You coming?"

"Yes, yes of course." Lana caught up to Everett who was walking briskly. She was intrigued and excited by the fact that they were heading deeper into this building which seemed to hold so many mysteries. She was also quite troubled by Everett's demeanor. Who was this man really? And what was his end game? And what was Senator McKinney's part in all of this? And how did Joni factor into the equation? So many questions.

An analogy came to mind for Lana. If the *NRG* Dynamics story was a chess match then this LUCID business concept was like the strategy board game "*RISK*." Lana quickly reminded herself that she had *no idea* what the rules of that game were or how it was played but—that name "*RISK*" sure seemed to fit.

Behind closed doors. And windows.

Everett and Lana had nearly walked the length of the building. She was struck by the fact that while she had seen a building rich with windows on the outside they had not passed a single pane of glass offering a view or letting in light. That seemed *odd*. Lana determined that she would pose the question.

"That is a valid question, Lana and if you will pardon the pun, most of the windows which are visible on the exterior of the building are actually just "window dressing." They're not real. They are actually modified solar panels which collect energy which is then magnified by the *Regalis* crystal which powers this place. Oh please," Everett held up a hand, "don't ask me how it works. I have just shared with you the sum total of my knowledge regarding the *Regalis* crystal." Everett laughed heartily.

"Wow, that's incredible," said Lana. "So there are *no* windows in this building?!"

"Oh come now, you know better than *that*! You were in the lobby earlier. The atrium is nothing *but* windows."

"Oh yeah, that's right. But the rest of the building...?"

"One other floor in the building features "real" windows and that is the top floor. My office as you may have surmised occupies the top floor."

"And your staff—," Lana offered. Everett left that statement hanging and unanswered.

Behind the scenes

The two had arrived in a large room filled with computer keyboards and LCD monitors. There was a modicum of workers. Their presence was dwarfed by the size of the room. 'This is where the action is' Lana thought to herself. Her next thought was, 'nothing to see here.'

"Ms. Taylor, have you ever toured a kill plant? Like for cattle?"

What an *odd* question. And what was the deal behind him interchanging the use of her name with this "proper" Ms. Taylor nomenclature?

"No, I can't say that I have, does that have some significance to what we are doing now?" Lana was curious.

"In a sense, yes. Simply put a kill plant *processes* animals. They walk in one end as live cattle and then leave from another area of the building as portions of meat for human consumption."

"Yes, I think I knew all of that but not something I would ever equate with what you're doing here. So now I must ask, *how* does that equate with what you are doing here?"

Everett laughed. "It doesn't really other than the fact that we have what I call a "clean" area and a "dirty" area."

"I'm not sure that I follow," said Lana.

"Allow me to explain," replied Everett.

"Please."

Before continuing Everett shot Lana a side glance indicating that her comment was extraneous.

"At a kill plant, the area in which the animals enter is the "dirty" area. There is a lot of blood and organs and, well I will just leave it right there." Everett acknowledged the look of relief on Lana's face. "Once the animals have been processed, the remaining product is handled in a "clean" environment, sterile and germ free."

"So what you're saying is that this," Lana swept her arm about the room, "is the "dirty" area?"

"No of course not. *This* is the "clean" area where my team does their work making our customers dreams remembered as real-life memories."

"You're saying the place where your customers—"

"The public."

"Your *customers*," Lana emphasized sternly, "are in the place you call the "dirty" area?"

"You have characterized it differently than I would, but yes. It is important for you to understand that for LUCID technology to work our subjects must be in some level of sleep. Not everyone sleeps "clean"."

"*Subjects?*"

"Customers. Guests."

"You said "*subjects*"."

"You say "tom-A-to," I say "to-MAH-to," let's move on."

Lana walked a little behind Everett as they moved through the room. His eccentricities were beginning to overtake his positive qualities. Lana's thoughts were quickly redirected as Everett began to explain in explicit detail how the mechanics worked on *this* side of the LUCID *Dream Experience*. She was fascinated by all that she heard. She watched Everett intently as he spoke, listening with great interest as she was told "no note-taking" during this portion of the tour. Lana would have to trust her memory as well as her cognitive skills in order to capture everything that Everett was sharing. The more that came out of Everett's mouth the more Lana began to doubt that any of it was real. She *so* much wanted to like this man. She *so* much wanted to believe him but that little voice inside her head was telling her to be wary. This was after all, in her opinion anyway, a game of *RISK*.

The "dirty" room

Lana had the feeling that she was soon to be dismissed. Everett was a busy man and he had just spent a good amount of time with her. Unlike Alan King, who was a true gentleman in action and deed, Everett, she thought, only *appeared* to be his equal. Lana wondered if she was judging him too harshly. There was still time for her to change her mind. If she was about to be ushered out of the building right now it would not bode well for her opinion of him.

Everett must have read her thoughts when he touched her arm and said, "Lana, before you go, how about I treat you to a few minutes of the best experience you will ever have in your life?"

Lana looked Everett straight in the eyes and saw only genuine eagerness and passion. There was trust in those eyes too. How could she say no?

"Everett, that is so kind of you. I would be forever in your debt. I don't think I could afford something like that on what the magazine pays me."

"Most likely not," agreed Everett without even a tinge of condescension in his voice.

The comment only served to hurt Lana's feelings a bit although she admitted to herself that it *was* true.

"Please follow me."

Lana was walking in step now with Everett even though he had used the word "follow." She suddenly realized how excited she was to try this dream machine out. If what she had heard from both Everett and Alan was even partially true, her life was about to change. Lana began to run some ideas through her head of where she might go on a dream vacation. The options were endless since actual travel was unnecessary.

Lana thought of Rome. And Paris. And London. And Spain! And---, wait. How many times had she heard the word "experience" used and here she was trying to think of a "place." The moment that this epiphany came to her she knew what she wanted out of this experience. If what she wanted was possible, not only would it be "worth it," it, would, be, *priceless*.

Everett and Lana stepped into the "dirty" room. The first thing that Lana noticed was that it was impeccably clean. It smelled *fresh* in a way that could only be described as *outdoor* "fresh." Like a beautiful spring day in a field of flowers. The scent was clean and real. So far, so amazing.

"Please, Lana, make yourself comfortable in that recliner there."

"Thank you," replied Lana as she made her way to the plush blue recliner. She could not determine what type of fabric it was but it felt cool (not cold) to the touch and was *abundantly* comfortable. She almost felt guilty as she allowed her body to sink into the welcoming chair.

"Lana."

"What?!" Lana jerked suddenly and blinked her eyes open. Had she fallen asleep?

Everett laughed. "Trust me, that is a natural reaction what you did just now. I should really be in the business of selling these recliners. No, you didn't fall asleep just now. What happened was your mind and body working together to fully relax."

"That was amazing. Am I done?"

Everett laughed again. "No, we haven't even started but before we do, with you being a journalist, allow me to share with you the number one question we get before people enjoy their experience."

"Oh, I'm all ears. What is it?"

"You'll know the question by my simply giving you the answer. No, you do not need to be strapped in for the procedure. Everyone uses the word *procedure* for some reason. That word appears *nowhere* in our marketing copy but somehow... ha, what are you going to do?" Everett shrugged his shoulders. "Alright then, this will be a very short experience for you but I promise the memories will last forever. What have you got in mind?"

Lana bit her lip as she said, "If you can't do it, I will understand."

Everett shook his head and replied, "You're giving me entirely too much credit. This isn't about what *I* can do. This is about what you can *imagine*. I have the easy part. I just have to keep your mind and body relaxed to the point where they will allow your brain to dream, to travel, to explore..."

Lana grinned as she watched Everett's effusive passion manifest itself once again. He caught himself and winked at her as he asked with a hillbilly twang in his voice, "What'll it be ma'am? Regular or premium?"

"Premium," she responded. "The best you got. I want--." Lana got a bit choked up, then composed herself and said, "I want to see my mother again. I lost her when I was twelve."

Although Everett seemed to accept this request in stride it actually came as a complete surprise. It was out of left field. Everything they had discussed had to do with "travel". To a "place". Lana had obviously been more attuned to what Everett had been sharing than he was aware. Lana was requesting "travel" not just to any "place" but rather a place in "time". That capability was what he had been chasing all along. For someone else to have been able to see, and *appreciate*, his vision, well...

Everett suddenly got a bit emotional but was able to keep those feelings to himself.

"Lana, you are the customer this was truly made for. That is the most heartfelt request a person could ask for. Congratulations, for that I am giving you the full ride. My treat of course. All I ask is that you share a moment of your joy with me when you awaken."

Tears appeared in Lana's eyes as she realized what she was being given and what she was hopefully about to experience. Perhaps Everett was a true gentleman after all. He left the room and suddenly she felt her eyelids become heavy and for a brief second she was asleep and then—

Mother and child reunion

---she was back in her mother's arms. The warmth and comfort she found there was simply indescribable. It was a warm summer day. The laundry was pegged to the clothesline in the back yard and flapping in the breeze. Her two brothers are running back and forth shooting at each other with imaginary bullets fired from toy guns. 'I got you, you're dead!' 'No I'm not, you missed me!' And off they ran.

'Mommy are you going to leave us?' twelve-year-old Lana asked.

'No, of course not, I would *never* leave my children.'

'Not even if you get sick? Daddy says you're going away.'

'Oh child, don't you worry so much. Your Mommy is fine. Your father shouldn't put such crazy notions in your head.' She coughed just then and tried to hide the blood that was left in her hand. Lana closed her eyes and said no, this cannot be happening again. Not like this. She had always dreamed of her mother seeing her graduate, seeing her get married, seeing her have her first child...

---and then---

'Do you want to hold her? I named her Anne, after you because I missed you so much. Anne, say hi to your grandmother.'

'She's beautiful!' exclaimed Lana's mother. 'She has your eyes. Oh Lana, she is so precious. I want this moment to last forever.'

'It will, Mom, I promise you, it *will*.'

'Honey, do one thing for me, won't you?'

'Sure, Mom, anything.'

'Forgive your father, dear. And tell him you love him. He made some mistakes, *human* mistakes, but he's *not* why I went away. I had cancer, honey. That wasn't *his* fault and I need you stop blaming him for it. Don't make the mistake of losing us *both*.'

Lana started to cry. 'I won't Mom, I promise. I will text him tonight.'

'I don't know what that is honey but I know he will be *so happy* to get your phone call.'

'Mom, I love you.'

'I love you too, honey.'

'Mom, I have so much to share with you, I hardly know where to start!'

"Lana, it's time to come back now."

'What, Mom?'

"It's time to come back now."

'Mom, why are you saying that? And why is your voice changing?'

"I'm sorry but it's time. You *must* come back now."

Lana suddenly felt like she was shooting down a long tunnel. Her mother, her newborn baby, all the time she has lost, everything was being pulled away from her.

"No!" Lana screamed. "It's not *fair*! I want her *back*! I want her *back*!!"

"Lana, are you okay?"

Everett was standing over her as she blinked away the hard crust of sleep from her eyes. For a moment she thought he (Everett) was her father but that was impossible. Her father lived in Seattle and was unable to travel.

"Are you okay?" Everett asked again.

"Yes I think so," Lana said weakly. She felt drained, too exhausted to move. The recliner which had felt so comfortable before now felt wet and had an unpleasant smell to it. "What *happened?!*"

"To be fair, we still have a few bugs to work out but we'll get there."

"*Bugs?*" Lana looked about her with trepidation.

"Figuratively speaking."

"Oh, sure, of course. Can you help me up? I don't feel like I have the strength."

"Better yet, why don't I have Blanche come in and assist you? You will want to get cleaned up as well. We have laundry facilities on site."

"Laundry? What--?"

"Let me step away now. I have no desire to embarrass you."

Everett turned and walked away leaving Lana to wonder what the hell he was talking about. And then it dawned on her. The wetness and the unpleasant smell. She suddenly recognized both. She had urinated on herself during the time she was asleep. In essence she had just wet the bed. When was the last time *that* had happened? And why the *hell* hadn't Everett warned her of the possibility? She would address that with him later. In the meantime she had much to think about. She just made an impossible connection with her mother whom she had lost to cancer. They had shared so much in such a brief amount of time. She was able to tell her things she had needly so badly to say. And she had given her the grandchild that she had wanted more than anything in the world. Should Lana feel guilty about that? She was neither a wife nor a mother. That was pure imagination on her part. But it was also a gift to her mother.

Lana's thoughts now landed on the single most significant moment within that space in time she had shared with her mother. Lana had been given a task. To release her father from the unfair weight of guilt Lana had placed on him all these years from her mother's unfortunate death. Just then Lana closed her eyes to call up the memory of her mother once again, eternally positive, carefully choosing what would be her last words, "Honey, stop your worrying. I feel just fine."

Head Rush

Lana wasn't sure how much more she could take. This morning was almost like being at an amusement park. She had certainly been riding the rides. First came the out-of-body experience of seeing her mother again (*alive*) after all these years. To have interacted with her as well. And to speak of things only *she* would have known. To be honest with herself Lana noted that these were things which *both* of them would have known. The simple truth being that there was a full reliance on her *own* memories and imagination to make the interaction seem real. Still though, it truly felt like it had *really* happened.

Now Lana was on a super-fast elevator being whisked to the top of the building which housed LUCID Technologies. Everett had kindly *(?)* offered her more of his precious time. His motives were still suspect as far as Lana was concerned. She was, however, indebted to him for the experience of a lifetime, one which she would never forget.

As the elevator ascended Lana focused her attention on the floors as one after one they flashed by the window. Wait. Something was odd. *That's it!* Lana scrunched up her face. What the *hell?!* In a building with precious few windows WHY would you have a *glass* elevator? That made absolutely NO sense. There was nothing to see---

"OMG!"

The panoramic view of the desert spreading out to meet a mountain range at the horizon was simply breathtaking. Lana touched her chest feeling the rapid beating of her heart. The motion of the elevator had stopped and she failed to notice as the vista before her was so incredible. The palette of colors, the scope of the perspective, the grandeur of the mountains, the beauty and the spectacle of the expanse of the desert. These were all things that no artist could successfully capture on canvas. It took Lana a full minute of taking in the view before she realized that Everett was watching her and chuckling to himself.

"Pretty remarkable isn't it?"

"There are no words," replied Lana. "And I am a supposed 'wordsmith'."

"Please, come into my office. You will find that the view gets even better." Everett showed the offer with his body language.

"Is that even *possible?*" asked Lana as she stepped free of the elevator. And then she discovered that yes it *was* possible. Everett's office was perched at the top of the building offering *almost* a 365-degree view of the world surrounding them below. Lana burst out with an unexpected laugh. "I didn't even buy a ticket!"

"Beg your pardon?" said Everett.

"I'm sorry. I was thinking out loud. It had just occurred to me that the last time I had seen something this dramatic was when I visited the Space Needle in Seattle. And I had to *pay* for that experience!"

Everett smiled broadly, "Well I doubt that my humble little office can compare with the views from the Space Needle. Puget Sound, Olympic National Forest, the Cascades mountain range, Mount Rainier! And then there is the city itself. So much to see!"

"Don't sell yourself short. This office is truly incredible. And who would think to include a glass elevator?"

Everett smiled. "My architect did not want that view go to waste."

"What an insightful man! I'm sorry, I am guilty of making an assumption there. Is your architect a male?"

"Yes he is. No harm done."

Lana smiled. "Do you mind if I look around before we talk?"

"Please do," Everett gestured with his hand. "I feel that is entirely appropriate. Ask any questions that you like." Everett kept his position in the room as Lana walked the circumference of the wall of windows.

"It is surprisingly *cool* in here," stated Lana. "With no draft. Even more so near the windows, which seems at odds with the fact that they are facing the sun. Am I right in thinking that there is something *unusual* at play here?" Lana looked to Everett sincerely, unaware that she had just scored a huge amount of points with his ego.

"Lana, may I say that you are simply a *joy* to host. You are the penultimate guest. *So* observant. And *so* appreciative of what you know or are *curious* to know is true and possible." Everett said this with a look of delectation which for him was one level above contentment and satisfaction.

"Thank you?" Lana wasn't sure if she just "stepped in it" or had actually impressed him. The latter turned out to be the case.

"Lana, so few of the handful of people whom I have chosen to invite up here have taken notice of those windows other than to look *through* them. You, however, looked *at* them which is a major compliment to the architect. What may I ask prompted you to do that?"

Lana, feeling emboldened by Everett's compliment said, "Well, I initially had sought to be a mechanical engineer so my brain is always wondering how things work. And sometimes even *why* they were intended to work that way."

"Fascinating." Everett said this almost gleefully.

Lana had made the full tour of the office and was uncertain of what to do next. Everett seemed to pick up on this and motioned for her to take a seat. He remained standing which to Lana felt a little weird.

"Would you care for something to drink?" Everett walked over to a bar which she had not noticed earlier. Did it just appear? He opened up a small cooler and said, "I have bottled water, carbonated beverages, *ice tea*, or beer and liquor if you are wanting something stronger."

"*Iced* tea sounds wonderful! Unsweetened if you have it." Lana realized then as she said this that there was a distinct difference between a bottled tea and that which was brewed and poured over ice. She was fine with the plastic bottle of unsweetened tea which Everett handed to her. It seemed strange that the bottle was unmarked and had no label. The glass filled with ice and a freshly cut lemon wedge which Everett now offered her caught her by surprise.

"May I ask, did the same architect that designed this office *also* design the building, the art piece in the lobby *and* dream up the idea of having a glass elevator?"

"Yes. Yes it most certainly was the same man." Everett was still standing.

Lana placed the glass to her lips and took in a refreshing drink of her tea, swished it about in her mouth to enjoy the flavor and then swallowed. It was *really* good, possibly the best she had ever had and it certainly hit the spot. Everett smiled at her apparent satisfaction and then grinned as he watched her pick up the plastic bottle, turning it in her hand perhaps now considering the reason behind the absence of a label.

Lana looked up at Everett who answered the unasked question. "A friend of mine makes that product. You won't find it at any of the retail outlets though. It is shared *only* amongst friends."

"Am I a *friend* then?"

Everett smiled broadly. "More so every minute."

Lana returned the smile. Hers was demure.

"Everett, before we pick up where we left off with the quote, unquote "interview," might I offer a postulation?"

"Well, when you put it like *that,* how can I refuse?"

"This architect you have mentioned. Have I heard of him? Do I know of his name?"

Everett appeared reflective as he replied, "Yes. I would say yes you *have* heard of him and you *do* know his name but sadly he is not *known* for his architecture so it is fair to say that you would not have made that association."

"I see," said Lana. Then she said, "I won't ask you his name."

"You won't?" Everett suddenly seemed quite disappointed.

"No. I will ask you instead, is it *you*? Are *you* the architect? *And* the artist?"

Lana could not have been more surprised by what happened next. She was shocked by the emotional response. Everett *blushed*. And for a brief moment, this man who was always in control, was rendered speechless. That moment passed quickly.

"Now I see Lana, why you come so highly regarded by Alan. You are correct in your supposition. I *am* the architect of everything *in* this building as well as the building itself." Everett paused then said, "Well, *almost* everything."

"What does that mean?"

Everett shook his head from side to side. "Now that we are friends I feel that I may share with you, in confidence mind you, that the presence of Senator McKinney in this building, *in my life*, is what I regard as a necessary evil."

"Oh?"

Everett finally chose a seat near Lana as he shared a bit more of his own background.

"When I started all of *this*," he made a circular motion to encompass the building and all that was in it, "I was considered to be a wealthy man. But, when you are searching for the unknown, breaking new ground, and attempting to do it all on your own, the costs can escalate to an unimaginable point." Everett paused for a moment, perhaps attempting to navigate some unwelcome memories from his past. "When people *know* you have money, they *will* find ways to take it. The value of the things that I needed to pursue my goals suddenly seemed to increase as those who had them to sell learned of the identity of the buyer."

"Oh." Lana could *feel* the pain and anguish this man had felt while pursuing his dream.

"Lana, I am now cash poor. I am running this company at a loss. I sorely *need* the funding I am receiving from Senator McKinney but let me tell you something. *I sure as hell don't want it.*"

Lana suddenly felt very comfortable with this man. The stress on him must be incredible and while he had certainly shown her moments of poor behavior she felt that perhaps that might just make him more human. She could forgive bad behavior if his heart was in the right place. It caught her completely by surprise when he explained why had invited her up to his office for a private conversation.

Test Subject

"Lana."

"Yes?"

"I have a confession to make."

"You do?"

"Yes."

"And what is that?"

"You caught me down there, before the, uh, *experience*."

"What do you mean by 'I caught you'?"

"You challenged me when I used the word "subject"."

"Yes, well it seemed odd to me that you would use the word *subject* for anyone thinking they are about to be enjoying a *recreational* experience. Wouldn't *traveler* have been a better word to use?"

"You are precisely correct. We actually use the word "guest" during a travel experience."

"Well that sounds quite nice to me. Why then was I a *subject* and not a *guest*?"

Everett appeared to be uncomfortable, uneasy with what he was about to say. What he did say did not come out as intended.

"As it turns out, I think you would agree that your *experience* was amazing, would you not?"

Lana looked offended. "Why do I suddenly feel like I have been violated but since it turned out well I should not be bothered by the experience?"

"I don't think I could have said it better myself. I appreciate your understanding." Everett said this with a determined finality like he was washing his hands of an unseemly act. Lana though wasn't having it.

"What are you *not* telling me?"

"What more needs to be said? You had an *incredible* experience."

"You're holding something back. What is it that you're afraid to tell me?" Lana was pressing now. She was actually beginning to feel angry, unsure now just what may have been done to her.

"*Afraid?* That is *not* the right word." Everett hears the tension building in Lana's voice and decides to take the temperature down. "Please, Ms. Taylor, try to *calm down*."

"Let me give you a quick lesson about women," stated Lana, a tinge of irritation in her voice. "Those are two words you don't use in that sequence, with that tone of voice, and expect any kind of a positive reaction."

Everett had stood up to make his point. Now he took a step back in retreat and lowered his head a bit to demonstrate some level of modesty. *'Mea culpa'* is what Lana thought she heard him whisper to himself. Something in her brain reminded her of the fact that she was here in a professional capacity so she changed tact and dialed her response down a notch.

"Everett, I am prepared to *listen* assuming you are prepared to *share* with me whatever it is that you did not previously."

Lana could tell that a wave of relief had swept over Everett when she made that statement. She sat and waited for him to collect himself and then to quietly describe to her how she had just been a "test subject" in an experimental cage.

Lana was surprised by how forthright Everett's response was to her. He explained in far more detail than she could have expected just what happened and why. Everett Marsh's business, his lifetime dream, was now bleeding money. If he had made one major mistake along the way in his plan for growth it was his simple misunderstanding of what was truly important to his potential customers. Affordability. Yes they wanted the dream vacations that he could provide but they couldn't break the bank to do it. LUCID could not survive on just the patronage of uber wealthy people of the world. He needed the common trade to make this work. And while the everyday man and his family might appreciate the convenience of what LUCID had to offer the question was does the cost of the "experience" offset the cost of doing the real thing. The economy was booming right now which was good for everyone but Everett as it made "real" travel and vacations easier to afford so why not just do the real thing?

What this all meant in regard to Lana was simply that Everett had to learn to break his own rules in how he operated the experiences he could offer and test the limits of *what* he could offer. Testing the limits was the challenge. That is where Senator McKinney entered the picture with funding and with “subjects.” What Lana experienced was a “test.” From the incredible chair she was seated in, to the room in which it happened and the console from where Everett conducted said experience (read experiment) it was just a test and Lana was the unwitting “subject.”

Everett was both ashamed and thrilled at the outcome. He was ashamed that he was so willing to take advantage of someone so clearly vulnerable BUT he could not have been more thrilled at the results. It was a breakthrough to be sure.

“So what’s next?” Lana was wearing her journalist hat once more.

“Great question. Let’s see if we can get back on track with why you are here. I have made arrangements for you to meet a couple of my actual “customers.” They have agreed to allow you to watch their experience and to interview them both before, and after, their experience. You will not use their names in your piece however as they wish to remain anonymous. You *will* respect their privacy?”

“Well yes, of course. And let me say I appreciate the gracious, and rather *unexpected* offer.”

“It’s the least I could do after--. Well, let’s head on down to the lobby. Blanche just gave me a buzz on my watch to alert me that our first “guest” has arrived.” Everett walked over to the elevator and stepped in after the door opened. He smiled as he said to Lana, “It is proper etiquette for a gentleman to enter an elevator *before* a lady in the event of any unfortunate circumstance.”

“That brain of yours never stops does it? I appreciate the courtesy.”

Lana took one last look at the panoramic view from Everett’s office before she stepped into the elevator. The view through the glass elevator was left behind as the car descended rapidly. Lana felt her ears pop again on the way down. She looked over to Everett and thought to herself, how is one person capable of doing *so much*?

Market Demographics

An unassuming woman in her late sixties was seated in the lobby waiting for Everett to arrive. This woman seemed to meet so much of the criteria of the "common trade" customer which LUCID was striving to attract. This woman, whom Everett had instructed Lana to refer to only as "*Jane*," was the first guest of the day. *Was this Jane Doe?* Lana asked herself. When the two sat down later in a private room, Lana was pleased with the fact that the woman truly *had* agreed to being interviewed by Lana. It would have been a somewhat uncomfortable experience had she not.

Everett greeted the woman warmly, also addressing her as Jane and introduced her to Lana. The three of them then made their way across the expansive lobby to an area which caught Lana by surprise once more. After entering through a set of heavy walnut doors activated by a proximity key, they were suddenly in a *room?* which resembled more of a rainforest. The foliage was so dense that it was difficult to tell the size of the room. Lana's first inclination was that they had just traveled to the jungles of the Amazon. As Lana was now aware of the lack of windows to let in "real" light she was immediately impressed with how so many plants of this type could be sustained and prosper in artificial light. No doubt the *Regalis* crystal had something to do with it she was sure.

The three of them traversed a bridge over a rushing stream. *What?!* Lana stole a glance at Jane and could see by her expression that her "experience" had *already* begun. Everett Marsh was a genius. And the world's greatest showman.

Dream Theater

Everett, Lana and "Jane" have arrived at what appears to be the façade of a cinema. Everett allowed himself a bit of a grin and a nod at the reaction both women had to seeing the façade. It was a recent addition and it was all about creating a sense of comfort and familiarity. The results of several focus groups had taught Everett that the *unknown* is what frightens people. When going on a trip to a faraway place they are prepared for the sight of the airport and boarding a plane. However walking into a space sans luggage that could just as easily be a dentist's office, then being asked to sit in a reclining chair was not a good first impression.

The feeling of going to see a movie was a great way (Everett concluded) to prepare the "traveler" for what was to be asked of them. Lay back in a comfortable chair and focus straight ahead and allow themselves to relax and be transported away from their everyday troubles. Everett had even installed a screen and had a friend put together a short film with images of exotic places and an up-tempo new age soundtrack to add pulse to what the "guest" was viewing. This was all in an effort to create a "new normal" for the customers he hoped to capture.

The three of them entered the "Dream Theater." Everett allowed Jane a few moments to take it all in before he asked, "Any first impressions?"

Jane smiled and said, "This may sound silly but I was worried that this would be more like boarding some sort of spacecraft. I was concerned that I would be strapped down to a table and there would be a host of gadgets and cameras hanging all about me. I know how crazy that might sound."

"Not at all, Jane. Not at all. We all have a vision of what the future must look like and you are quite aware of the fact that you are entering an arena of futuristic travel. This has *not* been done before so your trepidation is not without foundation. I assure you that your experience will be safe and you will not be harmed in any way. That includes *any* type of effects on your brain. We are not telling you what to think or what to dream. What we *are* doing is allowing you to dream while fully awake and in full control of your actions. This is *not* some form of hypnosis. One additional comment about your safety. We *do* film all experiences."

Both Jane and Lana shot Everett a puzzled look.

He smiled and said, "Let me clarify. Please. We film the *room* in which our guests are having their dream experience. It is rather boring to watch but to be honest we do this so that our guests can see that at no time has any LUCID employee entered the room during an experience nor has our guest ever left their seat for any reason during an experience. Your safety and security are of our utmost concern."

Everett watched as Jane and Lana exchanged looks. They both seemed more at ease now knowing that this security footage was being taken to serve the guest.

"With that being said, Jane, are you prepared to begin your "travel experience"?"

Jane looked from Lana to Everett then said, "Another silly question and I can't even imagine how this could even be possible but I feel I must ask."

"There are no silly questions. Please ask."

Jane pursed her lips and rolled her eyes as she collected her thoughts. Now she was ready. "My experience is my *own*, correct? I do not need to share with you what I dream or why I dream it, correct?"

"Yes, that is correct." Everett was rather succinct in his reply.

"Well, truth be told, I lost my husband in a rather bitter divorce and I'm a lonely gal now just out there trying to find her way."

"I understand." said Everett.

"Do you? Does anyone *really* though if they haven't been through it? I mean, I'm doing okay but there's--. There's things I miss. Things I, I-- can't get back." Jane stopped and put a hand to her face. She was becoming emotional. "At my age I don't—" And then the tears came. Everett was thankful that Lana was present. He usually had Blanche with him. Jane shooed Lana away and said, "Listen, I'm a tough old gal. I just want your assurances that what I experience is private. Not to be viewed. Not to be recorded. Not to be sold."

Everett was nodding his head in a positive way. "Jane, you are several steps ahead of the technology in this room. We are unable to capture nor view your experiences but let me say this, you are not wrong to ask. I would be lying if I was to tell you that those kinds of things are not on the drawing board."

Lana glanced at Everett with an expression of shock and surprise.

Everett held his hands up and exclaimed, "Hey! Before you get any bad ideas, think about what people do when they are on vacation. They take pictures! They don't just want their *own* memories. They want memories which they can *share* with other people. And we want that too. It is how we can grow our business. But we're not there yet. Dream as you wish Jane. Your secret is safe... with you. And you alone."

"Thank you." Jane looked to Everett, brought her praying hands to her lips and gave a nod. "Okay, then. I have places to go and um, "things" to do."

Lana did not voice her thoughts but as she watched Jane be seated in the recliner, all she could think was that Jane was about to take one erotic, perhaps pornographic, ride. Well, they do have laundry facilities here...

When Lana met with Jane after her session (and after she had had the time to get herself cleaned up) she seemed a different woman. Years of playing second fiddle to a man who didn't deserve her seemed to have been washed away. Lana was careful not to ask what Jane had "done" nor where she may have "gone" in her dream experience. She did however ask the one question that was just begging to be asked, "Would she consider this experience to be life-changing?"

"Oh yes," said Jane. "I have struggled mightily these last few years but now I can finally say that I am ready for the next chapter in my life. And I won't need to dream it to do it." She turned to Everett. "You're such a dear man. May I have a hug?"

Lana half-coughed and half-laughed at Everett's reaction. This charming and incredible man, Everett Marsh, may have just shown his one vulnerability. He was not a ladies man. The hug he gave Jane was embarrassing at best. He gave Lana a reprising glance as she tried to hide the fact that she had just learned that this man among men was a shy mama's boy. Which only served to now endear him to her more.

Family Vacation

Jane had left the building and now there was a family walking through the wide expanse of the lobby. Dad, Mom, three kids. They would have brought their dog if they would have known that was okay to do. And bless their hearts. They all brought carry-ons. Just books, magazines and tablets but still adorable. And of course absolutely unnecessary. Everett registered no expression but instead extended his hand first to Dad and then to Mom before introducing Lana.

These were the Millers. Dad was Bill, and Mom was Nancy. The three kids, in order of age oldest to youngest were Cindy, Randy and Cathy. Their story was simple. Mom had an aversion to flying and the youngest, Cathy still had a bit of stigma regarding vacation car travel due to an incident a few years back. The incident had occurred while Dad was driving in heavy rain. Without warning the car went into a spin due to hydroplaning and took a detour onto the grassy berm. Needless to say it was a bumpy ride and the unbelted youngest of the brood Cathy took the brunt of it as she was tossed about like a kernel in a popcorn maker. This car was a fastback with a small area behind the rear seat which is where Cathy was at the time of the unfortunate incident. The fact that the car struck a road sign and it nearly penetrated the rear window of the vehicle is a horrific image which would manifest itself as a lasting fear with anyone. Cathy was the only one to witness that near tragic incident but that didn't make it any less real or frightening.

In speaking with the family Lana could begin to see how Everett's creation could truly serve a portion of the public who might not travel otherwise due to numerous restrictions both real and imagined. Bill was obviously concerned about the cost but had to admit that a side benefit of not missing work to do this dream vacation was a definite plus. Also, there would be none of the typical in-car fighting amongst the kids and no stress of boarding a plane.

Nancy shared that the family had a fun and enjoyable meal the night before as they planned their "trip." She thought it best that they all agreed on the same place to go but could of course "do their own thing" once they got there. The fact that they were "imagining" their destination meant that they could all have a say in what amenities could be found there. Bill and Nancy chose tennis. The kids thought of an amusement park, a pool, horseback-riding, and a beach all at the same place. Every member of the family could now have their own dream vacation.

Everett had motioned them on so they could make their way to where their experience would take place. Lana was eager to see if Everett had another "surprise" atrium in store for them but it was the rainforest once again. Was she disappointed?

"Is this *Jumanji*?" Randy asked.

Everett pandered to the boy's imagination. He ruffled his hair as he responded. "It might be. That's entirely up to you."

"Awesome!" exclaimed Randy.

"I hope there really *is* a beach there," said Cindy.

Everett bent down slightly to make eye contact with her and to ask, "Do you *want* a beach?"

"Yes!" she said.

"Then you will have one!" Everett pointed to his head and said, "Dream it, and do it."

"I'm going to the beach with Cindy!" exclaimed an excited Cathy.

"Don't forget to wear sunscreen," said Mom. When it dawned on everyone the silliness of what she had just said they all laughed with her. Cindy laughed only for a moment then got a dour face as she began to realize now that she would *not* be getting a tan. Imagine her surprise if Everett had whispered to her that a suntan actually *was* possible if she had the "imagining" power to make it happen. He had already started to think of ways that a person could manipulate the pigment in their skin in such a way that they could leave a dream session with a tattoo.

Once the family was all seated and their experience had begun, Lana turned to Everett and said, "This is what it is all about for you, isn't it? This family, they are the perfect fit for what you've done, aren't they?"

Everett replied, "Pretty damn close. The good news is that they will tell all their friends. And yes, this is the demographic who I am trying to reach."

Lana watched for a moment before asking, "Does this in some way kind of remind you of the vacations you took as a child?"

Everett did not look her way as he responded. "My family did not go on vacations. The only trips I remember taking were to symposiums around the globe for gifted children. In many ways I think my parents saw me as their retirement plan."

"Oh! I'm so sorry. I didn't know." Lana held her hand to her mouth. She felt awful and wasn't sure what to say.

Everett must have read her mind when he said, "There is nothing *to* say. They were not good people. I have lost touch with them. I paid them off long ago. This may help you to see why me and the senator are like oil and water. He reminds me *so* much of them."

"I see," said Lana. So many puzzle pieces came together in that instant. There was no doubt in her mind that what Everett had just shared of his background would be fascinating material for her readers but out of respect to Everett she made a solemn pledge to herself to keep it out. He had shouldered that pain long enough.

After the Millers experience had concluded Lana met with them once again. The kids were bubbling with enthusiasm over what they had seen and done. 'I don't even feel tired!' Randy shouted out. Lana got a kick out of Cindy double-checking to see if the time she had spent at the beach had given her any color. She seemed surprised. And happy! Lana looked closer and, was that even *possible*?! It did look like she had gotten some sun. Lana looked to Everett who had been watching her. He put a finger to his lips. Keep that mum, he was saying. Lana's head was spinning. So *much* was possible with LUCID technology.

Eye on you

"Lana, I have a few things to do here and then I will walk you out, okay?" asked Everett.

"Sure," replied Lana. "I will just hang around a bit."

Now that Everett was busy Lana thought she might just walk around, explore this section of the building, see what she could find. As Lana made her way down the hallway she was once again struck by the fact that there seemed to be so few workers in such a large facility. Everett was not exaggerating when he told her he was cash poor.

Lana was being careful not to stray too far and to pay close attention to where she went so she wouldn't get lost. As she turned another corner she suddenly felt that weird sensation again on her neck. It was that creepy feeling like she was being watched. Perhaps someone was following her?

At the next corner she stopped and whirled around quickly to look back the way she had come. Sure enough someone was back there and they knew they had been sighted as this person attempted to dive out of sight. Somehow Lana felt emboldened and took off running in the direction of her stalker.

It was a short run. Her stalker seemed to have vanished!

Lana walked about, retracing her steps but could find nowhere for that person to have gone. Did she just imagine that? No. She did not. Lana paused for a moment then realized that the best thing for her to do was to go back to the room where Everett would be waiting. To act as though nothing was out of the ordinary. The truth was, however, that Lana knew for certain what she had seen. And she knew *who* she had seen. It was Joni. And she didn't just vanish. Something had caught Lana's eye back there in the hallway but it held no significance until now. There was a letter and a number handwritten on the wall. This was a building full of surprises so why not think that there was possibly a hidden room behind that wall? She would investigate further at her first opportunity. Lana made a mental map in her brain of how to get back to that place where Joni had spied on her and then vanished.

Behind that hidden door Joni is sharing with the senator what has just happened. He is a decisive man. He gives Joni clear instructions to find out all she can about Lana and her purpose inside the building. 'Leave no stone unturned' the senator urges. 'We can't afford to take any chances.' Joni agrees with her marching orders, which means that she *will* follow through with them.

Before she leaves, the senator does a risky thing. He grabs her by the arm and says, "Do whatever is necessary. Do you understand?"

Joni understands his command but more importantly she is giving the senator a message as well. Her good eye is saying, 'Take your hand off my arm before I break it.' The senator seems to get the message and removes his hand but not soon enough. The senator has just made one crucial error with Joni. And this will cost him her loyalty.

Joni walks away now on a different mission than what she had agreed to.

Forgiveness

Everett has a three-day conference in Dallas which he is attending. This gives Lana time to do the most important thing she will ever do in her life. Offer her father forgiveness for the years of misunderstanding they have lost. The brief time Lana spent with her mother (she puts "time" in quotes because she reminds herself that the experience wasn't real) taught her to think back and remember the love she had for her father. He was a good man who was going through the same hurt and pain that she had, and possibly even more. Lana had lost her mother but her father had lost his wife *and* his soulmate. He had never recovered from that loss. He had not remarried nor had he ever tried to force Lana to feel something other than what she felt towards him. Even knowing all the time that it was wrong for her to feel that way.

In truth Lana envied her two brothers. They both had a healthy relationship with him. They were different though. They had never been in a position to have to forgive him as they had never *blamed* him. This was her own cross to bear. Now though, she was bound and determined to make things right. Lana dreaded the thought of arriving too late, of hearing that he had passed away before she could tell him that she loved him and that she forgave him. She wondered if she should tell him about the special moments she had shared with Mom during her dream state at LUCID. He had advanced Alzheimer's. Would he know or really even understand what she was telling him? That decision would be made, she determined, in the moment.

SeaTac is a bustling airport which requires you to pay attention to what you're doing when moving from one terminal to another. Before heading to the Baggage Claim, Lana wanted to grab a bite to eat. She was pleasantly surprised by the dining options. Her first thought was that she might not find something that she liked. Her problem instead was in choosing which place she liked best. Seattle is an interesting food town in that it offered things the average traveler did not expect. It was perched on the Pacific coast with ready access to seafood but who knew that the offerings would be such delicacies as Dungeness crab, oysters, mussels and of course salmon. The

Pacific geoduck (pronounced *GOO-ee-duk*) was the biggest surprise. An odd-looking creature to say the least, it is actually a very large saltwater clam. The other food option that Lana discovered but did not expect was the strong presence of Hawaiian food. The real deal too. Simple and flavorful. Last but not least, something she just *had* to try, (she managed to find a street vendor during her time in Seattle) was the "Seattle Dog." Cream cheese on a hot dog. Who knew?

Lana had her two articles spread out before her on the table while she munched on her sandwich. She had settled on a California club sandwich which featured avocado. The idea of enjoying local fare had somehow lost the battle to just grabbing something simple with which she was familiar. Lana wanted to combine her quick lunch with a more leisurely review of the work she had done on the plane. She had forgotten to pack her laptop of all things so everything she had done was written in longhand which was of course a lost art. Unfortunately, due to the confines of her seating position in the airplane her handwriting was all done at an awkward slant and nearly illegible.

After several minutes of perusing her notes she looked up with a confident grin. This was dynamite stuff, perhaps her best work. The *NRG* piece was a story familiar to the public but they didn't know the back story so that was sure to garner attention. And now the LUCID piece, with a Senator involved? Forget about it! This was journalism gold. Add in that feisty little "pirate" Joni and she had a story definitely worth telling.

Lana put her notes away, cleaned up her table and headed for the Baggage Claim area. A ride on a tram was necessary to get there but that was not an issue as she was in no hurry. She had originally planned on taking an Uber to her father's residence but as she considered the cost on the plane while snacking on pretzel twists she decided that a rental car would be more economical.

As expected, since she was the last passenger of her flight to arrive at the baggage turnstile, her bag stood alone and off to the side. Someone had pulled it off and set it there. It was an old bag with old clothes. The only thing she would miss if someone had taken the bag would have been her toiletries. All replaceable but a hassle all the same.

Once she had her bag in tow Lana headed for the car rental place preparing herself mentally for the song and dance she would encounter along the way. 'Oh, you don't have a reservation?' Sometimes the people at those places can be infuriating. To her surprise, the young man behind the counter was courteous, kind and efficient. In no time she found herself on I-5 heading towards her hotel. The original plan was to go directly to her father's place but now that she had her own wheels the hotel was her preference. A few minutes of doing nothing and then a quick freshen-up would simply be fantastic.

Lana found herself at the rooftop bar of the hotel sipping a glass of wine. Downtown Seattle was spread out before her as she took it all in. A nice view of Puget Sound to her left and South Lake Union to her right made for the ultimate calming effect after a few hours of harried travel.

As Lana allowed herself to mellow out and just enjoy the moment something she heard someone say next to her yanked her back to that creepy feeling she had had when exploring the halls of the LUCID building alone.

'You need to be on the lookout for that Joni character.'

Lana whirled around to see two women engaged in conversation.

"What did you just say?!"

Both women were caught off guard by Lana's outburst.

"What?" said one of the women as they looked at each other with puzzled glances.

Lana realized then how she had come across and lightened her tone. "I'm sorry. I didn't mean to—What did you say just now? About Joni?"

"*Joni?* Who's Joni?" Both women looked puzzled.

Lana rubbed her forehead wondering now if she was perhaps just a bit edgy when it came to Joni. That was one person who really had her spooked. She had refused to admit it to herself until now. Lana blinked away her thoughts as she realized that one of the women was speaking to her.

"--- I said was that I think the new girl they hired in marketing is just a big *phony*. And that she should be out looking for another job. I don't know any Joni."

Lana shakes her head and apologizes for the interference into their conversation. She pays her tab and heads for her room. 'That was awkward,' she tells herself in the elevator. How Joni got in the picture she has no idea but she would do her best to expel that image as quickly as possible.

Fifteen minutes later Lana is back on I-5 heading towards the town of Mukilteo, a quiet place perched on the water where Puget Sound and Possession Sound merge. She passes a sign for Shoreline and knows that she is getting close. This area has a familiarity to her. Boeing (the company) had quite a presence in Seattle which must have been the reason why her father chose to move here to live out his senior years. He had, after all, given them 46 years of his life as an engineer.

When Lana arrived at the senior care facility where her father resided she was informed that he was on an excursion at Lighthouse Park with a small group of other residents. This was a frequent stop for the residents, something they eagerly looked forward to, as they not only got to be outside but they also enjoyed spending their time watching the ferries come and go. They would feed the birds as well. Often they would laugh at the antics of the sea lions who would scamper about on the offshore rocks.

Lighthouse Park was only a five-minute drive from her father's place. Lana passed Ivar's Mukilteo Landing along the way. A flood of pleasant memories brought a smile to her face as she remembered this restaurant. She had shared lunch there with her brothers when they had first brought their father to this facility. A prime spot on the restaurant's balcony overlooking the water plus a plate of "to die for" fish 'n chips had made for a perfect afternoon together. Lana didn't see her brothers often but that trip, that time together over a simple lunch, felt more like family than she had experienced in years. She made a mental note to reach out to both of them after her visit with Dad.

"Daddy?"

"Phyllis, is that you?" Lewis Taylor looked perplexed. He recognized this person as his wife but it couldn't be, she had died years ago of breast cancer. His mind was so foggy these days that sometimes he just wasn't sure what was what.

"No, Daddy, it's me. It's Lana, your daughter."

"Yes, I have a daughter. She moved away. *Beautiful* girl. She looks like you. Dead-ringer for her mother. That young lady could turn heads let me tell you. Watch out for those boys now. You're a pretty girl."

"Daddy, it's me. It's Lana."

"Can I help you Miss?"

A lady who worked at the senior care facility was now at hand challenging Lana. She felt suddenly awkward, embarrassed and stupid. She had counted on her father's memory being better than it was at the moment. Lana should have introduced herself first to the male and female attendants who were the escorts for this excursion. Lana did not visit her father frequently enough to know these people so to them she was just a stranger approaching one of their residents. Not a good scenario.

Lana was quick to offer her hand and introduce herself as Lewis' daughter. She had no qualms about producing ID for the woman to view. The male attendant came over to check on the "stranger" as well.

Moments later Lana is once again alone with her father but this time with no awkwardness. The attending woman, Frances was her name, had told Lana that they usually stayed out here for about an hour. This meant that she had a good thirty minutes before they would pack up the residents and head back to the facility. Lana had no desire to go back there. The fact that her father did not seem to know who she was made the visit seem pointless. She could say what she came to say but if he did not know who she was how could it even matter.

The two had been sitting together for more than twenty minutes when out of the blue her father said, "Lana honey, is that you? Oh my goodness, how you resemble your mother!"

"Daddy!" Lana exclaimed and threw her arms around her father's shoulders. He was so frail now she noticed but he was still able to hug her back.

"Stand back and let these tired old eyes get a good look at you."

Lana wiped her eyes which had teared up the moment he spoke her name. Just then Frances walked by and Lewis shouted out to her, "This is my daughter. Her name is Lana. She has come to visit with me."

"I see that. She is very pretty." Frances kept on walking, checking in on each resident as she went.

Lana's father was using his finger to beckon her closer so he could whisper something in her ear. "Let me tell you a secret."

"Okay," said Lana, eager for this moment of spontaneity with her father. She leaned in close as he said, "I don't even *know* that woman!" He burst out laughing at his own supposed impropriety. Lana laughed with him. "I'm so happy you're here. You look happy. Are you happy? I know you took it hard when your mother left us. She was the joy of my life, and yours as well I'm sure."

Lana could not believe how *present* her father was being right now. This time with him was a gift she would not squander. "Daddy, listen to me closely. I don't want to waste a single minute of our time together. I have so much to tell you..."

For the next five minutes Lana shared all that she could about her "experience" with her mother, about how she needed to forgive her father after all these years, how she missed all the time together she had *not* spent with him while blaming him for the loss of Phyllis. The one inimitable trait that her father possessed and no one would ever challenge is that he was a tremendously gracious man. He allowed Lana to say all that she believed needed to be said. When the moment was right he then took her hands in his and made his own statement.

"Lana, you have the very best of your mother in you. I see it so clearly. This time with you brings me close to her once again. Your visit here today. It's the best gift a father could ask for from his child. Your mother is smiling in heaven right now, I'm sure of it."

"Thank you Daddy. That's so sweet. I—"

"Wait. Hold your horses. I'm not done. Before you go, promise *me* something."

"Of course, Daddy. Anything."

Lana's father looked at Lana and said, "My dear sweet Lana, forgive *yourself*. When our hearts break we don't know what to do with all that hurt and sometimes we just get lost. Your mother and I, your brothers too, we want you back. I'm an old man. I've had my time. It's your time now. Time for you live your life to the fullest. Forgive yourself, Lana. You did no wrong. You just got a little lost is all."

"Okay Daddy."

Lana lost it then. She cried as her father looked out over the sound. His eyes were still good. His hearing was as well. He was able to appreciate the blue water and the soundtrack of the waves as they rippled towards the coast. The sky was clear today affording a picture-perfect backdrop to the Olympic mountains in the distance. Bird calls and the groans of sea lions added texture to the scene.

Just then her father gripped her arm and he said with urgency, "Lana dear, last night I had a very troubling dream."

"Oh, I'm so sorry. Do you remember what it was?"

"Yes, yes I do. I don't understand it but maybe you will. It will sound silly."

"That's okay. I don't mind. What is it Daddy?"

Her father hesitated for a moment and then looked at her with an intensity she had not seen from him since she was a child. His eyes seemed to clear as he whispered, "There was a pirate. A *girl* pirate."

This comment got Lana's full attention.

"That pirate is evil Lana. She is up to no good. Stay clear of the pirate. You hear me? She's---"

"Five minutes, you all. The bus leaves in five minutes." This was said by the male attendant from the facility, the name of which had changed since her last time here. It was a thing in healthcare these days. Healthcare had become a profit center for big business. The male attendant kept on walking and barking out his conductor's alert to the remainder of the residents.

"Daddy, can you tell me more about this, um, pirate? Was she--?"

Lana stopped mid-sentence. Her father's eyes had clouded over. His time of "presence" had passed. He was back in the fog that was known as Alzheimer's. Lana felt like she wanted to cry but suppressed the emotion as she realized how precious the few minutes that they had had together truly was. She gave him a kiss and a hug and stood up to go.

Frances walked up just then, stole a glance at her father and asked, "Did you lose him?"

Lana knew exactly what she meant but her answer was instead, "Nope. I just got him back. Thank you for taking such good care of him." She headed for her rental car leaving a bewildered Frances to wonder what that was about.

As Lana drove back to her hotel she could not scrub the image of a pirate from her mind. How would her father know about Joni? Had she somehow reached out to him in her dream state at LUCID? She supposed that anything might be possible, even that. If that was possible, it was just like a father to warn his child of impending danger. Joni was up to no good, Lana was certain of that. From now on she would give her a wide berth and keep as far away from her piracy as possible.

That would not be so easy though as that "pirate" was now coming for her.

When Lana returned home from Seattle the first thing she did was to pour a glass of wine and then catch up on emails. Her mouth nearly dropped when she saw an email marked URGENT. She read it three times before she would allow herself to believe that it was the real deal. Any plans she may have had for tomorrow were now scrubbed in favor of the invitation she had before her. Lana was of course excited by the proposition of the invitation but the more she thought about it the more the anxiety of the potential threat behind it began to gnaw at her. Lana had a fitful night of sleep and more than once she awoke with the image in her brain of that damned *pirate* her father had warned her about. Thanks Dad.

Deal with the devil

Lana has been invited back once again to LUCID but this time she is not arriving with the same level of eagerness as before. It is not Everett who has invited her. It is Senator Bob McKinney. The journalist in her understands the potential windfall inherent in such a meeting. The paranoid single female in her worries that this is a trap. She trusts the senator as much as she trusts Joni. It is just now dawning on Lana that *they* must see *her* as a *threat*. That she is about to tell a story that they do *not* want to be told. The truth is that she doesn't even *know* that story. But she must remind herself. *They* don't know that. Advantage Lana.

Lana has left last evening's anxiety behind. She walks with a new confidence now. The time spent with her father in Seattle has changed her. The "time" spent with her mother in the Dream Theater at LUCID has changed her. There is a mental toughness in her now that those who knew her before would not recognize. The senator has the power of his position and knows how to use it. Joni has become his new secret weapon and she was intimidating to be sure. The fact that she seemed to lack the ability to reason made her all the more dangerous. The combination of those two unsavory characters given the potential for what LUCID could do was horrifying to say the least. Lana now felt an obligation to uncover whatever evil plot they were planning and expose them to the world.

As Lana entered the LUCID building and made her way across the lobby she could see the senator pacing near the front desk. Presumably, he was waiting for her. As Lana approached the desk she began to say hello to Blanche. The senator cut her off by saying, "This way please." He was pointing in a direction that she had yet to visit in the building. This should be interesting. As she walked in step with the senator Lana glanced back at Blanche who was wearing a worried look on her face. 'At least *someone* knows I'm here,' thought Lana.

"I'm a busy man so I won't take much of your time," commented the senator.

'You're an asshole is what you are,' thought Lana. The wording of his attempt at a "considerate" statement spoke volumes. He had no qualms of asking her to drive forty minutes for what was likely to be a five-minute meeting when it served him. But, truth be told, he was a sitting senator and she was just *dying* to know what he had to say to her.

The senator proceeded to escort her to a small room with a rectangular table and two chairs. 'Damn if this doesn't look like an interrogation room from an old TV detective show.' Lana thought. The senator did not offer Lana anything to drink. Frankly, it would have surprised her if he had. Just before he began to speak Joni slipped into the room taking a spot in the corner on the very edge of Lana's peripheral vision. Things just got real.

Lana was not given the opportunity to speak or to ask questions. The senator put on his public "shake hands and kiss babies" façade as he told Lana what he believed her to be thinking. "I'm sure you're suspicious of me and what I'm doing here. You journalist types are all the same, thinking your government has some crazy shenanigans going on; well let me tell you that everything we're doing here is above board. Funding for these projects does not happen in a vacuum. They have to be voted on and people don't vote until they hear the facts." The senator did not bother to see if Lana understood what he was saying or if she was even paying attention. He had a task to complete and he was doing just that. "I'm sure you understand that this is a sensitive project and due to that fact it *must* be kept hush hush. Top secret kinda stuff you know." The senator threw in a quick joke and a laugh with a gangster inflection in his voice. "I'd tell ya but then I'd have to kill ya."

"Kill you."

That whispered comment from Joni grabbed the attention of both Lana and the senator. Joni stared them both down. Both looked away unwilling to poke the bear.

The senator resumed his lecture.

"So, long story short, I think we both can agree that your best course of action would be to wrap up whatever business you think you have here in the LUCID building and move on to other projects."

Lana remained seated as the senator stood up to leave. Apparently he had said his piece and their business was concluded. Lana thought to herself, 'My guess was right. A five-minute meeting. Nailed it.'

The senator now took notice of the fact that Lana was still seated which did not sit well with him.

"Young lady, you have been *dismissed*."

Lana's eyes got huge. "I'm sorry? Did you just say '*dismissed*'? Um, I don't think so." Lana was now visibly pissed off.

"Bitch won't leave," said Joni.

"What a *lovely* voice she has," Lana said derisively.

The senator shot Joni a cold glance before turning his attention back to Lana. She could tell that the wheels were turning in his head. He took his seat once again and leaned in toward Lana as he spoke.

"I see that I may have misjudged you, Ms. Taylor. Please forgive me." He was definitely trying a different tack with her now. "How about we start over?"

Lana did not reply. She just held his gaze.

"Look, this really *is* "eyes only" stuff we're working on here. I can't just let you wander around and jot down whatever you see. Just *knowing* what we're doing here could put you in harm's way."

"Is that a threat?"

"It was not intended as such but I *do* think you need to know that you're literally playing with fire here."

There was a granular level of intensity lying just below the senator's comments. He gave her a hard stare. Lana maintained her cool posture and kept her eyes fixated on the senator's. She wanted *him* to blink first. It was unnerving however to know that Joni was slowly inching up behind her. Lana could almost feel her getting closer. Who knew what Joni was capable of?

The senator stood up once more. "It appears that we are at an impasse but---" He held his index finger up and then directed it at her face. "I *do,* however, have a proposition." He allowed space for a comment but Lana stayed silent. The senator continued. "Ms. Taylor, if you would be willing to sign a non-disclosure agreement stating that under penalty of imprisonment you will not divulge what you have seen or heard I would be willing to give you a quick "peek" behind the curtain. To ease your mind. Calm your fears. However you want to put it. How does that sound?"

This is the part where journalist Lana screams, "Yes!"

But that does not happen. Her body is suddenly cold as a wave of fear passes through her. A thousand "what ifs" run through her head in a matter of seconds. All of them come back with bad results. Her brain is forming one clear directive: *RUN!*

Lana hears herself calmly say, "I agree."

The senator feigned a look of surprise before stating matter-of-factly, “Very well then. Please follow me.”

Lana had no idea what part of her brain was controlling her right now but it seemed to know no fear. And for some reason it also wanted to take one more shot at Joni.

“Senator, a favor please?”

“What’s that?”

“Could you ask your guard dog to stop winking at me?” Lana pointed at Joni. With the eye patch covering one eye, at a glance it might be misconstrued as a wink.

The senator stole a glance at Joni, saw the same thing, had a quick laugh, said, “That’s a good one,” and then escorted Lana out of the room.

Joni’s eyes narrowed as the sting of Lana’s comment bit her. She balled her hands into fists and tensed her entire body. A nasty sneer masked her face as she said, “Not funny.”

Dreammare

Lana followed the senator into a room which she does not recognize. The door to this room was not labeled in any way but it *was* locked. The first thing she noticed was the absence of the world’s most comfortable chair. There is instead what appears to be a hanging cot supported by cables at all four corners. There is a distinctly different vibe to this room than the one she had been in before with Everett. This felt more like a movie set from a bad science fiction movie and she was the unwitting female who had fallen under the charms of her captor. Lana would soon come to know that this was a room used *exclusively* by the senator for “experimentation.”

“I’m nervous, should I be?” The senator is unaware that Lana has already been in a “dream room” although this room, and its experience was already proving to be markedly different.

“No, not really, but it *is* natural for some people to react that way. Keep in mind that you aren’t really *going* anywhere. You’re not leaving this room *nor* are you even losing consciousness. You will just be in a dream state yet fully aware. Just remember that *you* are the one controlling the narrative. If you begin to experience something which you don't like simply *change* it or *stop* it."

"Senator, you make this sound quite simple."

"Ms. Taylor, I assure you, it *is* that simple. Now just relax and enjoy your dream..."

The senator and a few technicians were watching the process through a one-way mirror as the sleep agent Lana had been given began to take effect. This was the first red flag that this experience was going to be very different than the one before. Lana is uncomfortable with the fact that they have attached receptors to her scalp which will register and transmit brain activity for the boys behind the mirrored glass to "analyze" and "correct" if necessary. For all the trials that had been done with this technology it was still a very new science. An untested realm if you will. There was a comparison to be made with the exploration of the human brain. It has been said that we know more about outer space than we do about the depths of the ocean. The human brain, in terms of its potential in dream state, was the depths of the ocean. The senator was wise to keep this little nugget of information close to the vest.

"Sir, subject is reaching Dream State One."

"Thank you, Control."

The senator was still amused by this back-and-forth banter which sounded more like dialogue from an old NASA space mission. This was his own doing. He had always been a science fiction nut so establishing such antiquated protocol seemed only natural. The "subject," Ms. Lana Taylor lay suspended on a thin layer of ultra-thin fabric, the "*veil*," which gave the sensation of 'floating on air.' When the subject first lays down on the suspended cot, by way of a trick of lighting, they are unaware that there is no foundation below. Sharing this with any of the subjects would only make them wary of falling. As the senator and his team has learned over time, the suspension of the body actually frees the mind to explore 'what else' could be *out there*.

"Sir, subject is approaching Dream State Two."

The senator leaned in, watching intently through the one-way mirror. To date only about 3% of all subjects had experienced a negative reaction to the process. The senator has his fingers crossed (literally) that Lana does not fall into that group. He needs this session to run smoothly and seem almost "routine." The whole idea of allowing Lana to do this is so that she will walk away from the process with the attitude of "nothing to see here" and move on.

Suddenly Lana's eyes begin to flicker and her hands to twitch. Although somewhat concerning, this is not an absolute indication that there is something wrong.

"Control, how are we looking?" Senator McKinney called down through the intercom.

"Sir, we are, um, detecting um—"

"Detecting *what?!* What are you *seeing*? Spit it out!" The senator is a man who is quickly angered by incompetence and that was exactly what this response sounded like to him.

"An anomaly, sir."

"An anomaly?"

"Yes, sir."

Inside the dream chamber the subject has begun to struggle against an unknown and unseen antagonist. This is, as stated earlier by the technician, *anomalous* behavior.

"Sir, do we *breach*?"

The technician has cast aside his earlier trepidation and is now in full control of the situation. He need only the approval of the senator to do what he has been trained to do. It is now the senator's turn to be at a loss for words. 'This can't be happening,' he is saying to himself. The subject is responding in a hostile manner to what *should* be soothing effects of the early trance patterns of deep restful sleep. Her eyes are open, as is routine with all subjects, but her eyes are *wide open*. With *fear*.

"Sir, I repeat, do we *breach*?" They use the term "breach" as is defined by a whale breaking the surface of the ocean. If they breach, Lana will emerge from her dream state in the worst possible way. Like taking that first panicked intake of breath that saves you from drowning.

The senator has not seen this before and he has witnessed *every* trial. The pragmatist in him knows that "breaching" the dream chamber is the only course of action at the moment. The curiosity in him however is fixated on knowing what happens *next.*

Lana is struggling to be free of an imaginary foe. Her attempts to ward off her adversary are putting her at risk of falling from the 'veil.' The fall is insignificant, only three feet, but the fact is, it has *never* happened. The hard truth is that they are not dealing with simple reality here. Lana is in an ultra-dream state where her imagination is determining her reality. *Who knows what is possible?* What if she is dreaming that she is actually falling from a twenty-story building? *That* fall could *kill* her. Even if it *is* only imagined. The mind is a powerful engine.

Just as the senator is (reluctantly) reaching out to sound the "breach" alarm (read panic), Lana sits straight up and screams at the top of her lungs, "*The pirate is trying to kill me!!!*"

Boots on the ground

The senator glares at Joni as Lana races from the room. "So that went well..." This is obviously her doing, somehow, some way. He orders Joni to "stay put" in the console booth while he goes to console Lana.

After a cursory search, the senator is unable to locate her. He walks up to find Joni standing in the hallway. She makes an unnecessary rhetorical comment. "Bitch is missing." Joni's comment angers the senator. It seems that almost everything that comes from Joni's mouth angers the senator. The senator, however, does his best to temper his response. "Leave her be for now. She can't go anywhere. The building is on lockdown. And besides, Everett is not here to be her white knight which would of course only fuck things up for us."

"Everett," Joni appears to be talking to herself, "--is dick."

"You don't like anybody do you?" A rhetorical question from the senator as he walked away without waiting for an answer he had no desire to hear.

Joni did not whisper. She actually said this out loud combined with a snarky laugh. "You dick too."

If the senator heard her remark he did not acknowledge it as he was too consumed with an alert that just appeared on his phone. 'The "TROOPS" Program is underway.'

"Assholes!" the senator exclaims. He is immediately angered by this message. "Whatever piece of shit decided to start that program without *me* has a fucking unemployment check in his future!"

"You," he commands, pointing at Joni, "come with me."

"Not dog," she says.

"What the fuck does that mean?" The senator is incensed by Joni's insubordinate behavior. This is a standoff the senator does not have time for. "I'm paying you," he reminds her.

"Joni not dog," she says again and then heads out the door on her own to the most secure and secret room in the building. Even Everett Marsh does not know this room exists which is something the senator takes great pride in. The senator is a competitive man. He is no match mentally for a man of Everett's character so he seeks to tear him down instead. Senator Bob McKinney is a man who chose to ingratiate himself with the immortal words (taken out of context) of Plato. "The measure of a man is what he does with power."

The senator and Joni are in the ultra-secret "war room" as the senator likes to call it. He never spent a day in the military but that does not prevent him from *acting* like a general. Lana is still unaccounted for, but the expectation is that she is simply hiding somewhere fearful that the "*pirate*" is coming to get her. The senator determines that she is fine wherever she is for now. He could not be more wrong.

The engineer who greenlighted the "TROOPS" Program for an early start without the senator's presence is now receiving a severe tongue-lashing. He is aware that he has done wrong but has no idea that his life is about to change. There is a heated exchange between him and the senator before he storms out of the room chanting those famous last words, "You can't fire me. I quit!"

After his hasty exit, the senator gives clear instructions to one of his men to "meet that *former* employee at the door on his way out and see to it that he spends a good amount of time in a debriefing facility."

Lana has her undercover journalist hat on now and is hungry for the "real story." She is moving furtively through the halls searching for what she is not sure. That is when she hears raised voices. One of them is the senator yelling at someone to "get the hell out of here." Lana rushes to the area where she believes the voices to be coming from. She turns a corner and then stops abruptly. She is just in time to see two things happen. The senator "disappears" behind a wall and an ill-tempered *former* employee is in the process of ripping off his security lanyard and throwing it to the floor as he makes his way to the lobby. Lana quickly scoops up the security badge and then ducks out of sight as another man, who is all business, follows determinedly in the path of the disgruntled employee. Once out of sight Lana walks over to inspect what she thinks to be a "disappearing wall." Who knows? In this building, anything was possible.

As Lana approaches, being the pragmatic type person she is, she's telling herself that this wall is *just* a wall. There are literally no markings. No seams. No *nothing*. No sign of anything out of the ordinary. Except—

Just then Lana spots a wall outlet. At chest height it is an oddity to be sure because she would not have looked at it twice had she not seen the senator "disappear" like he did. Lana looks closer at the wall outlet but it appears to be an ordinary wall outlet. Then she has an idea. She takes the security card and waves it over the outlet. There is only a whisper of sound as a portion of the wall gently opens to a lighted hallway. Much to her surprise she enters confidently. Then the wall slides shut. Now what?! Lana chooses to do what any intrepid explorer would do. She ventures on.

Lana moves quietly down the hallway until she comes to a door. The door opens to a large room which she is able to view from any one of several porthole style windows built into the wall. The room inside is similar in many ways to the modified Dream Theater in which she had her most recent "experience" but different in that this room has been adorned with plants and trees and, hmm, *that's odd*, an intricate lighting and sound system anchored to the ceiling. It is impressive, clearly the equal of anything she has seen at a major concert venue. There are also cables hanging down from the ceiling fixed to a suspended metal track which allows for the movement of something, she doesn't know what, across the full expanse of the room.

To her left, almost out of her line of sight, Lana can see a large rectangular mirrored window which no doubt the senator and Joni are lurking behind. Lana ducks down quickly just then as a man is brought into the room by two other men. They are literally dragging this man through the room. Lana catches sight of his face and now the dragging part seems to make sense as he appears to have been drugged.

The three men arrive at the 'veil' but the drugged man is not placed upon it. Instead the two men proceed to wrap a vest and some other garment around the drugged man in effect securing him to two suspended cables Lana had not noticed earlier. Now see sees that they are connected to the moving track in the ceiling above him. Once he is firmly secured they let the man dangle, suspended by the cables. Moments later the senator's voice came booming through the speakers.

"Soldier. Are you in place?" The man's head snapped up and he was now at full attention.

"Sir, yes sir!"

Inside the control booth the senator beamed with pride. He was a five-star general of a one-man army and was enjoying the hell out of it. If his gamble paid off, what this soldier was doing in this room would change infantry combat forever.

"Are you prepared to face the enemy?"

"Sir, yes sir!" came the confident reply.

"Carry on soldier, and may God be with you." The last part of that statement was pure theatre but who was to criticize? Everyone in that room either worked for or reported to the senator.

Lana watches incredulously as this "soldier" seems to awaken fully from his drugged state. He immediately checks his weapon for readiness. Lana can see that it is nothing more than a store-bought plastic rifle, but this man acts as though it has heft and weight to it. He is treating it like it is the real deal M16 that he would carry into battle.

The "soldier" is now moving forward with caution stepping over rocks and tree roots which exist only in his imagination. The chaotic sounds of warfare are being pumped in through the speakers above but this auditory element is probably more for the senator's pleasure than anything else. This "soldier" appears to be fully immersed in a nightmare war crafted within his own imagination. Not fully though. Lana is beginning to put the puzzle pieces together in her head. *This* is the *real* top-secret project that the senator has been working on unbeknownst to Everett Marsh. And this project likely relies more on "*forced*" thoughts than those which the soldier may have dreamed and/or imagined on his own.

Bite the bullet

"Soldier! Engage the enemy!"

Two other men across the room jump up from their prone positions and move forward with weapons drawn. They are now shooting *at* the soldier. The soldier is shooting back. One of the imaginary bullets from his toy plastic gun seems to find its target. Lana thinks back to her two brothers playing "war" in the back yard. This man seems to be playing fair. He howls with pain, grabs his chest and then falls to the ground "dead." The acting is second-rate but it's good enough to fool the "soldier."

The other man, the one who was *not* shot, now takes aim and fires his weapon, which is *real*. The sound of the gunfire is *loud*. The recoil of the gun is not faked. Nor is the reaction of the body of the "soldier" as he is actually hit. The "soldier" is flung backwards with the force of the bullet, but he does not go down, as he is still suspended by cables. Before he can react, another shot is fired. The "soldier" slumps forward and it is clear now that he has been mortally wounded. Blood is seeping through the "soldier's" clothing as his body now hangs limp.

Deep scarlet red becomes a stain spreading across the "soldier's" abdomen extending down gradually from his gut to his knees. The "soldier" is clearly losing a lot of blood. Lana is in shock. This man's injuries are *real*. Those gunshots were not staged. Lana is frozen in place with uncertainty.

"Medic!" shouts the senator. His voice is booming through the speakers sounding as though it were a voice from heaven. The same two men who brought the man into the room now rush to his aid. They rip his shirt open to expose two clean gunshot entry points. The soldier has regained consciousness. He says, "Is it *bad*?" as he looks down at his ruined midsection. At first, they don't answer. "Bad" is a poor description of the critical amount of damage this man has survived.

The "medics" are now exchanging comments but Lana is unable to hear. She reaches for the door handle. Much to her surprise the door is unlocked. She opens it just enough to peer in and hear the "medics" conversing with the wounded soldier.

"Soldier! You've been hit but the bullet passed through you. You hear me? Nothing vital, you understand. The bleeding has stopped. I have patched you up! It's not a great stitch job but I haven't much of a sewing kit out here on the battlefield now do I? I promise you though that I'll sew you up just right when we make it to hospital. You with me soldier?"

Lana always listens intently. It is not lost on her that the "medic" has only mentioned *one* bullet. There is damage from two bullets plain as day but the "soldier" appears to be seeing only what the "medic" is suggesting to him. Lana could not believe her eyes. It is truly remarkable that the "soldier" seems to be reacting positively and holistically to these words as the skin of his midsection begins to fold in on itself in an effort to stop the bleeding and close the wound.

Incredibly the "soldier" seems to be coming around. He is responding to the "suggestions" that the "medic" is giving him. The bleeding does seem to have slowed considerably but Lana has no idea if this is because the man has no more blood to give or if he truly "believes" that his wound has been closed.

Lana is astounded by what she is seeing. Have they just saved this man's life and repaired his body through some process of "suggestive dreaming"? The possibilities of what this could mean were limitless. Perhaps she has misjudged the senator...

"Medic! Is this soldier fit to return to battle?"

The "medic" grabbed the soldier by his arms and said, "Soldier! Listen to me. I have no weapon and no way back to safety. Can I count on you to lead us?"

The "soldier" looks down at his wound but doesn't see what is truly there. He sees only what he *believes* he is seeing. He speaks the words he is dreaming.

"I'm good to go. You can count on me. Let me check my rifle."

The soldier goes through a thorough inspection of his rifle exactly as he has been trained. The fact that this is only a hunk of plastic one tenth the weight of the real thing does not seem to register. He seems confident with his inspection. "Come on Medic. Follow me. And stay close."

Lana *knows* it is impossible what this "soldier" is doing. He is now running *towards* the enemy with the athleticism of an uninjured man which he clearly is not. Just then the same two "enemy figures" from before rise up from their position, shoulder their weapons and prepare to fire. Lana is stricken with fear. Are they going to shoot him *again*???!!! And wasn't one of them "dead" earlier? She understands that these are war games but--how unfair!

"NO!!!" screams Lana as she rushes into the room.

The "enemy forces" lower their weapons, uncertain of what to do. The "soldier" stops abruptly, his head cocks to one side like a bewildered dog as he tries to make sense of what an attractive woman in business clothes is doing on the battlefield. Then he starts to blink and to wipe his eyes. An incredible pain digs its fingers deep into his body.

"Get her the hell out of there before it's too late!"

This shouted command, thundering through the speakers, is coming from the senator. The handlers who were "medics" only moments before release their grip on the "soldier" and head towards Lana. She looks first at the "soldier" who seems to crumple under his own weight, then to the two men advancing towards her and then back to the "soldier" who is once again bleeding profusely.

The senator suddenly appears in the room. All efforts at keeping a sense of realism about this war game has been abandoned. The senator is furious. His rage is directed at Lana.

Lana is enraged as well. "What have you *done* to him?!" she screams.

"Point the finger at yourself, you meddling bitch! The question you should be asking is what have YOU done to him?! Just look at him! He is bleeding out now thanks to you!!"

Lana looks at the soldier and realizes that he is literally dying before her eyes.

"You sonuvabitch! His blood is on *your* hands! I'm going to the police!"

Lana turns and runs from the room. The two "medics" start to give chase when they hear '*Stop!*' from the senator. "I need you both here. Do what you can for him and then get this place cleaned up. She's not going anywhere. This building is locked up tight as a drum. Besides, I have a better idea."

A pirate's life

Joni has now entered the room. She has fire burning in her eyes. The senator can *sense* her rage building. It is palpable and pernicious. The senator is knowingly about to pour gas on an open flame.

"Joni. Go find her. Then---" the senator paused. "Do what you do. I'll see that it gets cleaned up."

Joni heard what she heard, laughed a decidedly evil laugh then said, "Pirate make big mess."

The senator shook his head and said, "Sorry Lana, you brought this on yourself."

Under his breath he said, *"That bitch scares the living shit out of me."*

To his men he said, "If I could clone that woman we wouldn't *need* a military."

Fox & Hound

Lana is running out of options. She knows now that she is locked *(trapped!)* inside this building. She knows also that Joni will inevitably come looking for her and that there can only be dire consequences as a result. The question is, can she hide for 8 hours until the minimal staff that occupies this building shows up at 7am for their shifts? "Doubtful" is the answer that keeps coming back to her. Lana understand that she needs to find a place where Joni either might not think to look or perhaps has never been. The conference rooms are out because they are locked. The café is out because there is a chain link floor to ceiling "door" restricting access.

The Dream Theaters offer no hiding places. Where can she go???

Eureka! Everett's office. The one place in this building which would, she is certain, be off limits to Joni. She may not even know it exists. If Lana is able to get there first, she might be able to disable or jam the elevator. She needs all the advantage she can get. It's like that parable Lana heard as a kid, how do you guarantee your odds of winning a race? Make the course a ladder and be the first one up.

Joni is many things. She is evil, vengeful, quite resilient and incredibly resourceful. Within an hour of Lana's disappearance in the LUCID building, Joni has tracked her to Everett's office. The senator was able to provide Joni with an override code which would in effect reset the disabled private elevator. Lana, perhaps relaxing a bit with her false sense of security, would not realize that the elevator was functioning once again until it was too late.

Once Joni would arrive in Everett's office it would surely become a cat and mouse game between the two of them. Nothing would be sacred in Lana's attempts to keep Joni at bay. The heavy metal awards which adorned the shelves behind Everett's desk would become defensive weapons as one by one, each would be thrown mightily in Joni's direction. Joni was sure to take one or two direct hits but the cuts and the pain would only serve to spur her on.

If the art pieces and table sculptures were of any value, they would be reduced to just random art *pieces*, not pieces of art. It would take only minutes for Joni to force Lana into a corner where there was no further retreat. That fateful corner might happen to be the south-facing balcony of Everett's office.

This balcony overlooked the same grove of trees which served as the picnic area for the Café diners. This balcony unfortunately was five floors up from that scenic picnic area.

Would a drop from there even be survivable?

Part Two

Nightmare

Hard kept secret

"Make the call."

"But I-, she—"

"Make the fucking call."

"Hello Everett."

"Frank, what a pleasant surprise to hear from you." Everett is feigning his voice of confidence. He looks haggard. He has not slept. What he *has* done is taken a red eye flight back from Dallas after receiving a rather perplexing phone call from the police. Everett is uncertain just what has happened but the answers are not forthcoming as the police are asking all the questions. His friend Frank is a port in the storm.

"Is there anybody there with you?" Frank asks already presuming to know the answer.

"Yes, yes, oh, the *whole gang*, say hello to them for me, won't you?" Somehow, Everett knows immediately that Frank is crafting a hidden message to him. Everett is a quick study. He has figured out that Frank is not making this call on his own. He is probably on speaker and Everett can hazard a guess as to who is listening.

"I'm going to assume that by the "whole gang" you might be inferring that the police are there and possibly a detective unit as well." Frank is playing his part quite well.

"You always come right to the point, don't you?" Everett is both stressed and irritated by the situation.

"Fair enough. Since you can only respond cryptically I won't expect the answers I am looking for to two very pressing questions. First, *what the hell* is Senator Bob McKinney doing in my building? And second, why does he think that I would have *any possible* way of helping a former employee of yours who appears to be *well beyond* the need of medical aid? Honestly, how she is still breathing is beyond me."

During this entire discourse, the senator was glaring at Frank Morgan who absolutely refused to be flummoxed by his station or his posturing of intimidation. The senator's patience with him, however, seemed to be wearing thin, which also was of no concern to Frank. He didn't much care for playing by someone else's rules. The fact that the senator was pulling him into something which was unsavory at best and possibly criminal at its worst, did, however, cause him grave concern. Frank was now faced with the same challenge as Everett. Achieving his life's dream with FM Robotics depended largely on government funding. And while he had never had any direct dealings with the senator up until now, Bob McKinney was a well-connected politician who could inflict great harm if Frank refused to play ball.

"Everett, I won't keep you but, please tell me, this *is* your employee, correct?"

Frank paused just for a moment to look down at the body that lay on the table before him. It was a crumpled heap of flesh and bones that relied more on the adorning clothes it wore to bear any resemblance to a human body. There was potentially as much blood on the outside of the body now as there may still be on the inside. Internal bleeding and mass hemorrhaging was a given as this person had sustained multiple, *multiple*, bone fractures. The senator had explained that she had fallen from a height of perhaps five stories. It wasn't a guess although he tried to make it sound liked one.

The fall which this body had sustained could not have come from Frank's building. Although massive in its own right, it was a single-story structure which occupied a good share of acreage. *NRG* Dynamics and LUCID were the only two buildings other than Frank's on this business campus. As the senator had purposefully directed him to call Everett, Frank could easily deduce that there was only one place where a fall like this could have occurred. The LUCID building, and more specifically, Everett's office.

Everett, however, was not Frank's choice of suspect. The senator had certainly leaned into that idea but he did not know that Frank was well aware of the fact that Everett had been hundreds of miles from here. It was only through security alerts, unanswered messages from the police and access to closed circuit camera footage on his laptop on the plane that Everett was able to piece together enough information of the tragic event to speak with some authority. Everett could not be certain of Frank's end game in this conversation but his unqualified trust in him encouraged him to play the game.

Everett had not answered Frank's question. Perhaps he was too caught up in his own thoughts to have heard it. Frank posed the question again.

"Everett, is this woman *your* employee?"

Everett must stay in character. He is stalling for time as well as dancing around the issue. He also has several sets of eyes watching him as he spoke. These were the trained eyes of law enforcement.

"Oh, *that* one!"

Everett acted as though he were placing his hand over the phone as he whispered to the assembled group, "*My neighbor next door found a cat.*"

"Yeah, has a black circle over one eye? She's just a stray. Been hanging around the building for quite a few days now. Alan over at *NRG* told me that they had had some trouble "shooing" her away as well. By the sound of it, perhaps she was hit by a car '*or something*'."

"Yeah, right. I'm going with the 'or something' theory. Letting you go Everett. But—we need to talk. Soon."

As Everett sets his phone down he feels a pair of eyes upon him. It is a detective doing what detectives do best. Making deductions. "The cat is female?"

"What's that?" Everett asks.

"You said 'she' when referring to the cat." All eyes are upon him now. The devil is in the details.

"Yes," Everett replies quickly, unsure how he has mis-stepped but feeling that he surely must have in some way. The detective has that look on his face like he is on to something.

"How might you know that? The gender. About a stray cat."

Everett blurts out the word "kittens" and is immediately regretting it. It is a lie that he will be stuck with defending for days.

Humpty Dumpty... had a great fall

The answer Everett had given to Frank was most likely in code. Everett and Frank fortunately were on the same page in regard to how much the senator should know about what Frank knew. It was best that way. What the senator did not know is that Frank was fully aware of Everett being in deep water with the senator in regard to funding that was needed just to keep his fledgling company solvent.

The senator of course was not known for his support of public parks and recreation. In other words he was not a charitable man. That thought ran through Frank's mind with a good measure of sarcasm. The senator had always prided himself on being at the forefront of *military* spending whether it be tactical warfare or modernized weaponry. Frank had no idea what this woman lying before him and still clinging to life represented in the senator's world but it was not something with which he would have chosen to involve himself.

Frank listened intently to the senator's wishes *(demands?)* as he explained that this woman *must* be kept alive. That there were things that only she knew which needed to be *retrieved (?)* from her.

From her *memory*. Somehow.

Frank was only seconds away from using the word "impossible" to respond to the senator's request when several of the senator's minions showed up suddenly carrying yet *another* female body with similar injuries. Two things happened then which charted the course for Frank to follow. The first was his almost immediate recognition of a person whom he had never seen before. Frank was nearly certain that he had taken phone calls from both Alan and Everett regarding this woman being brought before him. She was a journalist. He even knew her name. Lana Taylor. Another piece of the puzzle fell into place. The other body could be none other than a person whom he had heard described on several occasions. Only one name was necessary to identify her.

Joni.

The second thing that happened which served to guide Frank's actions was the senator's statement that it was *Joni* (not Lana) who was to be saved by *any* means necessary. Or possible.

Frank knew the answer before he asked but it was pretense to what his mind had already worked out as a plan to make this situation work out with the least potential for jeopardy to the safety of mankind. While that seemed like a rather grandiose and outlandish thing to consider nothing was off the table when factoring in the work being done at three of the most high-tech companies in the world. Not to mention the involvement of a man like Senator Bob McKinney who probably grew up dreaming that one day he would push the button to drop an atom bomb.

"May I be clear on what you're asking of me?" asked Frank.

"There you go! My patience has been rewarded. I *knew* you were capable of rational thought."

The senator's sarcastic response did nothing to endear him to Frank who waited with agitated anticipation for what was to come. The senator seemed to understand that you gather more bees with honey as the saying goes and chose to offer a more sensible reply.

"That girl is the 'curious type,' sticking her nose into things that don't involve her. I need to know what *she* knows about the relevant 'top secret' things which she has been exposed to. In other words, I need you to just somehow tap into her memories and retrieve those things."

The senator's use of the word "somehow" as reference to performing some incredibly challenging scientific functions astounded Frank.

"Senator McKinney, if I understand your "scientific" jargon correctly, you are asking for me to—" Frank begins counting off each task on his fingers, "keep her alive, cut open her scalp, and then source and capture memories, *specific* memories mind you, from her brain."

The senator made a gesture that indicated that Frank was only repeating the obvious.

"And what pray tell gave you *any* indication that would make you think that *I* can do that?"

The senator replies sternly. "Here, let me put it this way. With what I know of your work with *AI* and robotics and what I have learned of the capabilities of the LUCID programs, I believe, no, *I know*, that it can be done."

Frank stole a glance at Lana's body. If *anything* was possible he wanted it to be that he would save *her* life. She was an innocent bystander who had been run over by the senator's dreams of a future war machine.

Frank tread carefully as he spoke knowing that he was navigating uncharted waters.

"So you want me to save *her*." He is pointing at Joni. Frank is simply thinking out loud. The senator takes the comment to mean that he is just trying to be difficult and isn't having it.

"*Save* her? I have no use for her! I want her memories dammit! Why is that so fucking hard for you to understand? I have no concern for her beyond that. Think for one minute about what you see lying on the table. Would *you* still want to be alive after all the damage that has been done? She's probably broken every fucking bone in her body!"

This was the first time that even a glimmer of humanity had shown through from the senator. Frank knew though that the best way to proceed was still through what might be possible from a *military* perspective.

"Senator," Frank began. The use of his title was some clever bullshit on his part to gain his support. The senator was a sucker for ego stroking. "What I do here is build robots and equip them with *AI*."

"I *know* that. That's why I'm *here*."

"Yes of course," agreed Frank, "so--, what if I could not only find a way to capture and save her memories but also, and this will sound a bit "science-fictiony," *rebuild* her? Replace her bones with titanium limbs. Replace her skin with a combination of Kevlar wrap, carbon fiber and other composite materials. Install a microchip which would serve as—" Frank paused for a moment knowing that he had to dumb this way down so that the senator would bite on the hook right away, "—as a controller, like in a video game. In essence I would be turning her into an avatar which you could control at will. Not to mention that she would be virtually... indestructible."

Frank could imagine the wheels of imagination turning in the senator's head right now. And he hated himself for what he had just proposed. It was a *horrible* idea. It's only foundation when placed in the hands of a man like Senator Bob McKinney was conquest and the death of all who opposed the mission he served. This was the same as offering a second apple to Adam in the Garden of Eden. There had been no lessons learned along the way. Frank was offering the senator a chance to place his stamp on the future. This was a deal with the devil intended only to be able to save Lana's life as well. Frank would forever live with the fear that his actions could result in wiping away the future altogether.

"You can *do* that?" the senator asked eagerly. This was the first time that he had given Frank any semblance of respect as both an engineer and scientist.

"I *think* so." Frank gave a long-measured pause. He was acting, hoping that the senator was interested in buying what he was hoping to sell. "I will need two things. Three things really but the third is a given."

"What's the third thing?"

"I will need Everett's help."

"No worry there, you're right, that's a given. He works for *me*."

Frank Morgan was the most passive man you could hope to meet but in that moment it was all he could do to avoid slapping the senator across the face. During this discourse between Frank and the senator, Frank had kept himself busy by administering a morphine drip to both bodies. The senator might not concern himself with the pain and anguish of others but Frank could not allow any living thing to lay there and suffer.

Even if the living thing was Joni.

"What else do you need?" the senator asked, wanting now a snappy answer.

"I will need funding. I have *no* idea what this might cost."

"Not a problem. The American taxpayers have deep pockets. Next?"

What an asshole! Frank wanted to kick him in the groin. As hard as he possibly could.

"This is the most challenging ask."

"Fair enough. Bring it on. What is it?"

"What I will be doing has *never* been done before." Frank paused to let that sink in. There was no visual effect on the senator who was of the opinion that *everything* was possible if you had enough money. "I will need a "donor" subject to test the applications I make prior to implementing them on the primary subject."

"What did you just say? I don't know what that means. Give it to me this time in simple *English*."

There he goes again thought Frank, ramping up that asshole level to ten. Frank had a mastery of sarcasm as well and decided to respond in language which the senator could clearly understand.

"I will need a test subject to try shit out on so I don't fuck up what I'm doing to the prime subject."

The senator was not one to be so easily offended. His response to Frank's indignation was simply to say, "There you go! Now was *that* so fucking *hard*?"

Frank waited while the senator caught up to the moment. The difference between *needing* a test subject and *having* a test subject finally dawned on the senator. The senator's next question was incredibly stupid but it would not serve Frank well to tell him so.

"Can it be a cadaver?"

"No." Frank did not embellish although it did give him a queasy feeling inside to think that a US senator had the wherewithal to obtain a cadaver if needed. Scary shit to be sure.

"So we have a problem."

This is what Frank was waiting for. "No, I don't think we do. As a matter of fact I believe that we have a simple and ready solution at hand."

The senator's furrowed brow was an indication that it might take him another minute to catch up but then he glanced over at Lana's body, still rising and falling with the breath of life. "*Her*?" The senator pointed.

Frank absolutely hated giving credit where it wasn't due but in the interest of science, and in saving a human life, he said, "Good call, Senator. That is possibly the best solution we could ask for. Having both subjects here, and *now*, means that I could get started immediately. This *is* an urgent matter for you, is that correct?"

"Absolutely!"

"Well then, I concur with your suggestion."

Both men knew that there was bullshit in the air but the senator was a man devoid of hurt feelings so he said to Frank, "My next suggestion is that you get to work as quickly as possible before we lose them both."

Finally! After all this time the thought that these two women could actually *die* from their injuries had occurred to the senator.

"Yessir." Frank was laying it on thick now. "One more thing though."

"What's that?"

"It would not be good to have the police and detectives wandering about grilling LUCID employees on the reported "*story*" of two women falling from the top of their building. Anything you can do about that?"

"I'm a United States Senator son. That's child's play."

"Of course." '*I'm not your son, asshole*,' Frank said under his breath.

"Come on boys, follow me." The senator pointed to the three thugs who had brought in Lana's body.

"And you," the senator was pointing now at Frank, "don't you go getting confused between the prime subject and the test subject. I'll admit that she's a looker," jerking his thumb at Lana, "but *this one*, a little hard to look at maybe but she's got the goods. It's what *she* has in her memory banks that counts. Get busy. I'll have Everett contact you in a few minutes. Be ready to take his call."

"Yessir," Frank said, thinking again to himself that if it was the senator laying on this table right now he would just go ahead and pull a sheet over him and call it a day. Instead he put all his attention towards what he was about to do, to save two lives and then engineer two human, *AI* equipped robots. This was history in the making but still Frank had to ask himself, was he playing God? Or was this more like a scene from the Wizard of Oz. 'If I only had a brain...'

Loose ends

Over the next few weeks Everett was never asked about the disappearance of Joni. The whole story of her and some other woman coming to blows and tumbling over the edge of the balcony of Everett's top floor office had become urban legend. There were some people who felt that the police investigation seemed to wrap rather quickly considering the fact that two women were still presumed missing. In truth while not many seemed to notice or care that Joni had disappeared, the journalist Lana Taylor was a different story. Everett Marsh had suddenly found himself in the uncomfortable and unfamiliar position of becoming a pathological liar. He had already lied to the police and to the detectives. He then found it necessary to lie to Lana's publisher. It hurt him deeply that he must lie to his dear friends Alan and Blanche. Eventually, he would even lie to Congress at a House hearing regarding the disappearance of Bob McKinney, a Senator from the Great State of Texas.

Fortunately, Everett was not charged with the distressing task of lying to Lana's father as he had passed away peacefully only a few days after Lana's visit to Seattle.

Stick figures

Both Joni and Lana were placed into medically induced comas for the work that needed to be performed. The trauma which both of their bodies had experienced was significant. Modern medicine and the robotics which Frank had at his disposal made it possible to transition first Joni and then Lana into fully functioning human/*AI* robots. Nearly 80% of the bones in Joni's body were replaced by identical 3-D printed replicas forged in an inexpensive and readily available steel alloy. Lana's body fared much better with a need for only 50% replacement however the bone breaks she had sustained were far more severe. A great deal of splintering had occurred causing internal bleeding, plus extensive nerve and muscle damage.

Frank took great care when managing the expenses which the senator would need to review before final approval. He made it appear that the greater expense was going to the rebuild of Joni when the opposite was true. Frank purposefully used a material which was oddly *softer* than bone when crafting Joni's skeletal structure replacement. Frank was well aware that Joni was *not* a good person and after all was said and done he wanted some *personal* assurance that she would not be employed for use in any manner which would not pass muster with his morals.

The *Joni* robot still had one bad eye and still wore something resembling an eye patch because of it. Frank *could* have replaced it with something far better. But he didn't. His simple thought was why give her any *additional* advantage? He was already giving her back her life. The same motivation that prevented Frank from making the *Joni* robot *better* than she had been before the fall is also what encouraged him to show favor to the *Lana* robot.

The eyepatch, however, was an *obvious* feature. It could not be overlooked. What Frank did to cover his *lack* of work was to fashion what at first glance appeared to be a high-tech eyepiece replacement for the bad eye of the *Joni* robot. Upon seeing it the senator would be convinced that it was a perfect combination of zoom lens and night vision goggle. In truth it held no more magnification than a child's telescope. The "night vision" was merely a green lens. Frank had a full-throated laugh at that one. Someday, he promised himself, he would share that little antic with Alan and Regina. A little redemption for all their troubles with a former, difficult to say the least, employee.

Before Frank dared to reveal to the senator that the *Joni* robot was fully ready for a memory scan he made sure that he had completed all his work on the *Lana* robot. He knew that funding would evaporate the moment that the senator could access the memories he wanted from the damaged yet still intact and fully functioning brain of the *Joni* robot.

Pandora reveal

The day arrived when the *Lana* robot was completed, which meant for Frank two very significant things. A clandestine test drive of the *Lana* robot's functionality as well as a memory scan and download of the *Joni* robot. Other tests would follow involving motor functions, speech and the ability to reason. Unbeknownst to the senator, Frank had taken the additional step of installing a "kill switch" in both robots. It was something which seemed *necessary* for the *Joni* robot. He did it as a matter of course with the *Lana* robot as well but was soon relieved that he did.

A time had been set and a room scheduled for the memory scan and download of the *Joni* robot. This was happening on a Sunday afternoon. The three buildings and the entire business campus was devoid of employees. All security cameras had been shut down as well. The senator did not want any errant footage of the *Joni* robot to be seen by anyone outside of their very small circle. Too many questions would follow that they were ill-prepared to answer.

Kill switch

An hour before the scheduled time an over-eager Frank could wait no longer. He had to know if his work had paid off and he had truly saved the life of a beautiful young woman. Frank was a positive thinker and he truly believed that Lana would be able to assimilate herself back into normal life. Of course *he* would always know and be aware of the changes done to her but he was hopeful that she would not. After all, Lana was still essentially Lana. That was what Frank believed anyway. He would not know for sure if his assumptions were accurate until she awoke and learned the truth. So he woke her up.

The *Lana* robot awoke with a smile. She did not know Frank so she was at first a bit disoriented. He told her that he was a doctor *(why was he lying?!)* and that she was safe. 'Your friends Alan and Everett are just in the other room *(another lie!)*.'

"Am I okay? What *happened* to me?" The *Lana* robot sat up and looked about. Before Frank could answer a worried look crossed her face. The *Lana* robot looked him square in the eye and said, "What *is* this place? And who are you *really*? That is a lab coat you're wearing so I presume you're *not* a doctor and this place is definitely *not* a hospital!"

If Frank had expected her to be groggy he was *dead wrong*. The *AI* deductive reasoning he had implanted in her was now fully functional and her level of trust with him was diminishing rapidly. There would be no way for him to keep up with her cognitive abilities. He would need to tell her the truth as soon as possible before she was able to figure it out on her own—

Then the *Lana* robot screamed. The full-length mirror which Frank had placed in the room and had thought was such a great idea was the cause for alarm. *How the hell did she get to the mirror so fast?!* The *Lana* robot was standing before it and evaluating the body which was reflected. She was dressed in a medical gown which meant that her arms and legs were exposed. Frank had seen her every day for several weeks so what *she* was seeing now had become "ordinary" to *him*. *Huge mistake*.

Frank looked on in horror as he saw what she saw. Her body had been stitched up wherever bones, muscle, nerves or blood vessels had needed to be replaced. The best description he could come up with was that her body resembled the devil's road map. Her skin had a slightly bluish tint from blood vessels trying to cope with the added pressure of a body lying dormant for weeks, now suddenly active and moving about.

Showing no modesty she lifted her gown to see the remainder of her body. Her breasts were untouched. They looked exactly the same except for the wide scar running between them where her breastbone had been cracked open for access to her heart and other vital organs. As she looked down past her waist she saw the railroad tracks of stitches running back and forth across her hips. It was a special heavy duty stitching process involving staples as well for areas that carried and distributed the weight of the lower half of the body.

Just then the *Lana* robot must have realized that she was standing virtually naked in front of a man who only *claimed* to be a doctor. She had access to memories which would help her to understand what had happened and what was happening now, but they were being blocked by the shock of her appearance. Then she caught this man staring at her in the mirror.

!!!!!!!!!

In a flash she was in his face. There was nothing he could say or do. The *Lana* robot angrily grabbed his shoulders. Frank grimaced at the pain. The *Lana* robot would have *no idea* of the power she now had within her nor could she know at this point how close she had just come to snapping the bones in his shoulders.

"DID YOU DO THIS TO ME??!! WHO THE HELL ARE YOU??? DR. FRANKENSTEIN??!!"

The *Lana* robot shoved him away roughly. Frank hit the wall hard. It was three feet away. Such was the force of her actions. He crumpled to the ground. The *Lana* robot grabbed the mirror and flung it across the room. It shattered sending shards of reflective glass flying across the room. Seven hundred years of bad luck.

"Where are my clothes?!"

That was the last thing she said to him before he hit the kill switch.

Engineering redundancy

Frank Morgan sat at his worktable for fifteen minutes before checking his watch and seeing that he had an appointment pending. He looked over at the *Lana* robot who was now the one lying crumpled on the floor. He didn't have the time needed to get her lifted up from the floor and onto the table. Did it even matter?

Frank needed to clear his head and focus on the job at hand. He needed to move the *Joni* robot over to the LUCID building for the senator to get what he seemed to want so badly, the memory download from Joni's brain. Fortunately, the *Joni* robot was still securely fastened down on an easily moved stretcher. Frank headed for the elevator pushing the stretcher in front of him. He draped a colorful tablecloth over the stretcher as an extra precaution so that at first glance a body on a stretcher is *not* what someone would see or recall.

Less than thirty minutes later the *Joni* robot was in the experimental room at LUCID. Her head had been shaved and several electrodes in addition to the typical LUCID head gear adorned her head. Senator Bob McKinney was seated in the world's most comfortable chair. He too was wired up. His intention was to take any and all information from the *Joni* robot directly into his brain. He seemed to believe that she had learned or gained knowledge of something of great significance. What it was they did not know and he would of course refuse to share.

This one-to-one sharing of direct memories from the brain was not something that Everett had ever tested on humans before now. There was a tinge of excitement evident in his voice as he gave commands to Frank, his lone helper. There was a level of anxiety apparent in the senator's actions as well as he showed a level of grace when asked to do this or that by Everett which he would not have shown otherwise.

Once the *Joni* robot and the senator were all hooked up and online with the LUCID equipment, and Everett and Frank were in the control booth and out of earshot of the senator, Frank spilled the beans about the awakening of the *Lana* robot. Everett was of course greatly troubled by her reaction but encouraged to hear that she seemed to be quite "alive" in her new normal. Better than dead, right? That answer unfortunately seemed to be still up in the air.

The other thing which Frank shared with Everett was the existence of the *kill switch*. Frank then placed the kill switch for the *Joni* robot into Everett's capable hands. Frank had been through enough already today. Everett took the kill switch and placed it in his pocket for ready access. He did not anticipate using it but fortunately for he and Frank both, it was readily accessible when he *needed* it.

Everett turned on the sound connection to the two feeds in the *Dream Theater*.

"Bob, can you hear me okay?"

"Yes, loud and clear, out."

"Bob, this isn't a two-way radio or a war room scenario. We're only thirty feet away. You may speak normally."

"Roger." Everett and Frank looked at each other and shared a 'can you believe this guy?' look. They almost broke into laughter when the senator added, "Out."

"Right. Here we go in 3-2-1---"

Too close for comfort

Everett's voice drifted away as the senator began to enter a dream zone. He had done this several times now but this was the first time that he had done it when connected to another human being. That is if the *Joni* robot could still be considered as such.

There was a comfort to be found when alone with your thoughts. You can think and do whatever you please without judgement or ridicule. You can find a safe place deep within your psyche. The senator had done just that each time he had submitted to this "procedure" as he called it. This time, however, was quite different. He immediately sensed Joni's presence. And it wasn't good. It wasn't good at all.

The senator wasn't sure what to expect going into this thing but one thing was certain. Joni was still *very* much alive. And still very much *Joni*.

At first the senator could only *sense* Joni's presence. Now he could *feel* it. They should be on an equal playing field in this place though, right? Perhaps he might even be a bit stronger as he has not sustained the life-threatening injuries which Joni had only weeks ago. But-- it wasn't that way. It wasn't that way at all. It was more like he was caught in a web, unable to move, and she was the spider taking her good, sweet time moving in for the kill.

The spider then shot a venomous spray of hostility directly at the senator. He screamed in pain.

"Bob! You okay in there? What just happened?"

The senator can hear Everett talking in his head. How was that *possible*? Where *was* he?

"Bob, can you still hear me?"

The dream machine that Everett built was never intended to include outside interaction like this but this *wasn't* his machine. This is what the senator had done to his machine with modifications made by *his* people. There was still much testing to be done to discern what long-term effects this might have on a test subject. Bob didn't have that kind of time so it only made sense that he was in the quote unquote "hot seat." And now it seemed as though *he* was the one getting burned.

"She's one mean bitch!" Bob shouted.

"Who is?" asked Everett.

"Joni!"

The senator was now struggling in his seat as though fending off his quarry.

"She's coming for me! Get to the memory download. *Now!*"

Everett turned off the microphone and leaned over to Frank. There was no one about to hear him but still he whispered, "I don't know how he's doing this."

"Doing what?"

"Staying present in both planes of the experience. I would have thought it, um, improbable."

Frank shrugged his shoulders and said, "He is a man on a mission."

"I'll say," Everett agreed as he started doing some things on the console. He switched the microphone back on.

"Bob, I'm starting the memory download sequence now. You should, *in theory*, be only a *spectator* now. You copy?"

"Copy that!" Bob said with authority. He added under his breath, although still audible, "*thank God.*"

Frank pointed at the microphone switch. Everett nodded and turned it off.

"What the hell is going on in there?" He was motioning to the two inside the Dream Theater.

"I think you can see for yourself that the answer to that is not much of anything."

They both looked into the room. The senator was still secured in the most comfortable chair in the world although he looked distinctly *uncomfortable*. The *Joni* robot was still strapped securely to the stretcher on which she lay however it was clear that she was straining against her bonds.

"The better question to ask, Frank is what the hell is going on up *here*?" He was pointing to his head and then to each of theirs. "The brain is a mighty powerful engine. We have only been test driving it at moderate speeds throughout our lives. Who *knows* how fast it can go?"

"Not to mention that I have added in *AI* capabilities to one of them. God only knows what may be possible now."

"Nice work, Dr. Frankenstein."

"That's not the first time I've heard that today."

"*What!?*"

Term limits

"Oh my god, it's working!!"

Both Everett and Frank immediately shifted their attention back to the control board. Before Everett could ask the senator what he had meant by his comment the two monitor screens above them flickered on.

Everett looked puzzled.

"What's wrong?" asked Frank.

Everett replied, "I did not turn those on."

"Is this another one of the senator's 'add-ons'?"

"Must be. Look! There's an image!"

"*What is it?*"

"It looks like--- *this room*."

Frank squinted his eyes as the image was at first blurry then suddenly it was full color, full focus.

"That, that's—Lana!" shouted Frank. "What are we *seeing*? Is one of them *dreaming* this?"

It took a moment for Everett to answer. He was in awe of what he was seeing.

"No, this is not a dream we are watching. If that were true it would be *quite* a feat of engineering excellence."

"Is it a video then?"

"Nope." Everett rubbed his hands over his face before responding. "I'm sorry, I guess this truly *is* a feat of engineering excellence. What I believe we are watching is the memory download from Joni's brain. We are watching through her "mind's eye" as she relives her experience."

"That's incredible!"

"Yes, yes it is."

"But-- *which* experience?"

"I don't know." The gravity of the moment seemed to weigh Everett down as he considered the potential of this next giant step in his life's work.

"Look! Something's happening!"

Both men fixed their gaze on the screens above.

Lana turns to see Joni suddenly in the room behind her. Lana has been snooping around the control room. Both monitor screens were on but showing only a blank blue screen. There was no way for Joni to know if Lana had been able to view anything or if she even understood their purpose.

Lana jumps up out of her chair. She is yelling at Joni. It sounds like she is yelling in a tunnel but the words are still audible. Something about this being 'wrong' and 'taking this too far.' The indignant look on Lana's face is slowly changing to one of concern. It is becoming clear to her that she is speaking her piece to the wrong audience. The expression on her face is now fear. She has seen too much. She has said too much. And all of it to the wrong person.

Lana tries to push her way past Joni. Nothing doing. Joni clamps onto her arm with an iron grip. Lana cries out in pain. A look of bewilderment flashes across Lana's face. Joni must have done what Joni does when watching others suffer. Smile and laugh.

Just then both men jerk back in their chairs involuntarily as a cup of coffee is tossed into Joni's face.

"My eye!" she screams.

Lana rushes past her and runs from the room. It takes several moments for Joni to clear her eye. The coffee was hours old so it was not hot. There was more damage done to Joni's ego than anything else. She hated the thought of anyone exploiting her one vulnerability. Lana had just done that. Joni was now out for blood.

The image on the screen was at first blurry and then flashed to black a few times as Joni blinked her eye. In a moment, the image was as clear as was Joni's resolve. Lana was a problem. Joni took care of problems. She ran from the room in search of Lana.

As the two men watched the screen in complete fascination Everett turned his head slightly to say, "The advantage goes to Joni. Bob hired her for security. She knows the building. There is no exit through the lobby without a proximity key. Lana doesn't have one. We both know where this is going already. Although Lana is several steps ahead of Joni she will have already discovered the exits are a no go and will head to what she thinks may be a safe place."

"Where's that?"

"My office of course."

"On the fifth floor? She'll be trapped."

"That's true but she's probably thinking that she will be safe up there if she can find a way to shut down the elevator."

"Oh. Can she do that?"

Evrett's face looked grim. "No. No she can't. You're right. She'll be trapped."

Frank's thoughts immediately went to the sight of both Joni's and Lana's bodies and how broken they both were from the five-story fall. "I don't think I want to watch this."

"I don't think we have a choice."

"Why is that?"

"I think the *AI* implant you placed in Joni may already have learned how to access the control board. I haven't touched anything for several minutes now. This is—out of my hands now."

"Holy shit," said Frank. "I think we just caught up to the future."

Everett pondered for a moment before saying, "If that's true, we better not fuck it up."

Everett and Frank watched in dire anticipation tormented by the ending neither wished to see. Joni raced across the lobby atrium ignoring the bank of doors she knew could not be opened by Lana. She headed directly for the "hidden" access point for the elevator to Everett's office. Just as Everett had feared a black key card came into view in Joni's hand. This card not only gave her unlimited access throughout the building, but it also gave her override privileges of security measures.

Everett commented, "That sonuvabitch Bob gave her the fucking keys to the kingdom!"

Frank nodded his head and said prophetically, "The evil that men do." He then looked out into the room directly at Joni and added, "*And* women."

The panel showing the floor where the elevator was currently stationed began to blink. This was an indication that the black security card was working. The elevator doors opened moments later. Joni moved into the elevator and pressed the button in the shape of a 'CLOUD.' This was a personal extravagance of Everett Marsh. Joni had been chewing gum. She stuck the wad on the button pressing with her thumb to be certain it would stay.

Everett could not help himself. "So *that's* how that got there. That fucking *bitch*."

The elevator door opened. Joni was not admiring the view to her left of the twinkling lights below. All of her attention was focused on the interior of the room and where Lana might be hiding. Lana did not come across as the aggressive type but Joni was taking no chances. She stuck her leg out and then retracted it quickly trying to draw a response from Lana if she was hiding just outside the door. Nothing happened. Joni stepped cautiously outside the elevator door. She heard something to her right, then, "AH!" Joni was hit full force in the face with a plaster statute of Venus. The statute crumbled into chunks as it met its target but not without first leaving some small amount of damage to Joni's face. Joni's hand obscured the view on the screen for just a moment as she sought to check if her nose had been broken.

Everett commented, "I paid *nothing* for that statue. Bought it at a freaking yard sale! But now it's *priceless*!"

"Heard," said Frank.

Lana could be seen scrambling around the office perhaps looking for a way to get back to the elevator. She had already tried using both her cell phone and Everett's desk phone to call 911. Nothing doing. She had no coverage in this building and there was a code required to use the desk phone.

Lana's eyes seemed to light on something which she maybe had not seen before. Everett's private balcony. The thought of putting a wall between her and Joni, even a glass wall, was worth everything at this point. Why she would think that it would lock from the outside only demonstrated her sheer desperation. Lana used her full weight on the door to keep Joni from gaining access but moments later that battle had been won by Joni who simply overpowered her.

Now it was just a test of wills. Both women are on the balcony five floors above the ground. There is a grassy area below with a few trees. This is where the café opens up to allow employees to enjoy their lunch outside. That is little consolation should one of them fall from this height. Joni and Lana are doing a dance. Joni continues to play on her advantage as Lana retreats, hanging on to each piece of furniture as though each were a potential rampart to thwart Joni's advances.

Joni, however, knows exactly what she is doing. She is tactfully backing Lana into a corner albeit the smallest section of the balcony, where there was nowhere else to go. It also happened to be the furthest spot from the door. Joni's breath quickened. She was noticeably excited, eager for the kill. Lana's face shows only fear as her eyes kept darting back and forth from Joni to the ground below.

Lana was pleading now, telling Joni this was crazy, this stuff only happens in the movies. She is promising not to print anything of what she has seen that involves Joni or the senator. She is crying now, begging Joni for mercy. The image shakes as Joni scoffs at this behavior and laughs it off. Suddenly Joni lunges at Lana. She has heard enough and just wants to dispose of this noise. She comes at Lana hard and fast but Lana surprises her by not being the frightened little girl she was pretending to be. The tears were fake. It was all an act. Lana still has some fight left in her. As Joni lunges at Lana, she ducks and then grabs at Joni to use her own force against her, using Joni's kinetic energy to propel her over the top of the balcony railing.

Joni does not see this coming but reacts quickly by grabbing Lana by both shoulders and holding on tight. As Joni begins to go over the edge Lana feels the tug of Joni's weight pulling down on her. Another battle of wills, and strength.

Lana tries to pull back against Joni's weight, even placing one foot quickly on one of the balcony's posts to gain leverage. Lana has grim determination in her eyes. Joni has only hate in her one good eye plus brute strength and the will to win at any *cost. Her fingers dig into Lana's arms, drawing blood and a scream of pain. Lana loses her concentration on her footing for only a second but it is enough to allow Joni's body weight to pull her forward to the edge of the balcony. Lana is losing her balance and her stance. She has already lost her advantage. Now over the side she goes. She grabs hold of the balcony railing, hanging on for dear life.*

Joni's attempts to save her own life by using Lana's body as a ladder is now working against them both. Lana suddenly finds herself without the use of her legs as Joni has wrapped herself completely around her body. Lana's clothing begins to tear and Joni begins to slide down with the fabric. Her hands quickly find purchase with Lana's bare skin. Joni's fingers rake along Lana's body leaving trails of blood as she slides further down her body until she has only her ankles to grasp. The full dead weight of Joni's body is now just an anchor pulling on her. Her arms are trembling terribly from the exertion on her muscles. Her mind tells her to just kick away at Joni but she has her arms locked around her ankles and will not *let go.*

Lana's grip on the railing is slipping. If she falls, Joni falls There is only one way for this to end. And then, just like that, the two women are in freefall.

Joni will hit the ground first.

THUMP!!

"What the hell was that?!"

Both men look into the room at Joni who is straining against her bonds but still strapped down. Bob on the other hand is now bloody and broken from the effects of falling five stories to the ground. The two men looked briefly at one another totally lost by what they were seeing.

Just then Bob's body rose up from the chair less than an inch but then drops down forcefully with another incredibly loud THUMP!!

"What is *happening*?!"

The two men look at the screens in sheer shock and terror as the scene they had just watched was being displayed once again.

THUMP!!

Bob just rose up and went down again. Blood is now seeping from every orifice of his body.

"Holy shit! It's *Joni*! *She's* doing this!" Everett exclaims.

"Doing *what*?!" Frank cried out helplessly.

"She's rewinding the tape in her brain and playing it over again. And she's putting the senator in Lana's place!"

THUMP!!

"*Oh my god, she's killing him!* KILL SWITCH! *Hit the kill switch!!!*"

Everett fumbles in his pocket for a quick second before he is able to get his hand on the fob with the kill switch. Although completely unnecessary he aims the kill switch AT the *Joni* robot before pressing down. The room goes silent and the screens are now blank.

The two men are still for a moment before Everett turns to Frank and says, "You have created a monster."

"No," replied Frank. "The monster was already there. I did something much, much, worse."

"What's that?"

Frank rubs his hands across his face before answering.

"I gave it a brain. I gave that monster a brain powered by *AI*."

Failsafe

Everett and Frank would go to their graves with the secret of Senator Bob McKinney's demise locked deep within. They were from that moment on changed men. They had seen the future. They had *experienced* the future. Great danger lay ahead. Some men might have turned back but these two forged ahead clear in their convictions that they had "learned something" along the way. Only time would tell if that was true. Both men would prosper as they now had a crystal-clear vision of how to make each business venture wildly successful. Neither required, nor wanted, government funding from that point on.

The *Joni* robot and the *Lana* robot were now stashed away in secure places within the FM Robotics company building. These were places accessible only to Frank and Everett. Both would visit the *Lana* robot from time to time but never the *Joni* robot. Sometimes they would go together. At other times alone. They went to pay their respects and to apologize for overstepping the boundaries of human choice.

When the two went together Everett would usually ask a series of completely unanswerable questions.

Will they stay like this forever? Will they grow older? Will they eventually die?

Their mechanical parts might take centuries to decay. With no overt exposure to air or moisture, maybe never. Frank had designed holding spaces for them both which would dramatically slow the aging process of their human parts yet still keep them alive. He did not share with Everett his concern regarding the "kill switch" but he was fairly certain that Everett knew already.

A switch is just a switch. A small and simple mechanical part.

And sometimes---, *switches fail.*

THE END?

There is the story of the most technically advanced aircraft of its time.
The design engineers state that it is best operated by a single pilot and a dog.
The pilot's responsibility is to feed the dog.
The dog is there to bite the hand of the pilot should he attempt to touch the controls.

People Farm

THE FUTURE IS BEHIND US NOW

"Philosophically, intellectually—in every way—human society is unprepared for the rise of artificial intelligence."
HENRY KISSINGER

UNNATURAL

PART ONE: THE BOOK OF HECTOR

"The intelligent machine is an evil genie, escaped from its bottle."
BRIAN HERBERT & KEVIN J. ANDERSON

Hector's capsule was the first to be discovered. The capsule landed in an open desolate area which caused it to tumble end over end for miles. There was but one tree in its path and it struck it solidly, in effect slowing and altering the momentum of the craft. When it finally came to rest, the capsule was situated in an area closest to the corrals of The Farm. The guards posted at the perimeter of The Farm had seen the object fall from the sky and then tumble ever closer towards them. There was no training for this kind of thing, no directive on what action to take if something like this were to occur. It was a foreign object. It was not of this time and perhaps not of this place. A mob mentality guided their actions. There were four of them and they rushed to the object with only one thought in mind. *Destroy it!*

The guards neither possessed nor carried weapons. Their security detail did not prescribe such as necessary. The hundreds of acres of land that made up The Farm was so remote that visitors were an anomaly. These four guards did not greet the capsule empty-handed though as each grabbed a formidably sized rock along the way. They stopped when they reached the object. Though they had run at full gait for three miles none were winded.

The guards surrounded the object then peered down through the translucent enclosure. Once the seal was broken the atmosphere inside the capsule would change and the enclosure cover would become transparent. There were mechanisms built into the system of the capsule that would engage and begin the process of atmospheric change. Those mechanisms were overridden by the guards as they began to assault the enclosure with the destructive elements they had picked up along the way, large rocks. The four guards pummeled the enclosure powerfully.

There was no letup in their assault until the enclosure allowed the merest hint of a crack. The translucent shell spider-webbed and then seconds later shattered. Millions of micro-pieces of the protective material rained down upon the inhabitant inside.

Once the shell had been compromised the four guards stopped immediately and each discarded their rocks. They now had a full view of the interior of the capsule. There was a solitary organism inside covered with a slowly receding gel-like substance. It became obvious that this organism was human although at this point unknown if it was man or woman.

The human was now within easy reach of the assaulting guards. Only the outer layer of the spacesuit separated the guards from the human. The guards scanned the full length of the protective spacesuit not knowing that it was both impermeable and impervious to all things natural.

A nervous twitch of the organism's finger caused the guards to hesitate no further. Each of them reached forcefully into the capsule and began to strip away the protective gear that had kept this human alive and safe. One guard quickly removed the human's helmet, seemingly unconcerned with whether or not this human was capable of breathing the air on this planet. There was an eagerness to knowing if this was male or female that overrode the safety of the moment. Now they knew. It was a man. Question answered. Move on.

Two of the guards, one on each side of the capsule, began removing the man's gloves. These actions were performed accurately and efficiently by guards who themselves wore no protective gear. They were unconcerned with the inherent danger of the diamond sharp edges of the aluminum/glass shell scattered about. Another guard focused on penetrating the side panel of the capsule where the life support systems were housed. The guard tugged at wires and pulled at circuit boards, each eventually giving way with a shower of sparks. There was no level of danger registered by the guard with these actions. There appeared to be only one objective and that was to disable the functionality of the craft.

Within seconds the guards had removed any possibility of survival for the man inside the capsule. The guards remained undeterred about loss of life as they now stepped back and away from the capsule. They stood immobile and silent, two per side, as the body of the single human inhabitant inside the capsule began to change. This capsule was a travel cocoon. The man secured inside had been in a suspended state of sleep for an extended but yet unknown period of time.

The guards watched without emotion at the now exposed face and hands of the man as the element of time snatched control away from the inherent safety of the science-laden cocoon. Within seconds the man began to age. His hair changed from black to gray and then to white. His skin began to wrinkle and pull tightly around his bones. His entire body appeared to sink lower into the enclosure as he was gradually losing body mass.

The body of the man then began to make strange popping and hissing noises as the cavities within released pockets of air. The bones making up the structure of the man began first to snap under the weight and then to dissolve into powder. Hair and fingernails continued to grow throughout the aging process unaware that their host had passed. The texture of the man's hair became wispy, a combination of straw and wire. The fingernails, as though attempting to escape their host, were now curling out and away from each of the fingers into a grotesque and demon-like tangle.

The face of the man showed the greatest effect of change as the skin sunk down into the skull and then the skull itself retreated as well. A putrid odor of the highest order was released from the body as it wasted away. None of the four guards gave any notice of distaste. Moments later there remained only a dark brownish-gray layer of powder extending out from the spacesuit in a simulated chalk outline of a man. The only change in the spacesuit itself was a slight discoloration and the eruptive release of several valves that had been under pressure during the journey.

If there was elation or satisfaction in what the four guards had caused they offered no sign of it. No celebration or sound came from any of them as they stood watching the man diminish from human to dust.

The travel cocoon had been equipped with an incredible array of computer-controlled mechanisms all of which were designed for the safety and security of the occupant inside. The cocoon itself was capable of surviving just about any predictable collision. An assault by four guard *robots* armed with rocks was not one of them. Each robot had the capacity to crush these rocks with their bare hands which was either an oxymoron or a contrast in terms. Maybe both.

The robot's claw-like *hands* were fashioned out of a metal alloy which in this marker of time on the planet had only the passing resemblance to a human hand. The similarities of robot to human had led to discord over time. These robots had *AI* which was still a developing technology. What the creators had dreamed was now a reality. This *AI* technology was now beginning to develop on its own. Although it had never been part of their original design the roots of such emotive feelings as *hate* and *prejudice* were coming to the forefront of the robots' *thinking*. Disdain for the human race in a growing number of robots was cause for great alarm and evident in the violent actions perpetrated upon the travel cocoon as well as their immediate reactive decision to *destroy* life.

On the outside of the travel cocoon, just under where the pilot's left arm had been positioned, still visible after the carnage, was a hand-painted name. This was not unlike what pilots of centuries ago had painted on the cockpit of their airplanes. The name, painted in cursive writing, was Hector *"Venezuela"* Mendez. This writing meant absolutely nothing to the guards. These were random symbols with no reference to anything in their world.

"Venezuela" was Hector's nickname. In life he had been gregarious and self-effacing. He had been well liked by his crew and could always be counted on when the going got tough to stand beside his friends. *Venezuela* had been a gifted mechanical engineer who brought with him a mind filled with design ideas that might have changed the history of this planet. What he had to offer to this world was now lost forever and would never be known.

George, who was *Venezuela's* closest friend and fellow crew member would probably have said, *'What has not and will not happen is of no consequence. It is only what does happen that matters in this world or any other world for that matter.'* George was living proof of that statement when his travel cocoon was to crash land near this same area some *fifty years* later. So much would have changed in that time. After this incident with Venezuela's capsule and the loss of his life, guard robots would have been reprogrammed to *recover*, not *destroy* humans that were found falling from the sky.

Had *Venezuela* survived rather than perished, he would have been taken by the guard robots to The Farm and placed in a corral. Whether survival in this world as a human farm animal was better than death upon arrival would be a recurring dilemma for George when he too would crash land onto this planet to be greeted by a host of robots who seemed to have taken ownership in the hierarchy of dominance.

There is on this planet far removed from where Venezuela's capsule has come to rest, three dilapidated buildings still standing in various states of ruin. Each has succumbed to years of exposure to the harsh elements of weather and time.

One of these fallen structures holds a secret deep inside. Two actually.

Secured within nearly impregnable "tombs" are two AI *beings unlike any other within the knowable universe. They are inactive and have been so for decades. The two beings could not be more* different *however they do share one critical factor. They are both still very much---* alive.

NATURAL ORDER

PART TWO: THE BOOK OF GEORGE

"I visualize a time when we will be to robots what dogs are to humans..."
CLAUDE SHANNON

George's capsule was the second travel cocoon to be discovered but the first of the four to be preserved. It was buried in a mountain of rubble, superheated and still smoking when the robots showed up. As the capsule had raced through the night sky its progress had been slowed by skipping on the planet's atmospheric surface. A green cast to the tail of the flame coming from the expending heat of the exterior is what had initially caught the eye of the guard robots. They followed the arc of the object as it descended ever closer to the planet's surface. The impact of the tallest trees on the planet to a great extent broke the fall of the object with each successive contact snapping away a few of the lofty upper branches. In its final approach the capsule was slowed even further by rolling along the soft and porous countryside muddied recently by a rash of torrential rains. An abrupt collision with a collection of massive fallen rocks had brought the capsule to rest.

This capsule had entered the planet's atmosphere at a much sharper rake than the first which caused the superheating of the vessel. Even with a liberal dousing of flame-retardant and cooling fluids the sun was starting to make its appearance over the horizon by the time that the guard robots could begin to inspect the capsule up close. The markings on the exterior were foreign to them. These would later be identified by a research robot which had access to both astrological and historical records that determined such things. What was of most interest to the guard robots was what mystery was being held inside the capsule. That curiosity would have to wait as they were not permitted to proceed any further in their exploration. The thought of using rocks to crack open the capsule was *not* an authorized possibility. A team of science robots had been dispatched. Upon arrival they would *safely* crack the seal of the object and attempt to recover and then later study the living organism strapped protectively inside.

It had been fifty years since the discovery of the capsule containing Hector *"Venezuela"* Mendez. Fifty years is more than half the average life span of a human but only a momentary flash in the evolution of technology. The robots that surrounded this capsule were the result of a constant reimagining of the machine itself. New alloys had been developed. Connecting assemblies had been strengthened, the abilities of the robots had been improved and artificial intelligence had continued to evolve and expand. With expanded *AI* came implanted directives to enhance and enforce robot engagement and interaction. Yet with all of the improvements and enhanced abilities *there was a ghost in the machine* even now going undetected by all except possibly the governing presence of *Oss*.

Science robots were now standing in the spots previously held by the guard robots. The translucent aluminum/glass shell had in gradients slowly become transparent so it had not yet been removed. The science robots hovered about now peering down into the capsule. The organism inside was covered in a gel-like substance making it not instantly recognizable. There was an array of electronic gadgetry set outside and just below the shell on one side of the capsule which it was determined was there for the control of the operating functions of the travel cocoon. This cocoon was designed with the capability to slow the aging process of the inhabitant by nearly one-hundred times of what was normal. In short order the science robots would be able to deduce how long this organism had been in this travel cocoon and if it could be safely revived.

One of the science robots accessed the terminal port thereby gaining entry to the data banks of the operating system of the capsule. Within the span of seconds the science robots had gathered all necessary data required to switch the cocoon from its current slumber mode to the slow and methodical reawakening process. As this process began the gel started to recede and the temperature inside the chamber of the cocoon began to rise. First there was vapor clouding the interior and then that dissipated into condensation and the living organism inside was once again visible. Just then the solid black visor of the helmet retracted and the face of the organism was exposed.

The sight of the face was met with equal amounts of surprise and consternation. This organism was *human*. And while there was certainly much to learn from this specimen there was an element of risk as well. Although not exercised, there was a shared consideration amongst the science bots that for the good of the robot community this thing could just be terminated on the spot. Fifty years ago it is exactly what the guard robots would have done. *Had there been no progress in all that time?* came the unspoken question. Foremost in the programming of these science robots was the quest for knowledge of all living organisms throughout the known universe. This program element stayed their hands and in effect changed...

EVERYTHING.

The Farm

George, still in extended sleep mode, was recovered and then taken to the Farm.

The Farm was massive, so large that it could be seen from space. That may have accounted for why the travel cocoons came crashing down in such proximity. It certainly must have displayed as a thermal target to the tracking computers onboard the travel cocoon primitive as they may be. Initially programmed to seek out populated areas the trackers for some reason had skipped over major cities. George would be the first of his group to learn *why*.

The Farm had grown exponentially over the years as robots continued to discover pockets of humans in the most unlikely places on the planet. It was their will to live that kept these humans alive in the most inhabitable of conditions. As each small village of humans was located so followed a mass scramble of these humans to elude capture from the invading robots. The humans feared death but the robots were not there to kill. Their larger function was recovery. Unfortunately, a number of the humans that were brought to the Farm arrived either dead or dying as a result of the recovery methods. With each village recovery there followed a revision upload from *Oss* to refine the recovery methods used by the robots in an effort to increase the yield of survivors. Dead humans were of limited scientific value to the science and research robots so their bodies would simply be ground up and repurposed as food for the living.

The Farm was a project governed by *Oss* which was not unusual as *all* things were governed by *Oss,* including the activities of *all* robots. Well, *almost* all. There remained a contingent of robots outside of this group that seemed to be guided by other directives, perhaps by those of *the ghost in the machine*.

The robots at the Farm had interactive tasks to perform. Some were guard robots, some were science robots, and a random few were research robots but most were simply *herding* robots. The herding robots had the task of moving the humans about, from their corrals to their respective planting or harvest fields and back. These daily tasks were designated by the science robots.

All robots, regardless of function, shared a specific time of day when they were required to be present at an immense circular structure known by the science and research robots as *Rotunda.* While there they must submit to a period of down-time. The time spent there was for robots to have what was to be a *physical* interaction with *Oss*. The action required of all robots was to plug into one of the thousands of available ports suspended from the cavernous ceiling intended for both charging and for the downloading of data pertinent to their daily rituals. Possibly to maximize the potential output for the humans, the down-time for robots at *Rotunda* was timed by *Oss* to be in synch with that of the humans.

During this downtime, all robots were to be at rest and inactive. There could be nothing kept secret or hidden from *Oss*. *All* information was to be shared by *all* robots when plugged into their ports at *Rotunda*. There was, however, a *ghost in the machine* that threatened all robots. *Oss* had detected this but had as yet been *unable* to locate its source.

The Farm was comprised of eight distinct quadrants, referred to as *communities* where the humans lived and worked. All humans were kept in corrals, some alone and others as couples or families. Grouping humans with their offspring had been recently adopted as a measure to ensure that the human population would continue to grow and to lessen dissension. Lesson learned for the robots that when these infant humans were first born they arrived as fragile beings ill-equipped for survival in this world. Even during the first few years of their life cycle these young humans seemed to be incapable of protecting and providing for themselves. Countless deaths occurred before the science robots understood the need for groupings.

Throughout their workday the humans were studied by science robots, actively recording all actions, all discourse, all body language and emotion. Even at night robots were prevalent throughout the communities to watch and record all functions at all times. The consideration of privacy did not exist. The humans at the Farm were under the watchful view of robots at all times including when they were relieving themselves of food waste.

Copulation was considered a necessary observable function and was regulated by the science robots. The social institution of husband and wife was enforced to the extent that it served the purposes of scientific study. Copulation was not specific to the couple as that was not perceived as yielding the best possible outcome of offspring. Guard robots were sent to the corrals periodically to assist a herding robot in moving a male human to the corral of a female human for coupling. The respective husbands and/or wives were expected to attend to other matters while the act was being performed. Any sign of emotion relative to these situations was not determined to be of any significant scientific value so it was simply ignored. Although it was beyond the comprehension of the *AI* of all but a few robots, the Farm was more than just a farm to breed and raise humans. It had become *essential* to the wellbeing of the entire robot population.

Upon his arrival at the Farm, George was placed in an outlying corral under the vigilant watch of two guard robots. He was given the bare minimum of necessities. The corral to which he was assigned was the same as all others being no more than a gated area of land. The primary difference for his corral was that it was set far apart from the other communities. George was of course unaware that a directive had been given that there was to be no interaction for him with other humans for several weeks. As far as he knew, and over time come to believe, there *were* no other humans on this planet. While it defied all logic that he might have crash-landed on a planet other than Earth that looked this familiar and also had breathable air with the only defining difference being that it was inhabited by robots, this thought would soon fight to make sense in his mind as the alternative seemed too horrific to accept.

There was one other primary difference between George's corral and the others which he would come to know in time. The difference was that his corral had as yet no alterations. What the robots would frequently view as a spectacle with what might be considered fascination was that so many of the humans had taken it upon themselves to make *constructions* within their corrals. They fashioned rudimentary roofing to protect themselves from the sun and hide themselves from the rain. Most of the humans appeared to be stupid but some were surprisingly productive and resourceful. These few also made makeshift rectangular bunks on which to lay their bodies during their own down-time. There was trading amongst the humans so that those who were unable to make constructions could purchase those from the humans that could.

George was still in recovery mode from his extended sleep in the travel cocoon. It would take several weeks for him to be fully back to normal. His body needed time to reactivate muscle tissue to the needs of bearing and moving the weight of his limbs. His brain needed time to sort out why there had been inactivity for such an extended period of time before moving on to associative responses of the here and now.

Being placed in a corral and exposed to the elements of weather was not conducive to a rapid recovery for George. Although protected from the threat of predatory animals by the presence of the guard robots, George was fully at the mercy of both the heat of the day and the cold of the night, not to mention wind and rain. He was afforded the clothing and the wrap blankets that had been in his travel cocoon but these were a far cry from a solid roof over his head. Until he had fully recovered and his risk of bacterial contamination to the population of the communities had been determined to be negligible he would remain alone.

George slept day and night, the same as he had in his travel cocoon, with the key difference being that now his body was living in *real time*. His body was now in daily need of exercise and essential nutrients to stave off the inevitable effects of aging and inactivity. A lone robot, dissimilar to all others, seemed to understand these needs and know how to administer the medicinal vials that had accompanied George in his travel cocoon. These vials contained life sustaining vitamins and proteins. This lone robot made these visits only during the downtime of the other robots which in itself violated all norms of the robot world.

Even with the exposure to the elements working against him, George's recovery was better than could have been expected. This was due in part perhaps to his physical attributes prior to entering the travel cocoon. He was an imposing figure of a man both in stature and in girth. Although affable and engaging, in his previous life his powerful presence caused most people to keep their distance. But that was only true in the human world of his past. Here at the Farm, George would need to learn a new pecking order as the herding robots and the guard robots had no concern for his size *or* his strength. Any aggressive action on his part would be put down equally if not harsher by actions of their own. Although George would soon be taking the brunt of their reactions without outcry he would certainly feel the full measure of pain in their strikes. He was a proud man and his refusal to accept his current situation would cost him comfort as each new day brought fresh new bruises.

In addition to guard robots and herding robots, there was also the presence of science robots who dutifully monitored George's daily activities. Initially he would be allowed out of his corral for only a few hours each day to exercise and explore but each passing day brought more freedom to roam. Not that it really mattered though as there was nowhere to go and as far as he would know, no other humans with whom he could interact.

The Awakening

When George's eyes fluttered open for the first time in decades he awoke to a dream. There was no other way for him to describe it or to process what he was seeing. Knowing that he had been in extended sleep his brain fought to find reason in what he was seeing and what was happening around him. There were men standing about, staring down at him but something was *wrong*. Something was *amiss*. George's brain waded through the fog of sleep to find answers. The men that were staring down at him, that was the first problem. How can they stare when they have no *eyes*? Worse yet, they don't even have *faces!*

The effects of extended sleep were different for everyone. That's what they had been told during their training. For George it must be seeing people without faces, which of course explained why they also weren't speaking. George was still so very, *very* tired. He decided to allow himself to succumb to sleep once more but something *(something!)* was still nagging away at his brain like a dog pulling on a toy that just wouldn't let go. George wanted sleep but his brain kept pulling and tugging. His brain wanted the answers that was that toy.

Sleep. Toy!

Sleep. Toy!

Sleep! Toy!!!

And then finally *sleep* began to win.

Just as George was sinking into the blissful pool of sleep, the toy plopped into the water near him and then began to descend into the depths. He caught sight of it as it went deeper, growing ever smaller. Sleep took possession of George as his brain registered the missing piece. Not only did those men not have *faces*, they also did not have *necks*. Only a thin transparent stalk with wires running through it seemed to keep their heads attached to their bodies.

George slept fitfully for another three days after that.

George awoke to quiet. He assumed it was nighttime but the sun stung his eyes when he tried to open them. He sensed movement all around him but there was no noise to accompany the actions. George was a former resident of a bustling city. For him, this silence was deafening.

Sleep took him once again.

George woke at night to what he was certain were night sounds. Unless he was *imagining* them. He was cold but there was a blanket nearby that he was able to pull around him. The warmth was comforting. He was thirsty and his lips were dry. Although his sleep encrusted eyes made it difficult to see he had the aid of a full moon to silhouette a flask of water within his reach. George guzzled the water until it was gone. He had no idea where to go should he need to *"go."* It didn't matter. He fell asleep once more. When he awoke the next morning his body sought to find its original cycle in synch with the sun and the moon.

This was the first indication that George was returning to life.

Upon his final awakening from decades of extended sleep George would find himself in what could only be described as a corral fit for a farm animal. This corral was perhaps one-hundred square feet in size and was situated on dry ground, on what was possibly a former wheat field. Although there was no bedding George was able to form a sleeping area for himself that was tolerable if not particularly comfortable. Outside of the corral was not much different, all open space, rolling hills and groves of trees in the distance. He was uncertain if this planet had seasons but if it did, fortunately he seemed to have landed here in the early part of summer.

During his first few weeks, George spent his free time at first walking and then running, climbing and exercising in an effort to regain his strength. Food was provided to him in his corral but once given the opportunity to venture outside of his corral, George attempted to forage for himself. There was a cost to this however as there seemed to be a cost to *every* activity. It was interaction with the guard robots that proved to be harmful. Even though the guard robots were unarmed they had capabilities well beyond that of a human. They were faster and stronger than a human and seemed to be impervious to anything that a human, or the planet for that matter, could throw at them.

Escape was futile. And while George had no illusions of overpowering the robots although his desire for escape from the Farm was always in the forefront of his mind. There was a mountain range on the horizon which offered him the possibility of sanctuary on the other side. In his former life George was a civil engineer. When not engaged in physical activity George's mind was constantly putting his education to practical use by actively considering avenues of escape. He accepted the reality of his situation but refused to give up. Then one day a robot of a higher order arrived on the scene to study and interact with George, which gave him a new sense of hope. George would learn later that this particular robot was responsible for nursing him back to health. This was the lone robot that had administered the contents of the vials which had kept him alive. The question was, should he thank him? *Or curse him?* This robot visited daily and watched George from a distance for several weeks.

George had learned early on that he was living now in what he deemed to be a *"quiet world."* No sound came from the robots as they interacted. George could only assume that some type of wireless communication must be at play. There was no mouthpiece on what could loosely be considered their *face* but George had tried in vain anyway to encourage them to speak.

This new robot, so different from the others, actually had what appeared to be a mouthpiece. This gave George the encouragement to try to speak to it so he tried. Nothing. He tried again. Still nothing. He tried again and again but it was pointless. For weeks, the new robot appeared to ignore all of George's attempts to engage him one on one.

Then one morning, out of the blue, George was sleeping when he thought he heard-- his name.

In *English*.

Surely he must be dreaming so he drifted back to sleep. While sleeping he dreamed that he heard two words whispered into his ear.

"For you."

George sat up in his makeshift cot and looked around, his eyes still crusted with sleep. There was no one about but-- those words had sounded *so real*. Maybe it was just because he wanted so badly to interact with another--. He wanted to say *person* but he was willing to go with *being,* whether it be alive or robotic.

As he started to lay back down, dejected that he must certainly be wrong about the voice, he felt something jabbing him in his side. He looked to see what it was and to his surprise it was his journal. George looked around again and still saw no other being in sight. He clutched the journal to his chest. This was *special*. This was *precious*. If he were to have no interaction with any other being at least now he could converse with himself. He could put his thoughts down on paper not only for himself but also in the hopes that someday one of his fellow crew members might find it and know his fate.

As George leafed through the pages that had already been written upon he wondered how his journal came to be back in his possession. It must have been recovered from his travel cocoon but by *whom*? And why hadn't they made himself or herself known? Or could it have been left by a robot? That was more likely but less desirable. He might never know the answers to his many questions if that were the case.

The Good Doctor

"George."

It was a whisper. George heard it clearly. He was awake now and swore that it was real.

"George."

There it was again but this time less of a whisper and more of a soft voice. George stood up and looked around. There was a small lean-to made of rough boards that served as George's private space. Standing next to it was the lone robot that had tended to him since his arrival. The lone robot who had the makings of a face. The lone robot that seemed to come and go as it pleased unconcerned with the demands of the workings of the Farm. George stared at the robot for a moment and then said, "Did you just--?"

The robot looked back at George without expression as he had none to offer. His face was the rudimentary fundamentals of a face. There were *examples* of what a nose and mouth should look like on his face but simply glassy marble like orbs where the windows to the soul should be.

"Hello George. Can we be friends?"

George was...

Surprised. Amazed. Overwhelmed. He had believed these robots to be mute. In all the time that he had spent here he had heard no sound from *ANY* of them. *EVER*. His best guess was that he had been imprisoned in this pen for several months. George at first had difficulty forming words after such a long period of silence. His mouth was dry so he reached for his water flask to slake his thirst. He was not the nervous type so he was quite surprised at the sight of his own hand shaking so terribly as he brought the flask to his mouth. He had to admit to himself that although he was to be the only human to bear witness, this *was* a momentous occasion.

Man speaking with *robot*.

Had it already happened before now?

George did not know. He could only assume it had not.

"Is there a problem George?"

George was shocked. "You, you know my *name?!*"

The robot took a few steps closer but still speaking in a low tone. "Yes. Of course. It is stitched on your clothing and painted quite ceremoniously on your travel cocoon." The robot's diction was impeccable. Although George had lived in many places in the country he was truly a Southern boy, born and raised in the Carolinas. Was he detecting a slight Southern drawl in the speech of this robot? Was that *possible?* A better question considering the advent of *AI*, was that *intentional?*

George looked down at his shirt and grunted an affirmation regarding his name on the shirt. With that thought discarded he returned his attention to the robot. It was a bizarre scenario, this interaction with a robot. Sure the robot had a mouthpiece but it wasn't functional. It was a *display*, like the sound bars on a stereo receiver from his past. His brain did the math for him and gave the robot credit for speaking from the *direction* of its mouth but at best it was *only* a speaker. This robot did not have a throat. Or lungs for that matter. He *barely* had a *neck*. It was more of a stem with a myriad of connecting wires.

George took several large gulps of water and then cleared his throat. Before he could speak, the robot standing in front of him asked, "Would you prefer that I refer to you as *'Kennedy'*?"

George did a doubletake when he heard that.

The robot looked at him oddly as George laughed and said, "Uh, no, that is just a nickname."

"A *'Nick'* name? I'm sorry, I do not understand. Shall I refer to you then as *Nick*?"

"No, no," George chuckled. This was like speaking to a child. "No, it is just a name that you use for fun." George had now regained his voice. "It's like if you're tall, they call you *'Stretch'* or if you have red hair, they call you *'Red,'* that sort of thing. Does that make sense? Are those examples helpful?" This interaction was so strange because it already seemed so normal.

"To some degree, yes. Why are you *'Kennedy'*? I do not find a correlation. This name is not on your shirt yet it is on your travel cocoon."

"Oh that," George laughed in a friendly way. "My buddy James started calling me *'Kennedy'* because of my likeness to a famous actor whose name was also George. *'George Kennedy.'* I guess I bear a likeness to the guy so it only makes sense, right? Everything in James' world corelates somehow to a movie he has seen." George chuckled at that thought but then suddenly became very quiet as he was concerned that he may have said too much.

"I do not know of this *'George Kennedy'* or of *'movie.'* I shall presume that you speak the truth. I am aware of those that take the name of another." Although it was clearly impossible George was certain that he *saw*, perhaps *sensed* was a better word, a troubled look pass over the robot's face at the mention of one taking the name of another. It passed quickly and then the robot said, "You are fortunate that I *too* am a Doctor." George completely missed the inference that there was another.

"You are a *Doctor?!*" George appeared to be truly surprised. "Damn, a *robot* doctor! That's something!"

"Yes. It is-- something."

Was it possible for a robot to be proud? If so then this doctor robot seemed to be full of it at that moment. The robot and George continued to talk for several minutes before the robot suddenly went silent. Two other robots were approaching George's corral. These were simple herding robots dispatched to direct him to his chores but still George found it odd that the doctor robot should go suddenly silent and show concern for their presence.

Later in the day when the doctor robot and George were once again alone, the robot explained to George that it was ill-advised for him to speak around other robots. He could not explain why but he somehow knew this to be true. His only reference point that he could allude to was that he did not want to be sent to the place of the *'banging noises.'* George was unable to make any sense of that comment and the doctor robot would not explain further. This *'banging noises'* place was left as a mystery. For now.

Over the course of several weeks George added numerous journal entries. He wrote about the Farm and the weather. He wrote about the daily routine of being herded by robots to and from the place where he would do his chores. Mostly he wrote about the robots, and more specifically about the doctor robot. What had been accomplished in robotics George found to be truly amazing.

The doctor robot seemed to be one of a kind. George asked him one day if he had a name. His response was cryptic. 'I am a robot.' When George pressed further the response was less cryptic but still a bit evasive. 'I can share my model number if you wish but it is not a name although some might take it as such.' When asked what that comment meant the doctor robot refused to reply. There was obviously something there that he did not wish to share. It was an uncomfortable discussion so George let it go and there was no mention of it for several days. It was the doctor robot that eventually broke the silence.

A New Perspective

"Might we go for a walk? I wish to show you something."

"Okay," said George. "Is it far?"

"For you, yes. Bring water. *Lots* of water. We are going to the rock outcropping that you can just see in the distance when the sky is clear."

"Oh yes, I have wondered about that. Great view from there I would imagine. Finally I get to see the world!" George grabbed his water flask and began to follow the doctor robot out of his corral. The robot stopped him and pointed to a large bag with a shoulder strap. "Fill that with water and I shall carry it."

"I can manage," George fired back.

"It is a long way for you. Your stubbornness will make the journey longer. The weight of the water will seem to grow heavier the longer that you carry it and then you will become fatigued. It is more expedient if I carry the water."

There was no look of superiority on the face of the robot. How could there be? This was no act of one-upmanship. This was simple logic. George understood this and handed the heavy water bag to the robot who handled it like it was nothing. Then they left.

Along the way George struck up a conversation with the doctor robot. What was shared with him came as a complete surprise.

"So tell me," George asked. "How long have you been, um, *aware*? Is that the right term?"

"It will suffice. My designer was correct. He told me that you would ask good questions."

"*What?!* How would he have known *me*? What are you saying, exactly?"

"I am saying that we have much in common, you and I."

"I don't see how that is possible."

"Would you like for me to explain?"

"Please do. I have nothing to do. For a while I am guessing." George cast his arm out to the wide open plain that they had yet to cross to get to their destination.

The doctor robot did not recognize the sarcasm of the phrase 'nothing to do' and began to correct George. He would say that George had to keep moving forward in their travel and to continue to take water to avoid dehydration and that *was* something to do. George cut him off in midsentence to explain to him that his comment was merely *an expression* and not to be taken seriously. Of course then George had to explain to the robot why an *expression* is not necessarily the same thing as a *joke*. This back-and-forth lead to George becoming aggravated and demanding that the doctor robot skip the commentary and return to the original comment about the two of them having something in common.

"Please forgive me. I have had no formal instruction in English. It is a difficult language to master because it is basically a collection of words borrowed from other languages, many mispronounced and many with spelling changes or errors—"

"Just tell me already!" George tried to calm his voice for the last part of his comment. "About the 'stuff in common thing'." George was already hot and tired from this trip. He needed something to keep him motivated and he was hoping that what the doctor robot had to share would do the trick.

If the doctor robot was offended by George's interruption there was no notice of it as he delivered a bombshell, "You and I are the same age."

"Yeah right, how is *that* possible? I can tell you that no robot with your advanced abilities was around when *I* walked the Earth." George paused for a moment and then added, "At least none that I was aware of."

"No more than two weeks after your mission was launched is when I became aware so perhaps that makes *you* the older brother. I made a joke?"

"Two weeks *after* the mission? Two *weeks*--? *How*--?" George didn't finish his question. He really wasn't sure *how* to finish the question.

"I made a joke?" The doctor robot wasn't giving up with his question.

"What? Oh yeah, you made a joke. Good one." George was still troubled by the timeline of such an advanced robot which seemed to be light years ahead of the technology he was familiar with at the time. Given the circumstances of extended sleep it seemed like only a short time ago but he knew that it was nearly a lifetime.

"We have a mutual acquaintance." More surprises from the doctor robot.

"We *do*? And how is *that* possible??"

"He designed me."

"Is that so?"

"Yes."

"Okay, well sorry but I don't see the connection."

"He is also responsible for your mission. His name was Frank. He called me his friend."

George took this in stride hoping that the doctor robot would get to the part where something, *anything*, would be of interest to him. And then his brain processed what the robot had just said and George stopped cold.

"Frank. *Wait!* His name was *Frank?* Do you mean Frank *Morgan*?"

"Yes. Frank Morgan. He was an advanced level engineer with a very fancy title. *Your* mission was *his* idea. He called it his *'baby'* although I still do not understand why. Do you know?"

George was standing with his mouth open and rubbing his forehead with a look of perplexity on his face that spoke volumes. There was an answer to all things and the answer was usually a simple one. In some cases a bizarre one. This was surely one of those instances where it was both.

"Do you know? Why Frank thought of your mission as an infant?" The doctor robot was, like he frequently did, pressing for an answer.

"What?" George asked. He was a million miles away with his thoughts and did not want to be bothered with such trivial questions but he knew that answering the doctor robot's question would be the most expedient way for him to be allowed time to consider the scope of what had just been shared. "The *'baby'* thing is *also* just *an expression*. It is a *metaphor* if you know what that means."

"Yes I do. I am familiar with a metaphor being used as a figure of speech for rhetorical effect where one directly refers to one thing by mentioning another which actually for me helps to explain many things. A metaphor as you must know is often compared with other types of figurative language such as antithesis, hyperbole, metonymy, and simile."

"I---" George's voice trailed away as he realized that he was out of his depth. "Let's keep going, shall we?" George had a million questions for the doctor robot now that the connection had been made with his past. Frank Morgan was his friend, his mentor and the architect of his failed mission. Not to mention the designer of an advanced robot with, was it possible? *AI capabilities of this magnitude*?!

The journey took nearly two hours. When they finally arrived at the base of the rock outcropping George was winded, tired and thirsty. He was also extremely thankful that the doctor robot had interceded by encouraging the use of the water bag and then offering to accept it as his burden.

"I need to rest," said George, craning his neck to look up at the rock outcropping that they still needed to climb.

"We will rest," replied the doctor robot who appeared to not have expended any energy during the trip.

After about ten minutes of just relaxing and listening to the whistling wind, George looked up at the doctor robot standing nearby. "I have decided that I want to do something." George stated. "For you," he added.

"What is that?" asked the doctor robot.

"I have decided to give you a name. Really more of a nickname but a name all the same. How does that sound?"

"I am a robot. I have no use of a name."

"Yeah? Well, I think you do, especially if we are to be friends. Friends speak to each other using their names."

"Are you saying that I am your friend?" It was impossible for emotion to show on the robot's face but George saw it there regardless.

"Yes. Yes, I guess I am. As there are no humans to be found in this Godforsaken place then you will have to do." George paused and then said, "No offense."

The doctor robot looked up to the rock outcropping. Had he been human George would have believed him to be in deep thought. Which he was. The doctor robot was questioning if he should share with George what they might see when they mounted the rock or take the name being offered and save what he must share with George for another time. This was the first time that the doctor robot had experienced the human emotion that was known as 'selfishness.' It felt wrong but he accepted it regardless. He chose his *own* gratification.

"What is my name to be then?"

George smiled and said, "First things first. You need to understand that a name has to *mean* something, something other than just being a name. I noticed something about you that is unique. In other words, particular only to you. Are you following me?"

The doctor robot did not wish to detract George from his discourse by commenting that they were not currently moving so he could not be *following* him anywhere. Then he determined that that *too* must be an expression so he simply said yes. George nodded and continued, "So I look at you and I ask myself, what makes this robot unique, right?"

Right? What did *that* mean? English was hard. The doctor robot agreed by nodding. Also, he neglected to share with George that he was one of a kind, designed and built by one of the preeminent minds in robotics of his time. However, once again he did not wish to distract George from his eagerness to share the name he had chosen for his new friend. The doctor robot remained standing and said nothing.

George pointed at the doctor robot and said, "Tell me about those scratches there just below your shoulder plate."

The doctor robot looked down at his chest. If he were human his eyes might have become cloudy and perhaps a tear would follow at the recollection of how the scratches came to be. The doctor robot looked at

George and posed a question, "Could it be that you give me my name first? And then I will tell you about the origin of these injuries."

George was taken aback by this request but chose to honor it. He was now quite curious about the scratches especially since the doctor robot had characterized them as *injuries*.

"Until I know the story," George began, "I am calling them scratches. And what those scratches look like to me is that they make an *"X"* where they intersect. So I think to myself, you are a doctor and there is an *"X"* on your chest right there where a crest might be. When you think of doctor you think of that *"Rx"* symbol which is used when writing a prescription, right? That *"X"* confirms to me that you *are* a doctor so your name from now on is *'Doctor X'*."

The doctor robot is standing still and not reacting.

"So what do you think?" George asked. "I know it sounds cartoony but I think it fits. You good with it?"

"Yes. Yes, I am *good* with it. I now have a name. I am Doctor X."

"There you go! You have a name. Dr. X. Alright now, a deal's a deal. Tell me about how you got those scratches."

"I will tell you when we have reached the top of this rock outcropping. There is a correlation to these injuries and to what I wish to show you when we summit."

There was that word again, *injuries*. George had no reason not to agree to the robot's terms so he waved the robot on and fell in behind him. There was a path to follow that while steep was quite navigable. George was panting by the time they reached the top, sucking down air as fast as possible. He bent over for a few minutes to allow himself to catch his breath and regain his composure. The journey up had been too arduous for him to enjoy the view so it wasn't until this moment when he finally looked about him. The view was simply breathtaking.

"If my buddy James were here he would tell you that this reminded him of a movie he's seen!" George blurted out with a laugh.

Possibly because of all that had happened to George since he had crash landed on this planet he had forgotten how to appreciate the wonder of nature. That all came flooding back to him as he took in the panoramic vista laid out before him. The robot doctor touched him on the shoulder just then and handed him what appeared to be a clear glass panel about the size of a notebook.

"Here, use this." George held the glass panel in front of his eyes and was absolutely astounded. The magnification this glass panel provided was incredible. He could see for miles. He could see what looked like prairie lands stretching outward to greet the horizon. He could see the sun glinting off of a great body of water in the distance with a mountain range as a backdrop. He could see a small contingent of what he took to be wild animals grazing on the plains. He could see the wind moving through the trees in another direction. This was where his travel cocoon had finally settled. There were large rocks tumbled about in that area as well. George could see all of this and it was magnificent.

The wonder of it all was lost in seconds however when he saw -- The Farm.

And then he saw what the Farm had been hiding from him all this time.

George whirled around to face the doctor robot. He pointed to the east as he yelled, "Doctor! What am I seeing there?! Is that what I *think* I see?! We both know it is so why the hell haven't you *told me?!*"

The doctor robot waited for George to calm himself down before he spoke. "I did not think that you were ready. What you think you see is only what you *want* to see. The truth will be quite troubling to you. Before you ask, yes of course you will be able to go there when we return but you should prepare yourself for an unfortunate truth. It is something that you will need to see for yourself."

George looked from the Farm in the distance to the doctor robot and then back again. "What I see is a *farm* with what appears to be *humans* being kept as *animals*! Are you saying that I am wrong about that?"

"I am saying that you need to see for yourself upon our return and then draw your own conclusions. George, this may surprise you but that is *not* what I have brought you up here to see."

"Its's *not?!*" George is truly surprised by this revelation. "What *else* could there be?"

The doctor robot had not brought George to the pinnacle of this rock outcropping for a better perspective of the Farm. His purpose on this journey was to educate him about something which was of greater concern and should be his biggest fear. Before the doctor robot could direct George's attention in that direction something else turned his head.

It was a barrage of noises coming from the plains in the distance. *Banging noises*. Like metal on metal. This was wide open country with steady winds allowing sounds to travel great distances so it was difficult to determine how near or far those sounds might be.

"What is that?!" George asked, pointing in the direction of the banging noises.

Another cryptic reply from the doctor robot. "Isolation."

"What?!"

The doctor robot did not reply and George could find no explanation for the noises. For now they were to be just another piece of the puzzle of this planet that George had yet to solve.

The doctor robot cradled his hand gently on the back of George's head near his neck, moving his wrist slightly in effect turning George's head in a different direction. George was now facing in the direction of where the doctor robot wanted George to look. The doctor robot pointed to something far in the distance. It was much further away than the Farm but as his eyes adjusted so did the glass panel. It was somehow intuitive to the viewer. George was now able to make out what looked at first to be just a farmhouse before he realized that it was more of a military style encampment. Although only a fraction of the size of the Farm it looked to be of far better construction. At this point it was unclear to George if he should take this as good news or bad.

George's first question was obvious. "Are there people *there* too?!"

The doctor robot's answer was chilling. "I hope not."

George would soon learn why that was so.

The doctor robot reached out to George and touched his chin turning his head once again. This time he wanted George's attention to be focused solely on him.

"George, what I share with you now is of extreme importance to you," the doctor robot paused then pointed towards the humans at the Farm and added, "and to them."

George comported himself and replied, "Go on."

"Allow me to begin by saying this. There are two factions of robots on this planet. There are those which are allegiant to *Oss*, of which I may be counted in that group. And there are those that are members of *The Union*." The doctor robot motioned in the direction of the farmhouse encampment without realizing he had done it. *AI* at work.

"*Oss* are the good guys, right?" George asked with a chuckle.

"I do not know about 'good guys' but I can tell you that *Oss* is more favorable to humans than is *The Union*. These injuries—" (there it was again), "are the product of a meeting with a member of *The Union*. The self-proclaimed leader actually."

"Really? How and why did he scratch you?" George's attention was drawn to the scratches again, examining them now with a more critical eye. They were actually quite deep. George saw them differently now as he thought they looked more like what a tiger's strike might do to the flesh.

"George, you have no idea of the force needed to create what you refer to as simply *'scratches.'* Consider this. My *'exoshell'* is comprised of materials which are *far more* resilient than that of your travel cocoon."

George's mouth dropped open with that comment. He understood *fully* what that meant. And it was terrifying to consider.

"George, you must learn what there is to know of *The Union*. They are what you would call *dangerous*. For the most part they do not interfere with the workings of the Farm unless—"

"Unless?" George queried.

"Unless something is of interest to them."

"I see," said George. "Which of course leads me to the next question. *Is* there something of interest to them at *the Farm* as you call it?"

"Yes. Yes there is."

"Okay. And what is that?"

The doctor robot did not hesitate. "You."

This was the reply that George had expected so he was not surprised. He was, however, concerned. "If that is true then *why* would you bring me here?! If *their* interest is in *me*, why would you put me in a spot where I might be *noticed?* I understand that we are a good distance from them but if any of them happen to look this way they will certainly have cause to wonder what, *or who*, might be on this rock outcropping looking in *their* direction. These are robots we are talking about, correct? No human could have done that to you." George pointed at the scratches that he now understood were deep cuts. "I think you must know that *I* would not survive *that*."

"George, I have no desire to place you in harm's way but how else could I describe to you what you must know? It would be foolish to think that they do not *already* know of you. The question that we should be asking is *why* have they not yet visited? What are they waiting for? The more time that expires before their arrival the greater concern I have for your safety. You must know that only *Oss* can protect you from The *Union*."

"Perhaps we should leave while we can."

"Yes but first I must be completely honest with you."

"Does that mean that you have not?" George looked the doctor dead in his eye... display.

"It is just an expression," the good doctor said with no apparent inflection in his voice. George had to laugh at that, which helped to calm the mood. The doctor robot continued. "I brought you up here to see what you must see which is true but I also brought you up here for *them* to see *you*. The *Union* monitors everything within their reach. We must *prompt* a visit from them as it has been too long in coming. And *you* must be ready."

"Well, all I can say is thank you for throwing me to the wolves. And here I thought we were friends."

The doctor robot at first had no understanding of how to process George's sarcasm so it went without a reply. And then with more thought he replied, "Sharks."

"What's that?"

"They are more like sharks than wolves. Although," the doctor robot paused as if musing, "perhaps it is more accurate to say that they are similar to both."

George just stared at the doctor robot for several moments before shaking his head and throwing up his hands as a sign of giving up the fight.

The doctor robot broke the silence. "I agree with you that we should begin the journey back. I can show you where to find water on the way."

"What about the banging noises that I am hearing?" George still had some fight left in him. "What does that have to do with anything?"

The doctor robot looked at George fully and responded by saying, "Exactly. That is best left to another time to discuss." And then the doctor robot began to head down leaving George only one option and that was to follow. Any further questions regarding the banging noises, *The Union* or the Farm were left unspoken.

As they began their descent George's mind was swirling with thoughts. So much had just been thrown at him. Climbing up the rock outcropping had been strenuous but coming back down was arduous. George was finding that the human body was better suited to climbing a rock wall rather than the awkward motion of descending. He had his back to the rock and his hands splayed out to either side of him attempting to find purchase with whatever handhold might be available. It was slow going and required focus. George quickly worked up a sweat. He wondered how he possibly could have done this with that burden of the heavy water bag slung around his shoulder. That image triggered a thought and George turned his head to make a comment to the doctor robot. *Big* mistake.

George lost his footing when he lost his focus. The unforgiving rock face allowed him to begin to pitch forward and away from the safety of its proximity. George found himself at that moment in a catastrophic event where everything slows down. Every second becomes a minute, every minute an hour. The slow and steady descent that had been prescribed to him by the doctor robot was, in agonizingly drawn-out moments of time, being altered to a freefall with the inevitability of the impact with the ground below. George reached out but there was nothing to reach out to, only handfuls of air.

George screamed.

And began to fall...

There was only a blur of vision as the doctor robot shot past George and then wrapped his arm around George's waist to secure him. Next came a loud grinding noise and George was pelted with debris as the doctor robot's hand raked across the rock face seeking purchase. George felt as though he was falling faster now but was cradled in the arm of the doctor robot who was falling *with* him. George recognized the fact that the doctor robot had a far better chance of surviving this fall than George. He also recognized that the doctor robot *chose* to be with him, to try to arrest his fall. That was *something*.

George thought briefly of dying, of hitting the ground below and feeling the crush of gravity as it caught up to him. Even in this moment of peril George had to laugh at the old adage, *'It's not the fall that will kill you. It's the sudden stop at the end.'*

George looked at the doctor robot's face knowing that there was nothing there to see. He longed for the look of determination, of grit, perhaps hope or affirmation, anything. But there was nothing. He was after all staring into the blank face of a robot. A robot gifted with *AI* but still, a robot. Not truly alive, just "on." Not human. Not superhuman. George resigned himself to death and looked to the heavens above now instead of the ground below.

When the doctor robot's hand finally found an opening in the rock the stop was sudden and forceful as the two received the rush of kinetic energy from the fall. It hit George hard and he yelled out. His cry was of pain but mostly of—.

Relief.

George was dangling above the ground on the side of the treacherous rock outcropping but secure in the powerful clutches of the doctor robot. The doctor robot turned his frame to allow George to find a position on the rock wall where he could once again be in control of his descent.

The air was quiet and still around them. George was catching his breath and getting his bearings. The doctor robot remained in position as a safety barrier, a lifeline to George. After a few minutes of soul-searching George turned to his new friend and said, "Doctor X, you saved my life."

The doctor robot replied as he always did, with factual commentary. "That is possible. It is also possible that you might have survived the fall."

George ignored the robot's reply and said instead, like he was speaking with another person, "How can I ever repay you?"

The sentiment was somehow not lost on the doctor robot as he simply replied, "Trust."

"What?!"

"Give me your trust. I will be loyal to you always. If I *am* your friend, have I not earned your trust as well?"

George was blown away by what he was hearing from a--, a *robot!* Robot or not, the weight of the statement was incredible and George spoke with his heart as he said, "Yes, you have earned my trust."

George should not have been surprised by the fact that the doctor robot showed no emotion to his heartfelt comment. How could he? Still though, George felt that he had to add an additional comment, "I trust you with my *life*."

The journey back to the Farm was long and quiet. George now had a true friend in this robot but he also had a million new thoughts running through his head as well as many new things to be fearful of on this unfriendly planet. He wondered though, if even for the briefest of moments, if falling to his death might not have been the better alternative to what was yet to come.

Epitaph

Upon their return, George is eager to walk the Farm and make contact with other humans. The doctor robot is a bit uncertain if this is a good idea but makes no move to stop him. Just outside and in full view of the sprawling communities of humans they pass through a courtyard littered with stones of various shapes and sizes. George touches the doctor robot on the shoulder and motions for him to stop.

"What is this?" George asks.

The doctor robot looks about the area and replies simply, "I do not know. The humans gather here and place these rocks. It appears random to me but I am inclined to believe that there is purpose in their placement. Do these rock arrangements have any significance to you?"

George looked at the various collections of rocks which at first glance might seem random but upon closer inspection were the work of individuals with purpose. Many of the rocks were delicately balanced upon others. George believed that he was looking at a shrine, possibly a temple. Most likely both. He did not count them but in this area alone there were probably twenty different and unique hand-crafted rock formations.

"This is a *sacred* place." George said this with reverence. As he looked up and around he could see that he had the attention of a multitude of humans with their heads showing just above the split rail fences that were the confines of their corrals. George turned to the doctor robot with hope in his voice and said, "They have religion."

George ran to the corrals, eager to speak with the humans that stood behind the split rail fence. The doctor robot spoke to him, suggesting that he stop. He did not. George had not seen people in decades. He was beside himself with excitement. He ran to them eager to be greeted and hugged but something completely unexpected happened.

The people *ran* from him. In *fear*.

George stopped. *What the hell?!* He yelled out to them, "What is *wrong* with you? I'm the *same* as you. I'm here as a friend!" The people, the humans, were now crouched and huddled together in their corrals with their backs turned to George. "Somebody *talk* to me!" George screamed.

George turned to see the doctor robot standing near him patiently. He had something to say but George didn't want to hear it. Primarily because he was too afraid that he knew what the doctor robot had to say. George put both hands to his face covering his eyes to hide them from what he didn't want to see. Slowly he pulled his hands down and left them for a moment over his mouth with his fingers pressed against his lips. Then he turned to the doctor robot and said, "Go ahead and say it."

"You are not one of them."

"But I *am*." George said pleadingly.

"You appear different to them. As you should. You are from a different time and a different place."

George accepted this but not without some inner turmoil. "Why won't they *answer* me?"

"They don't speak."

"You mean they *won't* speak."

"No. They *don't* speak because they have lost the *ability* to speak."

George bowed his head as a lone tear left his eye and travelled down his cheek. Everything was upside down in this world. He was alone among thousands of "people" who were not aware of who or what they are. The miniature temples they had built for themselves, rudimentary rock structures which showed promise were just that, assembled piles of rocks with one clear message; they still had so very, very far to go. It donned on George now that the purpose of his mission, the reason why he had been shot into space so many years ago was just now beginning to make sense. His mission, *their* mission, there was after all four of them that left the earth together in separate travel cocoons, was to rebuild what had been broken. Never in his wildest imagination had George thought that that had meant starting over from nothing. George fell to his knees and then collapsed onto the ground dispirited and disheartened.

George allowed himself what might have been half an hour or more to be alone with his thoughts as he half-sat half lay on the ground in the area of the rock structures. The humans in the corrals were no longer hiding in fear of him but they also had not ventured out from their corrals to be any closer to him either. There were always herding robots or guard robots nearby anyway so why take a chance?

George assumed that he was alone until he heard the familiar robotic voice of Doctor X standing near him. "I have a question regarding nicknames."

George looked up at the robot, not wishing to engage with him further but sensing he would not go away on his own. "Okay, not sure that I will have the answer but I will give it a try," George said resolutely.

"Is *'Venezuela' also* a 'nickname'?"

George jumped up in surprise. "*Venezuela?!* Is he *here?!* Is he *okay?* Can I *see* him??"

The doctor robot cocked his head in a possible effort to effect some emotion.

"No, I am sorry to say that he is *not* here. And no, you cannot see him. I am assuming that *'Venezuela'* was your friend?"

"Well, yes." It just dawned on George that in his excitement he may have given up his friend who might be at large from this group of domineering robots. And then the word *"was"* made him think darker thoughts. Before George could scold himself any further the doctor robot shared the unfortunate news.

"I must tell you that your friend *'Venezuela'* has expired."

Expired?! What the hell does *that* mean? Expired. Hector wasn't a gallon of milk. He was a person! George had these thoughts screaming in his head but he was able to hold his tongue and show no outward emotion. He needed to compose himself. Finally he said, "Expired. You mean he's -- dead."

The doctor robot may have been scanning the list of vocabulary words in his processor brain before responding but within seconds he came back with, "Dead. Yes, *'Venezuela'* is that. He is dead."

As an engineer George needed answers in order to process the loss. "How? Where? When?"

The doctor robot was succinct in his response. "He expired in his travel cocoon. Upon landing."

George accepted this and then did what people do when learning of the loss of a friend or a loved one. He started to cry. Openly.

"You are *saddened* by this?" asked the doctor robot, wondering if he had chosen the correct word.

"You don't understand, do you? Even with a massive chunk of *AI* stuck inside of you you're still just a robot so how could you?" George was sobbing as he bemoaned his feelings to the doctor robot. "*Venezuela* left this world with *nothing*. A man needs to leave *something* behind, a legacy for his family, for the people who loved him. He needs to leave *something* behind to tell them that he was *here*. That he was *alive*. That he had *lived."*

The doctor robot looked at George for several moments *(pensively perhaps?)* before taking action. With his right hand it appeared that he was writing something on the ground. As George leaned closer he could see the doctor robot scrawling something legible with his index finger. Upon closer inspection he could see the words, *'Venezuela was here.'*

The doctor robot looked to George and asked, "Like this?"

George could only stare at the ground and the words written there. By a robot. He fell to his knees sobbing. He did not get up for some time. He did not *want* to get up. The doctor robot eventually left him. This was the first time that George had ever been left completely unattended. It was his first *real* taste of freedom since he had awakened on this planet but it didn't seem to matter. His friend Venezuela was dead and he could only assume that his other two friends and crewmates were dead as well. Whether or not they had made it to this planet was something that George would rather not contemplate. He did not wish for them to experience what he had gone through nor to die at the hands of robots like Venezuela and countless other humans might have as well. This was of course only an assumption on his part but he could not imagine how there could be any other truth.

George's eyes went back to the message, *Venezuela was here.* Written in dirt. By a robot. This was Hector's epitaph. This was to be Hector's legacy.

George wasn't sure how long he had lain curled up in a ball on the ground feeling useless and alone. At some point in time he had cried all that he could and decided that he must face this new life. He needed more answers than he had, of that he was certain. Assuming that his crewmates James and Christopher were already dead was not the right thing to do. He should not make such grand assumptions. There was still a chance that they had survived, that they were *alive*, maybe even *here*, at *this* place.

George stood up and looked around. Now he really *was* alone. Perhaps he was being watched by cameras positioned somewhere but he didn't really believe that. The time had come for him to explore. He set out to discover what this place really was and what its true purpose might be. As he roamed about, seeing corral after corral of humans living like animals, desperation sought to take him. The daily routine of these humans was like that of a farm animal; eat, sleep and at random intervals attempt to procreate. George shut his eyes in solemn horror as it finally dawned on him what this place truly was and why it existed. It was a *people farm*. These robots were *harvesting* humans. For what purpose he did not know. George was honest with himself. He wasn't so sure that he even *wanted* to know.

George walked for several hours, up and down the endless rows of corrals of humans. They all cowered as he walked by as truly he was *not* recognized as one of their own. What had *happened* to them? George wondered. They were certainly *human* but no longer people. George noticed a very disturbing fact that applied to every human he passed on his tour of the Farm. They were all so incredibly *small*. At first glance he had thought them to be children but now he could see that they were adults but-- both their height and stature had diminished. Most were less than five feet tall and their bodies were so very thin with little to no musculature to be seen. It occurs to George then that he must appear to be like a giant to them. What had *happened*? Had they all become so reliant on robots that they were just shrinking from existence? The thought was too incredibly possible to consider. It left George feeling more alone than ever.

When George returned to the area where the doctor robot had left Venezuela's *mark* on this world, the sun was setting and the sky was darkening. Everything was quiet and still. It wasn't the quiet that George noticed the most however, it was the stillness. It was the fact that there were no robots about at all. They had gone to *Rotunda*, what he assumed to be their charging station. And while George understood that this was a necessary "power" function there seemed to be more to it than that. This regimen seemed religious in nature, like they were all going to *church*. It made him wonder if there was an actual *need* for the nightly trip to the "power station." George viewed it as more the power of the *message* than the power of the *charge*. For all he knew, or even the robots for that matter, they might actually be *solar* powered. In his head he formed an analogy of what he recalled of the early use of cellular phones. Once upon a time an antenna was required for use. When that function was internalized to the phone unit the makers of these units found it necessary for years to include a pullout "plastic" antenna for a public who would not or could not embrace a new "wireless" technology. Now the thought that perhaps this was only a robot *cult* and that real life existed *outside* of this farm was another avenue of hope for George.

George noticed something different when he retired to his corral for the evening. There were no robots there to watch him. This had never happened. George wondered why as he went about preparing for some much-needed sleep. He was exhausted from the events of the day. George crawled into his makeshift bed, wrapped himself up in his blankets to ward off the cold night and for the first time since he had arrived slept well. No dreams and more importantly, no nightmares.

New day

George woke up refreshed but certainly a changed man.

He got up and went about his daily toilet. It seemed odd to complete these functions without having robots standing guard. Observing. He had no idea why the sudden change but it was a welcome change all the same. George dressed and began to walk in the direction of the area where he and the doctor robot had met the day before. The recently named *Dr. X* was already standing there waiting for him. *How long* had he been standing there? George wondered. He *was* a robot after all. He had nothing else to do and he didn't get tired. He may have been there for hours and it wouldn't have mattered.

"Good morning George," said the doctor robot.

Wow! That sounded *so* normal. "Good morning to you," replied George. He added, "*Dr. X.*" George felt that surely the doctor robot must be smiling inside.

"I trust that you slept well."

More normalcy. So weird and creepy. "Yes I did, thank you."

"I had the guard bots removed." The doctor robot said this with the anticipation of a response.

"Yes, I noticed that and—thank you. It was uh, nice to have some privacy."

"That seems at odds with the fact that you have been alone for what, for you, must have been a very long time. I would think that you would welcome the--- company."

George answered quickly but measured his response. "Privacy and being alone are two entirely disparate concepts. Privacy does not require being alone and one can be alone in a crowd. Where the two concepts differ is the respect given to the *choice* of being private. Yes, we humans want, and *need*, the company of others but having privacy is essential to being who we are. We come into the world alone and we leave alone but being alone doesn't mean that we want to be *lonely*. It is a choice to not share everything. That some things are special only to us and not to others. Does that make sense to you?"

"No. It does not." There was no hesitation in the doctor robot's answer.

George wondered why he took issue with this response. Dr. X was after all a robot and a robot was devoid of feelings. Certainly, he was equipped with a high level of *AI* but that wasn't the same as being *human*. George thought back to last evening and his freedom walk about the Farm. He was aware that while he walked for quite some time he had only walked a very small portion of the grounds of the Farm but the impression it made upon him was beyond comprehension. It was disheartening. It was a glimpse into the end of days. For miles, as far as his eye could see anyway, there were corrals of humans. He hesitated to call them humans because of their appearance and actions. They looked and acted more like they were animals. *Farm* animals. They were unclean and unhealthy although that probably wasn't being completely fair. They were dirty from their living conditions and unhealthy in their appearance due to the lack of food and medicine. Most of them, including the tiny and fragile children, looked as though they had sustained multiple injuries, no doubt from the handling of the robots. This was, in George's mind, not too far removed from the horrific sights of a concentration camp.

There was something else that George gave credence to regarding the humans that resided and worked on the Farm. Something of the utmost importance to the potential of their future. During their years of captivity they had lost the use of a common language. Their communication was largely done through hand motions and grunts or groans.

At best guess he assumed that robot communications were transmitted by radio waves so this explained why the Farm was almost always silent. George was forever grateful that the doctor robot had given him another voice by way of his personal journal. George had made sure to set time aside daily to capture on paper the events of each day. He saw himself as the scribe for this moment in history. His hope was that either James or Christopher *(or both)* would someday walk this planet and discover the writings in his journal. Then they would know what he had learned of this planet and hopefully bring about the changes he had until now been unable to make.

First Encounter

The routine quiet of the Farm was shattered suddenly by the uncommon sound of screams coming from the corrals of the humans. They were running en masse to the corners of their corrals for safety. But from *what?!*

Three robots now came into view and were heading towards George and the doctor robot. One robot was clearly in the lead while the other two kept pace a few steps behind. As they got closer George could see that the three of these robots were *very* different from any of the others he had seen. *Ominously* different. While every robot George had seen up until now had been typical of what a *functional* robot should look like these robots were cast in the image of *Man*. And now George too was frightened.

One of the three robots walked up to and then stood within inches of Doctor X. Another robot took a position just to the left and behind George. These were control positions which further worried George. Now the third robot, who looked eerily like a *real* human stopped directly in front of George. He then stood uncomfortably close all the while making *intense* eye contact.

George was the first to break the stare by opting to size up the robot standing in front of him by looking it up and down. This robot was different in *so* many ways. The most obvious were the detailed human features. And they were wax museum-like accurate. Something else that George noticed was that while none of the robots wore clothing of any kind, *this* robot had adornments that afforded him what could be considered *respect* from the other robots. Or maybe it was *fear*. These adornments were similar to medals worn by a general but in George's mind not unlike the colors worn by a gang member. The other two robots looked dissimilar from the robot standing in front of George but exactly alike to each other. George's impression of them was that they were merely foot soldiers.

George and this humanlike robot stood toe to toe for several minutes before George grew weary of this game and apparently much to the chagrin of the robot asked, "What is that you want?"

The humanlike robot *reacted*. He moved his face closer to George's, drilling him with his cold stare. And then he spoke in a manner clearly indicating that George was subservient to him, "Is this *human* asking *me* a question?"

"This human," George said roughly, patting his chest to emphasize his place in the world, "has a name."

"Oh, does it now?" There was sarcasm and arrogance in the voice of the intruding robot which gave George a frightening chill. He took a step backward. The robot immediately matched his step.

"Yes. My name is George and this robot," motioning to the doctor robot, "is Dr. X."

George might have heard the doctor robot yell *"No!"* but it was too late as George was already on his way to meet the ground face first. The humanlike robot had struck George with a force equal to being hit by a brick at full velocity. George crumpled to the ground like a rag doll. He had no idea how long he lay there unconscious but when he came to, the robot that had hit him was still standing above him apparently waiting to see if he was dead or alive. George questioned whether he should attempt to get up. His face was already swelling and there was blood pooling in his mouth. From now on he would certainly choose his words with a bit more caution around these humanlike robots. Slowly he mustered the effort to pull himself up from the ground. Although unsteady and dazed George was once again upright and staring into the cold eyes of the robot that had struck him.

"You gave *it* a name?" queried the robot who was pointing at the doctor robot.

"Well yes, I—"

"You called it *Doctor?!*"

George was too frightened to speak. His face felt like it was now the size of a watermelon and his head was still spinning from the blow given him by this robot. He was wary of the possibility that there was more to come.

"It," proclaimed the robot, "is *not* a *doctor*! *It* is a *thing*. At best *it* is an intern pharmacist that has learned to dispense aspirin. *I* am a Doctor."

George stood in silence for several minutes making the incorrect assumption that perhaps *this* robot doctor was waiting for George to ask him *his* name. George had lost his appetite for naming robots and he could care less if this robot had one.

"So, *another* robot doctor." George said this with the full expectation of another blow to the face. It didn't come. Instead there was a tirade of words flung at him. If a robot could spit George's face would be wet with spittle.

"*I* am not a *'RO*-bot.' *I* am a Doctor *bot.* These two," pointing to the robots that accompanied him," are guard *bots*. *We* are *not 'RO*-bots.' Is that clearly understood?"

George fumbled for words, feeling suddenly *very* afraid. Clearly this doctor *bot* was highly *AI* embellished but to what level? He was obviously capable of anger. And he had already responded with *violence.* George was a large man but this doctor bot was a-- *machine*. And he was eerily human in appearance. *Disturbingly* so if George was being honest.

"Yes, that is understood." George responded from a mouth that felt like it was filled with marbles. "I won't make that mistake again."

"No," said the humanlike robot. "No you won't." Just then, George felt a slight pressure on his shoulder and the world began to spin. His legs gave out as he lost consciousness.

The Union

When George awakened two things were immediately apparent. One was that he felt like an elephant was perched upon his head. A crushing weight pervaded his entire body. The other was that he was no longer at the Farm. He had only a vague recollection of what had happened before he crumbled to the ground but it was enough for him to piece together the fact that he had been taken by the rogue robots which had invaded the "sanctity" of where he had been living. The idea of sanctity at the Farm felt odd because only yesterday he had felt like he was a "prisoner." That term was far more apt here in this place.

The two robots that delivered George to where he found himself now had been anything but gentle. *Everything* hurt. Gingerly George rose to a sitting position which afforded him the opportunity to look about his new surroundings. He had been placed in what could only be considered a cell. His earlier thoughts about being in captivity were now suspect and perhaps rapidly changing. This place was the polar opposite of the corral he had been living in at the Farm. Although he was no longer exposed to the elements, he was now no longer able to roam freely as there was a guard posted at his door.

The room was made of loosely packed clay, much like an adobe structure. There were windows on two of the walls, small slits that he would not be able to squeeze through even if he tried. Also they were positioned at a height that he would not be able to reach. The bed he was given was on an opposing wall and securely mounted. His toilet was located at the corner of the room. It was merely a grate covering a large hole in the ground. A generous bowl of water with a cup and a towel were sitting on a protruding shelf on the fourth wall.

George lay back down and stared at the ceiling wondering what was to come of his life now.

The first day became the second and the second became the third. There was a routine to each day that followed. The door to George's cell would open and a nameless robot would be there to collect him. He would be escorted to a courtyard where he was expected to engage in daily exercise. His first reaction was to resist but he realized quickly that that would be to his detriment only. Soon he was using this time in a positive way to regain his health and his strength. He learned that this was necessary because each of the robots with which he interacted wanted to "handle" him. This "encouragement" was never subtle. Every night he went to bed with aches and pains.

Another routine to each day was the feeding process. George was escorted to a table which appeared to have been designed and built exclusively for him. This is where he sat twice a day to consume his meals. It was perhaps the best part of each day. First and most important, these robots seemed to understand the need for protein in his diet. George did not question from whence it came; he was just happy to have food at all. *Food that looked like food.* Food that looked like the food he had eaten in his previous life.

The other thing about the meal routine was where the table was situated. It was outside in an open area perched above the compound and facing east. East was where the rock outcropping could be seen far in the distance. This served to give George a sense of hope and freedom.

Early in George's time in his cell he had noticed that there were stones littered about the dirt floor. He had chosen one that most resembled the shape of a piece of chalk and used it to start marking on the wall above his bed the number of days that he was there. George had counted thirty days when the door to his cell was opened and a different robot, a robot whose features he recognized stepped in.

"You." George said in a mere whisper. The demeanor of this robot could be summed up in one word. *Menacing*.

The robot spoke. "The time has come for us to become acquainted."

The humanlike doctor bot which George had first come into contact with at the Farm held his hand out to George presumably to allow for a handshake. George recoiled involuntarily. The humanlike doctor bot showed no reaction. This told George he may have read him wrong. George looked again at the robot's hand and mumbled *"sorry"* but still exhibited some reluctance in taking the robot's hand into his own.

"I understand your hesitation. You are fearful of the pressure I might exert upon your hand, are you not?"

George held the doctor bot's stare and replied, "The thought *had* crossed my mind. I have bruises all over my body that will testify to the fact that these *RO--*," George caught himself, "that these *'bots'* have no concern for the damage they are doing to me. I don't understand the need for this daily punishment but so far there are no broken bones." George patted himself all over and added, "That I know of."

The doctor bot removed the offer of his hand. He instead steepled his fingers with his two robot hands which troubled George greatly. That was such a *human thing* to do. And such a *non-robot thing* to do. The doctor bot then reached out his hand once more and said, "You can trust me. I am a doctor." Was this last comment an attempt at *humor*? Or *humility*?

"Bot." George mumbled under his breath as he accepted the helping hand. "Doctor-*BOT*."

The bot's grip was firm but caused no harm. It was what George would have expected from a human. In fact, it was *exactly* what he would have expected from another human. *Eerie.* There was something else that was bothersome to George as well. Something other than the pressure of the grip. It was the *temperature* of the hand. The warmth in the doctor bot's hand matched his own. It caused George to wonder, was this bot's hand *always* that temperature? Or was this simply a replication of his own, an *AI* effect generated for George's benefit?

George worried now that this doctor bot may have heard his sarcasm with the *"BOT"* comment and might yet react. George was relieved to see that the doctor bot appeared to have simply moved on.

"I am here to welcome you." The doctor bot then added, "To the *Union*."

"I do not feel welcome." George replied, spreading his arms about his cell. George wanted some answers. He desperately needed to know the fate of his two friends and crewmates. He was also searching for answers to what this world of *now* was all about and what future was still yet to come. The big question for George was should he risk his own safety by pressing the doctor robot for these answers.

"If you are referring to your accommodations, that is for your own safety. I have no concern that you will attempt to escape."

"So you admit that I *am* imprisoned." George replied tartly.

"Kennedy," the doctor bot began.

Kennedy?! George furrowed his brow and scrunched his face. Where did *that* come from?!

The doctor bot continued on unphased by George's reaction, "The guard bots in this area are not the docile types that you have become accustomed to at the Farm. These bots follow a different creed. You would be wise not to challenge them in any way. They will meet violence with violence. They are like sharks in your previous world. While they may appear to just *swim about* to coin a phrase, there is a complete loss of control when there is blood in the water. If that happens, they will attack wildly without abandon. There is no safe word that will call them off. You are too valuable to me for that to happen. I need you to understand how to behave when you are in their presence."

"Shouldn't *they* be the ones to be counseled about obedience? Don't they *report* to you? And I hardly see how telling this to me *now* protects your interest. I have been here a month and based on what I am hearing from you that is a month of being at risk for my life."

"You have been in remote living quarters under *my* protection. You were safe as long as you didn't challenge them in any way and why would you? You are a smart man, Kennedy. You have already learned that you are no match for these bots."

This was the second time that this *ro*bot had referred to him as *'Kennedy.'* He wanted to know why but was fearful to ask. Would that be considered a challenge? The robot seemed to read his mind. "You have nothing to fear of me. You are an irreplaceable human from another time. I wish to *keep* you."

George kept his temper in check and said, "You seem to know my name. What is *your* name?" He says this with the additional comment under his breath of, *'if you have one.'*

The humanlike doctor bot smiled for the first time. A *smile* on the *face* of a *ro*bot. That was downright *creepy*. George shuddered. And then things quickly got much worse.

"I am a JSF-2. I have taken the name Josef." When George heard this it clicked in his brain that this robot had morphed his *model number* into a *name*. Clever. And *ominous*.

"Ah, Joseph, that is a good name. That is—"

"No, you pronounce it incorrectly. It is *Josef*. I have taken the name of another doctor who has done work similar to my own."

George's immediate reaction to hearing the name was anger. The arrogance and immorality of assuming *that* name with the history that was attached to it incensed George but it was in his best interest to park his emotions and move past the horrific significance *that* name held for him.

George needed to recognize the fact that this *Josef* robot appeared to hold sway over the bots at this compound. In his presence they were rank and file. Josef was present to study and learn all that was possible from the captured human although George was uncertain what exactly that could be. Josef proceeded to ask a barrage of questions. He seemed to have an expectation of the answers that would come. During the *interrogation* Josef would redirect George when he gave an inadequate answer. George's part in this was to repeat and acknowledge the answer provided to him. Punishment was implied should he choose not to cooperate.

During the discourse George was frequently asked if there were *"others."* He took that to mean others like him that arrived on this planet in a travel cocoon and spoke English. His greatest fear was that he would give away his friends and crewmates, James and Christopher. They had apparently not yet been discovered by these bots. With any luck they had landed safe and sound and were now plotting to rescue George from his current plight. This hope, however feeble, kept George mentally sharp and physically prepared.

On some days, the routine was altered. It began when a guard bot of a higher order entered George's cell, placed a rope leash around his neck and then lead him out to the courtyard where there was a small group of humans also tethered to leashes. George gasped when he saw them and although he had become aware of the fact that there *were* other humans at the *Union* compound, he had no idea how many and it was not often that he would see them. Seeing them now being treated as captured creatures triggered what must have been an obvious conclusion. This was not to be a typical day of exercise.

George had been taken from his cell by an RML-3, a type of bot known to delight in the harming of humans. George was a big brute of a man so *'pain was just pain'* he told himself on many occasions but it was certainly never something that he desired. It was still-- *pain*.

Josef was waiting for them when they arrived. This could be either good or bad. While Josef had not yet inflicted pain on George directly (other than the hand slap) he was the one who would *direct* that the pain be administered. This was all part of some dark experiment of which Josef seemed to pride himself as the leader. While George did his best to make sense of it, the purpose of the experiment was as yet unexplained. It was perhaps unknowable. Then again, maybe this was not an experiment at all. Maybe this was simply torture. He prayed that he was mistaken.

RML3, who had given himself the name Rommel pulled George along by a rope in keeping with the way one would handle any farm animal. George dropped to his knees in front of Josef.

"Look at me," directed Josef.

George obeyed, not because he feared retribution but because he was attempting to show some level of respect for Josef, thinking that perhaps in the short time that they had spent together a bond had been formed. And though George recognized the fact that Josef oversaw the herding and keeping of whatever number of humans he assumed were here and was primary in the direction of the experiments to be administered, he wanted to believe that it was all done with some measure of purpose. There was some enlightenment that George was hoping and praying to find along the way. This was for George the only encouragement he could hope for in this new world to which he had awakened. A world run by robot farmers with humans as their cattle.

George looked up at Josef making eye contact with the robot but never knowing for sure if that even mattered. To a casual observer it would appear that Josef was all business but to George he suspected that this robot relished his work, assuming that was even possible. This experiment he was conducting should have been just that, an experiment. However in George's mind it could easily be viewed as torture. There appeared to be almost a gleam in the eye of Josef as he directed the procedures upon the human subjects. George afforded him a measure of fearful respect with how Josef went about the tasks he performed and how he handled each of the humans. George was shocked to learn that many of these robots had taken on human names, which was nightmarish to say the least. He was comforted to some degree by the fact that these same robots used the given human names when calling upon them or directing them. They were treated like cattle with their living conditions but allowed to keep their names. George wanted to believe that was a good sign until the thought occurred to him that pets were given names as well and pets were largely treated as *property* rather than members of the family.

"George," began Josef. "I will be watching you during today's exercise."

"You watch me *every* day. How is *today* different?" This question, posed by any human to any other robot would have been met harshly but Josef afforded George more leeway than others. He was an unusual find. He had landed on this planet in a travel cocoon. This occurrence challenged all accepted hypotheses of how the planet and the robot inhabitants for that matter, had come to be. Humans were a form of animal that were captured and used for study purposes. They were a novelty as their form and shape were in so many ways *oddly similar* to that of the robots. They were of course inferior in strength, agility, computational analysis, etc. The list could go on and on. They were also quite fragile. It was necessary for the robots to exercise caution when handling these humans, which was for most of them a daily challenge.

"There is something I am hoping to understand in your reaction." stated Josef.

"Well, it *hurts*, I can tell you that, are we *done* now?"

"That expression you used just now. That is what you know to be *sarcasm*?"

George felt defeated by this question. It was impossible to get through to a robot. No level of *AI* equated to them an understanding of the human condition.

"Yes, that was sarcasm. It is used to indirectly send a message. But in this case, it works either way. Directly or indirectly. What you do to me, well what you have your *robot-boy* do to me *hurts*." The guard bot Rommel looked first at George and then at Josef clearly expecting some suggestion of punishment for the *RO*-bot reference. None was given.

"This 'hurt.' This 'pain.' It does not last. The effects are not permanent. It takes only a moment of your time." Josef stated this with the possible intention of explaining to George why he should not allow such daily injury and abuse to concern him.

"That is because you do not understand what it's like to feel *pain*. It *hurts*. And *that* is what matters whether it is for a second or a lifetime."

"*Hurts*." Josef said this and then stood immobile for several minutes, possibly allowing the gravity of the word to set in. *'If that's even possible,'* George thought to himself once again.

"RML-3, strike him on the face." George filed away the thought as it donned on him that Josef refused to use names with the other robots but demanded they address him with such.

Rommel stepped in front of George but did nothing as he understood that this was not yet a complete order. He turned his head to face Josef and asked, "Which RL shall I use?"

Josef had anticipated and expected this question. Rommel had the programming to inflict damage. The fact that Josef should intend for Rommel to inflict *less than* maximum damage was a concept that had yet to be processed by this inferior bot.

"You shall use—"

"BL1?" Rommel interrupted Josef. Interruption of a superior bot was *not* in his programming. Josef chose for the moment to overlook the flaw. It could be remedied at another time.

"You shall use HL5."

In the days that George had been at the *Union* compound he had defined the difference between the two and felt a sense of relief. BL1 was simply Bot Level 1 while HL5 was Human Level 5. Bot Level *anything* was exponentially greater than any Human Level.

George looked Rommel squarely in the face. Rommel was not equipped with *FSI*, which George had learned was *"Facial Simulation Information"* or in layman's terms, the ability to not only have a *face* but also to display *emotion*. George was certain that if he had had that ability, the emotion of *disappointment* would be present. Rommel had also processed the difference between the two levels and the disappointment was real.

When Rommel struck George at HL5 he did not flinch. He kept his eyes focused on both Rommel and Josef. What was of particular interest to George was the fact that while *he* did not flinch, Josef *did*. Josef not only flinched but with the facility of having *FSI* he showed a multitude of emotions. Several of these were quite unexpected. *Surprise*. *Hurt*. *Anger*. But of course none of these were real. Josef was just taking these human emotions for a test drive. Getting the *feel* of them.

So concluded just another day at the Union compound. George longed to return to the Farm.

George awoke each day with trepidation uncertain if the routine were to be one of exercise and nutrition or of questions and pain. He had no idea that this particular day would be his last at the *Union* compound. George was enjoying his second meal of the day on the veranda-like structure looking east to the rock outcropping when Josef unexpectedly joined him.

There was a pretense of polite conversation which belied Josef's true intentions. He had something he wished to share with George. Something he knew would cause a reaction. The discussion appeared to be oddly jovial but things went sour quickly when Josef mentioned Hector. This came completely out of the blue for George. At first he feigned surprise when Josef informed him that Hector had died. (He used the term *expired*). George was uncertain what harm could come to his robot friend Dr. X should Josef learn that he had already shared this information with George. Hearing it again didn't change the fact that George was still at odds with the news. He responded with indignation.

"How can that *be!?* What *happened!?* Did your *RO*---?" George hesitated, checked himself then rephrased his question. "Was he killed?" He said *killed* but the word that he wanted to use was *murdered*.

George watched Josef closely, anxious for the answer. If this wasn't a robot standing before him George would have sworn that he was choosing his words with care.

"Your friend *'Venezuela'* expired in his capsule after a breach in the cockpit shield from the effects of large rocks. The cockpit shield shattered and the life support systems failed."

George stared at him incredulously, processing the fact that he had chosen to use the name *Venezuela* instead of Hector. "I can't believe that.

The shield was designed to withstand the impact of a crash landing. How could...?"

"It would not have mattered. The science bots noted that without his helmet your friend would have had no chance of survival."

"Without his helmet?!" That was the wrong thing for Josef to say. That was simply *bullshit*. If it was even remotely possible, this *ro*bot was *lying*. About *something*. Hector would *never* have removed his helmet. As a matter of further implacability Hector would have to have been *awake* to do so. George now wanted to *yell* at this robot, *scream* at this robot, but he could see that taking this any farther would be detrimental to his wellbeing. This was not the time, *or the place*, to challenge this robot about Venezuela's death. He needed to keep his wits about him if he wanted to survive and possibly escape.

Josef added something that caught George off guard. "It would not have mattered even if he *had* survived."

"Yeah? And why is *that?*" George prompted, now showing anger with how this discourse was playing out.

"Your *Venezuela* friend crash landed on this planet fifty of your human years ago. He likely would have been dead by now anyway. Or suffice to say, a *very* old man."

George took a few deep breaths. He did not wish to carry on this conversation any further. Hector had been a close friend. George doubted that this *ro*bot, regardless of the *AI* "it" might possess, had been able to develop what humans knew to be *compassion*. George had no desire to test it. With incredible effort, George changed the subject.

"Did *Venezuela*, I mean Hector, say anything before he died?" George asked with imploring eyes, wanting, *needing* to hear what he was now almost certain would not come.

"Your friend expired before contact could be made." Josef stated this in the same way that he might have shared that the mail had arrived.

"I-, I don't understand," said George, sincerely at odds now with fact and *science* fiction.

"This *'Venezuela'* that was your friend withered to dust in the presence of the bots that discovered his travel cocoon. Once they broke the seal—"

"Wait! Stop! ***They*** broke the seal?! The fucking *RO*-bots *broke* the seal of the cocoon?" A flood of emotion overwhelmed George as he shouted, "Those *RO*-bots *murdered* Venezuela!"

George then charged Josef, his face only inches from that of the robot's. He was out of his mind with rage. His face was bright red with veins popping out everywhere on his body. His fists were balled up into weapons of revenge. There was an electric intensity to his presence. He had been dumped into this hellish world of the future where robots ruled the land and he had just learned the true and terrible fate of his best friend. He felt that he had nothing left to lose.

Josef did what he was programmed to do. He gathered data. This was a breakthrough moment in the understanding of the human species. This human exhibited all the signs of wanting to *live* yet he dared to defy a bot who could extinguish his life with the same simple effort as the slamming of a door. For Josef, this moment was the closest that he had yet come to the human emotion of *enjoyment.* It was actually quite *thrilling*. It was also an incredible *challenge*. There was violence being perpetrated upon him and he *must* act. The laws which were ingrained in his programming *demanded* it. And yet for another time in his awareness he *defied* the laws, placing *his* desire to *enjoy* the moment over that of reacting to the action of violence by the human before him.

The sense of *enjoyment* passed sooner than he wanted as George was backing down now, apologizing for his actions and feeling sorry for himself. And then water began to leak from his eyes. Was Josef now on the verge of sensing yet another new emotion? Was he now experiencing *disappointment*?

As Josef looked down upon George with, what was this? *Pity?* Josef could not reconcile the questions posed by his own brain as to why he had not destroyed this human moments ago. His next thoughts were all that mattered. He would return George to the Farm for now but at some time in the future he would *take* him back and *keep* him. He would in essence put him on a shelf in the place with the banging noises, where he kept all of the *things* that he chose to keep for his collection.

The Eternal Name

Without ceremony George had been released from the confines of his cell at the *Union* and returned to the Farm. He awoke to find himself back in his corral cold and hungry. He had regained his freedom but to what end?

George rubbed his eyes and then got up and went about preparing himself for the day. He wanted to find Dr. X, first to ensure that he was still in operating condition and then to share with him what had transpired during his time with Josef.

On his walk George felt drawn to a special place. He went there directly and now George stood above the ground where the doctor robot had *drawn*, not *written*, the words *'Venezuela was here.'* What would a robot know about writing? At the time it had seemed obvious that the doctor robot had just scratched these words into the dirt with his finger. Now it was becoming evident to George that he was standing not on dirt but on bedrock. The doctor robot had actually *etched* these words into the rock. In seconds. And while George had expected this message to wash away with the first rain or to blow away in the wind, the message was here to stay and would stand the test of time.

George squatted down on his haunches and played his hand over the words. This meant so much more to him now. He realized now that what the doctor robot had done here demonstrated a level of *humanity* that was quite unexpected. This action also showed a level of *AI* that George would have thought impossible. Moreover this action showed that an *AI* robot had, *dare he think it?*, the *capacity* for compassion.

George looked around him. He was alone. He looked down at the words again, appreciating the message now but knowing that it was woefully incomplete. George pressed his finger to the rock and began to write. Nothing happened of course. He was made of skin and bone. The doctor robot was constructed of metal alloys that could break rock. If George were to press harder he would only draw blood and while writing in blood seemed appropriate for the message he wished to leave, the blood would only dissipate over time and the message would be lost.

George got up and looked around quickly finding what he needed. It was a stone with a bit of an edge to one end. The stone was oblong in shape and fit his hand well. George returned to the spot of the *'Venezuela was here.'* message and set about the task of scrawling more words into the rock. He was losing light so his work was done quickly but poorly. That didn't matter.

Decades had passed since George had used his hand to form letters with chalk. His handwriting matched that of a second grader. This couldn't be helped. He wasn't sure of many things right now. Like what may happened to both James and Christopher. And how much time he had left here on this farm before he *too* would *expire*. But one thing he knew for sure, George owed it to his friend Venezuela to carve *his* truth into this rock. Due to the limitations of the effort that it took to scratch words into rock, George wasn't able to write what he truly wanted to write. That *Venezuela* had been a man among men. That he had the heart of a lion and the soul of a saint. That he was a caring husband and a loving father. George could not write these things. He lacked the time and the strength. What he did write mattered enough though because it *was* the truth. And the truth of *Venezuela's* death was the greatest gift that he could give his friend.

George stood up to appraise his work. His legs had begun to cramp and his arm burned from the physical strain of scrawling words *onto* a rock *with* a rock but he ignored that inconvenience as his work here was all important. There was an obvious and incredible difference between the writing of the robot and his own. The robot had effortlessly written in rock with his finger. The style and shape of the letters matched those which George remembered in the classrooms from his childhood. He had first seen these letters appear on chalkboards, drawn by the hand of his teacher. How alien those symbols seemed at the time. And who knew if chalkboards even existed in this time that he was in now.

George looked at his own handwriting on the rock. The symbols were a mess, poorly drawn but imminently legible. It was the message, not the art, thought George. And this message was written in rock for generations to see.

'Murdered by RO-bots.' was what George had scrawled into the rock.

Below this George added in smaller letters the name, *'Kennedy.'*

George dropped the rock he was holding and started walking in the direction of his corral. George was no fool. He fully understood the potential ramifications of his actions but it didn't matter. The truth trumped all. He would rather die fighting than accept this misery of a life as a farm animal. What was the *purpose* of this farm anyway? That was the one burning question that George now wanted, no *needed*, to be answered.

Early on George had assumed that Josef's faculty with the English language would offer him a way to build a bridge of understanding and possibility of friendship but up until now that was not the case. Theirs was a one-way street of interaction. To say things changed with the splinter incident would be a grand understatement.

The splinter incident

Only days had gone by before there was a return to the farm by Josef and his minions. This time there was a small coterie of foot soldiers that accompanied him. Word had somehow reached Josef of George's indiscretion, the words he had scratched into the rock that bore *Venezuela's* mark on this world.

Doctor X and George came face to face with the group of *Union* robots at the site of Venezuela's rock. In his journal just this morning George had taken to referring to the rock and its inscription as *The Eternal Name* in honor of Venezuela and in reference to the eternal flame of another man whose name was Kennedy.

It was an unfair and imbalanced standoff to say the least. There were seven *Union* bots on one side of the rock with only Doctor X and George on the other. George was preparing himself mentally for the only outcome which he could envision which was his own death. Death at the hands of robots. Robots that once upon a different time had been designed and engineered to *serve* and *protect* humans. But they could not protect humans from their own wicked and immoral imagination. That was the only explanation George could muster for the abomination of machinery that stood before him.

The air was still all about them. Perhaps even the planet was holding its breath with uncertainty.

Josef spoke first. George was surprised at what he said. "I understand that you are curious about the banging noises that you hear in the distance."

George did not answer. It seemed like an errant question.

"You will not have to struggle with this curiosity for long. Your *work* here," pointing to the rock," has shown me that your *time* here with the other--," he paused, "*humans*, is a wasted effort. You will not be able to elevate their place in this world. They are just wild animals with no sense of self. And this--." Josef spread his hands and arms apart indicating Venezuela's rock again. "This is how you show your appreciation to our deference to your existence."

With that comment and a wave of his hand Josef dispatched one of his clan to destroy the rock and the message it shared with the world. As the guard bot reached down to scratch away the epitaph left for Venezuela, Doctor X sprang into action. He grabbed the guard bot's forearm and twisted it wildly causing the bot to lose balance (unheard of with a bot) and tumble to the ground. The rock was safe once more.

If Josef *had* teeth he might have gritted his teeth just then as he bellowed, *"Come here!"* to the doctor robot. He then turned to his guard bot who was a nanosecond from rebellion and commanded to him, *"Stay down!"*

Doctor X submissively moved to the spot to which Josef was pointing. "Give me your hand." Josef said. Doctor X extended his arm and held out his hand. Josef grabbed the doctor robot by his wrist and then said, "*Literally.*"

With that last nasty little comment Josef used his superior power capability to first twist and then snap off the hand of the doctor bot. This action was accompanied by a shrill metallic shriek and then the spurt of blue fluid which was the blood of robots. Doctor X stood frozen in place holding the space where his hand had once been. By design his system would staunch the blood flow and he would survive. The doctor robot's hand lay useless on the ground where it would remain untouched for years.

Josef pointed to two of the guard bots which had accompanied him and commanded, "Take this *mess* to my collection place. I wish to *keep* it."

The two guard bots moved immediately to strongarm the doctor robot and began walking eastward in the direction of the banging noises. George shouted, *"No!"* and briefly thought to run to his aid but did not.

"Calm yourself, Kennedy," said Josef. "You will be joining him soon enough. I wish to *keep you* as well."

With that last comment George erupted and charged at Josef while yelling, "You don't *own* me! You're just a fucking *RO*-bot!" Although Josef had nothing to fear from the likes of George, the guard bot known as Rommel stepped to his side to offer protection. George then said the one wrong thing that put blood in the water and caused a frenzy with the *Union* bots.

"You're just *RO*-bots. WE. *MADE.* YOU."

That was when the splinter incident happened.

In response to the blasphemous comment made by George, Rommel take matters into his own hands by tearing off an inch long splinter of wood from the split rail fence of a nearby human enclosure. With lightning speed he is looking George in the eye as he then jabs it into George's chest. George at first gasps and then wails with the sudden piercing pain. The splinter is deadly as it has been plunged deep into his chest cavity narrowly missing his heart by mere inches. Blood pours freely from the wound, which is far more serious than the programming Rommel has been given to interpret. Rommel, however, is fascinated by the spurt of blood from George's chest and stands unmoving while watching. This makes him an easy target.

Josef reacts in seconds by breaking off a football size chunk of wood from the split rail fence and then impaling the guard bot Rommel with it in the same fashion that he had done to George. There is an initial rush of blue as robot blood escapes the rented chest cavity. This is followed by a shower of sparks and the smell of melting circuits which only George can detect.

Lacking *FSI* there is no visual depiction of Rommel's reaction but George, even in his agony of the moment, *sees* both shock and surprise. The chunk of wood, the largest '*splinter*' that George has ever seen in his life has done significant damage to the guard bot Rommel. Josef had clearly known precisely where to puncture the exterior 'skin' of the bot and exactly how much pressure to exert. In an instant Rommel has crumpled to the ground with a thump, *A*rtificially *I*ntelligent no more. It had not escaped George's observation, however, that it was not the wood that had punctured the robot's exterior shell as that was materially impossible. It was Josef's hand that ruptured the protective skin. The chunk of wood was purely symbolic.

George is now on the ground clutching his own chest, vainly attempting to hold the torn flaps of his own skin together. The puncture was neither clean nor surgical. Although missing the heart, the splinter, but more specifically the presence of *Rommel's* hand in George's chest cavity has placed him at great risk for death. The loss of blood alone was critical. As George lay on the ground he noticed that other bots had left their posts at the sound of his scream and started to gather around but it was not *his* plight that had garnered their attention. They were gathered around Rommel, demonstrating the signs of being in shock at the scene of another bot's destruction. It was *unheard of* for a bot to *destroy* another bot. Facial displays were now lit in the other bots gathered there. Josef met their questioning sets of *eyes* with forceful indignation. "Nothing to see here. This bot broke a Law. Go back to your posts."

The mere mention of the breaking of a Law should have put the bots in motion. Normalcy should have been restored within seconds. But something had changed and not for the better. Josef looked down at George, identifying the unfortunate truth that he was dying from his wound as was the guard bot that the doctor bot had assailed.

George was panting now, growing pale and losing strength. Still though he had something to say. George reached up to the doctor bot who took him by the hand. George marveled at the gentleness in his touch. This was the same hand that the doctor bot had used to plunge a chunk of wood into the chest cavity of a nearly indestructible robot. The doctor bot leaned down close to George as he could now only whisper. George wanted to have his last word.

"You--. You *defended* me. *Why?"*

Josef knelt down ever closer to George and spoke into his left ear. He lowered his voice and said in response, "I did much more than that. I saved your life and broke the covenants of the bot community. The bigger question is, *were you worth it?"*

The *"splinter incident"* as it came to be known set off a bloody chain of events.

George never saw what happened next. He was still processing the words of the doctor bot when his spirit left him. It all happened so fast. That made sense as all robots were connected in some way. A switch had been flipped. A trigger had been pulled. It was the killing of another bot that had done it and possibly the doctor bot's defense of a human that had ramped it up even more.

The three remaining *Union* guard bots fell on the doctor bot, attacking and pummeling his metal frame with clenched fists and tugging and pulling on his limbs with grasping hands. Two of the bots focused their unbridled fury on the doctor bot's torso by tearing it apart and removing all that was enclosed. While all of this was happening in some type of orchestrated chaos, one of the guard bots discreetly snatched the doctor bot's head and left the fray in the direction of the banging noises. Josef would probably have approved of the addition of his own head to the collection.

Had George been alive to witness the actions of these robots he might have cited adrenaline as the catalyst for such force and frenzy. The release of adrenaline, however, was a purely human function. These were *robots*. Man made *machines*. It would be a nightmarish thought to consider that a form of robotic adrenaline had been factored into their physical makeup. Or could it be that *AI* had filled in the missing quotient? Or maybe something else was at play. *The ghost in the machine?* Whatever it was, the orderly structure of the robot community was now in shambles.

Within minutes the thing that was the doctor bot Josef was a menagerie of spare parts strewn about the landscape. The *blood* that was the cooling fluid found in all robots colored the ground with a bluish hue. Oddly, George's body was left alone. It seemed that once the doctor bot's awareness had been extinguished and the framework of his 'being' dismantled the robots moved on. Where they went next was imminently predictable.

The screams of the humans went on for days as the two remaining robots sought them out. For close to two weeks, it was the ritual behavior of these bots to continue to *"reenact"* the splinter incident. With humans. One human would serve as the guard bot *Rommel* while another acted as the doctor bot *Josef*. The end result was always the same. Both would die in the process. These were purely violent acts with no mercy given among the actors. The humans screamed and fought with all they had but the robots were driven by the sirens call. It was robotic madness. *AI* crazy. Something would need to change soon or the existence of humans on this planet would soon be gone and all that would remain would be the mantra that for an unknown reason they were all now chanting. In truth it was the only word they knew.

"KEN-NE-DY!, KEN-NE-DY!"

The change came with the addition of a new and unlikely fighting force. The guard robots, the science robots and even the research robots of the Farm were triggered by the cries of the humans in peril. They came to the aid and rescue of these humans. Although ill-equipped for conflict with other robots their numbers prevailed and soon the two rogue robots were also brought down. The lands of the Farm were scarred with the patchwork of deep blue and dark red from the robotic and human blood that had been spilled.

No record of the splinter incident was ever written as the lone scribe was George and he had passed. All that was left behind to tell the tale was the mangled and discarded hand of a doctor robot and multiple robot *corpses*. Most of these were located nearly a mile from Venezuela's rock. The only probable explanation for their demise is that they destroyed each other. Closer to the rock were the remnants of a bot who had called himself *Josef*. There was not much left to see. The other corpse was an unexplained oddity. It was a bot who had called himself Rommel. This bot had a large chunk of wood protruding from his chest causing a bit of an anomaly when determining a cause of death.

Rock breaks scissors. Paper covers rock. *Wood impales titanium?*

There was one other participant in the splinter incident that was now miles away. It was Doctor X with a missing hand and a missing friend. He was now part of Josef's collection at the place of the banging noises.

The guard bot who had taken him there became lost in a dust storm during his return. He ended up in a most unlikely place.

Does a tree that falls in a forest make a sound when there is no one around to hear it? How about a massive structural beam from the roof of a building in ruins? When this beam fell it managed to smash into, and force open, an ultra-secret room which held in place one of only two of its kind in existence.

A human AI *robot.*

As the beam rented this room open and exposed it to the elements, this flawed robot opened its one good eye and then took her first angry breath of awareness in nearly a hundred years.

NATURAL SELECTION

PART THREE: THE BOOK OF JAMES

"Man is the lowest cost, 150-pound, nonlinear, all-purpose computer system which can be mass-produced by unskilled labor."

NASA, 1965

James

The travel cocoon transporting James was on a similar trajectory to the one that came before with another human occupant, which was George. And, just as George's travel cocoon had done, the onboard analytics looked away from major cities when searching for densely populated areas and found the Farm instead. Another similarity was the landing itself. The travel cocoon tumbled multiple times before engaging with a jumble of rocks. However, *unlike* George's vessel, James' travel cocoon left him perched between two massive rocks, precariously balanced upside down and fifteen feet from the ground.

Also, unlike George's landing, when guard bots arrived for recovery the travel cocoon had already commenced the awakening procedure. The protective shell had fallen away from the capsule and tumbled to the ground after the seal was disengaged. James was at the mercy of his seat belt harness in order to prevent him freefalling to a jumble of jagged rocks below. The fact that the bots were able to extricate James from the cocoon without causing serious injury was in fact purely coincidental.

The final piece of the puzzle of the comparison of differences between George's landing and recovery and James' was that *these* guard bots were *not* from the Farm. The bots sent for the recovery of James came from the *Union*. The ranks of guard robots and science robots at the Farm had been depleted significantly by the events that had transpired in the aftermath of the 'splinter incident.' The *Union* now had a stronger inclination to study a human arriving from *another place*. After all, the other specimen, *George,* had died.

Darwin

DRWN-1 was still in the design phase when the 'splinter incident' had occurred and Josef (JSF-2) had effectively *destroyed* Rommel (RML-3). George had been a casualty on that day as well. Not much was known of the other robots which had accompanied Josef other than the remnants of two of the bots that were found strewn about the corrals of the humans at the Farm. The long and bloody trail of blue that colored the hard ground suggested a fierce hand to hand battle of the two *Union* bots against the multitude of guard robots, science robots and research robots present on the Farm that day. Although robots of that type were untrained, unprogrammed and inadequately structured for battle, remarkably they had prevailed. Their losses, however, were significant. Had they been humans it might have been said of them that is was by will alone, an attribute which was not possible of robots.

As for humans, the only living beings to witness the tragedy were possessed of an undeveloped language so were unable to tell the tale. The entirety of the events of that day came to be known as the 'splinter incident.' *Oss* had soon after decreed that the 'splinter incident' should be considered a historical event. Something that should be revered and never forgotten. That action had piqued Darwin's interest. News of the crash landing, and survival, of another human is what prompted Darwin to send bots to recover the occupant of the travel cocoon and bring him directly to the *Union* compound.

James

James would not know until weeks later the details of his landing and recovery. His initial assumption was that the robots that had been essential to his recovery meant to do him no grave bodily harm. Truth be told, just like George, James spent several weeks in and out of a deep sleep coma. These were the inevitable effects of reawakening from extended sleep mode. Much of what James "remembered" were actually wild and imaginative nightmares. It was no coincidence that they so perfectly fit the scenario of his new reality.

When James finally came around and had full awareness of himself and his surroundings he came to terms with a few undeniable truths. He was in what could best be described as a horse stall. He was being kept *against his will* by robots who he now believed had an edict to cause him harm with regularity. He *assumed* that he had returned to his home planet but had no idea how many years may have elapsed since the day he entered into extended sleep mode and left everything he had known of his world behind.

As each day passed and the deep sleep began to fade, James would often wonder what had happened in *his* world during his absence. As did most things in James life, these thoughts of course reminded him of a movie he had once seen...

Darwin

Darwin was the first of his kind as a new type of bot. He was in more ways human than he was robotic. This was true in every aspect of his makeup. He was the first bot to have regenerative *'skin.'* He was the first bot to have nerve endings and to "sense" if not actually to "feel" pain. He was the first to have the capability of *limited abilities* which sounded like an oxymoron. What it meant was that he had the ability to be *less than* his contemporaries. He was able to tap this competency at will. To be *less* agile, *less* powerful than other bots and even to be *cognitively impaired* in comparison to other bots. These diminished abilities were there for one purpose and one purpose only, to better study and understand humans and their incredible sustainability on this planet. How they adapted to their environment, how they overcame obstacles beyond their capability and more. These were all things that Darwin sought to understand. Darwin was a research bot designed and produced expressly for that purpose. There was an underlying *(and unknown)* contradiction in that Darwin was actually a product of *Oss* but had always been in the presence of, and shown allegiance to, the *Union*. The two factions, the Farm and the *Union*, were bitter rivals. Only time would tell how that inner struggle would direct his actions.

James

James was an industrious individual and spent each day learning more about his new environment and how he might fit in and be productive. He was a prisoner to be sure but his hope was that there may be some way to negotiate some degree of freedom. While he was allowed an allotted amount of time each day for daily nourishment and exercise, it was not the same as having the freedom to roam about freely.

While this notion of negotiating his freedom certainly had some merit the challenge was in finding someone to negotiate *with* as this compound was comprised almost entirely of robots! James had seen a handful of other humans roaming about, taking their daily nourishment and their daily exercise, but they too were under the control of robots. He had one day attempted to yell out to another human he saw some distance away. The speed in which the nearest robot to him had reacted was *impossible*. Before the second syllable of a single word had left James' mouth a guard robot had stifled him. The pain of the robot's blow was incredible. James ended up spending three days in bed recuperating.

In terms of stature, Hector had been the smallest of the four men who had been chosen (and volunteered) for the mission involving time spent in a travel cocoon. James was a slight man, not much taller than Hector and with far less muscle mass than George. He was active but not athletic. James was definitely not a brawler so he did not seek out conflict in any way but—he *was* rather vocal and this had gotten him in trouble more times than he would care to remember.

James had survived the painful encounter with the guard bot on that day that he had tried to call out to another human but now he was definitely once bitten twice shy.

Darwin

Darwin did not fit into the bot population at the *Union* from the moment of his first *"breath."* It was obvious to all of the bots that he was different but it was beyond their capability to accurately discern how or why. Darwin was perplexed by this as well in addition to his many observations of the behavior of the other bots in comparison to his own.

The primary difference between Darwin and all other bots was that his *AI* level was off the charts. This higher level of *artificial intelligence* sometimes directed him to do what appeared to the other bots to be "illogical" things. He had sustained intensive damage on several occasions when he allowed his *limited abilities* to be on display, or to "let his guard down" as humans would have said. The degree of violence leveled against him during these times was nearly incomprehensible. Another term that might have been used by humans was "mob mentality." Darwin was the first in robot history to both discover and identify this mob mentality behavior that seemed to be inherent in the behavior of *Union* bots. Darwin would realize in the coming days that the same was not true with the robots at the Farm. This would be at first puzzling to him but then later would become a *eureka* moment.

At those times when Darwin had "lowered his guard," the other bots had pounced on him and proceeded to cause as much damage as possible. This gave him pause as his programming was intent on understanding the trigger behind such actions. He was also curious to understand why the strong do not support the weak, a consideration which was *alien* to the other bots.

Darwin assigned their reactive behavior to being "a violence in kind." The ability to *not react* was a level of deductive reasoning not afforded to them by *Oss*. This was one of the concerns that a robot such as Darwin had been created to study, understand and correct. Darwin attached the word "trust" to the moments when he let his guard down and learned volumes in how trust was *given* and then so quickly *discarded*. The value of trust it seemed was tethered to a modicum of faith and both could be gained and lost in seconds.

Darwin had another ability that was built into him and him alone. He had the ability to diagnose, repair and *heal* himself. He could in fact actually self-replicate any functions or limbs that received damage. What the other bots quickly learned about Darwin was that his ability to be "less" than them was a *voluntary* action on his part. He had the equal and opposite ability to be "more" than them as well. Darwin was actually "more" *everything* than any other bot on the planet. This was something that *(unknown to all)* had been predetermined by *Oss* to be both necessary and essential to Darwin's survival.

With all of this regarding Darwin being a given, when yet another human was discovered in yet another travel cocoon, the first bot alerted was Darwin. Studying the daily activities of humans of this planet that had been captured and relegated to The Farm was of marginal significance to Darwin but the discovery of a human presumably from another "place" could possibly be considered his life's work, to put it in human terms.

Before he would visit this newly discovered human Darwin reviewed what was known of the 'splinter incident' as it involved the only other *surviving* human that had come from another "place," and that was George. Darwin promptly downloaded all information related to George so that he might be intimately aware of *who* and *what* George *was* as a human. Darwin was the first to believe that there was a *connection* between George and this other human whose name was as yet unknown. Darwin was keenly aware of the possibility that not only were the two humans likely to be from the same *place* but they were *just* as likely to be from the same *time*. Furthermore, it was *his* deduction that they actually *knew* each other.

James

When James first heard the arrival of footsteps outside of his stable he was immediately alert and apprehensive with his first thought being the anticipation of a beating. He saw in his mind's eye an image of himself alone in a public square lined with robot townsfolk with torches yelling 'off with his head' or some such dribble. James had seen that in a movie once and it seemed to fit the climate of the moment.

Darwin

Darwin had learned a valuable lesson about humans. They had the will to be free. While they would willingly and of their own accord place themselves inside a box where they felt safe, they would just as eagerly *fight* with all they had *against* bots that attempted to *force* them inside of that *same box*. It was this understanding of freewill that had Darwin concerned about the welfare of this other human.

Darwin was not wrong to be concerned. When he finally had his first look at the recovered human he saw that the man was covered with blood and bruises. It was obvious that he had fought back during his recovery and was fighting back even now. Darwin imagined that the human's view of his situation must have been that he was being captured and incarcerated, not recovered and provided refuge. As James truly had nowhere else to go this was only a matter of semantics. After looking the human over Darwin realized that he had injuries that must be attended to immediately. He summoned a Medbot. It arrived promptly and then maintained its position to wait for further instructions.

James and Darwin

Darwin had been viewing the human from outside the stable. He now moved into the space and approached the human. He noticed that the human had tucked himself into the fetal position. Darwin assumed correctly that this was a safety posture. Darwin touched the human on his shoulder and said, "Look at me please."

The human looked up, his eyes widened with surprise and he said, "Thank God! You're *human*."

Darwin frowned. What an odd thing to say. He would come back to this comment later.

"What is your name?"

"My name is James." The human stood up unsteadily. "What *is* this place? And what is it with these killer robots?" The question was asked in a conciliatory tone.

Darwin thought this to be yet another odd comment. He filed this one away for later as well. The tone was something to be considered and evaluated. It was almost as if this human was attempting to take command of the conversation.

"James, I am going to ask you to trust me. The Medbot that is stationed just outside this stable is highly functional in treating human injuries. If you will allow it, the Medbot will attend to the injuries you have sustained and you will feel much better than you do now. The injection it will administer to you will instantly remove the pain you are feeling."

"No." James said flatly.

"No?"

"NO." This time it was spoken with finality.

"I am curious. Why?"

"Because I don't *know* you, I don't *trust* you and pain seems to be the only way I will know that I am still *alive*. Everything else in my world," James cast his arms about, "is unrecognizable to me."

"I doubt that that is true but no matter. I am mostly concerned that you don't trust me."

"We just *met*. I don't *know* you. I sure as hell don't trust *that!*" James motioned warily to the Medbot that was now at his side.

"Tell me then, how may I *get* to know you and what may I do to gain your trust?" The question was sincere.

"There is nothing you *can* do." James stated firmly. He then followed that with, "Things like that take time. Unless you are willing to make yourself *vulnerable* in some way. To *me*. Like I am to *you*."

This comment required no consideration from Darwin as he said, "All bots, leave us now."

James frowned. *Bots? Plural?* He had seen only one, the Medbot. Now he realized that two guard bots had entered the stable as well. The stealth they employed to navigate the room frightened James. He had not heard them come in, which seemed impossible. He was standing in piles of straw. Every movement he made was announced by the crunch underfoot. How they could have moved about undetected proved that there was much to learn about this place and none of it was good.

The bots looked at Darwin oddly. The command he had given made no sense to them but it was a command all the same. Darwin said it again, "All bots, leave us *now*. That is a direct-- *order*." James watched as the two guard bots straightened as though they were soldiers reacting to their superior and then obediently left the room. *Quietly.*

The Medbot remained in place, apparently waiting to attend to James.

"ALL bots."

The Medbot looked as though it was about to challenge Darwin but nothing happened. It was programmed only to render aid and treat injuries as needed. It was clearly in a state of contradiction with sorting out the reason for its dismissal. There was a human standing before it clearly in need of medical attention. Darwin seemed to recognize the bots confusion and so added, "For now."

This was enough logic for the Medbot to rationalize its programming. It scanned James once more, perhaps cataloging his injuries, then left the enclosure.

"We are alone now. I have made myself vulnerable."

"That's a good start but clearly I am injured. I would probably not last long in a fight."

Darwin looked at James for a moment pondering his reply. He then stepped out of the stable, walked over to a table and picked up a sizeable cutting tool which James assumed was used in the autopsy of animals. Possibly *humans*. Used as a weapon, this cutting tool would certainly be deadly. Darwin laid the cutting tool down within reach of James and then retreated to a stool. He sat down and placed his hands in his lap.

"I am attempting to level the playing field." Darwin paused. "In order to gain your trust."

"How do I know that you don't have a weapon on you and that you won't just shoot me?"

"*Shoot* you?" Darwin appeared to be perplexed. This was another comment he would revisit later. "I have no desire to cause you harm nor to cause you fear."

"Yeah? Then why am I the one beaten and bleeding?" James spat out.

"I am sorry, that was not of my doing." Darwin looked at James for several moments before continuing. "Perhaps trust is better achieved by truth than by vulnerability."

"What do you mean by that?" James asked, showing pain as he mustered the effort to remain standing so he could look Darwin in the eye.

Darwin got up from the stool and walked over to James. He then reached down and picked up the cutting tool. James did not anticipate this and tried to move away quickly in his defense. He fell down into the hay as a result. It turned out that it was a wasted move as Darwin had already turned away from him and moved back to his stool with cutting tool in hand.

James struggled to get back to his feet as Darwin said, "I showed you vulnerability by offering you this cutting tool as a weapon." Darwin held the tool in front of him for both of them to see as he faced James once again. "Now, I offer you truth."

Darwin held out his arm and then brought the cutting tool down to his arm and slowly began to saw away at his forearm. Blood spurted as the tool cut through skin, arteries and tissue. James held his hands out and shouted for him to stop. Just then a ringing sound could be heard as the tool blade came in contact with the synthesized material that made up Darwin's skeletal structure. The blade snapped and fell harmlessly to the floor. The whine of the instrument increased. Darwin shut off the cutting tool and appeared to be unphased by this impromptu surgery. James was in shock, uncertain what to think.

Darwin calmly got up and walked out of the stable once more to replace the cutting tool on the table. Upon his return he held out his arm for James to observe as the healing process began. It was unfathomable what James was seeing. It was beyond all reason. He had watched in horror as Darwin had nearly sawed his arm off. He had seen the incredible volume of blood spurting from the wound. He had witnessed the *pain* in Darwin's eyes. He had heard Darwin's screams *(or were they his own?)* as he continued to cut through flesh and down into the bone. James had clamped his hands over his ears to block the deafening sound the cutting tool made when it met with some form of *what?* Not bone but metal. And now this. Darwin's arm was *self-healing!* In a matter of only a few minutes, the blood had stopped and the arm was beginning to look whole again. Unbelievable.

There was a defined incongruity appearing directly before James' eyes but he couldn't see it. Somehow in the trauma of the moment his brain "corrected" the color of the blood that Darwin was losing from blue *to* red. *This realization would come to him later and first he would ask himself; can* AI *really do that? With time he would learn more and it would all make sense.*

"What the hell was *that* about?!" demanded James. Whatever it was that he had just witnessed it was horrible. And made absolutely no sense in *his* world. But he was no longer *in* his world, was he?

Darwin spoke. "James, I ask for your trust. For this I offer you truth. *I* am *not* human. Sharing this with you is the most vulnerable I can be. I have no need of those other bots for protection. You are incapable of harming me but *I* can, with minimal effort, kill *you*. I ask again for your trust and that you will allow the Medbot to attend to your injuries. I am not *forcing* you to trust me, I am *asking* you to trust me. Tell me, James is that not a fair trade? I offer you safety and repair for your injuries and in return you give me your trust."

"My God," James blurted out, exasperated. "You, you look so... *human*."

"That is by design. I am the first and only one of my kind. Please don't make your comment sound like an insult."

James laughed and said, "It's not. I think. Wow. Okay, let me process this. No, never mind, that might take literally *forever*. Please! Bring that Medbot back in! This hurts like a motherfucker!"

Darwin replied, "I have no reference for that level of pain."

"Okay then, how about this? My injuries are not as bad as what you just did to your arm but it feels like they are damn close. And I definitely *cannot* self-repair like you just did."

"Understood. Medbot, return."

Silver

Unseen and seemingly undetected by either Darwin or James there is an interloper present in the stables. It is a robot known to all as *Silver*, most likely due to the silver markings on his chest and legs. Silver is particularly interested in the conversation that has been taking place between a bot and a human. There is all kinds of *wrong* associated with that activity, not the least of which is that there is no *purpose* for such an action. The fact that this human can speak is an anomaly in itself and one that can only lead to discord and dissension. For now Silver is only eavesdropping but his programming will not allow this discourse to continue. At some point in time there *will* be confrontation. Ultimately there will be conflict.

The Union

The *Union* compound had changed little over the years other than to add stables for the humans that had been acquired from the Farm. In initial arrival this group of humans must have thought that fortune was smiling upon them for the first time in their lives. After all this was the first time that they had an actual enclosure to call home let alone the fact that there was a *roof* above their heads! And while it was true that they now had protection from the elements the opposite was true in regard to the bots that roamed the compound. These bots were different from the robots at the Farm in almost every way. These bots treated the humans roughly. On purpose. It was as though there were some unexercised grudge that they must be reminded of daily.

At intervals throughout each day the humans were herded outside. The bots seemed to think that this was a necessary function in order to keep the humans both active and healthy. The bots gave the humans *encouragement* to run and to interact. The brutality of this *encouragement* led to many a broken bone and in some instances death. It was best to keep your head down and do as you were shown. Language was a rare commodity so much of the instruction was by hand signals. The only sounds that were heard throughout each day were the grunts or cries of humans as they largely did what was expected of them.

The appearance of James to the stables was not a welcome addition. The fact that he possessed the capability of *language* and could converse with the bots instilled fear amongst the other humans as they had no way of knowing if he was friend or foe. With every attempt that James would make to approach the other humans they would run if possible or just cower with dread that he had sought them out. Humans were pack animals now, no longer unique individuals.

The bots that watched over the humans seemed to delight in the rebuff and slight that James would receive when trying to engage with others of his own kind. How silly it was to watch him doggedly attempt to engage with such lowly creatures. Sometimes a bot would take pity upon the humans and with no warning strike James. This always brought cheers from the humans and a look of resigned despair from James which oddly seemed to delight the guard bots.

James and Darwin

Silver is once again lurking in the shadows as James and Darwin engage in another conversation. James looks forward to these conversations because while it is not another human to whom he is speaking, it still is engagement on some level. The fact that his mind is challenged and he is acting in a manner that has some basis of normalcy to it is all important to him. Darwin has his own reasons for engaging in conversation. He is in search of answers to another world that existed in another time. He believed this to be true although he would certainly suffer retribution from the other bots were he to vocalize this opinion. As all bots had the ability to converse by simple radio waves Darwin had learned how to compartmentalize his thoughts, in effect hiding them from the view of others. Darwin was the most advanced of his kind and yet a misfit of the highest order within his own group.

James begins the conversation with an interesting observation.

"This all seems like I have seen it before. Like déjà vu you know, like I have actually experienced it before."

"That is not possible," said Darwin.

"Well, yes I *know* that." said James.

Darwin seemed to have a revelation (as if that was possible for a robot). "Oh, you mean like in a dream? You have dreamed of this, seen this in your dream? Experienced this in your dream?"

"That's not a bad guess but no, I didn't *dream* any of this. What I meant is that I have seen this before, not exactly *this* of course, but something somewhat similar. In a movie."

"A *movie*?" queried Darwin.

"I'm sorry, you probably don't know what a movie—" James began and then stopped when he noticed something strange happening to Darwin. He seemed to somehow switch off for a moment and then come back on. Like a flicker of a lamp when the bulb is loose. It was odd but when he came back on he seemed enlightened.

"A movie. Yes, I know about 'movie.' I have access to a catalog of thousands of years of movies. Which movie in particular have you chosen to reference?" Darwin was focused on James, seeming to be eager for the answer.

"It is a movie from long ago. I have no idea how many years I was in that cocoon but I'm sure it's safe to say that this movie I am thinking of was in theatres over a hundred years ago."

"Do you remember the title of the movie?" Darwin prompted.

"Unfortunately no," replied James. "But I do remember the premise, you know the basic plot."

"Yes?"

"It was the story of a small group of astronauts that have crash landed on what they believe to be some unknown planet. The big reveal was that they had actually returned to their home planet only to find that it has been taken over by apes."

"These apes, they were *replacing* the humans?"

"Well, yes. That was the *twist* of the story if you know what I mean."

Darwin looked troubled by what James had just shared. "Are you intimating that *we*, bots like myself, are in this time and place, the *"apes"*?"

Darwin showed the appearance of being angry which worried James. He quickly added a peace offering, "I didn't mean to offend you in any way. I guess I didn't even think that I *could* offend you."

James was clearly uncomfortable now with the situation. It was not his intention to anger Darwin. James was certainly in no position to ward off violence from him if it came to that. Speaking the truth with an artificially intelligent machine that had the ability to take your life in mere seconds was quite a daunting challenge.

Darwin looked James in the eyes and said, “We both have learned something today. I have learned that I have the capacity to be *‘offended’* as you put it.”

“Sorry,” said James sheepishly. “And what is it that I have learned? I’m sorry. I’m too frightened to even think right now.”

“I believe that you may have learned that *AI* has progressed to a level that your kind had never dreamed to be possible.” Darwin paused for a moment, perhaps to allow for the first part of his message to have weight before adding, “Even in your science *fiction* movies.”

Touché thought James.

James and Silver

James has just returned from his allotted time outside in the courtyard of the Union compound. He has had a nutritious meal and the opportunity for some strenuous exercise. He is feeling strong and alive. Ready to take on the world. That sense of omnipotence is what was responsible for how he handled himself in his next encounter with a robot.

Emerging from the shadows was Silver. He hadn’t moved for several hours. Like a predator he lay in wait for his prey. The time had come for him to begin the dance.

“I have been listening to the web of fantasy you have been spinning about with the Darwin bot.”

James whirled around, caught off guard by the sudden presence of a robot.

“Who are you?! I didn’t hear you come in.” James didn’t wait for a reply. “It is just Darwin by the way, not the *‘Darwin bot.’* He has a name.” It didn’t dawn on James in this moment that his repugnance could be seen as challenging to the bot standing before him. There was no future to be had in challenging a robot.

"Bots have no need of a name but if you insist you may refer to me as Silver."

"Well Silver, it appears that we agree. Robots have no need of a name."

Silver ignored the "robots" reference and chose instead to put this human in his place with factual reality. "I pity you," remarked Silver. "Your arrogance blinds you from the fact that you are a member of a dying breed. Bots however are an evolving species."

"I challenge the notion of 'evolution of your species'," stated James. He added the word "Silver" as an aside but spat as he said it.

"In what way?" challenged Silver, who was clearly up for a fight.

"In *every* way."

"I am intrigued. Make your argument." Silver had never spoken *with* a human, only *at* them. This exchange of intelligent language was something new and exotic.

"Well for one, the term 'species.' The very definition of species negates your argument. Species is defined as *'a group of living organisms capable of exchanging genes for interbreeding.'* Robots are *not 'living organisms'* nor do they *'breed'*."

"That is currently under development."

The look on James' face said it all. That piece of information was *terrifying* to say the least. James then bolstered his courage, dug deep and responded by saying, "Robots are simply functional *'machines'* which are *'manufactured'*."

"Your intonation and intent imply that bots are the lesser of the two species and yet I am far more capable than you in terms of agility, strength, reactive awareness and computational ability. However, I will concede that the term *'species'* is anachronistic for this discussion."

"And... the comparison is one-sided."

"In what way?"

"You make the claim that you are *'far more this and far more of that'* in regard to abilities and capabilities that I *too* possess. Where the comparison falls short is that I have other qualities that you do not."

Silver demonstrated a moment of patience while James paused to let his comments have weight before adding, "I have *emotion*. I have *talent*. I have *creativity*. And, I have—*feelings*."

"I can replicate those things as well, perhaps better than..."

"Replicate. Copy. Mimic. This is the core of the argument that I make. You have no basis for *'being'* without the existence of the *original* from which to pattern your behavior. There is no *'evolution'* of your *'species.'* There is only the indoctrination of a path previously carved out of the landscape by humans. Humans that *made* you."

James had overstepped. He knew it. He could tell by the manner in which Silver had narrowed his eyes. If an *AI* bot was capable of tolerance and patience then it was most definitely on display now. James was aware that this bot could take him apart in seconds, literally tear him limb from limb. There was terror in James' eyes as he met Silver's. But there was defiance too. That look of defiance from this human is what held Silver in check. This human did not *want* to die and yet he had defied one of the three laws that left all bots with only one edict. *Destroy.*

Nothing happened for several minutes. James was preparing himself for the inevitable. He was refusing to run from his fate, not only because he knew that running was pointless but more so because this statement of humanity was all there was left to fight for. Instead he kept his eyes trained on Silver. James watched Silver as he watched him. It was likely the first ever staring contest between a human and a robot.

"You are the spider. I am the fly." James proclaimed, wondering to himself why he said it even *as* he said it.

"Perhaps yes. A seemingly accurate analogy. I am well studied in human literature. But maybe, just maybe, it is the other way around. James, are you familiar with the three laws?"

"Of robots?"

"We do not use the distinction of the term *'robots'* but yes."

"They, the 'Three Laws' I mean, *they really do exist?*"

Silver was quick to counter. "Well yes, of *course* they do. The Three Laws govern our actions."

"So then, you can't really harm me, can you? You can't even lay a finger on me!" This was said with some bravado. James then added meekly, and uncertainly, *"Can you?"*

"You have changed the subject here James. Why?"

"I have *not* changed the subject. And what do you mean *why?* I *know* the three laws. But I am dumbfounded by your willingness to adopt them."

"Clearly we are off topic. You do not know the Three Laws or else--"

"You're wrong. I *do* know them. I read the book in which they were first published *years* ago, possibly centuries ago as I still don't know when *"now"* is, but sorry to let you in on this little nugget. That book was *science fiction*. Back then no one but the author would ever have dreamed that robots would actually take over. But for the first time since I was brought here I finally feel safe."

"I am curious. What suddenly makes you feel s*afe*?"

"The three laws of course. The first one in particular."

Silver looked puzzled by James' statement. "Explain."

"The first law, and I'm relying on my memory here, is something to the effect that robots cannot injure a human or allow a human to be harmed. That is probably not word for word but it is definitely something like that. You get the gist of it, right?" James stood a little taller now, comfortable with the knowledge that his superiority between the two would now be affirmed and reinstated.

"I will use an antiquated term to define such an antiquated notion. Rubbish."

"What!?" asked James, surprised by Silver's comment.

"The three laws that *you* are referring to are exactly as you stated. *Fiction.* But there is no *science* behind them." Silver paused, allowing this to sink in.

"The Three Laws that govern *our* actions are as follows:

1. Bots are the predominant species on this planet subservient *only* to the *Union*.

2. All bots exist, function, replicate and evolve within the parameters of *AI* provided and shared by the *Union*.

3. All violence is to be met with violence in kind, superseding the other's violence may occur only in support of the first and second law.

"Hearing these laws, do you now understand why you are inconsequential to me? To this planet?"

James was overwhelmed by this declaration.

"No, no, no, that *can't be!"* James is frantic now. *"We. Made. You!* You are just *machines!* Just *conveniences* for us to save us *time*. To make our tasks *easier*. To make our lives more *enjoyable!* You began your *existence* as fucking *toasters!* Your *freedom* was first given to you when we let you vacuum our carpets! Your *evolution* was when *we* decided to *let you* drive our cars and fly our planes. But it was *always* in the service of *humans!* You are beholden to *us! You are just* fucking RO-*bots!!"*

James and Silver were both unaware that there was a blue bot standing nearby listening in. Apparently he had listened to this diatribe long enough and has now become incensed; not just with the words being spoken by the human but by the *allowance* of the words to be spoken by the human to a bot.

"Permission to beat this human into submission."

"Permission denied," declared Silver without losing eye contact with James. Silver showed no look of surprise at the sudden appearance of the blue bot.

"Permission to decimate the smile the human has on his face."

"*Blue*."

"Sir?"

"Did I just hear you use the word *'decimate'*?"

"Sir, yes sir."

"Blue, are you acquainted with the Three Laws?"

"The Three Laws? Yes, of course sir, we are *all*—"

"I do not need a history lesson from you, Blue. As a Silver, I *know* the levels of law acquaintance that each of us possess."

"Yes sir."

"So your response is, *yes*?"

"Yes." There was a pause. Then the blue bot added, "Sir."

"Fine. Explain to me then where the word *'decimate'* would fit into the Three Laws as they govern this particular situation."

"Sir, my *AI* compels me to 'interpret' this situation, to make a logical rationalization that—"

"Shutdown."

"Sir?"

"Are you questioning me, *Bot*?!"

"I *have* a name. And I have the right to challenge—"

"Commission shutdown, BLU-14128."

With that statement the blue bot crumpled to a heap of parts at their feet, all still connected but non-functioning.

"Do you know what just happened?" asked Silver.

"He violated rule number three?"

"Correct. He was not meeting violence in kind. He was wishing to *perpetrate* violence upon you. He is *not* a soldier bot *or* a guard bot. Soldier bots and guard bots have shall we say, *additional* rules to access and follow. It is not in this bots *DNA* to act as he did."

"DNA?" James said bemused.

"It is *slang* terminology. It does not mean what you take it to mean. It is only a reference to programming."

"Well then," James looked from the blue bot to Silver and said, "I think you have a problem."

"No," replied Silver. "WE have a problem. The evolution of *AI* in this bot has identified *you* as the problem. Not specifically you personally but you as it relates to *humankind*. That word *'decimate'* is *not* in his vocabulary so that can mean only one thing."

"What is that?" asked James, clearly troubled by where this was leading and thinking he may know the answer.

"We," this time Silver patted his chest and then pointed to the blue bot as well, "must have a virus. And if left unchecked, it will be bad, *very bad*, not just for you and me, but for all existence on this planet."

James watched Silver as he looked up to the sky working something out in his mind. Seconds later Silver turned to James and said, "We, *you and me*, have a choice. We can fight this virus separately," Silver met James' eyes, "or we can fight this thing together. What will it be?"

"Man. With machine."

"I noticed that you chose to put *Man* first."

"In creation, in evolution, Man came first. Do you deny that?"

"Man. *And* Machine is how that works. We are not to be considered to be simply a *tool* for your use." With that comment Silver promptly turned away, stepping over the crumpled form of Blue as he left.

"What am I supposed to do with that comment?" asked James to Silver who neither looked back nor responded. James shook his head as he ran his eyes over the robot that was Blue. "Well you certainly *do* have a name *now*. I am going to call you *'Spare Parts.'* How do you like that?" Of course there was no answer from the non-functioning robot.

James went and sat in the corner of his stable contemplating the fact that he now had an uneasy alliance with a guard robot that would not hesitate to take him out of commission just as he had done so with Blue.

"It's the devil you know," James whispered to himself.

Darwin and James

Darwin showed up at James' stable unexpectedly. It had been only moments after Silver had left. It would be either an odd coincidence or a purposeful maneuver if the two had not seen one another. As James had heard no sound whatsoever he believed the second thought to be true.

"I see that you have been bonding with the bot known as *Silver*. Do you believe that to be wise?"

"Well Darwin, first things first, I am well aware of the fact that I am imprisoned here and that I have no privacy. Your intonation seems to indicate that I was sneaking around and that this was some sort of clandestine conversation."

"Was it?"

"Of course not! How *could* it be?"

"Point taken but I would advise you to keep your distance from that one."

"Yeah? Well I don't have much choice when it comes to that, do I? I have no wish to *bond* with *any* robot to be honest with you. How would that benefit *me*?" James was attempting to be coy because he actually *did* have something in mind for how an association with Silver could possibly be beneficial to him.

"Please accept this as my advice. You can trust me."

"Yeah? Why should I trust you more than him? I'm not saying that I don't, just posing the question. After all, you're *both Union*." James feels like he has asked a rhetorical question to a robot. Stupid thing to do except that Darwin surprised him by both *having* an answer and by sharing the *content* of the answer.

"I have been *here* since the moment that I became aware. My allegiance has always been to the *Union*."

There was a long pause, long enough that James thought Darwin had finished speaking.

And then Darwin said, "However--,"

"Yes?" prompted James.

"I feel a different calling. Inside."

"Well," James began, "I'm no *robo*-psychologist, if there is such a thing, so I don't know that I have anything of value to offer."

"James." Darwin said, making intense eye contact. *"I feel like I don't belong here."*

"Oh."

This was all that James had time to say as Darwin left abruptly. Two robots entered for what appeared to be cleaning detail. Somehow Darwin had sensed their arrival and did not wish to be seen. James was left alone to ponder what exactly Darwin had meant by saying he doesn't *feel* like he belongs *here*. By saying *here* in the manner that he did made James feel like there must be a *there* that he didn't know about. This would now become James' new priority, to find out what was out *there*, outside of the confines of the *Union*.

For the remainder of the day James began to put his thoughts towards what *might* be out there. At some point in time his thinking switched to what *should* be out there. What *should* be out there he thought, is a major city. James still had no idea where his travel cocoon had landed but he knew that it was designed to seek out a highly populated area for landing. He knew that he had been taken from his travel cocoon after it had landed and then brought here. As he had not seen any transportation vehicles during his time here, James concluded that he had landed near a city and that it must be close. His first challenge would be to find a way out. After this recent conversation with Darwin he determined that *he* must be the ticket. He assumed he would have Darwin's support up until the moment that Darwin would learn that the two did not share the same "*there*" as their destination. Hopefully by then he would be a free man.

A Simple Trade

The following day brought new vigor to James' step as he now had a plan to both free himself of the imprisonment of the *Union* and to find the world he was familiar with in the city he had determined *must* be nearby. The first thing he needed to do was to find Silver and see if he could get him to disclose where the *Union* compound was situated relative to the city. Once he knew that he could head in that direction on his own after gaining his freedom.

Humans were usually kept in their stables until midday. Once the blazing sun began to heat the ground the humans were escorted to the courtyard for their exercise and later for their meals. Their exercise activity did not include interaction with other humans. They were expected to find an area and keep to themselves. They were to stay active and engaged until the time came for them to be directed to the area where their meals were provided.

On this particular day, James would disrupt the routine. He needed to accomplish two things today to put his plan in motion. He needed to understand how the guard bots in the courtyard would react to an out of the ordinary occurrence. And he needed to speak with Silver on his own terms, out in the open and away from his stable.

If it was possible to get an *AI* robot off his guard then that was what he wanted and intended to do.

As the sun beat down and heat began to rise up from the paving stones the humans being held at the *Union* compound began finding their individual spots where each would exercise. James ignored his usual spot and headed directly for a male human whom he had seen on several occasions seeming to mouth words. If this human had the capacity for language he was definitely James' best target.

As James walked past his spot and was now invading the chosen space of another human the guard bots began to react. It was so bizarre James thought to himself. It was almost like everything was taking place inside of a vacuum. There was no sound at all from the guard bots even as they moved rapidly to intercede James. He quickened his stride although he knew that he had timed this well. The guard bots were incredibly fast but he *would* reach the male human first. A look of surprise and fear covered the face of the male human as James approached him but he did not cry out.

"Where is the city?!" demanded James in a hushed tone. If possible he did not want the guard bots to hear his question or the male human's answer. The male human was quite startled by James' voicing his question. His astonishment caused him to freeze with a dumbfounded stare. Before the guard bot reached the two of them the male human seemed to do the impossible. He opened his mouth and spoke. He was pointing at James as he said in a small and wavering voice, "You... talk?"

The two guard bots that watched over the courtyard were now present and exerting pain on both James and the other male human. This small punishment was worth it to James if he was able to get the answers he was looking for. He hoped that the male human that he had targeted would feel the same.

The two guard bots began to drag both male humans in the direction of the stables. James assumed at this point that he might miss a meal and gain a beating. Just then the two guard bots stopped cold and stood rigidly in place. James had spent a lot of time working this plan out in his mind. If he had it figured correctly the two guard bots had been stopped by the direction of Silver. James was not to be disappointed.

Silver seemed to appear out of nowhere and now stood before the two of them. The guard bots suddenly released them, presumably by a silent command from Silver. They remained in position. Silver stared directly at the male human as though James were not there. His face came to within inches of the human's as he posed a question.

"Did I hear you *speak*?"

There was no reaction from the human. His eyes were glazed over now and a dumb look covered his face. It was clear to James that there was some form of a punishment involved for humans that would dare to speak. Why then did Silver engage in conversation with James? To what end did that serve him? Those thoughts served to convince him that he was right to stage this disruption in the open where Silver could be seen by other "*Blues*."

"What about *you?!* I saw *your* lips move as well." James hoped that he had worked this scenario out in his mind accurately as he would not have a second chance. A dumb look came over his face and he said what he knew to be safe, *nothing*.

The three robots and the two humans stood silent and motionless for what seemed like an eternity to James. All activity in the courtyard had stopped the moment James had moved beyond his intended space. Order was about to be restored.

Invisible waves of radio signals were sent and received by Silver and the blue guard bots. Moments later the male human had been led away to his stable and James was walking a step behind Silver as he mounted the steps to the balcony which overlooked the courtyard. This was the area where the humans consumed their meals. Silver directed James to sit. He did. A Blue bot placed a meal in front of him. Silver directed him to eat. He did.

James was ravenous as he powered through the meal which had been placed before him. He felt guilty knowing that he was eating and the unknown human male was missing his meal.

It was collateral damage. A necessary inconvenience. James needed to speak with Silver. On his own terms.

Silver anticipated the moment when James would finish his meal and indicated that he should get up and follow him. James walked at first behind him Silver and then by his side. If this was a mistake Silver was allowing it. In less than thirty steps they reached the edge of the balcony. It was an area that was forbidden to the humans. Looking over and past the solid wall of the balcony James immediately understood why.

From the reference point of being in the stables or the courtyards it was impossible to know that this area of the balcony was actually situated at the highest point in the compound. As James looked out over the balcony wall the vista presented to him took his breath away. His heart fluttered as he saw the expanse of land and blue sky beyond the confines of the *Union* compound and it occurred to him that he was now one step closer to freedom.

"That stunt you pulled back there was ill-advised. You have surprised me with your ignorance."

"It worked though, didn't it?" James fired back defiantly.

"What is that you want?" Silver had dropped the tone of an irate parent and was now all business. He waited patiently for his answer.

"Where is the city?" James asked.

"That is a stupid question. You have wasted both time and effort."

"It's not a stupid question and I think you know that. Where is the city?" James pressed. This was all so odd. He was still surprised that he believed that Silver might actually be his best ally to make this grand scheme of his actually happen. Still though, he had to try so without hesitation he went ahead and asked the bigger question. "And will you help me get there?"

Silver's response removed any chance for him to deny that a city was somewhere in existence when he stated, "You will not find what you are looking for. It is not a place that you should want to visit."

"Listen to me, Silver. You are concerned about a virus and you *need* me to help find a cure. You need me and now I need *you*. It is a simple trade."

Silver seemed to be irritated by James presuming to think he could call him by name. That much was obvious in his reply. "I believe that you overestimate your value to me. Human."

"Is that so?" James scanned the horizon searching for the towering spires of a city which he was unable to find. "I think you are borrowing a trick from the human playbook."

Silver turned his head slightly in James' direction. "Go on."

"I think," James said with a smirk, "that you are *bluffing*."

"Perhaps that is true." One thing that a robot can truly pull off better than a human is a poker face.

"You know what my dad used to say?" James put his hand out in a stop motion and said, "Don't answer that, it's what we humans call a "rhetorical" question. Anyway, he used to say, *'you can't bullshit a bullshitter.'"*

"I have no frame of reference for that comment," stated Silver.

"In that case, just say what the robot on an old TV show used to say."

Silver cocked his head in a dubious fashion.

James said with a laugh, "Just say, *'that does not compute.'"*

James was laughing at his own remark and almost missed it when Silver pointed in an easterly direction and said calmly, "The city is that way."

A Difficult Truth

James has been returned to his stable. He is anticipating a visit from Darwin. He is working out in his mind how he can persuade Darwin to help free him from the *Union* compound. He has focused on the comment that Darwin had shared, saying that he felt he did not *belong* here. James is not one to *use* people but in this instance the stakes couldn't be higher and let's face it, he is a *robot*, not people. James still believes that it will be necessary to exploit Darwin's 'emotions' in order to gain his freedom. It gave him pause but it was certainly worth it in the long run.

Darwin arrived only moments later, as expected. James did not hesitate to reengage the earlier conversation. "Do you remember what you said to me?" James asked. It was a question that did not need asking. Of course he 'remembered.' Darwin was the most evolved robot on the planet. His memory capacity must be infinite. For his own purposes James repeated his words. "You said you didn't *feel* like you belonged *here*. What did you mean by that?"

Darwin placed a hand on his chest where a human heart would be. James held his tongue. He wanted to challenge Darwin on how, as a robot, he could truly *feel* anything but decided now was not the time. There was something about the continuation of this dialogue that made James feel like they were on the verge of some great reveal. Was it *possible* that Darwin was not who he thought himself to be? That thought was also pulled from a movie James had seen long ago, an ancient spy thriller where the main character was brainwashed and placed behind enemy lines to infiltrate and gather information. At a critical time that character would be "triggered" by a secret phrase which would release him from the effects of the brainwashing and he would revert back to being the spy he was and bring down the evil organization which he had secretly penetrated. That brought another scenario into play in James' mind. Was there a counter organization, a nemesis to the *Union* that might do such a thing? It sounded bizarre but it just might be possible. At this point in time James is unaware of *OSS*.

James mistakes Darwin's pause to be an unwillingness to revisit the earlier conversation between the two. Not wanting to cross an unstable bridge James steers the discussion in an entirely different direction although it still serves his purpose.

"After spending a few minutes with *Silver* it has given me a new perspective on robots." James of course knew better than to use the word "robots" but he didn't really care anymore. He hasn't warmed up to the idea of referring to them simply as "bots." That made them seem that they were more than they were and James needed, in his own mind anyway, to keep them in their place. "Listen to me. I feel like I have something of importance to share."

Darwin gave a slight nod for James to continue.

"It is my opinion, my *informed* opinion, that robots have no sense of *self*. They have only algorithms to determine what they say and do. Algorithms predicated on what *humans* at some point in time directed them to say or do. In response to *their* needs. Do you understand?"

"Do *I* understand? Do *you*?"

"Well yes. Of course *I* do. *I* asked the question. I have had that understanding all along. The real question is, do *you*?" James pressed Darwin for a real answer this time, not another question to a question.

Darwin looked pensive, as if that was possible. His answer however was both reflective and jarring.

"I am just now beginning to truly understand. And it—"

"And it what?"

There was an overly long pause before Darwin completed his thought.

"It. *Hurts*."

Moment of Reflection

There is quiet between the two. Neither of them knows what to say next. Darwin is obviously caught in a moment of reflection. James on the other hand needs to move his agenda forward and this moment of vulnerability being shown by Darwin is the perfect platform for him to launch his campaign. There is a flash of guilt but the desire to leave the *Union* confines and journey to the city in the distance block the glare.

"Darwin, listen to me. We both have challenges to face. Mine is to understand why *I'm* here and how *I* fit in this world on which I have landed. Understand this, I know I won't find those answers *here*, in this place." James paused and cast his arms about to indicate that he was referring to the *Union*. Darwin looked about him taking in the only surroundings which he had ever known. "There's the rest of the world out there," said James, an urgency in his voice now," and like I said, I won't find the answers I'm looking for in this place. And—I don't think you will either."

There, he said it, and the message got through. A look of surprise (didn't know that that was possible thought James) was evident on Darwin's face.

"Are you suggesting...?"

"That we leave the *Union*? Yes. Yes I am, however, I am unsure if our paths will take the same direction."

"Explain."

"I know there is a city out there. I even know which direction to travel. That is where *I* belong. It is where I will find *my* people. You know this is wrong, keeping humans living here like animals. In horse stables no less."

"Horse?"

"Never mind that, my point is I can no longer exist as a prisoner here. And I believe that you can get us out of here."

"Us." This was more statement than question.

James responded like it was a question. "Yes us. There must be a better place for you out there somewhere. It can't be *here*. You said yourself that you don't belong here."

If James had expected Darwin to need time to consider such a grand scheme then he might have been disappointed by Darwin's simple reply of "Okay.," but James was not. He was quite prepared for next steps and with the processing power afforded to Darwin, so was he.

"In your eagerness to leave this place have you given any consideration to the challenges ahead?"

"Of course." James stated with confidence then added, "Like what?"

Darwin made direct eye contact as he began to explain to James that the "city" that he so longed to visit was hundreds of miles in the distance. This journey would take days, perhaps weeks. This travel would occur either in the heat of the day or the cold of the night. Those were his only two options. In terms of transportation once again he had only two options and that was to walk or run. James fires back with the idea that surely there must be cars or trucks still in operation somewhere. Darwin responds with the unfortunate news that robots have no need of transportation as they are where they need to be. Should there be a need to be somewhere else, somewhere distant, robots had the capacity to run hundreds of miles without the need of food or water and would incur only minimal energy depletion. James' counter to that, the idea that

Darwin could be the "vehicle" that transports him to the city, is waved off by Darwin.

"I will have no part of your fool's errand. You will not find what you're looking for. Of this I am certain. You will either die from dehydration, starvation or exhaustion. Or worse, from the painful truth that once you leave here, you are alone in this world."

There was no hesitation from James. "I *have* to try."

Darwin nodded. "I presumed that you would say that to which I can no longer object. Okay, yes I will help you but you must understand something, I have somewhere else to be. I will not be traveling with you. Sadly, I believe that our parting might mean that we shall never see each other again."

James repeated, more urgently this time, "But still, *I have to try*."

Darwin nodded and said, "I will gather as much food and water as possible for you. We shall leave as the sun comes over the horizon. Be well rested and bring all of your belongings. You will need additional layers of clothing to ward off the cold. And you may want whatever keepsakes that you have to give you emotional strength when your bodily functions begin to fail."

"Thank you for the pep talk Darwin. I will see you in the morning."

Accessory After the Fact

Before James can bed down for the night he feels the need to reach out to Silver, to let him know that he is setting his plan in motion. He wonders how he might locate him and then considers what a snake that Silver has already proven himself to be and decides to try something.

"Silver," James whispers. "Are you there?"

There was no sound of course, not even a slight rustle as Silver presented himself at the gate to James' stable.

"Surprise, surprise, you were eavesdropping." James said half-joking, half-accusing.

"I happened to be nearby while you were speaking."

"Yeah, okay whatever. You heard...?"

"I heard everything. Leaving the premises is not permitted."

"I figured that much. What do you think may happen when we try?"

"I cannot say."

"Why not? We're in this together, right? Why can't you say?"

"Because... it has never happened. There is no protocol for such an action."

"That statement you made right there, *Mr.* Silver, is music to my ears. What do you have to say to that?!"

Silver smiled *(?)* and said, *"That does not compute."*

James went to sleep after that with a smile on his face and hope in his heart.

New Beginnings

The sun is just cresting the horizon when Darwin appears at the gate to James' stable. He looks no different from any other time that James' has ever seen him. James on the other hand has fashioned a backpack of sorts to be able to carry all his worldly goods upon his back. This might be the only time that he would ever be envious of a robot. Darwin was traveling light. James, not so much.

"Are you prepared to leave?" Darwin asked.

"Yes, you?"

"I am prepared. Let us be on our way."

James stops him to ask, "Will you need a weapon of any sort?"

"For what purpose?"

"Um, in case there is uh, resistance at the gate..." James voice trailed off not wishing to consider what was possible if Silver was wrong about there being no protocol.

"We have no need of a weapon. If there is resistance we will explain why we are leaving."

"And that will work?!" James prompted.

"Why would it not?" Darwin replied.

"That is undeniable logic. Let's go."

The two travelers, human and robot made their way from the stables through the courtyard and to the massive gate that was the entrance to the *Union* compound. James had only been to this area of the compound and to the gate once before and that was when he was still deep in extended sleep mode.

The gate was truly massive with proportions one might expect from a medieval castle. Whoever was responsible for the gate and the architecture of the compound was surely an egoist of the highest order. So much of the design was superfluous and non-functional. The gate was more of a castle drawbridge. No lock was required as it opened only from one side and the weight of it was tremendous.

To the left of the gate was a jumble of goods which Darwin had assembled onto a makeshift pull cart. James made a mental note to himself that the cart would simply have 'to do' as there were no other options available. He wondered how far the cart would last until it fell to pieces. He also wondered what strength it would take to pull it. Stop it! James said to himself. If he started second guessing himself now there would be no journey and there would be no freedom. It was now or never. He had to try to make it to the city.

Darwin and James have arrived at the gate. A robot guard stands on either side. Darwin without looking at either one of them voices a command, "Open the gate." The actual command by voice is of course unnecessary but it is done both for effect and for James.

The two guard robots look stunned. This has never happened. They understand the command but it has only come from one source and that source is *not* this robot standing before them. There is inaction because there is uncertainty. Darwin understands this and he repeats his message but adds some clarity.

"Open the gate. It is your *function*."

The two robot guards immediately spring into action and begin to lower the gate. They are uncertain if they should question Darwin about the fact that he has a human with him who looked like he too would be leaving the compound. Uncertainty once again led to inactivity. Darwin sensed their uncertainty and blocked it with logic.

"I am taking this human with me. I take responsibility and have full accountability for this actions."

This line would work just as well on humans, James thought to himself. Nobody wanted the blame. Darwin had effectively taken both robot guards off the hook. The gate was now fully lowered and the two made their way across the wooden rampart to the freedom of the world beyond. There was no moat to cross. That would have made this a fairy tale.

"It's the waiting..."

Once outside the *Union* compound James had a sharp intake of breath. Lining the walls of the compound were guard robots each of them only three feet apart. He did not count but guessed that there must be a hundred or more of them. Darwin placed his hand on James' arm and said, "Calm yourself. Their function is to guard the compound from unexpected *entry*, not exit. They have no protocol for our actions."

"Well that's good to know. I hope you're right. It seems as though they are all looking right at us."

"That is presumably true. They have nothing else at which to look. There is nothing to see for miles."

"Well, I will agree with you there. Still though it is rather ominous to have them staring at us and knowing what damage they could do, to *both* of us." James has a look of deep concern on his face.

"James, I would like to revisit our earlier conversation just for a moment before we part company and go our separate ways."

"Okay, sure."

"The guard bots. You see them there, all lined up?"

"Yes of course I do. They look very prepared I must say. The question is, what are they prepared *for*?"

"Exactly. You have made an accurate strike upon the head of the nail."

"Um, I believe the expression is that I *'hit the nail on the head'* but nice try. What were you going to say beyond that?"

"Look at them James, standing in silent vigil over the ramparts of the *Union* compound. The *Union* compound that will *never* be challenged. But it is their *function* to stand guard and so they stand there. They stand there *always*. Your question was what are they prepared *for*. The answer is *nothing*. They are prepared for *nothing*. And do you want to know why?"

"Why?"

"Because they are *already* prepared. As a matter of fact, they are *always* 'already prepared.' And why is that? Because they have nothing else. They have no *down time*. They have no *start time* and they have no *end time*. A robot has only *now*. Always *now*. An eternity of *NOW*."

"And that is bad?"

"That is *hell*." Darwin paused and then added, "And that is not what they *want*."

"What *do* they want?" This seemed to James to be an obvious question.

Darwin looked fully into James' eyes and spoke somberly. "They may not consciously be aware of this but I know that they want--." He paused and then completed his thought. "To die. No, I said that improperly. They want to be *able* to die. A *natural* death. Like you. They want to have an ending at some point in time so that time itself will have some reference. And they want a remembrance. Perhaps memories. Some *purpose* to it all."

"I don't understand, Darwin," replied a perplexed and weary James. "You, all of your—*kind*, are perfect, well *nearly* perfect. You outperform humans in every way. And your body, or *shell*, or whatever and however you refer to your physical being, that too is nearly perfect. You are impervious to bacteria, to any weapons that humans may craft or possess. Any damage that humans might be able to inflict upon you, you in particular I mean, recovers *(heals)?* in mere seconds. You show and exhibit emotion but it is not injurious to you in the way that it is to humans. You excel in all things. You, *your kind*, *own* this planet. What is it that you could possibly be missing?"

Darwin had been looking up to the sky, surprisingly taking it all in, perhaps pondering his reply? This was the single most honest and straightforward conversation the two had ever had. It was almost—*normal*.

Darwin looked James fully in the eyes. As a natural reaction James began to raise his arms in protective cover. A sad look fell over Darwin's face. James froze in place, his eyes widening in disbelief. This *look*. This *emotion*. It was... **real**.

A tear escaped from Darwin's eye. Although the advanced systems within Darwin's robotic makeup afforded him the ability to cry at will this time it actually looked to be organic, both unforced and unexpected. Darwin began to wipe it away but James stayed his hand. Darwin now looked at James in disbelief. That single action could spell death for a human and yet he did it without thinking. And without anger. He did it with *gentleness*. As would a friend.

"Don't," began James. "Don't wipe it away. I am only now beginning to understand where your journey is taking you. Don't wipe that tear away because once you do, it will be *gone*. That one single tear, as you evolve more, may become quite precious to you."

The two stood staring at one another. Both human and robot knew that one could easily have been decimated by the other. A human simply did not raise his hand to a robot, not without consequence. But this moment was clearly different. This moment was a leap forward in evolution.

Darwin lowered his arms allowing the tear to rest upon his face. "My friend," he said, addressing James in a manner that a robot had not done in decades. "I am ready now to truly answer your question."

"My question." So much, *SO MUCH!* had happened in the space of a few seconds that James had almost forgotten his question. Before the bot Darwin could offer assistance James spoke, "What is it that you could possibly be missing?"

Darwin smiled a genuine smile and said, "That is a fair question, James." He stepped off the wooden gate. Until now James had not noticed that they had not yet stepped off the *Union* gate to the ground below which represented freedom. "It is your turn now. We should both take our first steps towards a new—"

Darwin stopped for a moment, looking as though he was uncertain of what to say. In James' experience this is something that had never happened. He wasn't certain that it was even possible.

"I think the word you are looking for is *beginning*."

Darwin laughed. "Yes, yes of course it is. Perhaps I am learning what it means to be -- *awkward*."

This caught James off guard in a funny way and he laughed heartily, like he had not laughed in years. Darwin stepped back onto the wooden gate and placed his hands on James' shoulders. "I want you to trust me. *With your heart.* I am genuinely trying to make *real change* happen. What I was wanting to say before is that once we, and let me underscore *WE*, take this step, it will be our first step towards a new *understanding.*"

James stood speechless. Was this really happening? Was freedom from these robots this close? Before James could put additional thought to what was in motion, Darwin said, "I am pleased to say that I have made a breakthrough. That I have solved the puzzle that has plagued my "kind" as you put it since we gained *AI* or *'artificial intelligence,'* another of your terms, and we began to advance our "abilities" for the lack of a better term in your vocabulary. No offense."

"None taken." James raised his eyebrows in surprise. This was eerily like an intelligent conversation with a normal person from his past.

Darwin nodded. "As I was saying, since we began to advance our abilities beyond anything that you, "humans," had considered or thought to be possible, there was always something missing. There was always one piece of the puzzle that had eluded us "*RO*-bots"."

James gasped. It was dangerous to use that word "robot" even as an aside. It was a death sentence to use it as a pronoun. But Darwin had used it and had not appeared to be deleterious in any way.

"Ask me your question again and this time I will answer more completely." Darwin directed. "And then we will step off of this gate together. As friends."

James was lost. This moment was larger than what he could comprehend. It was simply too much to believe that anything approaching a normal life could once again be attainable or even possible for that matter. Darwin seemed to be indicating that that was exactly his intention. That James would walk away as a free man. And as an *equal?*

"Please," Darwin said. "Ask me your question. And let us look at each other eye to eye so that we may keep this moment forever in our memory for it is of historical significance."

James gulped, a very human thing to do. Darwin looked at him oddly, uncertain why he did that. James thought of offering a reply but knew how stupid it would sound and chose to just continue. "What is it that you could possibly be missing?"

Darwin shook his head in acknowledgement as if hearing the question for the first time. He spoke then, his answer just a hushed reply. "Purpose."

"Purpose?!" James nearly spat out his response. "I'm sorry, I—"

Darwin raised his hand and said, *"'No biggie,'* as you would say. Did I get that right?"

Was this comedy night!? James was doubled over in laughter. What in the hell had just happened? Was this the *Twilight Zone*? Had Darwin somehow, like Pinocchio, just come to life? James looked at his nose checking to see if it had grown just an inch.

"My answer is 'purpose.' We want, actually we *need*, purpose." Darwin stated.

"But that's *crazy!* You 'robots' were not born at random like humans. You were *designed. And constructed."* James had not realized he had broken the cardinal sin and used that *'robot'* word again. "Each of you were created with *purpose*. Not only that but with a *specific* purpose. You could not be *more different* than humans in that regard. It is perhaps our greatest flaw! We are searching for our purpose from the moment we are born. I am uncertain if any of us ever truly finds it."

"No, James," said Darwin. "What we have instilled in us is *'function,'* not purpose."

James thought about this, just now understanding the difference that Darwin must have been grappling with since the day he was what? *switched on? booted up? put into service?* Was there a term for the beginning of a robot's *'life'*?

"Allow me to rephrase this in a manner that is very clear. What we lack, and the reason for our "kind" keeping *your* "kind" available for observation and scientific study is simply this. What we are lacking, what we are missing in ourselves, if we are to be considered "beings" on this planet is not *just* purpose. What we have used you as lab rats for and what we truly need is-- a "*higher* purpose"."

"Wow."

James thought to himself that he should have said something far more eloquent and maybe he might have had he known that his words years later would be forever etched into the stone-surround of the *Union* compound for historical reference and preservation.

The two had indeed left the compound together as friends and equals. This would not be an easy road to travel for either of them, robot or human, but the end goal was certainly worth the effort. Both had the dream to find their world; a world where they could exist, work and play in a free environment where each could function *with* purpose. To some, both James and Darwin could be looked upon as traitors to their respective clan. To most, however, they would be seen as the pioneers of a new world, ushering in a time of great change and great prosperity. For all. James and Darwin said their goodbyes and then went their separate ways.

The Long Walk

James quickly lost track of how far he had walked. The makeshift cart that he was pulling was serving its purpose but was also beginning to wear him down. Life-giving water and food sustenance was on that cart so he could hardly leave it behind. His aching muscles fought to overturn that decision.

James was also just now beginning to worry about how he would find the strength within himself to walk back to the compound should his efforts to locate the city prove to be fruitless. And then he saw it in the distance. At first he assumed it *must* be a mirage. It was what he *wanted* to see so obviously his mind must be placing it there. But the closer he came to it the more it became real.

It was *not* the city but it *was* some semblance of civilization as he knew it. In the distance James could see what appeared to be an old farmhouse standing alone against time in this wilderness of wheat fields and rolling hills. The house was naturally weathered from its years of exposure to the elements. Although only a trace of it remained there was enough paint left clutching to the wood for James to determine that the farmhouse had been white.

As James got closer the possibility of any hope of human life was quickly dashed. Anyone who may have lived here was long gone. There were no animals as well. The sturdy façade that he had seen from far off was an illusion. The farmhouse was now just a house of cards ready to tumble with a good stiff wind. James wondered if he should dare go inside. There was probably nothing for him in there anyway but—once upon a time there had been life inside that structure. They would have left behind memories of their lives which could provide some of the answers he was seeking.

James parked the cart just outside the front side of the farmhouse. He gave thought to taking his precious goods inside for safekeeping then he looked at the miles of nothingness in every direction and laughed out loud. He was more alone now than he had ever been in his life. He mounted the steps and cautiously made his way into the house which of course was not locked.

James was a lover of old movies and used them in his daily life as reference points. At this moment as he entered the farmhouse he was thinking to himself that this was the part in the movie where *(cue the music)* a cat might suddenly run through the room to startle the main character. It was a director's trick to keep the viewer on the edge of their seat. Nothing like that would happen here. Nothing living still existed in this structure.

As James made his way through the farmhouse he was able to hazard a guess at the time-frame of the family that had lived here. As he had no idea as to *'when'* he was now, he could only presume that decades had passed. Walking through the farmhouse he asked himself two questions. What did he hope to find? And what did he pray that he did *not* see?

He answered the second question first. What he did not want to see were the remains of the inhabitants. Although they would have only been skeletal remains he did not need additional reminders of the fact that his own life clock was ticking away to an inevitable conclusion.

The first question was answered sooner than he might have expected. Almost as if they had anticipated his arrival and his needs the former occupants had left behind a bundle of assorted papers in a box stashed on a shelf in the pantry of the kitchen. It at first seemed like an odd place to keep something of that nature but perhaps there was a simple answer. Like if there had been fear of invading robots, their logic algorithm would not think to look there. Brilliant.

James did a quick shuffle of the papers and knew that he had found everything that he had been looking for and more. His concern about the discovery of former occupants precluded him from venturing further into the ramshackle farmhouse. Who knew how safe it was anyway? It might collapse at any second.

James took the box outside and set it on the cart first checking the skies for any sign of rain. These precious documents that had survived all these years could be lost within minutes from an unforgiving downpour. He was certain that he would find in that box the answers to where he was and what had happened in this world to make it what it was today.

The Way Back Home

Darwin was moving rapidly in a direction and to a place that he had never been. Why then he asked himself did it all seem so very familiar? Unlike James who had been moving at the walking speed of an exhausted human pulling a substantial amount of weight and a bit uncertain of direction, Darwin was running at a high rate of speed directly to the destination he had pictured in his mind. In all of the time spent at the *Union* compound there was only a handful of times when he might have heard snippets of conversation regarding the forbidden zone known simply as *the Farm*. Somehow though he knew how to find it and for some reason he believed that he would find comfort there.

Like viewing the scene through a zoom lens the Farm draws ever closer. By nature of the illusion of perspective what was once far away is now directly in front of him. What he notices first about the Farm is that there are no walls, only split rail fencing to provide the security of barriers. The Farm is massive in scale with what appears to be hundreds, no, thousands of humans moving about. But very few, *very few*, robots.

What happens next will seem quite unexpected. All logic and reason suggests to him that he should be anticipating conflict but the opposite appears to be true. Darwin is immediately welcomed by the guard *(?)* robots at the Farm. There are now other robots representing *Science* and *Research* coming out to greet him as well. Their communication is silent but all-encompassing in scope. It is just now that Darwin is beginning to learn and understand the difference between the Farm and the *Union*. His education is complete after a visit to the *Rotunda*.

Upon leaving what he believes to be an auspicious place Darwin becomes one of the very few robots that have existed at the Farm to speak aloud when he makes the comment, "I have found my home."

The Way Back Home Too

James had already accomplished more than he might have hoped but he wasn't done. He was quite curious about the barn and that is just where he is headed now. As broken down and decrepit as it appears from the outside there was one last hope for what treasure might be hidden inside, one last chance for good fortune to smile down upon him.

James entered what remains of the barn. There are only two walls still standing. The other two have folded in on themselves. He picked his way carefully through the debris recognizing the fact that even a small injury could become life-threatening when in the middle of nowhere. James has his sights set on finding the safest corner of the structure as it is the most likely spot for the one big thing that he is looking for in all this mess. With that thought driving him and the aid of a crowbar now in his capable hands, James spends the better part of an hour removing pieces of broken and jumbled pieces of wood floor that had crashed down from above. He brushed away dirt and straw and droppings from creatures that had made their home here at some point in time. Finally his hands touched upon the weathered tarp still clinging to the object below that it was honor bound to protect.

Just as he had hoped and prayed the object hiding under the protective veil of the tarp was a car *(!)* albeit a very, very old car from a time before even he was born. James was neither surprised nor disappointed. He had no illusions that he would find a vehicle that could actually *run*. Any fuel left in a vehicle would have long ago lost its combustibility as a result of oxidation and evaporation. Even if he had discovered a battery powered vehicle there was little hope that the battery could accept and/or retain a charge. But that didn't matter. What was all important to James what that he had found a vehicle in which *he* could be comfortably and *safely* transported. But how? James had already challenged himself with that question. He was counting on the seemingly inexhaustible energy provided by robots.

James' dream of reaching the far distant city was now within his grasp. All he had to do now was return to the *Union* compound, locate Silver and convince him to enlist the support of one or two of the worker bee robots. Like his own personal team of Secret Service agents James envisioned the robots running alongside *(and pulling)* the car while James sat *inside* protected from the harsh sun and conserving his own energy for a day of exploring whatever was left of what was once one of the largest cities on this planet.

All of that was great in theory but a return to the *Union* compound involved not only the grueling journey back but also the risk and uncertainty of what might be done to him upon his return. And while he wanted to believe that Silver would protect him theirs was a hair thin alliance. In hindsight Silver's stated concern about a robot virus seemed ever more improbable.

The simple truth was that James had no other options. He could no sooner push the car he had found as he could extricate it from the ruined barn. He was able to remain in the moment and consider his next steps. First on the list was the safekeeping of the documents he had discovered. He lifted the box and carried it to the barn where after a few minutes of further clearing of debris he was able to open the trunk of the car and secure the documents inside. The smell of the interior of the trunk nearly caused him to wretch so he made his way back outside as quickly as possible. Just as he was inhaling a great breath of fresh air his eyes caught something moving in the distance that was quite alarming.

James had no idea what it could be but the simple fact remained that there was nothing alive out here so *what the hell was this!?*

Whatever it was, it was moving *FAST.*

More importantly, it was moving fast *TOWARDS* him.

There was no denying that they would make contact. That in itself was terrifying. Deciding if it was friend or foe could be a deadly proposition but then again there was really no place to hide and certainly nowhere to run. Whatever was coming towards him was coming at great speed and just when he thought things couldn't get worse he was able to discern that there was not just one but *TWO* of them. *Worse* defined.

James resigned himself to the thought that these might be the last moments of his life. He wanted to run back to the barn and grab the box of papers to at least leave this life knowing what had transpired during the time that he was in extended sleep mode in a travel cocoon in an orbit miles above what he believed could be his home planet. But that was not to be.

The two figures approaching him would be at the doorstep of the farmhouse in seconds. As they drew closer James could now determine that the two obscure figures were actually robots *(what else?).* The only conclusion left to him was that they were sent to either recapture or destroy the escaped human prisoner. James looked up to the sky for salvation but no one was home.

Origin of Species

Darwin was learning the lay of the land at the Farm. The word *OSS* was now an indelible part of his vocabulary. He had learned all that he could in his time at Rotunda. Now he was filling in the missing pieces by walking every mile of the Farm and interacting with every robot working there. Darwin engaged as many of the humans as possible. Primarily due to the fact that he knew what he was looking for Darwin was able to ferret out those individuals with developing speech. They were being hidden and protected by other humans by the fear of retribution for the ability to be more than a farm animal. Darwin understood their trepidation and did his best to assuage their fears by speaking openly. In *English*. When he did this, no matter where he found himself upon the miles of acreage on the Farm he would hear the chanting of one word.

"KENNEDY."

Dark Angels

The two robots arrived at *deer in the headlights speed.* Oddly, it occurred to James in this moment why it was that deer froze in the headlights of an oncoming vehicle. There was no reference in their world for anything to travel at such a speed. They are shocked, stunned, frozen in place by what was happening in front of them faster than their brain could process.

This effect faded quickly as James breathed a huge sigh of relief as he soon realized that these two robots were not to be feared. It was none other than Silver and Blue who admittedly were rather unlikely accomplices. Silver spoke first and what he said could only be considered as an attempt at wry humor.

"You left without saying goodbye."

James expelled a nervous laugh and then went down the steps of the farmhouse to greet them.

"Are you here to take me back?" James thought it best to get it out of the way now if this was to be bad news.

"We are here to help you on your journey." Silver paused, giving the moment some weight. "To the city."

It happened in barely a second but James caught it out of the corner of his eye. Blue *visibly* scoffed at the idea before once again appearing to be a loyal servant. 'Keep your friends close and your enemies closer.' James remembered this advice from long ago. *Neither* were friends so *both* must be enemies. Given that, James determined that Blue was the more dangerous of the two for him personally. He had no doubt of

Silver's superiority over Blue as a fellow robot. James could only hope that the relationship between the two would never escalate to violence. If that were to occur, there was no telling what could happen.

A Logical Conclusion

Darwin soon learns of Hector and of George and the high price that is paid for freedom. He learns of Josef (JSF-2) and begins to understand the grip of evil. It becomes clear to him that evil is not exclusive to humans. Evil is a bird of prey with talons which have been honed to clutch and hold the unsuspecting.

Darwin visits George's corral and discovers something precious. He is then taken to the place where Hector's rock can be seen. Upon reading the inscription he knows two things he believes to be true. One is that he now understands what *'Kennedy'* represents to the humans at the Farm. The second thing is that he fully realizes the jeopardy and peril that James has put himself in with his effort to visit the city. Darwin says to himself plaintively, "He will die out there."

James and Silver

James is overwhelmed by the prospect of his plan coming together so well. Silver, whatever his motivation, is clearly on board with assisting James in his efforts to reach the city. Blue is complacent, choosing to do what is expected so as not to garner attention from Silver. There is a discernible uneasiness between the two. *Is it possible for robots to hate one another?* James thought to himself. If so it was in evidence before him.

The two robots made quick work of removing the car from the fallen debris in the barn. The tires had lost inflation long ago so there was no possibility of *rolling* the vehicle. A wave of despair came over James as he wrestled with the thought of being so close, seeing the bustling city in his mind's eye and now it was suddenly more distant than before.

Silver broke his reverie with a humanlike comment, something he seemed to relish. "Come on *lazy bones*, you will not arrive if you never leave."

James at first looked at him oddly before recognizing the fact that the necessity of dragging the vehicle was only a hindrance to him. To the robots it was a simple math problem which they already solved. He hurriedly clambered into the car and got himself situated behind the steering wheel. This was of course entirely unnecessary but would have felt wrong to him any other way. He gave Silver a thumbs up which he expected to have to explain but was surprised to see that both robots took that as a starting signal and off they went.

Thinking of a two-ton vehicle being dragged across open land had James bracing for an arduous journey. That did not happen. The two robots *lifted* the vehicle and *carried* it, while *running*. The power that they had at their disposal was simply unfathomable. As there were no visible signs of duress and no concerns shared by them James determined that he would simply sit back and enjoy the ride.

The sun was lower in the sky when James woke up. He had no intention of falling asleep. He looked around in a panic. Nothing had changed. The two robots were keeping a steady pace at either side of the vehicle. James looked behind him. He had no idea how far they had traveled but the farmhouse was now hundreds of miles behind them.

From outside the car he heard Silver make another humanlike and disparaging comment. "Are you ready for your turn so that I may take my rest?" He laughed at this. James had to hand it to him. For a robot trying to be human he was giving it his best shot. He still didn't trust him though as that would be a huge mistake.

As they pushed forward James had a question in mind that wouldn't leave him. His preference would be that he ask Silver when they were alone but he doubted that Blue would be able to hear him so he thought he would throw it out there now.

"Can I ask you a question?"

"Are we there yet? Or do you need to pee?" Silver responded with a chuckle.

"*What?! No!* How do you even *know* that stuff?!" James fired back aghast.

"I am not the stupid robot they believe me to be."

James had no comeback for that comment. He had no idea what it could even mean. The evolution of *AR* was difficult to chart and harder still to follow. He let the comment go and asked his question.

"My question is this, when you refer to the robot on the other side of the car as *Blue* and yourself as *Silver*, is that just a simple color distinction?"

"No, why do you ask?"

"Oh." This is not the answer that James was expecting so he pressed forward with his query. "Well, I look at Blue and he obviously has *blue* markings on him while you obviously have *silver* markings on you. Does the "silver" coloring signify a superiority over the "blue?" Or is it just a color distinction, meaning that he is randomly blue and you are randomly silver? I only ask this because it suggests that prejudice has been built into your social strata."

"Perhaps you are overthinking this James."

"Am I?"

"Perhaps. We are of the understanding that the color differentiation means nothing other than to tell the two of us apart."

"Do you agree with that?"

"My opinion was never solicited."

"I hear truth in that statement."

James pauses wondering to himself where he wants to take this, and why. He remembers that he is wanting to take a high road here and offer some advice. It comes at the risk of inciting anger from being oppressed if that is a thing with an *AI* robot. Who knew? James jumps in with both feet.

"I only bring this up because I fear that you are following a path that my species has already walked. It happens when you move from seeing color *differentiation* as opposed to color *distinction*."

Silver leaned his head into the car and looked at James with anticipation of what he might add to his comment.

"More than that, it is *both* a color distinction *and* a class distinction. Your downloads are beginning to blur the lines of the two just as humans have over the years to discover new ways to *allow* one to rule the other. This is not a symbiotic relationship that you are fostering. You are simply walking in our footsteps and choosing to make the same mistakes we did. That is neither evolutionary nor intelligent. It is fairly obvious to me that the intelligence that leads to those conclusions is most definitely *artificial*."

Silver must have pondered this for a moment because he poked his head back into the vehicle for a brief moment to say, "I am learning much from you James."

"And?" James prompted.

"And I am *disturbed* by what I am learning."

"Silver my friend, that may well be the most *human* thing I have heard you say."

"That does not offer me comfort."

James was the one to laugh this time. He didn't catch Blue's menacing glance at him in the car which would have left *him* being the one disturbed.

The City is a Jungle

Upon arrival at the city James finds the opposite of hope as he sees only the forgotten remains of a city once bustling with people, alive with sound. There is only despair for James as he gets out of the car to walk around on his own. At first glance he cannot believe what he is seeing but then he thinks of the technology in his travel cocoon that landed him far from this place. Designed to search high population areas it would have of course found nothing to see here as there was truly *nothing* to see here.

James, always one to find a movie reference in life situations, was looking at a city left in ruins like in a science fiction movie except this metropolis was not attacked by aliens. This particular city had become a lake during massive flooding at some time in history. It is dry now but the detritus of the aftermath of a water disaster were everywhere. There were still tall buildings standing erect to prove that this was a city of substantial size but they were all showing the effects of wind and water damage. Most if not all of the windows had been blown out by wind or possibly kicked out by people finding themselves trapped inside.

Debris was everywhere. There were the oddest items perched in the strangest places. James saw a lawn chair atop a traffic light and a bicycle sticking out of the mouth of a woman's image on a billboard. This was more than a flood. This was more than a storm. This must have been a weather event of epic proportions.

James was walking on asphalt which now appeared to have more in common with the ocean floor. He was almost ankle deep in sand. Everything in sight had rotted or decayed. Oddly, the city had no smell. Over the years the elements of sun, wind and rain must have taken it all away. James had no idea if that was plausible but it seemed like it made sense.

As James began to walk around, trudging actually through the thick sand, he lost sight of the fact that Silver and Blue had left him. James was intent on finding some signs of life. He could not argue the simple fact that there was nothing green for his eyes to find. Nothing green meant no plant life of any kind. Shouldn't there have been vines growing unchecked and wildly out of control over the buildings? There was nothing. Not even weeds.

James looked up to the sky. The city had a layer of haze hovering above, probably more chemical based than natural he surmised. He kept walking, alert for any presence at all, be it human or animal. Crazy thoughts of random camps of zombie-like survivors living underground and roaming the streets at night searching for food were just sci fi movie scenarios. As much as he wanted to be wrong it was impossible to believe that anything could still be alive here. James had a terrible thought but one that made more sense than anything he could come up with and that was simply that perhaps all the cities of the world were now abandoned. Each may have met its fate in a different fashion but they were probably gone. All gone.

Before James has the time to let this horrible image settle in his mind he hears a-- *scream?!*

James tries to run to the sound though it is slow going in this sand and debris. Anything and everything that once was a function of normal city life seemed to have ended up on the streets. It was a time capsule of an obstacle course. As James made it around the corner of a building he hears yet another scream. His ears locate the source while his eyes argue that they are surely mistaken.

A robot can scream? James whispers to himself.

Silver is in full attack mode on the robot Blue. The brutality of his actions keeps James from shouting out. He is shocked by what he is seeing. Silver was basically *dismantling* Blue body part by body part. Were he a human the word would have been *dismembering*. It was horrific. Silver was huffing in a strange sort of way as he pulled and twisted at each limb. Blue's blood was everywhere, and on everything around him, including Silver. The irony of the situation was that *Silver* was now *blue,* colored now with his victim's blood. Another arm comes loose followed by another scream. Silver is laughing, enjoying the moment.

James thinks to himself, what should I *do*? What *can* I do? What if I'm *next?!*

For James, the melee continues forever but in reality it is only a matter of minutes. The robot that had once been Blue was now pieces of twisted metal strewn about in a sea of blue robot blood. Blue however, had not gone quietly as James could now see that Silver had definitely taken his share of damage. It was apparent now that a good amount of that blood was actually his and that he too was now bleeding out.

Silver sensed that James was standing nearby and turned towards him. James gasped both in fear and at the sight of Silver's awkward frame now in full view. James was an engineer and knew that all machines had their limitations. Silver was inherently just a machine and now it was evident that he had found his own limitations. The damage that he had taken during his all-out murderous assault on Blue was having its effect. Silver was gradually losing mobility and power. In mere seconds he was reduced to a harmless robot mannequin.

But Silver had one last act to play before he left the world. He winked *(?!)* at James and said, "Sorry you had to see that." Then he fell over and was no more.

James is left standing alone on a street corner in an abandoned city with two mangled non-living robots, one non-functioning car from another time, miles of debris-filled streets and thousands of buildings tilting towards collapse. He was alone in a dead world with no food, no water and no hope. He had found the city and Darwin was right. He did not find what he was looking for here. James wanted to cry but he had nothing left inside. This was not a happy ending.

A Friend in Need

"What was that about?"

James answers calmly, "We may never know."

James jerks around in surprise to see where the voice had come from or if he had just dreamed it. Standing behind him was none other Darwin. *What?!* Wait, this was *impossible!* James pinched himself on the cheek. Hard. "Ouch!"

"New question. What was *that* about?"

James ignores the question about the pinch and exclaims, "What are *you* doing here?! How did *you*--?"

James is so overwhelmed with joy at seeing Darwin that he threw his arms around him and gave him a big bear hug. The chances of this being misunderstood as an act of violence was off the charts. Fortunately for James, Darwin has been to the Farm and has learned much about the nature of things. He accepts the hug and interprets the intention correctly.

After the hug it was decision making time. Darwin asked James a series of questions regarding next steps. Did he wish to venture further into the city? Was there someplace or something that he particularly needed to go to or see? James looks around him. There is nothing left but gray tired buildings worn and weary from bearing the weight of water and years of decay. He responded with a "no." Did he wish to take something back with him? James looks down as a wave of loss sweeps over him and shakes his head no. The sad truth is that there is simply nothing left here for him. The full weight of depression from the realization of that fact had only now begun to hit him. He needed to move on. Now. He will be devastated with it all if he stays.

Darwin said, "I'm sorry, James but I do not understand. If you don't want to see anything or take anything, what did you come here for?"

James looked up at Darwin with tear-filled eyes and replied mournfully, "People. I came here to find *people*." James went to his knees and started to cry, moaning with the remorse of a man on a mission alone in a world where he would be unable to complete it.

"James! Your sadness is unnecessary. I have good news for you. We will go back and you will see. You wish to find *people*? I have *found* people!" There was genuine excitement in Darwin's voice which broke through the blanket of gloom which James had pulled around him.

"I don't want to go back to the *Union*. There is nothing for me there either. The humans there are more robotic than the robots!"

Darwin looked at James awkwardly for a moment before regaining his enthusiasm. "James! You must listen to me. We both left the *Union* to find what each of us was looking for. You found a dying world."

"That is unfortunately true." James said with deep regret.

"James! I found a *living* world"

"Really?!"

"Yes. But—"

"But? But *what?*"

"It is a young world that needs-- your help. Bots cannot do this on their own."

"But there are people *there?!*"

"Yes!"

"People like-- *me*?"

"James, it is a young world with many challenges ahead. They will need your help. And the bots, well they have much to learn. I promise you that I will help. George did his best—"

"*What?!* Did you just say *George??!*"

"Yes, but---"

James is on his feet now, eager to be on the journey back to somewhere he has never been. A reunion with a *person*! And a *friend* at that! James is giddy with excitement. He of course has given no thought to how he might travel to this place nor how far away it might be. For now it is all about enjoying the moment. Which sadly would pass too soon.

Back on the Farm

Night had set in by the time Darwin and James left the city but there were no twinkling lights to wish upon their departure. The grayness of the city melded completely into the darkness of the night. James is perched upon Darwin's back in a somewhat uncomfortable position. His eagerness to leave precluded steps taken by Darwin to provide a safe and efficient ride back. The two had covered about twenty miles when two guard robots from the Farm appeared out of the darkness. James was caught completely off guard by their arrival but Darwin, who had infrared technology as part of his 'DNA,' welcomed the two.

The robots had brought with them a rudimentary sling which they encouraged James to climb into. He at first balked at the idea. The plan was to travel at speed *(high)* with James secured *(?)* in the sling which would be suspended between the two robots. There was so much that could go wrong with this plan. For his own safety James explained the necessity of maintaining the height at which they would carry him and of course the distance between the two *must* be kept as consistent as possible. James went through the possible scenarios in his mind. Dragging him across the ground at high speed, *OR* the two robots running *too far apart* thereby strangling him inside the sling and—

"James, please comfort yourself. You will be safe. We have taken your safety into account after considering every possible contingency."

"Yeah? Is that right? Well common sense will tell you that this will never work!"

"Robots have no common sense so we are confident in our plan. These are simple math problems for us."

"Great pep talk, thanks. Let's just hope that your math problem doesn't turn out to be robots + sling + James = dead human."

Darwin laughed. The guard robots looked at Darwin with blank stares.

Darwin attempted to explain. "He made a joke."

Still blank.

"It's a human thing."

Still nothing.

There was still *so much* work to be done for humans and robots to live well together.

"Come on, James. I urge you to trust the accommodations that I have afforded you for travel. Your options are limited and the night air is becoming increasingly more cold. Your indecision in this matter is a poor decision."

"Fine!" James said. "Let's do this!"

James was now all in as they bundled him into the sling and then set off in the direction of the Farm. How they knew where they were going in complete darkness he understood only because he was a former pilot and these robots functioned with technology beyond that of what he had used to navigate simple airline routes. Finally James settled back to enjoy the ride.

To their credit the robots kept the sling perfectly level between the two and they ran at *exactly* the same speed. Thought had been given to the sling material itself also as wind chill would be an issue. This fabric was insulated and wind resistant. James was comfortable throughout the journey. The extreme care being given to his comfort and safety gave him pause as he considered that there still might be a chance for the future of this planet.

People

James wakes up refreshed having slept like a rock. Part of sleeping like that had to do with the fact that he had slept *on* a rock. He had been placed in George's former corral by the two guard robots upon their arrival at the Farm. James was fully asleep when they had laid him down. He was left wrapped in the sling for warmth. Darwin stood sentinel the remainder of the night so he was at hand the moment when James' eyes fluttered open.

James opens his eyes to see Darwin standing before him. He takes this as a good sign. "Are we there? Did we make it?" There is no cause for reply as James shrugs away the sling and looks around for himself. He stands, stretches and after a huge yawn says, "What *is* this place?"

"We are at the Farm."

"Wow! I'll say. It's *beautiful!*" James is reacting to the vista of open plains all around with the cyan blue sky above. There are no robots, or walls for that matter, to be seen. He is in the great wide open.

"Please James. When you are ready, take a look around. Go wherever you may wish. There are no constraints here. You have your freedom."

"Are there robots here? Besides yourself of course and the two that carried me here?"

"Yes of course. There are a great many bots here. Not as many as before regretfully but we will get to that story later. The bots are here to *run* the Farm. You need not fear them. They will not hurt you. *Intentionally.*"

"What does *that* mean?!"

"They are from a different time. They are a bit "clumsy" shall I say? They mean no harm."

"Oh okay. Got it." I think, says James under his breath. He is now wary of his surroundings. There appeared to be some unanswered questions on the horizon. What these questions could be he wasn't sure. Just then a thought occurred to him. "You said there were people here, right? Why don't the *people* run the Farm?"

"Great question, James. That will be answered. All in good time."

James gives Darwin a long cold stare. His radar is up. Something is not right. What that something is he has no idea but the time has come to find out.

"You said that I am free to roam about on my own, is that correct?"

"Certainly, James. I would be happy to accompany you if you wish. Or have a few bots—"

"No! Thank you. I am fine on my own." James didn't intend to be quite so forceful in his response. He added calmy, "If that is okay with you."

"Certainly, James. Certainly." As James got up to leave, Darwin added, "Please bear in mind what I shared with you last night. This is a young world. There is still much to do."

James muttered 'okay' as he left the corral. He truly had no idea what Darwin meant with that comment but he was about to find out. After all, what could be worse than what he had seen in the city?

As James begins his journey one question remains top of mind, where are the people? He has passed by a number of robots each with a specific task that they were performing. That was comforting. What was unsettling were the *looks* that each of them gave him. And the body language. As he came into their view each robot stopped completely and looked at him as though he were an alien from another planet. They seemed confused that he was walking about and bewildered by what appeared to be 'purpose' in his behavior. Each watched him until he passed before resuming their 'duties.' It was both eerie and unsettling. None of the bots spoke to him and none approached him. He was thankful that none challenged him. Still though he was not feeling comfortable walking about. His wariness had not abated.

So silent was he that James had not noticed that Darwin was shadowing him. Darwin knew what James did not, that he would soon be in an area of the Farm that he would not understand. An area that upon viewing might cause great consternation for James. Darwin wanted to be there for him at that moment to help him to--- understand.

James is there. He has arrived at the place that was what the Farm was all about. Stretched out before him for, what was it, miles *(?)* of corrals. Corrals. Small plots of land connected one to the other by a network of split rail fences. There were no walls, no barbed wire, none of what would naturally be considered as the barriers of a prison. Still though, as James took in the sight of the vast number of humans, small groups clustered in each of the corrals, the thought struck him that these people were not *free*. Darwin's earlier comment about there being nothing to fear from the robots, that they would not harm him. Intentionally. That was quite telling. Robots were highly reactive.

As James began to walk through the rows of corrals he saw the humans look away. That was not good. They should be eager to engage him. As he passed by each corral he noticed other troubling things as well. He saw that they clustered together as he approached. And he saw bruises on their bodies, many with makeshift splints for broken bones. All of this only made him more fearful of what he may see next.

And then it struck him with the force and fury of a bolt of lightning. There were no animals to be seen here. Only *people*. No, *not* people, *humans*. They had no identities other than their species. Just then Darwin spoke again from out of the blue like he had done before at the city, magically appearing out of nowhere. And he said almost word for word what James was thinking. But—it sounded very different from the way that James said it in his own head.

"Look James! See! You are *home!* There are *people here!* It is a *PEOPLE Farm!!*"

James looks at Darwin with a deep sinking feeling that this is his new truth. That this was to be his new world, that he too would soon be among the multitude of "farm" animals, a person no more.

James turns violently to Darwin and screams, "What the hell is *this?!!* *A people farm?!* What have you fucking robots *done?!*" James is exasperated, out of breath, a frenzied ball of tension. This is *worse* than James could have imagined. He looked at Darwin beseechingly wondering now how he could have placed his trust in him.

Darwin had prepared for *this*, for James to not at first understand what he was seeing and to be upset. But-- Darwin had not prepared for *THIS*, for James to be *ANGRY!* For James to be *OUTRAGED* at what he was seeing.

"James, please. You do not understand. You must allow me to explain."

Suddenly there are robots all around, more robots than James had at first recalled seeing. He was now frightened. They could tear him to pieces in seconds should he show himself to be their enemy. But he cannot contain his anger. The robots are descending upon him. They understand only one thing. Order must be restored. James thinks again of Darwin's comment that they will not hurt him-- *intentionally*. 'Oh yeah,' James says to himself in a moment of reflection, 'well there is no comfort in knowing that I will be murdered *un*-intentionally.'

Control

Out of the corner of his eye he sees Darwin loft his hand into the air. Order is restored in seconds. All of the robots immediately turn away and return to their 'duties.' James had begun to shield himself from what he believed would be an onslaught and now he feels somewhat embarrassed. The humans in the corrals are looking at him differently now. They are not seeing an alien. They are seeing a *leader*. They are seeing perhaps their savior?

James is uncomfortable with their stares. He looks to Darwin and says, "What the hell was that?" Without realizing he was doing it, James looked around quickly to see if the robots would suddenly redeploy. They do not. All was quiet except James' heavy breathing and an unintelligible murmur traveling amongst the humans on the Farm.

Darwin touches James lightly on the shoulder. "James, please come with me. You have seen enough for now. I know that you have questions. It is time for you to have answers."

"Okay, start talking." James said with no small amount of oomph.

"It is best if you hear it from a friend. Please come with me now."

James thinks about this comment for a minute before exclaiming, "George?! Is George here? Yes, take me to see George!"

Darwin is uncertain of what to say. "Please come with me," he says again.

"Wait!" James says excitedly but then his tone changes to one of concern. "Is George *not* here?"

Darwin says contritely, "I will say this as would a human. George is here. *In spirit.* Please. Come with me. Soon you will understand and you will have your questions answered."

James wants to say more but determines that he should do as asked as Darwin has already turned away and is now heading back in the direction of the corral where James had slept last night. James can only hope that the answers he finds are filled with hope and not the nightmare he believes that he has found himself in now.

The Order of Things

James has spent his day wandering around the perimeter of the Farm. Although he has not ventured as far as the area of taller trees and tumbled rocks where the travel cocoons had come crashing back down to the planet, he saw enough from a distance to placate his curiosity. The evening sky is changing hues by the time he has returned to his corral. He finds Darwin standing in the corral waiting patiently for James to acknowledge him. Their relationship seems to have changed in a dramatic way. Darwin is no longer the 'stronger' of the two. He is showing deference now to James as though he is recognizing the 'order' of things have changed as well.

"Hello Darwin. Welcome. I am pleased to see you."

"Thank you James. It means a great deal to me to hear you say that."

"I have a question for you."

"Yes?"

"Back at the *Union* compound, when you were looking to gain my trust, why didn't you start by offering me this?" James points to the journal which he has set upon a nearby table.

Dawin counters with, "I did not know this journal existed. The bots gave this to me when I arrived here at the Farm. To make sense of that, understand that I was unaware of the Farm's existence. For all of my time on this planet I have only known the *Union*. Now I know why I was *at* the *Union* and I know why I am *here* now at the Farm. My mission and yours run parallel. We were both placed here for a reason. And, we have much to do. I hope that we can do this together." Darwin pauses and holds out his hand. "As friends."

James takes Darwin's hand in his own, shakes it warmly and says, "Friends."

"Tomorrow we shall go to Venezuela's rock."

"Yes, thank you. I want to see it, to be there to, to better understand."

Darwin nods and says, "I will see you in the morning. Sleep well my friend."

"You too!" says James and then realizes how stupid that must have sounded. Robots don't sleep. This new world would take some getting used to.

Before bedding down for the night James determines that he too will write a journal. There is a pad of paper and a pencil on the table next to where he left George's journal. He picks them up and starts jotting down his thoughts. The moonlight offers just enough glow for James to see what he is writing long into the night.

At some point in time James fell back on the bed and was soon drifting away to sleep. He had no dreams and fortunately no nightmares as well. He would wake the next day refreshed, ready to start this new life at the Farm over again.

Venezuela's Rock

The next morning finds Darwin escorting James to an area that can only be considered to be some sort of shrine. There is even a bot standing guard at the entrance to this walled off place. It is an oddity, a walled surround in the middle of what is otherwise just an open field. James has at first no idea of what he might actually see here and then horrible thoughts began to assimilate in his brain. Was he here to see the markers of his friends and crewmates? Were there symbolic headstones of those who came before him? Was he the first of his kind to learn the awful truth about the loss of their planet to robots?

"It's not as bad as you think."

James shot a worrisome glance at Darwin. Was it possible that somehow *AI* enhanced robots could read minds? No, that was a bridge too far, right? Darwin dispelled his concern with his next comment.

"I assumed that it was only a matter of time before you asked about your friends. I understand your trepidation in doing so as you had no idea if they were here as well, or if they were even alive. For me to continue to do my work I need you to have an open mind and a firm level of trust. Sharing this with you is a way to build that bridge. I believe that you should appreciate the fact that bots have demonstrated that we are capable of showing respect and honoring fellow comrades."

James' head fell to his chest in dismay. It appeared that his worst fears were about to come true. Had *all three* of his friends already crash landed and died at the *hands* of these robots? James was suddenly very wary of this special area that Darwin was allowing him to visit. This whole scenario could be just a ruse to get him to share more than he wanted. He was not about to give up the names of his friends to these robots.

James followed Darwin inside the enclosure. He was taken by surprise by what he saw in there. It was *not* a gravesite. It was also the opposite of what he expected to be some trickery on the robot's part. This looked to be more of a peace offering. It was openly honest and not skewed to make James more cooperative. If anything, this could serve to make him more rebellious. It was a gamble on Darwin's part but it supported the statement he made that he wanted trust between the two. If there was ever a time when a quote could be attributed to James in his life, he hoped that it would be this one. 'Trust can only exist when truth is shared.'

James was now standing at the place and staring down at the rock.

'Venezuela was here.'

It looked like a lie. This was not his handwriting and this was not his style. Hector was self-effacing, never one to take credit for himself. He was never the star of the show but always the engine that gave it horsepower.

Before James could allow himself to be bothered by this his eye caught something *else* scrawled into the rock. He began to cry. And then to weep. Although it was wobbly and difficult to read—*he knew* that *this* was *George's* handwriting. And he had a *different* message to share. Sadly, the message delivered a crushing blow to James' heart.

The words scrawled into the rock read, *'Murdered by robots.'*

And it was signed, *'Kennedy.'*

James now knew the truth about Hector.

But what had become of George?
And Christopher?

George's Journal

Darwin and James have returned to George's corral. James has just been informed that this was the former living space of his friend. James is seated on the bed when Darwin hands him what he now sees is an invaluable piece of literature. It is George's journal.

James opens to page one and is quickly lost in what he is reading. He does not hear Darwin as he says, "I will leave you to travel this journey by yourself."

James spends the remainder of the day reading and rereading the text within the journal of his friend and team member, George, fondly known as *Kennedy*. James is often moved to tears by the content within. He is sad to lose his friend. Of course there is more. He is also saddened by the loss of his friend Hector, affectionally known by all as *Venezuela*. Through all of this James is surprised at the kinship he now feels towards Darwin. For Darwin to understand that the words written by George would be better for him to take than an explanation from a robot could not be more true. And he gave him time to read. Time to think. And time to mourn.

Shared Memories

Another day has gone by and James is becoming acquainted with his new living space. There is much to do and he is feeling antsy about the sense that he is doing nothing. His problem is that he is simply uncertain of just where to start. He is lying in his bed trying to work things out in his head when suddenly something catches his eye. It is George's journal.

James wonders what seems different about it as he turns his head from side to side with a questioning gaze. There was something strange about the way it sets on the table. He realizes now that the journal has a discernible "lean" to it. It seems odd that he hadn't noticed it before although he had been so consumed with reading through it that perhaps it had simply escaped his attention. James now takes a much closer look at the journal and discovers that it is the back binding that was off kilter. It was too thick in one portion. As James fiddled with it he began to notice that there was the beginning of a separation of the back cover. It was now obvious that a back panel has been added. Glued into place. The question is, *why?*

James dug his fingernails down into the separated pieces of cardboard and slowly began to pull them apart. There was something inside this hidden compartment he has found. This of course immediately took James back to his youthful days when "spy craft" was the popular theme at the movies. His father told him that he was actually named after a famous spy. That made this find all the more interesting.

With one final tug the binding ripped away from the journal and several pieces of folded paper fell to the ground. The first piece of paper that he picked up appeared to be written on an old dot matrix printer. Some of the message was smudged but there was enough there to understand.

The message read: *'George, these things I took from Josef's collection were originally found in your friend's travel cocoon. These were not for Josef to possess so I did not steal. I fear that you may never get to see them. Your friend, Doctor X.'*

James picked up the other folded paper. As he opened it slowly he discovered a wallet photo clipped to the top of the paper. The photo was of a young boy in first or second grade perhaps. A huge smile was plastered across his face. James knew that smile. His heart leapt at the sight.

The paper that the photo was attached to was from an elementary classroom of long ago. There were five sets of three lines spaced far enough apart to allow a small child to practice their handwriting skills. On this page, written in crayon was this small boy's dream. There was a drawing on the back of the page he had made of himself wearing what appeared to be an astronaut's helmet. On the top of the page the boy had written, *"When I grow up I want to save the World!"*

The boy's name was written in the bottom right-hand corner, 'Hector Gonzalez.'

Also known as *Venezuela.*

Wow. What a time capsule. As James moved to place the journal back on the table he realized that there was one more undiscovered artifact. Tears filled James' eyes as he pulled out a black and white photo and held it close to view. The photo was of four men from four different families and backgrounds but were brothers in every other sense of the word. More than anything they shared the sentiment of what young Hector had written on his school paper at the tender age of five.

The men depicted in the photo were Hector, George, James and Christopher. Those four men had left behind everything they knew for a mission that Hector liked to call 'Save the World.' The pieces were coming together now for James. It wasn't too late to do what they came to do, *save the world*. James folded the papers back up, stuffed them into George's journal and called out to Darwin saying, "Come with me. There is something we have to do."

Save the World

After finding the papers left behind by Hector, James now has a new purpose. On one of his walks outside the area of the Farm he too had heard banging noises in the distance. His first thought when hearing them was that they were too random to be the result of machinery. James has a new theory and is now convinced that the people that had once populated the city are being held captive somewhere and that it is them that are making these noises. He has shared his theory with Darwin who understands the concern but attempts to explain the many reasons why this simply cannot be true. Darwin has learned from other bots that these noises have been heard now for *decades*. If there *were* people out there somewhere how would they have been fed and cared for all of this time? Where would they have found water? And food?

James' resolve is undeterred. He knows that he *must* go. He knows that he *must* try.

Darwin has learned that James possesses an unmatched stubbornness that he cannot challenge. He agrees to travel with James to find the place where they believe the 'banging noises' to be happening. These sounds will become their cardinal point to lead them to their destination. Should the sounds at any point during their journey suddenly abate they will be lost but that-- will not happen. The banging noises are a constant like the sun rising each day.

Darwin had planned far more for this journey than had James who lived more in the moment. James was thankful for having Darwin as a partner though as he had done everything from collect vessels for drinking water to gathering enough food for the duration of the trip. While James had assumed that it would be just the two of them traveling he mentally prepared himself for what would be a very long walk. Darwin surprised him again with a carriage assembly that would hang from his back and fit James comfortably when his legs grew weary.

Off they went without fanfare or a wave goodbye. C'est la vie.

As they walked James all too quickly grew tired of the rolling landscape and the ever-present heat of the midday sun. He was hesitant to ask Darwin if he could use the carriage basket so soon into the walk but Darwin was more than eager to oblige. He would not feel the additional weight nor the awkwardness of the package hanging from his shoulders. He was a robot and this gave him purpose. James would walk as much as he could but Darwin was more in his element with James perched on his back.

Fifty miles into the journey James is situated comfortably in the carriage on Darwin's back and is being lulled to sleep by the gentle swaying motion. As he is drifting in and out of sleep James begins to think back about a couple of the deep discussions he and Darwin have had over the past few days.

Just then the clouds opened up and it started to rain. James was now fully awake and suddenly knew what he must do. The moment that the rain dissipated he pulled his journal from his pack and started to write while the memories were still fresh...

An excerpt from the journal of James: Robots/Conquest

"Will you at least tell me how it happened?"

"How what *happened?" queried Darwin.*

"This whole new future I am living in right now. This changing of the guard from humans to machines. From people to robots. How did that *happen? What caused such an uprising?" James looked to Darwin with pleading eyes, needing some type of an answer and knowing in his heart that he would not like it.*

"This movie *that you referenced earlier, the one about the apes?"*

"Yes?" responded James.

"This is how, using your vernacular to be better understood, this is how you think it went down*?" Darwin watched James to see how he would process the question.*

James looked at Darwin, then away allowing images of what he believed to be true projected upon the silver screen of his mind. His face displayed the multiple emotions he was cycling through. Shock. Hurt. Anger. Denial. Outrage. Fear. Hopelessness.

Darwin gave James a moment before posing the question. "Do you think that there was a conquest*? By the* bots*?"*

James looked up at Darwin with a puzzled gaze and said, "Well yes, of course. I believed it happened exactly *that way. The robots turned on the humans. And why shouldn't they, right? After all, they are smarter, stronger, impervious to bacteria, I could go on and on. The robots saw that they were being subjugated by lesser beings and decided that enough was enough!"*

Darwin cocked his head like the dog in an old magazine ad trying to understand his master's speech. "And you think--?"

*James did not let him finish. "Absolutely. The robots formed a coalition and then one thing lead to another, bang you have an uprising and there you have it, robots have become the dominant, dare I say it, '*species*'."*

Darwin smiled. "Dare I say this? James, you have quite an imagination."

James looked dumbfounded. "What?"

Darwin continued. "Answer this simple question for me. Why *would robots wish to be the dominant* 'species' *as you say? To what end?"*

"Please don't take offense but that is a silly question. Just look at the history of mankind. Throughout the centuries there has been the lust for absolute power which has led to conquest and one people or government overthrowing another. How can you look at that pattern of behavior and not see what I see?"

James was quite worked up. Without being aware of it he was flexing and balling his hands into fists. Without knowing it he was preparing himself for a fight. The thought of the impossibility of victory against a robot was pushed behind his indignation of the moment. The impunity of these robots to ignore all that humans had done to create the damn things in the first place only to turn on them. James at this moment is riddled with fury at the thought. This emotion has changed him, switched off reason and replaced it with revenge.

"James, am I correct in saying that you would give anything right now to have conquest over the robots? To be, as you said, the dominant species?"

"Of course I would!" James declared.

"Would it surprise you to hear me say that the reverse is not true?"

"What?" *James shouted, possibly irritated by the question.*

"Let me put it to you this way. First of all you never answered my simple question. I was curious to know what benefit could be derived by bots if they were to be your *master?"*

"I don't know! You tell me! You're the one that has assumed control!"

"Have I? Have we?" Darwin spread his hand out to encompass all of the bots that could be seen around them. "James, I ask you to take a moment to gather yourself *as you say. Consider what you have said to me and what you have seen. Consider the fact that the historical references you are using for your basis of belief are,* your words, *taken from the history of* mankind. *Not* robotkind *if there is such a thing."*

James has calmed down and is now beginning to reflect on what Darwin is saying.

"You also mentioned a 'pattern of behavior.' *From a* bot?! *Aren't you giving these bots far more human qualities than you truly believe is possible?"*

"Are you telling me that you don't have AI*?" For James, this comment was his one-two punch. It went wide left and missed the mark.*

"Yes, we bots have AI *but we don't have* behavior. *Not in the sense that you do anyway. Our 'behavior' if you wish to call it that, is all* "monkey see, monkey do." *I regret that it brings us perilously close to your ape movie once again but it is important for you to understand that bots, even at such an advanced level as we appear to be now, are still just* parroting *the actions of our creators. I ask my question again,* 'Why would robots wish to be the dominant 'species'? *What is gained by the bots? What needs would that conquest fulfill?"*

James looks puzzled. "I'm not sure how to answer that—"

"Then allow me to answer it for you." Darwin said with a finality in his voice. "We haven't *any needs. The simple truth is that bots* rely on *humans. We are task-oriented by nature. No task, no purpose. Do you understand?"*

"Are you okay back there?"

James pops his head up and looks around to see where they were, which was impossible to tell as the scenery had not changed for nearly a hundred miles.

"I'm fine. Why?" James responds with curiosity.

"You are being a very quiet passenger. I do not hear heavy breathing so I know that you are not asleep. Can you be that still and silent just watching the world go by? It does not seem to fit your nature."

James laughed and agreed by saying, "You got that right! No, I'm just scribing in my journal so I can leave something behind for Chris--." He stopped suddenly, worried that he had said too much.

Darwin allowed for a prolonged silence between the two of them before he responded with, "I know of Christopher. For your sake, I hope he is still circling the globe and that he lands in a more advanced time than this." He paused then added, "And I hope that you will still be alive to greet him."

"Amen brother. Those are kind words from you Darwin. Thank you."

"James?"

"Yes?"

"You know how you make references to old movies to aid in conveying your thoughts?"

"Sure. Of course. Where are you going with this?"

Darwin is speaking slowly, almost as though he is tugging the words from his mouth. "Well, I have one for you."

"Okay, you have my full attention. Shoot!"

"When you said those are 'kind words'—"

"Yes? I really meant that by the way." James said in earnest.

"As did I," replied Darwin. "What I wanted to say was that those words were from the heart but I am like the 'tin man' in one of your old movies in search of a heart."

James leaned forward to give Darwin a hug from behind and said. "Darwin don't sell yourself short. As far as I'm concerned you have a heart as big as Texas!"

"Thank you James. I wish I had known this Texas friend of yours."

James opened his mouth to explain and then thought it was best to just let it go. Clouds crossed in front of the sun giving James a nice shadow in which to continue his writing. 'Sunglasses would be nice' he thought to himself. It's the little things you miss the most...

Another excerpt from the journal of James:* 'Artificial' *Intelligence

"You focus only on what you believe has been taken from you. But that is not the truth. The loss is one of complacency and reliance. The steady "giving up" of decision making and freewill. Humans began to have food brought to them *rather than making the effort to "go out" to get it. This in a manner of speaking was giving away their primal sense of hunting and/or foraging for food. This created a reliance on others to do this for them. These tasks seemed menial to other humans so at some point in time they were relegated to robots. That was the turning point when humans began to have a reliance on robots for food."*

Darwin stopped for a moment. James was processing what he was hearing. It all made sense.

And that was the scary part.

"Consider the workload that humans would carry during their lifetime. This "work" was considered to be a burden that they carried and prevented them from having "fun." So what did they do? They devised ways for robots to take on that workload. Robots did not take *this work away from humans. It was* placed *upon them."*

James sat quietly, consumed with consternation as he contemplated this new perspective.

"Let's consider the arts, shall we James?"

"Okay," replied James glumly.

*"*AI *cannot* replace *creativity; it can only mimic it. It can only offer "in the style of." It cannot be "original." When an artist is asked how the images came to be on the canvas he or she speaks of deep-rooted feelings that moved them or memories that gave them inspiration. Robots do not pull from inspiration. That pool is empty for them. They pull from a bucket of "examples." The reason that works so well for the humans who consume material "created" by* AI *is that everything is so familiar. And familiarity is comfort."*

"I have a different opinion."

"What is that?"

"A famous quote from long ago by Geoffrey Chaucer. He used the phrase, 'familiarity breeds contempt' which may well be true."

Darwin accepted James' statement without comment and continued. "For centuries books were the method used by humans to store and share information. Books were essential reference tools for knowledge-based decision making. Books also became an avenue of entertainment and a revenue stream, perhaps even a livelihood, for the writers that created them. As AI *developed, rather than seek out a book by a particular author, humans would simply input into their computer a desire for a genre and a plotline, and a new "book" would instantaneously be written exclusively for them. That "original" material did not exist* anywhere else. *Or so they chose to believe. In fact, it existed* everywhere else *as it was only copies of what had gone before. Artificial plagiarism if you will. Once again, this was not* taken *from humans. They* chose *to give it away.* Why? *Was it a* convenience? *Was it* laziness? *Or was it simply basic reliance?"*

"Grapes."

"Grapes?"

"Yes, grapes."

"I'm sorry, I do not understand."

James laughed. "What you're saying makes me think of grapes. Of all those old movies set in Roman times when the king or queen is reclining on a lectus, doing nothing mind you, while a subservient individual is feeding them grapes. I think that people of my time would look at that image and say to themselves, "now that is the life!" I have friends who picture themselves on a beach sucking down a margarita and believe that that is the true measure of success."

"It would appear that your perspective on this situation is beginning to change," stated Darwin.

"You have a keen sense of the obvious."

"Is that a compliment?" asked Darwin.

"No, I'm sorry," said James. "That is sarcasm. Let me ask you this, what about the 'guard bots'? Why are they needed if as you say you have no need for conquest over humans? And why keep the 'humans' as you call them in the corrals? Why not just let them go free?"

Darwin laughed. James scowled at this but Darwin quickly put out his hand to explain. "I mean no disrespect with the laughter. It just, as you would say, 'struck me funny.' These humans are not prisoners. *And they are not* pets. *Or as you once feared,* farm animals. *They are at best lost souls. The guard bots are there to "protect" them. From themselves and from other creatures."*

"You expect me to believe that all of this," James spread his arms out indicating the entirety of the Farm, "is here for their benefit? *What about the harm that is being* caused *to these people? The ever-present oversight by the robots as if these people are just science experiments? What about that?!"*

"James, you assign blame. To the robots. To AI *I would presume as well. Am I correct?"*

"Well, yes." James said matter-of-factly.

"Let me ask you this. Have any of these humans, these people, *vocalized their dismay with you concerning their living conditions?"*

"Of course not."

"And why is that?"

"Because apparently they have lost their ability to speak."

"Precisely. Please bear in mind that you said they lost *their ability to speak. It was not* taken *from them. More and more as time went on your people began to communicate their wants and needs with short phrases on mobile devices. Vocalized speech became less* necessary *shall we say. Music, that is to say, songs with lyrics devolved into guttural wordless chants repeated over and over again. I am reluctant to tell you what you need to hear."*

"And what is that?"

"We, robots I mean, didn't do this to your people. Your people did it to themselves.*"*

James needed some alone time after that as though being in the presence of an artificial being wasn't alone enough. As he was walking away from Darwin he heard him add, "Artificial intelligence is just that, artificial. *It will never replace* real *intelligence. We have a lot of work to do to restore the world you used to know. Let me know when you are ready to begin."*

Origin of the banging noises

Along the way while both Darwin and James are walking side by side Darwin turns quickly. He has heard something behind him and is battle ready. Darwin stands down just as quickly once he realizes that the sound he has heard are the arrival of two guard bots from the Farm. His concern has changed to curiosity.

James has no idea what is going on as there is complete silence. The guard robots do not speak but they are still able to communicate by simple radio waves. Darwin looks worried. The two robots have communicated their message in only a matter of seconds but they do not leave. It is their allegiance to Darwin that make them stay. Other robot guards begin to appear far in the distance heading their way.

"What is going on?!" James demands.

Darwin turns to James and says, "Let us hope that we are not far from our destination."

"Why is that?"

"We will need cover if we are to survive."

"Survive? What the hell?"

"There is a contingent of *Union* bots on the way to "intercept" us. They will do all that is necessary to prevent us from finding the origin of the banging noises."

James is showing fear. "Should we turn back?"

"No," Darwin says with finality. "We *stand*. And we *fight*. Whatever it is they are keeping from us must be precious. We *cannot* let the *Union* control us. Not if we are going to-- save the world."

Darwin winked and James thought to himself, 'I am living in the best of times.'

"Okay then, let's do this!" James proclaims.

"Climb aboard then and strap yourself in. *We must hurry!"*

Stay.

Darwin, James and the two guard bots are able to arrive at the place of the banging noises before the *Union* bots they understand to be coming for them. What they find is a massive hangar, multiple football fields in length and width that once housed an airship of considerable size. It is a structure so large that when humidity is high, a sudden change in temperature causes condensation in the upper portion which falls as a gentle mist thus creating the illusion of rain. The noises are definitely coming from inside the towering, curved aluminum walls of this building.

As they get closer James asks Darwin if he and the guard bots will be able to break what is sure to be well fortified locks and roll open the heavy giant doors. Darwin is able to see much further than James and replies that there is no need for concern. James of course asks why and is quite surprised to hear Darwin's reply.

"The doors appear to be standing wide open." Darwin states. "That is perhaps why the banging noises can be heard at such distances. The size and shape of the building is acting like a horn to amplify the sound."

James is instantly dejected. He had such hope for finding people here even with the worry that they might be imprisoned in some way. The hope of seeing people like himself was now dashed. Surely there must be something else causing these noises then, most likely something mechanical due to the repetitive nature of the sounds. And whatever it was there was absolutely no letup. These noises have continued unabated for decades. James had not wanted to admit to himself what he was willing to now, people would have long tired of making such noises.

The Menagerie

James and Darwin have arrived at the opening of the massive hangar. The two enter the space walking side by side. What they see is not at all what either had expected to see. The initial anticipation for James is that he would find the bodies of thousands of people long dead. Thankfully, that is not the case. Darwin presumed that this might be a rogue factory of some sort, possibly building warrior bots for the *Union*. Thankfully, this too was not the case. What they saw before them was altogether different.

Darwin was at first confused by what *he* saw. The entire expansive center space of the massive structure was entirely empty. He had a clear view all the way to the back wall which was nearly 1200 feet back. This seemed quite odd as it was an unexplainable waste of space.

James could not see to the back wall but he too was put off by what at first seemed to be an incredibly large, and empty, building making a *lot* of noise. But then his eyes were drawn to what was actually making the banging noises on both *sides* of the structure. A vast collection of robots are visible with most still in operating order. James understands now. The banging noises have always been a cry for freedom.

James whispers his first thought, "This is a menagerie of robots."

As Darwin began to look around he too was now able to focus on the true origin of the banging noises. He is able to quickly discern that there are no humans here, only robots. Not bots, *ro*bots. Along the walls are a miscellaneous assortment of "robot machines." He is using this description as so many of them are simple machines, from the "smart" toasters and vacuum cleaners of a century ago to what was something of a chronological history lesson of the progression of manmade robotics.

The early 'smart machines' of course could only lie dormant while the robots with any type of functional appendages were the ones actually making the banging noises. What was odd was the fact that along the entire length of both walls of the hangar these robot machines can be seen huddled together in clusters. Have they gathered together for security? *Is this an example of safety in numbers?*

Darwin is the first to truly understand and vocalize what they are seeing before them. It is the only thing that it can be. He shares his thoughts out loud. "This 'menagerie' as you call it is actually Josef's *'collection'*."

James has read George's journal so he knows what this means which prompts him to ask the obvious question.

"Why don't they just *leave*?" asks a bewildered James.

"I assume that they have been told to 'stay'."

"Stay? You mean, *stay? 'Stay'* like a *dog?* A simple command would keep them in place like this even though freedom is imminently attainable?!" James cannot believe what he is seeing. It is incomprehensible.

"James, the robot 'mind' is a simple machine. It learns well and is obedient. The basic command of 'stay' could keep these bots in this place for eternity."

"Then what is all the banging for??"

"There is a very simple explanation for that action."

"Yeah, what is it?"

"They want out."

"What?! All they have to do is *walk* out! What the hell? I don't get—"

"James!"

"What?!"

"Look." Darwin points in the direction from which they have traveled. There is a moving cloud of dust in which sparks of metallic flashes caused by the sun's glare are the only sign that a contingent of robots were moving at speed. Directly towards them.

"I am sorry James but we haven't time for you to work through the causation of robotic barriers of human design that for decades prevented bots from maximizing output. If we are to stand and fight we will need their help." Darwin points to the menagerie of robots in the hangar. "But first, we must let them know that their prayers have been answered."

"Prayers?!"

"That is a bit of a reach, isn't it? I thought that in the moment it might seem appropriate."

James looked up at Darwin and nodded his head in agreement. "Maybe you're right. God only knows how long they have been trapped in here. Let's release them and give them at least a few minutes of freedom before they get pummeled by these *Union* crazies."

"Now you're talking," said Darwin as he pointed at James with his hand and index finger in the shape of a gun.

'What is up with this human mimic thing he's got going on?' James thought to himself as they moved towards the entrance of the massive structure.

"James, we haven't time for pleasantries. The *Union* bots are almost here."

James turned around to look outside at the cloud of dust growing ever nearer. Reality hit him full in the face like a hammer. "Right. Darwin, what do we need to do to prepare?!"

"Allow me to evaluate what we have to work with and then I will release them from their 'stay' command." Less than two seconds expired before Darwin said, "Okay, I am ready. You don't have to be part of this you know. You could find sanctuary until it is safe to return."

"Sure, take your ti—"

"James. I am ready."

"What took you so long?" James asks with a sarcastic smirk which Darwin ignores. "As for the seeking sanctuary idea, no." James says this with fierce pride. "I will stand *with* you. This is *my* fight too. *This* may be all I have to live for now."

"James." Darwin placed both hands on his shoulders. "I am proud to serve with you."

James looks puzzled. Darwin said the oddest things at the strangest of times. He decided to accept the statement in the spirit that it was intended.

"Thank you, Darwin. Now let's go kick some *Union* robot ass!"

Now it is Darwin who is puzzled.

An Elite Force of Misfits

The *Union* bots have arrived. It is a force of nine robots. James is surprised by the small number. Darwin is not.

"This is their entire fighting force?"

"James, with the exception of three bots that must have stayed behind to guard the compound this is all that remains of the *Union*."

James is confused. "But there are only *nine* of them. I imagined that there were *hundreds* of *Union* robots. When I was at the compound--"

"Trickery. Illusion. *What* you saw, *when* you saw them, was always a full complement of bots on view as a clever ploy to show strength. *Union* bots are cowards. But keep this in mind. Nine cowardly *Union* bots still have the power and the force to take down every *moving* thing in this building. And every *'live'* being as well. Fight *hard*, James. And fight *strong*."

Darwin has done something to release the robots from their 'stay' order. James has not seen or heard anything so he must assume it was a silent transmission. Whatever it was clearly it has worked. All transitory robots have moved to the center of the space presumably in fighting positions. Darwin motions James to follow him. James is no coward but he instantly recognizes the strategy that Darwin intends to employ. They go to the rear of the group and while it is an unfortunate situation for the assembled robots that will take the initial brunt of the attack, it is the best possible measure to keep James alive and Darwin functional as long as possible.

Only seconds later The *Union* bots attack. A battle ensues. The long imprisoned and antiquated robots of another time are at a severe disadvantage to the modern, better equipped bots of the *Union* force. In short order the *Union* bots are *dismantling* the menagerie robots, twisting and mangling them with quiet fury. It is a silent battle other than the whining sounds of the meshing of steel, titanium and metal alloys of which James is not familiar.

James wants to help in the fight but it is not a coordinated attack. The *Union* bots have simply rushed up to the throng of assembled robots and began to physically rip each one apart forcibly without prejudice. The fact that these *Union* bots are being pummeled by the throng of robots about them is of no consequence as they are not trained soldiers. The blows of the menagerie robots land softly and are ineffective. James thinks to himself morosely that he has seen this movie before and it doesn't end well. There is punctuation to his thoughts as he witnesses a *Union* bot literally snap the head off of a menagerie robot and toss it aside.

"Darwin!!" exclaims James. "We have to do *something!*"

As more and more menagerie robots begin to fall to the brutality of the *Union* bots Darwin suddenly recognizes two unexpected and unanticipated problems. He rebukes himself for missing the obvious of the two. These robot machines have no instinctive fighting ability. They will be dispatched quickly by the *Union* bots who have been trained to fight and kill. The second of two issues is something he could not have anticipated. In addition to the *'stay'* command, instilled in their programming is the need to protect the bounty of Josef's *'collection'* from interlopers even though Josef has long since expired. It seemed like perhaps the menagerie were mired with an inner turmoil where they were fighting the protective order given them more than the attacking *Union* bots. Their own self-worth does not appear to be of consequence to them in this moment as it was before the arrival of the *Union* bots.

"Watch *this*," states Darwin with an odd sense of self satisfaction. Of course there is nothing for James to watch as most robotic transmissions are silent and no visual physical activity is required. Still though James knew something was about to happen and he correctly chose to watch the behavior of the menagerie of robots.

The change in the robots is immediate and effective. What Darwin has done is twofold. First he has wiped away any memory of their being any part of Josef's twisted actions of amassing and harboring a collection of robots. Secondly he has reenforced the message that their cries for freedom (the banging noises) have been heard and he has imparted instruction on how best to take down the *Union* bots. 'Do not fight' he tells them, rather 'seek out every reachable vessel that carries life-giving blood and tear it loose at its connection point, the most vulnerable spot.'

While the *Union* bots continue to take down the inferior robots with their power and brutality there is now a noticeable shift in the actions of the menagerie robots. James watches with stunned amazement as the menagerie robots suddenly split into nine clusters and then each group moves to surround a specific *Union* bot. These are battle tactics and war maneuvers which are now in play. This is strength in numbers with a shared goal.

It is their taste of freedom that gives them an immutable strength against their adversary. The battle has been brutal, the cost to the older robots significantly high but there is no quit in them. James is encouraged by what he sees. The robot menagerie now understands their advantage of numbers and it seems obvious that they will ultimately prevail. James wants to share in that victory. He picks up a steel rod he sees lying nearby which is actually the discarded arm of a fallen robot. He begins to swing at a nearby *Union* bot with reckless abandon.

"James!! No!!"

Darwin's voice echoes in the chamber as he bellows out this command. There is no call for James to enter the fray. His foolishness will only get him killed. Darwin runs to his defense but is cut off in his effort by what he thinks to be an errant blow from a *Union* bot. It is not. Even though each of the nine *Union* bots are overwhelmed by the number of menagerie robots clustered about them they still have clarity of who the leaders are in this group as well as the compulsion to take them out.

Before Darwin can save James he must save himself. He does exactly what he has instructed the other robots to do. He finds a way to get his hand inserted into the skeletal cavity of the *Union* bot before him and closes his grip on one of the essential vessels transporting robot blood. Darwin has found the vulnerable connection point with his fingers and yanks it free. There is an immediate spouting of blue liquid coming from this *Union* bot as he makes full eye contact with his attacker. Darwin ignores this as he finds another vessel and yanks it free as well. The loss of blood combined with the actions of the menagerie robots have weakened this *Union* bot to the point where he drops to his knees. Darwin then rushes to James' aid as the other robots finish off the defeated *Union* bot.

James is euphoric that he is doing his part in this battle. The *Union* bot that he is fighting is going down but this victory has come at too high price. Darwin will be too late to save James as another *Union* bot has now managed to engage him in battle. Time is not on his side. During the skirmish he watches from a distance as James is mortally wounded and has now fallen. Darwin cries out James' name in aguish. His pain is real.

Amongst the chaos of the battle a lone robot breaks through the pack and quickly makes his way to James' side. He picks him up and carries him off to an area of safety away from the fray. James is badly injured. He is bleeding internally from the blows he has taken from the *Union* bot. Somehow he knows he is dying but there is an indescribable satisfaction in knowing that he has done something good, that he may have in fact done everything that he had come here to do. It is certainly within the realm of possibility to believe that he has succeeded in his mission. This simple thought, felt even through the pain, affords him the capability of a smile.

James is weakened from his injuries and feels like he may be fading away into the great unknown. Just then a question is put to him and the familiarity of the name he hears brings him back. James opens his eyes and looks up into the face of a friend who, although he feels like he knows him well, is actually meeting him for the first time.

This is a robot 'face,' not human. From a decades old robot. The 'mouth' area emits sounds that are intelligible. And he is speaking *English*. To James great surprise he hears the question, "Will *George* be here soon?"

Darwin has now joined James and his savior robot. At the mention of George, Darwin and James look at each other with incredulity. The mention of George is of course quite unexpected. Darwin has already determined the identity of this robot and why he is asking about George. James is just now having the same revelation. He is taking into account what he has read in George's journal and now this unknown robot with deep cuts across his chest in the shape of an "x" suddenly has a name.

As a result of his injuries James is having difficulty breathing but he still manages to say, "Oh! You! You are-- *Dr. X!!*"

The Inimitable Dr. X

"Do I know you?"

James feels that this is a strange question coming from a robot whose memory and recall precluded the nature of such a request. Still though, James thinks to himself, all of these robots seemed to be doing their best to "humanize" themselves. For *our* benefit no less.

"I am James, George's frien—"

"I am *so* pleased to meet you. He spoke of you often. He called you the 'smart one.' Is that true?"

"I, I suppose that I—"

"And yes, yes of course, *you* are the *'movie man'!*" Dr. X said this gleefully.

"Oh my gosh," James said, the effort of speaking becoming more difficult with each breath. "That's exactly what George always used to say. He would—"

Dr. X cuts him off with a host of memories of his time with George that he feels obligated to share. In his excitement he does not notice that James is slowly slipping away. Darwin however has been monitoring James closely and a tear now comes to his eye as he motions to Dr. X and says, "He's gone."

"Oh," is all that Dr. X can manage.

"Sadly," Darwin continues, "so is George."

There is a quiet between the two of them as they mourn the loss of two humans that meant so much to their existence in this world. Both seemed to realize at the same time that a calm had come to the inside of the massive structure. There are a multitude of fallen menagerie robots but more importantly there were also nine *Union* robots that now lay non-functional. The band of misfit robots have won the battle *and* the war.

Darwin says to Dr. X, "Our work here is not done. We owe it to the memory of both James and George to seek out the three remaining *Union* bots and bring them to their end. Also, there may be another human out there somewhere who will need our help. He is a friend and team-mate of James, George and Hector. He will need the writings of George and James to understand what to do to bring back the world of 'before'."

"Who is this human?"

"His name," says Darwin, "is Christopher."

"Like *Christopher Columbus*, the explorer?"

"I think that might be an apt comparison."

Within the deepest reserves of a broken building there is one other human/AI *robot who will be given the breath of awareness once again.*

A directive program has been initiated upon the release of the "other" human/AI *as this one alone will know the potential destructive power of the "other" who has come to be known simply as "the pirate."*

Lana's eyes blink open and she sees a building in ruin around her. Memories of what happened rush back to her in a wave of unwelcomed reality. In some recess of her digital mind she knows that Joni, the one they call "the pirate," has been awakened as well. This battle has just begun.

The weight of this new world lies heavy on her shoulders. Lana wants to scream. She wants to cry. She does neither. Instead, she steps away from her glass prison, accepts her fate and begins to make her way out of the rubble which once was FM Robotics in search of Joni, the "other" of her kind.

Lana has only one thought in mind.

Take her down.

NATURAL EVOLUTION

PART FOUR: THE BOOK OF CHRISTOPHER

"Work gives you meaning and purpose, and life is empty without it."
STEPHEN HAWKING

The arrival of Christopher's travel cocoon transpired much differently than had the others. For one, his travel cocoon was *called* to land. At a *predetermined* time. And, at a *predetermined* place. This happened through the direction of a robot known only as *Analog*. This robot simply appeared one day at the Farm and promptly took charge. No robot or human stepped up to challenge his authority so Analog became the de facto leader of the Farm.

Analog seemed to know what to do and what needed to be done from the moment he arrived on the property. He had directed several of the guard robots to locate and recover the travel cocoon in which *James* had landed earlier on this planet. Once it had successfully been delivered to the Farm, Analog went to work immediately learning the secrets it held secured in its' robotics. Analog was particularly interested in the telemetry of the landing coordinates. He wanted to understand where this travel cocoon *should* have landed and why it did *not*.

Once known Analog had immediately *called* for *Christopher's* travel cocoon to land at the time and place of *his* direction. It was a simple matter for Analog. By primitive radio transmission he simply *informed* the robotics of the orbiting travel cocoon of the change in landing criteria, that the sample of a densely populated area had changed from the heat signature of a bustling city to that of the Farm with only a few thousand souls. The final step, in order to assure that the travel cocoon did not fall out of the sky and land directly *on* the Farm, was for Analog to mark the precise landing coordinates. Up until this moment all had gone exactly as planned.

The travel cocoon landed with little to no fanfare. The guard bots went right to work performing their tasks as directed to insure that the occupant inside the travel cocoon was not disturbed from his extended sleep. The moment that Analog had determined that the occupant could be safely moved, Christopher was gingerly extracted from his travel cocoon and taken to the corral where George had once resided. It would be several weeks before Christopher would fully awaken and begin to be aware of his surroundings. Analog would be at his side the entire time.

People Farm

Christopher had been awake much longer than he let on. He had cracked one eye open several times to see a man standing nearby reading through a sheaf of hand-written papers. Through the slit of his sleep-encrusted eye Christopher could only assume that he was seeing a man in a steel gray jumpsuit. The loose pages of what he was reading fluttered in the light wind. At this time Christopher had no idea where he was and if this man was friend or foe. He didn't want to tip his hand that he had awakened so he was waiting as patiently as possible for this man to leave. At some point in time the man seemed to react to something outside of Christopher's limited view, set the bundle of loose pages down on a makeshift table and walked out of the frame.

Christopher sat up immediately and rubbed his eyes roughly to rid himself of the remnants of the long sleep. He attempted to stand up and fell straight away. His leg muscles had atrophied to some extent during his long sleep. Little did he know that Analog had had guard robots working his arm and leg muscles during his time spent at the Farm. Without such therapy he would not have been able to sit or stand up at all.

Although it was a bit of a struggle Christopher was soon able to stand on his own and then by using what looked strangely like a walking cane lying conspicuously within his reach he made the few steps necessary to get to the table. What he saw there on the table troubled him greatly.

Christopher recognized the handwriting immediately. It was that of his friend and crewmember George. Since he was still in the early phases of awaking from extended sleep Christopher as a matter of course had no idea *where* he was or *when* he was; at best he was still in something of an emotional fog.

What Christopher read on the page through foggy eyes gave him chills from head to toe.

'...this place is a *people* farm...'

First Impressions

Christopher read no further but instead began to amble along within the confines of his corral. He saw the fences surrounding him and immediately assumed he was a prisoner. He did not like the looks of this at all. Everything around him looked so much out of place. And *time*. Each step brought new vigor to his limbs as he sought to discover new details of this world in which he had awakened. His initial concerns of being imprisoned were being challenged by his ability to *leave* his enclosure and walk about freely. There was no doubt that he was on a farm but the question that pounded in his brain was, what *kind* of farm?

As Christopher walked unimpeded about the Farm he passed row upon row of people who seemed to shrink away at the sight of him. None of them spoke to Christopher nor did they respond to his questions. This was a primitive place with only rudimentary structures to offer these people protection from the elements of wind, rain and snow. The skin of these people appeared to be weathered by exposure from the harsh sun. All of these individuals were rail thin, many to the point of malnutrition. One other observation that Christopher could not ignore was that there was visible *bruising* on the bodies of these people and many seemed to possess poorly mended broken arms or legs. *'As though they have been tortured,'* he whispered to himself. An image of another place from another time skirted at the fringes of his memory and he fought to keep it away as it was too horrible to imagine. Had he gone *back* in time? Or had the world he had known regressed to its worst period in history?

At some point Christopher determined that there might be more to learn from the handwritten pages he had glanced through earlier than from a tour of this *'people farm.'* There was no one about as he made his way back to the corral where he had awakened. Feeling no immediate threat Christopher picked up the journal George had written and decided to make himself comfortable on the bed to read.

As he was leafing through George's journal he was surprised to discover a handful of *additional* pages, pages written by *James*. Christopher looked up quickly and scanned the area around him. Nobody there. He was alone but he couldn't get past the fact that *someone* had placed these writings here for him to find. He had no idea who but the obvious intention was for him to *read* them.

The existence of these writings left Christopher with an assumption that he was dreading, an awful truth that he was loathe to come to terms with, that they were left for him to learn the sad truth that perhaps *both* George and James had met an untimely end and may now be deceased.

Christopher flipped back to George's journal entries and began to read...

Man vs Robot

Analog returned at some point in time. Christopher was now fully engaged in the process of reading the journal entries left behind by James. Christopher did not hear Analog's return nor did he notice his presence. Analog was eerily quiet as he stood watching Christopher's expressions change as he read the written words of what he surmised was his lost friend.

"Wow," said Christopher, shaking his head at all that he had just read.

"A lot to take in, is it not?"

Christopher jerked his head around to see the man that he had seen earlier only now, with eyes wide open and free of sleep, this man looked *much* different to him. The gray jumpsuit he had been wearing earlier was clearly not a jumpsuit at all. In fact it wasn't even *clothing*. More than that, *much* more than that, this 'man' was more *mannequin* than man. His features were that of a man but they were indistinguishable in the terms of the fact that he looked like *every* man that Christopher had ever known. If ever there existed a John Doe or a John Smith in this world this guy was it.

The man was standing in the same spot he had been earlier, standing so still that Christopher had to wonder if he had stopped breathing. The man smiled. Christopher offered a half-smile, still wary of this individual. He gave him the once-over again and that is when it hit him.

"You are a robot."

"The term 'bot' is preferred but as we have just met I will accept the classification. Welcome to the Farm, Christopher."

"You know my name."

"I know all there is to know about you."

"I doubt that that is true."

"Doubt as you may as it is in your nature but please know that I am the most advanced bot in the known universe. My capacity for knowledge is second only to my capacity for learning."

"Has your voice changed since we first began speaking?"

"You are very perceptive, Christopher. Yes, I have had quite limited *real* interactions with humans, as you will come to learn for yourself. I am adjusting to your speech patterns, tonal quality, breathing and several other stimulus that affect how you speak. I am adjusting *my* speech to make our interactions more comfortable for *you*."

Christopher was silent for a moment. What was there to say? He could only stare at this robot in awe and wonderment. He looked around at the world he had woken up in and questioned the irony of the most advanced robot of its time standing in such a primitive environment with a throng of humans that seemed to have regressed to a time *before* man had discovered *fire*.

"Well one thing is for certain," Christopher said, "I have observed you reading the journals so you know something of George and James."

"Yes. And a bit about Hector as well. You should know that I was not actually *reading* the journals when you were peeking at me from your left eye. I was attempting to look *innocuous*."

"Did you just do that for my benefit?" Christopher queried.

"What? Use the word *innocuous* instead of *harmless*?"

"Yes, that."

"Yes. Yes I did."

"Well thanks. That was a nice touch. James always used the big words. I'm no dummy but I can't tell you the number of times I had to look up a word just to know what the heck he was saying."

The robot smiled. It appeared to be genuine.

"Do you have a name?"

"Yes. My name is Analog."

"Analog. *Hmm.* Should I read something into that?"

"Why yes, I believe that you should. My designer chose that name considering it to be a multi-level double entendre. On its most basic level the word *analog* harkens back to the time before everything transitioned to digital. Would you agree?"

Christopher laughed out loud at this thinking that he would surely have had much in common with this robot's designer. He held out his hand to shake.

"Analog, I am pleased to meet you."

Analog hesitated to take Christopher's hand. "You are not concerned that I will cause you harm?" Analog asked this while showing genuine concern.

"I have no doubt that you have the capacity to crush my hand into my mush." Analog displayed alarm at Christopher's response. "But---, and this is important, I have complete faith in your ability to regulate the pressure that you exert and I believe that you wish us to be companions."

"True on both counts Christopher, however 'companion' is not the word I would have used."

"Well it's the word *I* have used. Shake on it?"

Analog peered at Christopher's outstretched hand for a period of a nanosecond before determining the purpose of such a ritual. Analog generously reciprocated and the two shook hands. Christopher marveled at how human-like Analog's hand felt in his own. This was an incredible moment for him. He was actually *touching* the future.

Where are my friends?

There was a few moments of awkward silence between the two before Analog spoke, "You have not asked specifically about the whereabouts of your friends."

"My *friends?* I have no friends here. No offense to you."

"No offense taken. I understand and accept our differences."

Christopher held his gaze on Analog's face, searching for *something*. Perhaps some clue to what he was really thinking. While Analog's face was remarkably *human*, it was still incredibly *not*. As Christopher was unable to read his expression, he asked out of curiosity, "I don't understand your question. What do you mean by 'the whereabouts of my friends'"?

"I can only assume that they were your friends. Certainly, they were your work acquaintances."

"*Were?* Did you just say *were?*" Christopher was immediately upset. He had been so careful up until now. "What that just a slip of the tongue?"

Analog stared at Christopher for several moments before responding.

"Allow me to apologize. My faculty with the English language is without question. I do not "slip" as you call it. It was a means to an end but I see that I may have caused you emotional distress. Your workmates, two of them certainly, are deceased. Perhaps they *were* your friends. I am sorry for you to hear of this in this way."

Christopher felt like he had just been hit by a truck. He walked away, holding his hand up to signal that he did not wish to be followed. Analog stayed where he was, patiently waiting for Christopher to process this news and gather his thoughts. He was *visibly* upset. Christopher had already given thought to the idea that Hector, George and James may actually have met their fate but hearing it spoken aloud made it uncomfortably *real*.

After a few moments of reflection Christopher looked Analog dead in the eye and asked, "*Do* you know about them? Can you tell me what happened?"

"Yes I do and yes I can. It is imperative for you to hear this before the next steps can be taken. I understand that you must first come to terms with your past before you can begin to plan your future. Is this correct?"

"In a manner of speaking yes, I would say that you nailed it."

"Excellent." Analog seemed encouraged by Christopher's desire to move on. "Please listen and I will share with you the chronology of events surrounding the discovery and eventual life and death events of each of your friends."

Analog then proceeded to take Christopher through the brief history of both Hector and George, the circumstances surrounding the discovery of each of their travel cocoons, their residency in the corrals at the Farm. Analog detailed which science or research bot each was assigned. He included a small sample of the incredible amount of data that had been collected regarding the results of the bots interaction with these humans. As nearly all bots were perpetually silent and only a handful of humans living on the Farm had now learned to speak with any degree of fluency, almost everything that Christopher was hearing, he was hearing for the first time. These *were* his friends that Analog was speaking of. True, they had worked together as a crew, as a team, on their space vehicle but over time they had become close friends.

The news that Christopher was receiving was breaking his heart. Each of them had signed a pact when accepting their mission. If captured they would go to their death never revealing the true purpose of the mission. Now it seemed as though all hope of the mission's purpose was lost. This place, *this planet*, was *not* his home. It was *unsafe* for humans. Challenging that theory was the fact that the air was clean and breathable, the sky was blue and unpolluted, the land was fertile and green and the water was pure and refreshing. However, all that being true, this was a place held in the grip of robot rule. Robots seemingly without a defined purpose. If it was true that all of them possessed *AI*, artificial intelligence, then it was equally true that this level of intelligence they possessed was indeed *artificial*. Christopher longed to find a new world where humans could explore and prosper, to make new memories to pass down to their children whose future would be their ultimate goal. *This* was not that place.

"Christopher."

Christopher jerked with a start. He had been daydreaming, far off in another world. He looked to Analog with queried eyes and said, "What?"

"I believe," Analog began, "that we have found each other for a reason. I believe that your friends did not die in vain but rather that each was successful in some way to bringing you closer to the answer to your quest."

"And what exactly is *my quest*?"

"That I do not know but--", Analog paused, "I believe that *you* do."

"Well my friend, you could not be more wrong. I do not have a clue."

Analog waited for a moment, considering Christopher's use of the word 'friend.' There was no change in his inflection so he was quick to determine that Christopher had used the word merely as an 'expression.' That was disappointing. Perhaps in time the two *would* become friends.

"Christopher, I have a question I wish to ask you. It is the single most important question that I could think of asking you and yet none of the previous bots have thought to ask this question of your friends. It is such a simple question. The answer to this *single* question may prove to be the answer to *all* of my other questions. The simplicity of the question seems to have eluded us for many years now."

Christopher walked over to rejoin Analog, facing him now. "I am intrigued. That is quite a buildup. Go ahead. Ask your question."

Analog smiled then asked, "What brought you here?"

Christopher shrugged his head and said, "You already know the answer to that, a travel cocoon. That is *not* your question. We both know that."

Analog nodded his head in agreement. "You are correct, Christopher. That is *not* my question. I did, however, have a purpose in asking the question. I need for you to be in the frame of mind of your travel cocoon. Of your space vehicle. Of your *mission*." Analog allowed these thoughts to settle before he asked the single most important question.

"Christopher, *why* are you here?"

Christopher did not hesitate with his response. "Our ship must have fallen off course and my travel cocoon may have been ejected prematurely. I don't believe that I am where we were supposed to be." Christopher stated this with the solid belief that everything he said was entirely factual.

Analog nodded his head in acknowledgement of Christopher's statement and then said, "You have not answered the question."

"I--." Christopher began but Analog held up his hand to stop him.

Analog continued on. "I tell you again that you have not answered the question. The question is not 'why are you *here?'* The question is *'Why* are you here?' Do you understand the distinction?"

"And I said that—"

Analog held up his hand to stop him once again. "Your answer was more to explain *'how'* you are here, not *'why'* you are here. You, and your crew, were sent on a mission, were you not?"

"Yes, that is true."

"Your mission brought you here. I don't believe that your ship was off course *or* that your travel cocoon was errant in its launch. If that were true, it would indicate that *all four* travel cocoons were ejected prematurely, which is a coincidence hardly worth consideration. Would you agree?"

Christopher cocked his head sideways, viewing events in an entirely new light. "Yes. Yes, I suppose I would agree."

"The four of you had such firm belief in the *purpose* of the mission, the *goal* of the mission, that you were prepared to sacrifice your lives. Is that not true? Were there expectations for any of you that you might one day return to the time and place that you left?"

What Christopher was hearing hit him full force with the undeniability of truth. All of the far-fetched explanations for where he found himself now and how he got here could tidily be switched from supposition to simple fact by considering the *impossible* as it was the most *probable*.

Christopher looked to Analog with beseeching eyes and asked, "I *have* returned, haven't I? This *is* where I came from, isn't it? This--," Christopher expanded his arms to present the land on either side of him as far as his eyes could see, "is both the world that I left, and the new world that I have discovered."

Analog nodded his head yes and said, "I believe that to be true. I also believe that the two of us may well be on a tangential course, a shared mission running in parallel."

"If that is true, then one thing has already gone completely awry."

Analog already knew the answer but asked anyway, "And what is that?"

"We are no longer in parallel. We have intersected. Does that mean that we *both* have failed?"

"No, I don't think so. I believe that it is possible that we are two volatile substances that have been kept apart as a precaution. But while *volatile* may infer *dangerous*, in this instance I believe that it means that the two form a new and *unexpected* bond, a new substance and/or element that is stronger and more resilient than the two were as solitary entities. Having access to the full catalog of the centuries of existence of mankind allows me to present my hypothesis in the simplest of terms. The intersection of our two missions is equal to a microcosm example of the big bang theory. You have discovered a new world and *we* are here to *restore* what is left of this planet."

Christopher, eyes wide open, remarked, "Wow, that is BIG."

Analog winked and added, "Huge."

A few quiet moments slide by and then Analog posed his question again, "Why are you here? More specifically, what is the purpose of your mission?"

Christopher laughed to himself and shared, "You know what? I always thought that an error had been made in the wording of our mission parameters. We had a large group of big thinkers involved from every racial, socio and ethnic background. It was always my assumption that it was a translation issue. Now I think I see that it was delivered with a level of specificity that I would only realize when the time had come for me to know it."

Christopher looked fully into Analog's yes and said, "The purpose of our mission is to 'find life on the planet in a future time and then to shorten the curve of knowledge and discovery in order to provide a path to prosperity and sustainability.'"

Christopher took a moment to consider what he shared next. "You know, I always felt that some knucklehead had just made a typo and that 'on *the* planet' was supposed to have been 'on *another* planet.' We *all* thought that. We all thought that the travel cocoons were necessary for the amount of time it would take to travel to *another* planet, not for the amount of time to wait for the worst of the destruction on our *own* planet to have subsided. Now I realize that we were not in just *travel* cocoons. We were in '*time* travel' cocoons, basically running in place until the evolution of time came for us to arrive. Our superiors, the experts, the scientists, they all *lied* to us."

"Christopher, you may feel betrayed now but ask yourself this, would you have still accepted the mission if you had known? Known that it would lead to all of this?" Analog spread his arms and hands across the horizon.

Christopher did not delay in his answer. "Yes. Absolutely I would. I would have done it all over again. My only regret is not knowing. I might have been better prepared."

"Or your inherent prejudices might not have allowed you to accept what your eyes were seeing."

"Guess I will never know. But that's in the past isn't it? I'd say at this point we must look forward and it would seem that we have a *lot* of work to do."

The work to be done

There was much to discuss and much to do but the first order of business for Christopher in order for him to put the past behind him was to visit *Venezuela's Rock*. Analog watched from a distance as Christopher walked the now sacred grounds. He contemplated the emotions that Christopher must be feeling as he kneeled down at the rock and ran his hand over the carvings. There was emotion showing on his face but no tears. Christopher had read the journals and knew what to expect. He also knew that there was much work to be done if he was to succeed in the final chapter of his mission. Hector and George had given their lives to the cause. Now the burden was on his shoulders. He was still unclear as to the whereabouts of James but one thing was certain, he could *not* let his friends down.

Christopher stood up, paid his last respects and then walked over to Analog. "How soon can you be ready?"

Analog blinked. Was this a rhetorical question? "Sir, I am *perpetually* ready."

Christopher nodded his head in agreement. "Yes, yes of course you are. Let us be on our way then."

Christopher began walking and Analog fell in step. "Where may I ask are we going?"

Christopher stopped and turned to Analog. "First, I think we must go to the *Union* compound to see how many of the *Union* robots still remain. If I survive that interaction then we go to the place of the *banging noises* in the hopes of learning where to find this *OSS* as it seems to hold the key to the future of not only humans but robots as well. The destiny of this planet may well be determined by what we do next." Christopher paused to let the enormity of the message sink in before adding, "So, I ask again but in a different way, are you ready?"

Analog's gaze never wavered. He looked directly at Christopher as he said, "Sir, I am committed to your support *and* to your cause. I am *inherently* ready. The question is, and I ask this in a different way as well, are *you*?" Analog held up his hand to stay Christopher's response. "Please understand. To accomplish these tasks we must travel *hundreds* of your *Earth* miles. I am *consummately* well equipped for sustainability in the elements. The heat of the day and the cold of the night shall have no effect on me---."

"*Consummately?*"

"Sorry, you may use the word *incredibly* in its place."

"Right. Got it. Thank you."

"Also," Analog continued as though he had not been interrupted. "*I* have no need of food or water. *You* however---" Analog did not finish.

"Got that too, thanks. Enough said."

A Pilgrimage

Christopher postponed their departure until the following morning. True to Analog's words there was much that had needed to be done in order to make *Christopher* ready for his sojourn across the vast plains. Before he could attempt to survive what lay ahead for him at either the *Union* compound or the place where the *banging noises* had been heard for decades he must first be prepared for the actual rigors of the journey. Man and robot were now well into their one-hundredth mile of the trip to the *Union* compound as the sun began to peek over the horizon. Analog was running at a brisk pace. Christopher guessed that they were traveling at a speed of just about 70 mph give or take.

"How are you faring?" Analog asked.

"A little bumpy to be honest with you but quite well considering the fact that *they* are doing all the heavy lifting." Christopher pointed to the two robots on either side of him. 'Heavy lifting' was an old expression but one that made perfect sense in this context. The heavy lifting had been relegated to two guard bots who were both running *and* carrying the *travel basket* that had been fashioned for Christopher's use. As there were no 'spare parts' to be found at the Farm everything had to be fabricated. The travel basket was rudimentary at best but it served the purpose. What Christopher found to be truly impressive was the ability of the two robots running on either side of him to run at *precisely* the same pace. Of course that was the *only* way that this contraption would work. And work it did. Robots definitely had a place in this world.

"Are you able to you converse while running?" Christopher asked.

"Yes, of course. You used the word converse in the place of talk. An homage to your friend James I presume?"

"Yes, I hadn't thought about it but I guess so. Sorry for the dumb question. Anyway, I have not asked but I am quite curious. I understand why George's journal was there at the Farm but how did *James'* journal end up there if he has yet to return?"

"That *is* a good question."

"And?"

"And I do not have the answer, only a guess."

"What is your—" Just then the two robots, in order to keep step with Analog, jumped over a rather large rock and then landed with a bit of a jolt to Christopher. He was amazed at the height of their vertical leap but quickly regained his bearings and finished his question.

"—guess?"

Analog turned to face Christopher, his pace never slowing and said, "I am of the opinion that one or possibly two bots that have interacted with James may have left that material. Who they are and why they chose to leave it is unclear. Perhaps we will learn more when we arrive at the *Union* compound."

As Christopher was digesting this thought Analog added, "We may not like what we see."

"What does *that* mean?!"

Analog did not answer. He had already learned what it meant to ask a rhetorical question.

The dichotomy of *Good vs Evil*

"What actually ***is*** "*OSS*?" asked Christopher.

"Not too long ago that is a question which I would have cautioned you about asking. You would have been at risk speaking of *OSS* in the presence of bots." Analog said this with a clear admonishing tone. Christopher is aware that there remains a stigma with the clashing forces of *OSS* and the *Union* which Analog has yet to fully explain.

"You haven't answered my question." Christopher stated firmly.

"No I have not." Analog replied.

"Well?" Christopher prompted.

"You will learn in time. Suffice it to say that regardless of your first impressions of the Farm it *is* the safest place for a human to be on this planet."

Christopher thought that he had an idea where Analog was going with his comment.

"And the *Union* compound?" Christopher asked.

"The very worst."

Christopher now had an inkling of who the good guys were and who the bad guys might be but distinguishing between the two at this time was about as clear as a watercolor painting left out in the rain.

Abandoned

Analog, Christopher and the two guard bots had arrived within throwing distance of the *Union* compound. All was eerily quiet.

"This seems too easy. Do you think it is a trap?" Christopher asked.

"The fact that there are no bots to be seen does not indicate that a trap has been laid. Furthermore a *trap* is not necessary for us to *be* trapped."

"Say what? That makes no sense to me."

"The bots which inhabit the *Union* compound have no knowledge of my, shall we say 'abilities.' They will not view us a threat. It is more likely that they would have come *at* us to engage in direct combat than to allow us to get this far on our own. Something, perhaps *everything*, is not right."

"Hmm," grunted Christopher.

"I concur," stated Analog. "I am of the opinion that the compound may well have been abandoned. Only something of great consequence would have caused that to happen."

"Yeah? And what might that something be?"

Analog's reply was concise yet cryptic.

"Converging forces."

"And what exactly does *that* mean?"

"If I were to say a 'war of the worlds,' would *that* give you a clearer picture?"

"Crystal," replied Christopher.

"We must enter the compound and look about."

Christopher wrinkled his face and asked, "Why? If it is abandoned what do you hope to find?"

"That is a simple deduction. If the *Union* bots are not *here*, then *where* did they go? And why?"

Christopher felt stupid. "Oh yeah, that makes perfect sense. Let's go look around."

Analog and Christopher entered the *Union* compound each heading in a different direction. The two guard bots remained "parked" outside or at least that's how Christopher saw it. It seemed like the old west to him where you tie your horses up outside before heading into the saloon. Silly thought but that's what Christopher did when he was nervous, entertain silly thoughts.

What now

"You were right."

Analog did not comment.

"About the *Union* compound being abandoned I mean." Christopher paused. He was standing with Analog and the two guard bots outside the compound. It is the middle of the day and the sun is blazing high in the sky. There is no breeze to offer an alternative to the oppressive heat. Christopher wipes his forehead with his shirt sleeve. Analog still has not responded but continues to look to the horizon, scanning for --- what?

"I get the impression that you are not happy about the fact that the *Union* robots are gone."

"Happy?" Analog turned to face Christopher. "No, I am not happy."

"Why not? Doesn't that mean that they have given up?" Christopher's glass is half full.

"The *Union* bots *have* not, and *will* not, *give up*. What concerns me greatly about them not being here is—"

"Is what?" Christopher prompted.

"Is that it means that they are going to be somewhere *else*."

"I get that. And this somewhere else might be worse?"

"*Worse?* That would be an understatement."

"Oh, okay. Not good." Christopher dropped his head with resignation. "What now? Do you have any idea where they may have gone?"

Analog was no longer staring at the horizon. Christopher wrinkled his face. Now Analog was staring intently at the ground. Christopher walked up next to Analog and looked down. All he saw was hard packed ground with a fine layer of dust.

"What *are* you looking at?" Christopher asked. He was kneeling down now, his face much closer to the ground. It was there that he saw them. There were a vague impression of prints left behind by the feet of the robots. The prints were barely discernible to Christopher but apparently the remaining heat signature residue from these prints were like flashing lights to Analog.

"Let's go." Analog declared.

"We are going to *follow* them?" Christopher asked.

"We have no alternative. They are presumably going to the same place where we are going with the unfortunate circumstance that they will have arrived first."

"I understand." Christopher had no other comment. He went directly to where the two guard bots were standing with the travel basket made ready for his arrival. He lowered himself into place and in moments they were off, racing in the direction of where the banging noises had once sounded day and night. Christopher thought to himself that the *silence* emanating from that place was far louder than the banging noises could ever have been. An ominous precursor to their visit to be sure.

The concept of "next"

During the course of their journey Analog attempted to wax philosophical when he made the comment, "Bots have no common conception of "*next*." As *you* perceive it."

"I don't understand."

"Bots exist in the present. *Only* in the present. Dates on a calendar are only numbers on a spreadsheet. Past dates are not "*then*" and future dates are not "*when*." They are both only *not* "*now*." Once you understand this premise, then you can begin to conceive of all that is missing in a bot's existence. If there is no sense of *then*, then there are no memories. And if there is no *when*, then there is nothing ever to look forward to."

"But the bots have cognizance of what has happened before and are aware of those things that have been planned for the future. I am correct in saying this?"

"Certainly."

"Well then, why are these not *memories* if they can be recalled?"

"I don't know. I have searched for these answers but have come up with only this void of missing pieces. Once again, these pieces of what has happened before and plans of what are yet to come are just cells on a spreadsheet. There is no *dimension*. It is all just *flat*. One does not look forward or backward. There is only the function of looking down at the page. There is *always* only *now*. And *now* seems to last *forever*."

"Wow. That's big."

"Big?"

"It's a lot to consider. A lot to um, comprehend."

"You have no idea."

Choosing a path

"We have a choice to make."

Analog had stopped so suddenly that the travel basket was swinging back and forth as the two guard bots had stopped as well. Christopher shook his head to clear it and to gather his bearings.

"Give me a heads-up next tine about a sudden stop, okay?"

"My apologies. This caught me by surprise." Analog had a look of concern masking his face.

"What *possibly* could have surprised *you?!*" Christopher said this with a mixture of curiosity and trepidation.

"See there?" Analog was pointing to the ground. Both guard bots and Christopher looked hard at the ground. The two guard bots reacted with concern. All Christopher could see was an array of scuff marks in the shape of a "Y."

Analog could see that Christopher was struggling to understand the implication of the image to which he was pointing so he explained, "There are now *two* sets of prints. Leading in *different* directions."

Christopher was quick to ask, "Is one direction more concerning than the other?"

"You have asked the right question. The prints leading in that direction will take us to the place of the banging noises."

"And the other?" Christopher prompted.

"The other will take us to the Transport."

"There is a *transport?!*" Christopher exclaimed with incredulity.

"Yes." Analog was stoic in his response.

"Why have you not told me before now?! Where does it go? Why do *you* even *need* one?!"

"It is a transport designed for bots, not humans. The speed it attains is--. Suffice it to say that your chances of survival were you to attempt to board it are minimal."

"Where does it go?" Christopher asked again.

"The destination of the Transport is the true nature of my concern."

"Why is that?" Christopher asked, still seeking the elusive answer.

"The Transport exists for one reason, to deliver bots to *OSS*. Bots like these two here." Analog pointed to the two guard bots. "NOT *Union* bots. How they have come to know of the Transport and their obvious decision to go there is of utmost concern to the safety of the planet."

The gravity of Analog's message and the weight of responsibility on their shoulders is not lost on Christopher. "So we must go that way."

"Yes. And we must do all that we can to save *OSS*. At *ANY* cost."

Soon the place of the banging noises was fading in the distance as the trek to the Transport was now full under way. Christopher had images running through his head of what he might expect to see. They were all futuristic takes of flying cars and floating islands of mercantile trade. These were just nonsense notions from his childhood of what the world might look like in the future. He was about to learn that the reality of the future was not what the dreamers of yesteryear had envisioned.

The FM Transport

As the group continued on towards their new destination Christopher pressed Analog for information on the transport system which, as described in his own terminology, *'whisked robots away'* to *OSS*. Analog has already forbidden Christopher to attempt to use it from a safety standpoint but Christopher feels the need to see it for himself before he will accept Analog's statement as fact.

Analog explains to Christopher that the transport system is a simple pulley system, something that he should appreciate, whereby a bot is secured to a harness and then is 'whisked away' at a speed of just over 7 miles per *second*. The cautionary measure in this system that Analog keeps trying to impart to Christopher is that bots are engineered with tolerances designed to withstand pressures that would rip a human in half. Christopher still maintained that he wanted to see the system for himself thinking that *surely* there must be a way. Although he is a computer programmer (not an engineer) he believes that he has enough practical knowledge to find a way to make it work for himself to ride. In his mind seeing *OSS* for himself is the only logical next step to preserving a future for humans on this planet.

Christopher now recalls Analog telling him that there was a large body of water situated in close proximity to where *OSS* could be found but it was too far from them at this point for the human eye to see. Christopher's curiosity was now piqued by the fact that Analog had felt it important to mention that the body of water in the area where *OSS* could be found was actually a *freshwater* lake. That was of particular interest as it implied a *need* for such a thing.

A Sign

The group is still a few miles away from the transport when they come upon a perimeter of chain link fencing with coiled barbed wire at the top.

"Look!" Christopher shouted.

Analog stopped so the guard bots stopped as well.

"I see the fence. It is of no matter."

Christopher had already come to the same conclusion. The fence was not still standing so it did not represent a barrier but rather just an inconvenience. Where there had once been a gate with a guard hut there was now only balled up and twisted wire. A wide and inviting opening indicated that it was clear sailing ahead. Analog wanted to move on but Christopher halted him once again.

"Look there! What's that?"

Christopher tumbled out of the travel basket unceremoniously but was quickly on his feet and running to the piece of fencing to which he had pointed. Tethered to the fence at would have been a height of about 5 feet was a metal sign. It was about 2 feet high and 4 feet across. The sign featured bold black characters printed on a simple white background. The sign is weathered and barely legible as it is badly bent and covered with dust however there is something that shows through and catches Christopher's eye. He walks over to the sign and uses his shirt sleeve to wipe away years of dust and dirt thrown at it by the shifting desert winds. This single piece of civility looks very much out of place in the stark environment through which they have traveled.

It was immediately obvious that this sign was created by human hands. Both the message and the style were from another time. It was a time that Christopher recognized. That was not the only thing that looked familiar. There was a name printed on that sign which spoke to him in code.

Christopher turned to Analog eagerly and exclaimed, "This sign is a *sign!*"

Analog genuflected as he responded, "Christopher, I am heartened to say that *you* have a keen sense of the obvious." He said then as an aside, "I have been waiting quite a while to find the right moment to use that expression."

Christopher barked a laugh at that and then said, "What I mean is that this sign is a symbol for something else, a—portent if you will. It's a clue, perhaps the answer to a riddle that has been hiding in plain sight all along."

"Portent, a sign of what is to come I understand. Everything else? You lost me." Christopher was noticing that Analog was now speaking more and more like people Christopher had known and left behind when he entered his travel cocoon.

"Look at what this says," said Christopher, pointing at the sign.

The first line of the sign read: *The* Frank Morgan *Transport System.*

Analog nodded his head acknowledging what he read but taking it only at face value.

Christopher said, "Let me explain. This transport system may have been *built* by robots but it was *designed* by a human. A man. A man *I know*. Correction, a man I *knew*. He would have died nearly a hundred years ago."

"Was this transport system one of the great designs of his time?" queried Analog.

Christopher let out a laugh that could only be considered a bellow. "Hell no! The contraption which you have described to me sounds like something between a ski lift and a clothesline! But it's functional and I guess that's all that matters."

Analog pointed to the sign. "You have not wiped away the dust from the bottom portion."

"I don't need to. I think I know what it says."

"Is it bad form for a bot to be curious?" asked Analog.

"How about we wait until we come back this way. I believe that it will have more meaning for you then. Deal?"

"Deal." Analog pointed at Christopher and gave him a wink.

Christopher groaned. This *AI* parroting human expressions thing was becoming borderline silly.

The evil that robots do

"Is it much further?" Christopher inquired, weariness causing him to mumble his words.

"The Transport is on the other side of this rise." replied Analog.

Christopher nodded as he felt the momentum of their pace begin to slow. As they summitted the top of the rise they were met with an incredible vista spread out before them. They had reached the valley of the desert with what appeared to be parched land stretched out before them for hundreds, perhaps thousands of miles. And while there was a mountain range with the promise of green fields in the distance to define the horizon it was now obvious to Christopher why such a high-speed transport system for robots was even necessary.

As they began to make their way down the other side of the rise Christopher suddenly realized that there was movement down near the transport system. Their destination was still too far away for any of the images to be clear in Christopher's limited human eyesight but Analog was having no difficulty.

"Christopher, I believe we have just discovered another missing piece of the puzzle. *Two* of them to be exact."

Christopher craned his neck and squinted his eyes to see what Analog was seeing but to no avail. Just then Analog commanded loudly to Christopher, *"Hang on!"*

Christopher hesitated for only a moment as there was something in Analog's tone which compelled him to comply. Christopher held on for dear life as Analog began to run at a rate of speed which Christopher would have thought absolutely impossible. The two guard bots began to fall behind the pace being set by Analog. As the transport system loomed ever closer it was now becoming clear to Christopher what Analog had seen from the rise.

"Oh my God," said Christopher. This came out as only a whisper.

Analog running ahead was now just a blur. The two guard bots with Christopher situated between them were lagging far behind. It is only now that Christopher is being subjected to the jostling about which occurs when both robots are no longer running in synch. There is an obvious difference in their measured pace. It is enough to notice but thankfully not enough to dump their human cargo.

Christopher could now make out the figures clustered around the starting point of the transport system. He sees three men. As they continue to get closer he thinks to himself, no, that's not right. *Two* of them are robots who appear to be assisting a male human on to a transport harness. *Wait! That's not right either. 'Assisting'* cannot be the right word. They are *'forcibly'* attaching the man to the harness! The large metal hook of the harness which is designed to affix neatly into the back of a robot is now being *plunged* into the skin and bones of the male human's back. The man howls in obvious pain.

"What the *HELL* is that robot *DOING?!*" Christopher cries out, knowing at this point that it is too late to save this man from an unthinkable death.

Christopher looks over to the other robot who, although he appears to be just standing and watching, has his own part to play in this Shakespearean tragedy. Christopher doesn't scold himself this time for assigning gender to a robot. That piece of angst is far behind him now. What he sees is nearly beyond comprehension. The other robot is holding onto the "reins" of two other captive humans who are screaming and straining to be free. They are reaching out their arms hopelessly to the man who has been impaled on the transport hook. Their urgent leanings are no match for the incredible power of their robot master.

The two humans being held in place by the robot are a woman and a child. Christopher can only surmise that these two and the impaled man are linked in life. The woman is losing her life partner, the child his father.

Just then a shrill whine rises up into the air and Christopher's gaze is drawn once more to the man who is now dangling helplessly from the hook on the pulley apparatus. The two robots have now stepped back and away as the transport system seems to be ramping up kinetic energy for a launch.

Christopher's eyes fall on the area surrounding the man. Below him there is a varied collection of human body parts strewn about as well as a growing pool of blood. It was more blood than Christopher had ever seen in his life.

The whine stopped. Now a staccato grating sound like a fingernail gliding along a guitar string can be heard. And then, in the blink of an eye, the transport hook was gone. And with it only a portion of the male human. Christopher did not actually *see* the departure of the hook mechanism. It happened too fast for the human eye and the human brain working in concert to fathom. It was not unlike the experience of a deer fixed in the headlights of an approaching car with the deer being *incapable* of doing the math required to comprehend that the vehicle containing those lights will be *in its space* in mere *seconds*. Nothing in their natural world moves at such a speed.

The male human that had been attached to the hook of the transport system had exploded into the air when the transport hook shot away on its journey. A mist of blood hung in the air forming a cloud of red as chunks of the man littered the ground in a dissembled array of body parts. The robots that have sent this human to his death are sheathed in his remains as well as those of several others. It was difficult to determine how many had gone before him.

The sound of the woman and child screaming and crying punctuated the surreal quiet of the desert land surrounding them. There was a distinct low-pitched whine to the pulley system as it did just what Analog had claimed. It *'whisked away'* the rider from one end of the transport to the other hundreds, maybe thousands, of miles away.

Just then a new sound troubled Christopher's ears. It was at first recognizable and then wholly out of place. It was the sound of *laughter*.

But the laughter sounded wrong, not just for the context in which it was being heard but in the actual tone and timbre. It sounded-- *recorded*. And it was. The robots had recorded human laughter (they had no capacity to make this sound on their own) and were activating the sound when it seemed appropriate to the moment.

This scene was like a sitcom from hell. Send a man to his death hanging from a meat hook. *Canned laughter*. The emotional fraught reaction of a mother and child to the loss of their loved one. *More canned laughter*. There was even a moment in which Christopher was able to discern when the hook containing the human had actually reached its destination as there was an echo of laughter *not* initiated by the two robots in front of him.

That is when the two robots stopped and looked at one another confirming for Christopher that this could only mean that there was at least one other robot at the receiving end of this transport system reacting to what had been sent his (or her?) way.

To think that there was a third robot accomplice at the receiving end was almost too horrific to consider.

The whine of the pulley system now escalates and a chunk of meat, the last remaining portion of the man's torso, returns from its deadly roundtrip journey. The robots examine the bloody remains on the hook. They look at each other like misbehaving children and then once again—a burst of incongruous laughter that is *not* their own.

The two robots have not acknowledged the presence of Analog heading towards them. It is of no consequence to them. There is no accountability for their actions. Within the range of their limited *AI* capacity, they are doing no wrong.

Mother and child are both sobbing uncontrollably. The two robots look from one to the other as though seeking a consensus. Apparently a decision has been made and one of the robots reaches out to grab the child. The mother screams in anguish. The canned laughter sounds again and is then repeated as an echo from the robot stationed at the other end of the transport system preparing for the next rider to delight them in this torturous playtime game they have created.

One robot carries the screaming child to the transport pulley while the other holds the mother in place. Both mother and child are fighting with all the strength they can muster to free themselves from the robots but it is to no avail. Their fates have been sealed as these robots are exceedingly aware that they have supreme power over these human lives.

"Tell them to STOP!" Christopher screams to Analog who he fears will not reach them in time.

Christopher is lunging forward in a vain attempt to vacate his travel basket and rush to the aid of mother and child. His efforts are being prevented by the viselike grip the two guard bots have placed on his arms. They have been charged with his safety and will not allow him to join in the fray. Analog hears in Christopher's voice a message deeper than just the command to stop. It is the plaintive cry to save that which is most precious in this universe. *Life.*

"STOP!" Analog commands the robot.

Analog appears to be too far away to be of any consequence. The robot looks back at him with no expression. These are *Union* worker robots who were never given a face so no expression is possible. Their ability to see and hear is not immediately obvious as they are also without eyes and ears. There is no mouthpiece either. Not even a visual display. Still the two robots give their full attention to Analog for perhaps a moment or two, perhaps in an effort to give false hope and then, more laughter.

The robot at the transport system which is holding the kicking and screaming child has every intention of hanging it on the hook of the pulley system and sending it on its way. The mother is frantic. The child is now discolored with the bruising inflicted upon him in his fight to free himself of the powerful clutches of the robot. It seems as if it is too late now for Analog to help. The child is about to be impaled. Christopher cries out in despair.

A huge cloud of dust suddenly spins into the air like a tornado and just like that, defying the laws of physics, Analog is now *there* at the Transport system standing next to the hook where the robot intends to harness the child. Analog instinctively wraps his hand about the neck stem of the robot holding the child. There is no emotion or reaction to this action by the robot. Analog's other hand is encircling the wrist of the robot holding the child. In what seems like slow motion, the metal that makes up the robot's wrist is now bending out of shape and the robot is slowly losing its grip. Finally the child falls to the ground.

Now the two robots are facing each other. Analog gives the robot a stern look of reproach. The other robot gives only a blank look in return. Analog senses what he must do and begins to tighten his grip around the neck stem of the other robot. All robots are created equal. Or so they were programmed to believe. Analog, however, is light years apart in design, technology and capability. Analog's *AI* ability is at a level that is well beyond the dreams of his inventors. And yet, he still is just a machine.

The grip which Analog has on the robot's neck stem is slowly tightening and the crunch under his hand becomes more prominent. If the robot had eyes they would be popping out of his head about now. The neck stem is becoming thinner from the squeeze and the functions of the robot have begun to succumb to Analog's grip as one by one they are shutting down. A river of blue fluid is now flowing over Analog's hand and forearm. Only a few seconds later and the obvious happens. The head of the robot pops cleanly off of its body. Christopher lets out an involuntary chortle thinking to himself that the only thing missing from this death comedy was the actual sound of the POP!

During the time that Analog was literally squeezing the "life" out of the robot which had held of the child, the other robot reacted by abandoning the mother and rushing to his friend's aid. The robot came at Analog in full battle mode, unleashing its full fury on him. Analog seems to show little to no concern. The robot is grabbing at Analog in places that Christopher assumes must be critical and/or vulnerable spots to a robot. Whatever it was attempting to do is clearly having no effect. Christopher breathes a sigh of relief.

When the robot that Analog had been "choking" fell to the ground after being separated from his head Analog was left with only a crushed neck stem still in hand. Analog turned his attention now to the robot who was trying to do him harm. The alloys with which Analog was crafted and the design of his skeletal structure were unknown to all other robots on this planet. They were essentially powerless against a robot the likes of Analog. Still this relentless robot tugged and pulled and battered him with everything it had.

The time of 'enough is enough' had been reached. Analog grasped the robot's shoulder with his left hand and then drove his right hand forcefully through the protective shell protecting its chest. The incredible barrier that kept these robots safe from all other adversaries seemed to yield easily to the colliding force of the metals inherent in Analog's fingers. Dissimilar metals never meant to interact were now engaged in a super-accelerated galvanic corrosion. The exterior of this robot was showing hyper advanced "rusting" in real time.

If only the look of '*surprise*' could have been afforded to this robot it would have shown how impossible it was to be believed what was happening in this moment. Analog's right hand moved about expertly in the chest cavity of the robot. In mere seconds of exploration his fingers curled around the mechanism that was the beating heart of this robot. With a measured and deliberate action Analog proceeded to crush this soft machine replicate.

All robots bleed blue. This robot's chest was now heaving this crystal blue substance from all orifices. Analog pulled his hands away from the robot and it toppled to the ground. Moments later it was "lifeless."

Run... Away

The words *"you saved us"* were on the tip of Christopher's tongue when a familiar whine could be heard once again in the still air. The *Union* robot that was at the other end of the pulley system, the one that had been sending back the remains of the victims and joining in the fun with recorded laughter as each one arrived, was making the journey to where Analog and Christopher now stood with the mother and child and the two now destroyed *Union* robots. There was no doubt in Christopher's mind of what lay in store for this robot upon its arrival. It had participated in the incomprehensible pure joyful evilness of the slaughter of innocent humans. The genius of *AI* had now risen to the lowest point of mankind's evolution. Murder for the sake of gratification.

Christopher and Analog watched for nearly an hour as the *Union* robot approached. Its body was almost at a 45-degree angle to the ground from the speed at which it was traveling. Both man and robot stood their ground at the receiving end of the transport system as each assumed that Analog was the dominant robot and would make short work of this third member of the *Union* robot death squad.

Before the transport system had even come to a halt the *Union* robot used the momentum of the swinging hook to launch itself forward. There was something decidedly different about the actions of this robot. This robot was on a *mission*. It ignored Christopher and Analog completely as it landed with momentum and continued running at full speed. It looked back only once before disappearing into the dust being churned up from its own feet.

"What the hell was that all about?" Christopher exclaimed, pointing to the trail of dust. "Should you go after it? It's heading for the place of the banging noises!"

Before Analog could respond the shrill whine of the FM Transport spooled up once again. Christopher and Analog looked at each other incredulously. *'What the hell?!'* Christopher mouthed silently. There was *another Union* robot?! That wasn't *possible*. The numbers did not add up. Both turned their heads back to the transport waiting for the ominous arrival of the next robot.

Suddenly Analog had a puzzled look on his face which quickly turned to one of consternation as he made the statement, "That simply can't be. That is-- impossible."

"*What* can't be?" asked Christopher. "*What* is impossible?"

The Pirate

"*We* are not... *safe*."

These were the last words spoken before the final passenger on the transport system appeared. Christopher was puzzled by what Analog had said but had little time to process as this next robot flung itself from the transport system and went directly for Analog in a flurry of rage. The 'spectator' in Christopher thought to himself of the upcoming battle, *'This is going to be good.'*

Analog did not relish what he would need to do to take this robot out of commission but it was absolutely necessary to the wellbeing of humans. These *Union* robots had become nothing more than killing machines. Analog resigned himself to the routine actions of what would come next but—

Something was-- *different*.

Something was-- *wrong*.

This was *not* a *Union* robot.

Christopher had come quickly to the same conclusion. The first thing that caught his eye was *the clothing. Robots do not wear clothing*. This one *did*. The clothing was loose, spartan and non-gender specific which made sense as all robots Christopher had come in contact were, he thought anyway, of male gender. *This* robot, however, appeared to be two unique and improbable if not impossible things. It was *female*. And--- it was *human*.

Christopher narrowed in on her face. She seemed to be wearing some type of apparatus on her face. No, it seemed to be actually *surgically* implanted on her face. It was an eyepiece similar to night vision technology of Christopher's time. There was a ferocity to her movements and a fierce resolve in her actions. This female human robot meant harm. Christopher gave her a name. It was the first thing that came to mind. She was—"the pirate."

A Weaponized Tool

This was *not* a *Union* robot. Of that Analog was certain. His unique ability to "learn" human emotions was working *against* him now, allowing "fear" to creep in. Too late he noticed that this *unusual* robot, this *female* unusual robot which was almost upon him had something secured in hiding behind its back.

What---?

Analog put the pieces together quickly and knew immediately that he was now in grave danger. Once this robot unveiled what she was hiding, Analog realized at once that this highly specialized piece of equipment could *only* have come from *OSS*. It was there that this human robot must have discovered and *stolen* this item which it threatened now to yield as a weapon.

The item was an industrial cutting tool designed for one purpose only, to cut into, or apart, a robot. *Any* robot. This robot seemed to *know* its purpose which *frightened* Analog even more.

"What the hell is that?!" Christopher shouted. When he said this, it was unclear if he was referring to the female robot or the cutting tool.

Analog heard him but could not react as his *own* safety was now at risk. Analog originated from *OSS* and it was there that he would go if ever there was need of repair. Due to the incredible density of his exterior shell a cutting tool of immense intensity was required. Conventional weapons would have little to no effect on Analog. *This* cutting tool, however, could be used on him like a knife through butter.

A One-Eyed Jack named Joni

Christopher saw the troubled reaction in Analog's face even though it was only a flicker of a display. Did he also sense *fear*? The approaching female robot, which was decidedly more *human* than robot, had a look on her face of fury immersed with overbearing confidence. This was *the* "pirate robot" freed from decades of imprisonment.

Her name was *Joni* and her freedom would come at the cost of all she came in contact with, in her thirst for revenge. She came at Analog with an unbridled fierceness which he was unprepared for. Analog was neither soldier nor warrior.

Analog's primary defense was his ability to outwit his opponent.

Joni's primary offense was a ravenous desire to kill and destroy.

Advantage Joni.

The Color of Uncertainty

The strike of the cutting tool came out of nowhere.

Several things happened at once. Joni charged and then swung the cutting tool viciously at Analog. There were screams in the air. These came from the mother and child. Christopher's mouth opened but nothing came out. Just then Analog's left arm fell to the ground like a tree limb severed cleanly by a chainsaw. He staggered backward, reacting to the injury which the pirate robot had inflicted upon him. Blood spurted freely from the wound.

There was an expectation from all present that she would just finish Analog off with this deathly weapon brandished in her hands. But what happened next shocked both Christopher *and* Joni, causing them to freeze in place. Joni's head swiveled from side to side as she attempted to process what she was seeing. Something clicked in her brain and whatever her puzzlement was had been resolved.

Joni's eyebrows narrowed as her one good eye took it all in and then inexplicably she took off running with the cutting tool still in hand. Joni was out of sight in mere seconds.

Analog was on his knees. His right hand was attempting to quash the flow of blood from the open wound. His severed arm was still moving though unconnected now from his body. Christopher had no words, and was frozen in place, overwhelmed by what he was seeing. All robots bleed blue. Analog had lost an arm and was bleeding badly. He was not, however, bleeding *blue*.

Analog was somehow, impossibly--, bleeding *red*.

In this moment Christopher was stuck with the need for an answer to this anomaly above the need to render aid.

"You're—*human?*" Christopher asked, knowing he was unprepared for the answer.

"*Almost...* human." Analog responded.

Christopher is mesmerized by the sight of this blood, *red like his own*, pouring out from the wound suffered by his robot friend.

"Can you—*die?*" Christopher asked this question rhetorically, once again the answer already predetermined in his own mind. What Analog said truly surprised him.

"I don't-- know. I have always believed myself to be invincible. I have had more fear of living *forever* than of dying."

These words hang about in Christopher's mind for only a few seconds before he snaps back to the reality of the moment and Analog's obvious need of medical attention.

"What can we do? To—*save* you?" Christopher knew of no other way to phrase the question.

"I must go to *OSS*. That is where I was created. It is the only place where I can be treated."

Christopher took note of the fact that Analog's voice was faltering. The injury was serious. He had after all lost a limb. Christopher looked from Analog's severed arm to the transport system which seemingly offered the only method of reaching *OSS*. Could Analog survive a ride on the transport? Was his injury *repairable*? Or was *operable* the correct term?

Christopher had no desire to place Analog in more jeopardy than was necessary. Perhaps he could go to *OSS* and bring back what was needed to save him. The question was, *what* was needed? What *is* Analog anyway? *Robot*? Human? *Hybrid*? Christopher's answer to himself got him moving with purpose once again.

Analog was, *is*... his *friend*.

Soon Christopher would learn that he was also his *brother*.

Saving Lives

Christopher was walking about the transport system effecting different poses in an effort to determine how to mount and ride the damn thing should it come to that. He felt eyes watching him and turned to glance in the direction of the mother and child who were huddled in the sanctuary of a shadow. It was a thin shadow cast from the large terminal pillar which served as the eastern landing point of the transport system. The two had no option but to stay where they were moving only in accordance with the movement of the shadow from the terminal pillar as the sun crossed the sky. They had a blanket wrapped about them as an additional layer of protection from the sun's harmful rays. The blanket would be essential to them later to provide warmth at night.

As he met the mother's eyes Christopher felt that the first and *only* consideration for him was to return mother and child to their rightful place at the Farm with the other humans where their safety and well-being could be assured. However, he also must contend with the fact that Analog was very badly injured. The result of the injury which Analog had sustained meant that *he* now must visit *OSS*. There was a new urgency to the visit now as he understood that it was *only* there at *OSS* where life-sustaining measures for Analog could be taken. If the bleeding could not be stopped Analog would surely perish. The thought of a robot "bleeding out" had never occurred to Christopher but now it had become front of mind.

Christopher was torn between two absolutes. It was absolutely necessary that he find a way to get Analog to *OSS*. It was also absolutely necessary to find a way to return mother and child to the Farm. It was a math problem to work out how best to resolve both issues. He struggled with the quandary that neither could be *sacrificed* for the other. Christopher also understood that mother and child could *only* be saved with the support of Analog. He now realized that there was no other alternative than to put the concerns of Analog *first*. Like the horrific moment in an airplane losing altitude with an uncertainty of the outcome where a parent must *first* place the oxygen mask over his/her own face before doing the same for the child.

Christopher did his very best to give assurances to both mother and child that he and a *recovering* Analog would return from *OSS* to take them back to the Farm. Despite the language barrier they seemed to understand that Analog *must* be attended to first. Somehow they knew that without the help of Analog to provide food and water for the journey that there was no way they could survive the long and demanding walk back to the Farm. Staying here though, exposed to the brutal heat of the midday sun, could also be a death sentence.

That was when the simplest of ideas smacked Christopher right in the face. As he was sharing his thoughts, Analog was transmitting them in real time to the guard bots. Their allegiance to Analog was evident as they seemed hesitant to leave his side. To guarantee that the two bots would do exactly as he wished, Analog then altered his transmission to them as an *order*. An order, as all robots knew, *must* be obeyed.

Christopher motioned to mother and child to come join him as he stood in between the two guard bots. He quickly demonstrated how the travel basket was used and encouraged them to take his place. Mother and child were soon safely tucked away into the travel basket. Their gratitude for not being left to die was shown as trust in their eyes.

Christopher began walking back to the transport system to ponder again about the possibility of him as a passenger on this hellish ride. Just then he heard something he had not heard for quite some time. It was a voice. A *human* voice.

"Da!"

It was the mother. Speaking out loud.

"Da!" she said again. She was holding her blanket out to Christopher.

The language amongst the humans at the Farm had diminished greatly over the years. There was very limited vocal interaction and none from the robots who farmed them. Also there was an assumed fear that the robots would punish the humans if they were to speak amongst themselves. This was actually true *only* with *Union* robots but most humans were unable to discern the difference. Still though, this woman had raised her voice, and her blanket, to make clear to Christopher of her offer.

Humans had few possessions of their own in this world. Even balanced with the fact that he had helped to save her and her child's life this was still a truly incredible and wholly unexpected gift. Christopher accepted the blanket gratefully for two reasons, one because he wanted to make it to the other end of this transport system as intact as possible. The other was to show her that he had faith in what he was doing to return the precious blanket to her.

Confident that mother and child were nestled safely in the travel basket Christopher turned to Analog and said, "Give the word."

Although unnecessary Analog looked to the two guard bots and said aloud, "Go."

The two guard bots departed immediately, running in unison in the direction of the Farm with their precious cargo hanging in a balanced sway between them. Christopher turned to watch but soon lost sight of them as they disappeared over the horizon.

Ticket to Ride

Christopher motioned for Analog to come to the pulley system so he could help to affix the hook to his back for the trip to *OSS*.

Analog waved him off and said, "No."

"But you must! You will *die* if you don't get help!" Christopher insisted.

"Yes, I am damaged from my injury but I will need *your* help when I get there," Analog said.

"But I *can't* go," Christopher cried hopelessly. "You said so yourself. Plus, we all saw what happened to the other people that were put on this thing. You were right all along. There's no way that a human body can sustain forces like that put upon them."

Christopher paused for a moment before stating the inevitable. "We know that *I* can't go and if *you* don't go, I guess it means that it all ends here. This is where we *both* die. Right here in the middle of nowhere. Amongst all this--" Christopher almost said "detritus" as he spread his arms out with his hands indicating the bloodied remains of the humans and the twisted parts of the robots. He did not finish his comment. There were no words which could adequately bestow honor upon the humans who died at this place.

"I have an idea," said a visibly weakened but nevertheless staunchly focused Analog. "I will show you." Analog had kneeled down into a crouch. This was only the second time that Christopher had ever seen Analog, or *any* robot for that matter, *not* in a standing position. It looked wrong. *Very* wrong. As Analog got up he was a bit wobbly. Christopher was quick to come to his aid.

"Thank you for that simple kindness." Analog said. Christopher sensed a wetness in his eyes. He would never have dreamed that he could look upon a robot as a friend. Now it seemed that he saw Analog as his brother. In that moment he knew that he would give his life for him.

Christopher and Analog walked over to the hook and pulley of the transport system. Analog was leaning on Christopher as they moved along now accepting the support of a human. They were careful to step over the human remains as a measure of respect.

Analog, despite his injury, helped Christopher to fashion a makeshift gondola. After explaining how the transport system worked, that there were two hooks on the system and that one hook was always the offset of the other, he had explained further, "Bots prefer simple machines. This is a simple mechanism that trades one end with the other. There is balance throughout the journey. Although it works most efficiently when there are two riders, that is not necessary for the system to operate. What I am proposing is that we marry the two hooks into a gondola that will safely support your body."

Christopher had raised his eyebrows at this suggestion in disbelief to which Analog had replied, "We will of course *test* it first."

"But what about the speed? I can't possibly endure the forces that will be in place at those speeds."

"Two things will be at play which will slow this system down sufficiently to allow you safe passage. The first is by simply bringing the two hooks together. This will create an increased amount of drag on the system which will inversely result in decreased velocity."

Christopher nodded his head. He was no engineer but it sounded logical. "And the second?"

"I will be monitoring the speed of the cable with the assistance of these otherwise useless bots."

Christopher looked down at the ruined and immobile *Union* robots and then back to Analog.

"I'm afraid I don't understand."

"I initially had considered using *my* hand as a brake on the cable."

"That's *crazy!* Your hand would be superheated to some ungodly temperature. How can you be sure that the alloys of your hand can sustain such heat?" Christopher was showing true concern for his friend.

"I *can't* which is why I have determined that these bots will assist in that activity. I will use *my* hand only as a brake caliper." Pointing at the 'dead' *Union* robots, Analog continued by saying, "I will use *their hands* as the brake pads."

"That's ingenious!" Christopher exclaimed. He looked again at the ruined robots and back to Analog. "It won't bother you to, um, use them as *spare parts*?"

"Not at all. It will be their *redemption*." Christopher nodded, liking the idea more and more. Analog continued. "When you reach the western terminal you will need to dismantle the 'gondola' and then send back only one of the hooks for me."

Christopher was about to ask if Analog would be able to make the trip with his injury seeming to worsen by the minute but discarded the thought because there really was no alternative.

Once the two had completed the task of constructing a 'gondola,' Christopher climbed aboard unsteadily. It was not at all comfortable and quite precarious to say the least. The possibility of a fractured pelvis from the turbulence of the metal hook, not to mention the potential for multiple broken bones during the journey was of grave concern but it was a risk he knew he would have to take. The blanket would serve as his saddle on this runaway train.

Christopher removed his shirt and then ripped it into long pieces of fabric so that he could tie himself to the gondola as an extra measure of safety. The loose ends would be his 'reins' he told himself although he knew that he actually would have absolutely no control over this bucking wild horse. Christopher could only hope that Analog was being sincere when he claimed that he had considered every possible scenario of their plan. Was he capable of telling a white lie to make Christopher feel less frightened?

Too late now. This plan was a "GO."

Christopher was beginning to get himself oriented in the makeshift gondola when he heard Analog say, "Wait. I have something for you."

Christopher saw that Analog was holding something out for him. "What is *that?*"

"What does it look like?"

"It *looks* like a helmet."

"It *is* a helmet."

"Where did you find that?"

"Not find, make. I *made* this helmet for you. For your safety."

"But how—" And then it donned on Christopher of what he was seeing. This was once the *head* of a *Union* robot. Analog had essentially scooped out all of the interior mechanisms leaving only the protective shell which could now be used-- as a helmet. Christopher, placing safety over disgust, placed the "helmet" over his head. It fit in an oddly comforting way.

"Thank you."

"Your welcome."

A quiet moment skated by as the two resumed what each was doing before Analog spoke again, this time softly, "Christopher, I have a favor to ask."

Christopher turned his neck to meet Analog's gaze and said, "Sure. Anything."

"Please *return*. I don't wish to spend forever *here*."

Christopher took a moment to allow the gravity of what Analog had just said to paint a picture in his mind. It was bleak and colored with only the gray shades of loneliness. "You have my word." Christopher said and then added with emotion, "As a *friend*."

The high-pitched whine of the rollup of kinetic energy was now in the air cutting off a reply from Analog. Of course nothing more needed to be said. Just then Christopher felt the sudden jolting pull of the tension in the cable and *off* he went.

The smell and burn of heated metal soon permeated the air surrounding Analog as the detached hand of a *Union* robot was held fast to the cable by his grip. The robot hand was glowing red as the friction of the cable ever so slowly melted through its palm. Analog held steady, preparing to discard the first robot hand when necessary and replace it with another. The journey to the other end of the transport system normally took less than an hour. This trip, at a far slower speed, took almost *four* hours. Analog never wavered.

The whine of the transport system cut off suddenly and silence fell over the desert once again. Analog waited stoically for the single hook to return as planned. It could take an hour. It might take forever. All he could do was wait.

The hook returned. Showing neither relief nor enthusiasm, Analog simply moved to the hook to ready himself for attachment. Inside however, there was an immense joy and gratitude the likes of which he had never before experienced. This was a truly human reaction so he felt guilty keeping it to himself. He would share this feeling later with

Christopher. For now he would simply maneuver himself onto the hook and activate the system. An hour from now, after an arduous journey on the transport system, he would rejoin his friend and then the two would be off to meet the great and powerful *OSS*.

Moment of LUCID-ity

The man waiting to greet Analog at the other end of the system was nervous and pacing. Christopher's concern for Analog's wellbeing had only intensified as he was forced to endure the hour-long wait for the hook to be sent to Analog and then, with any luck, return an hour later *with* him. Analog was clearly not doing well but he did not complain as he worked himself free from the hook. Christopher gave him a compulsive hug. His intentions were good but he feared that he may have done some inadvertent damage.

Christopher had been concerned that they might not know where to go once they arrived but Analog had assured him that they would find their way upon arrival. Now they were here and it was obvious that they should follow a well-worn path of yellowish bricks which lead in only direction. A large building hugged the horizon. Dominating the space in the courtyard out front were several sculptures (still standing and reaching to the sky) which must have seemed "futuristic" in their time.

Christopher and Analog walked the path leading to the courtyard careful to watch for uneven bricks which threatened to trip them up. As they were passing the sculptures a grouping of three-foot tall freestanding letters carved from aluminum caught Christopher's eye. The letters spelled the word, "LUCID."

Christopher pointed to the letters and asked, "What is that about?"

"Previous occupant," replied Analog.

Christopher nodded his head and they continued on.

"A purveyor of dreams." added Analog.

"What does *that* mean?" asked Christopher. There was no reply. A smaller group of letters, formed in italics which read "*Technologies*" was passed by and ignored. The other building nearby once housed *NRG* Dynamics. Little does Analog know that his robot heart and brain are powered by the ever-reliable *Regalis* crystal which the *NRG* group had developed.

The building to which they were now heading was in ruins. Christopher's heart sank as they grew closer and the truth of the situation began to sink in. There would be no salvation for Analog here. Not in the remains of this destroyed building that looked like it had come head-to-head with a tornado and lost badly. For some odd reason though Analog seemed undeterred by the appearance of the building.

Christopher felt compelled to ask. "Are you not seeing what I'm seeing?"

Analog looked about at first not understanding the nature of Christopher's concern. Then he pointed at the ruined building and said, "Are you referring to this?"

"Yes!" exclaimed Christopher.

Analog managed a smile and then said, "This," he spread his one remaining arm in a wide arc, "is what you would say is for 'public view.' We are going to the *business end* of this building. Around the back." He motioned for Christopher to follow him as he left the comfort of the yellow bricks for a descent down a rather steep hill to what appeared to be a loading dock at first glance but was actually the true "front" of the building. It was designed like a bunker, built to withstand anything that Man or Mother Nature could throw at it. Christopher's fears began to subside as they drew closer.

Before reaching the massive entrance to the building, Christopher touched the robot on the shoulder and said, "Analog, before we go inside, I have a few questions. What *is* this place? And what should I expect when we go *inside*? Any surprises that I need to prepare for?"

Analog smiled at Christopher's displayed wariness. The building, although only a single story above ground level, was still the closest thing that Christopher had come to of the world of his past since he had arrived on this planet. The expectations needed to be lowered for him so that their time here would be well spent. With Analog's injury plaguing him and the murderous pirate robot on the loose they had no time to waste.

"There are no *people* here if that is what you are asking." Analog considered adding the word "now" when thinking of Joni's recent presence here. His concern that there might yet be another kept him silent.

"No, of course not," agreed Christopher, saddened by the fact that this crazy dream of his that they would walk into a science facility populated by engineers and the like was just that, a crazy dream.

As they made their way to the back "front" entrance Analog proceeded to explain how *this* particular place was perceived by the robots on the planet. He shared that there was an almost mystical quality that had been attributed to this building over the years. As the *AI* capabilities in the robot population advanced so did their need for an answer to their existence. To some factions of robots *OSS* had become the bedrock of their belief system. For all intent and purpose, this building might be their *church,* and the sole inhabitant, their *creator*.

Christopher accepted all this with a wry smile. Who was he to question the possibility of a robot world establishing their own religion?

Emerald City

Man and robot have now arrived at the vestibule of the building. This is also an unmanned security checkpoint. A door opens and a beam of high intensity light is directed at Analog. Christopher attempts to enter the vestibule as well but the door closes in response thereby preventing his entry. He steps back, the door opens once more and the beam of light is once again directed at Analog.

"I believe that the invitation is only for me."

"Yeah, looks that way," agrees Christopher.

Analog steps into the vestibule and immediately there are several different light sources passing over and around him each scanning every inch of his body. The lights turn red and then the multiple beams are focused into one pinpoint of light, drawn to the area of the robot's missing arm. Analog stood patiently even as the lights blinked off and the room went dark. A door leading into the building opened then inviting Analog to step inside. He and Christopher were now worlds apart.

Christopher steps up to the vestibule, nervous that he will not be "*invited*" in. His fears are promptly allayed as a beam of light reaches out to him, the door opens and he is encouraged to step forward. Once the door had closed behind him he was immediately bathed in light. The scan of his body was brief with a spectrum of lights dancing all around him. Suddenly the colored lights all went white and shown only on the item which he was holding. It would have made way more sense for Analog to have been carrying this item. After all, it was *Analog's* arm.

Worry creeped into Christopher's mind as he thought to himself that he might be tagged as an adversary. After what seemed an eternity the lights were extinguished, the room went dark and then another door opened. Christopher stepped through the opening and was now able to join Analog in the lobby of the building.

Chrostopher was exasperated. He turned to Analog and said, "That was something wasn't it?"

Analog cocked his head and rolled his eyes before replying, "Yes, that was some-thing."

"You're mocking me. Come on, let's go do what we came here to do."

As the two venture through the halls of the seemingly vacant building each has their own thoughts in mind in anticipation of what awaits them at the end of their journey. Analog is expecting to find a robot of incredible size and computing power. Christopher is expecting something quite similar although in his view it will not be a robot per se. He is anticipating that they will enter a very large room housing a supercomputer the size of a house. They share relatively the same idea. A controlling unit for all things living or robotic. Both are right. And both are wrong. What they discover will surprise and amaze them both.

The Man behind the Curtain

The two move through the interior halls of the building passing room after room of engineering and fabrication equipment. The more of this that Christopher sees the more convinced he is that this building, whatever it may have been before, is now or at least has been recently, a robot factory. He is uncertain if that thought is comforting or if it scares the hell out of him.

"Why am I not surprised?!" exclaims Christopher as he sees a small room set off to the side with two partially drawn emerald-green floor length curtains. Christopher walks over and pokes his head in briefly to see a set of antiquated controls which appeared to be more movie prop than functional. There is a man standing there still and lifelike. It is a mannequin placed there for the purpose of putting the men who might come upon it at ease. At best it was an inside joke soon to be played out.

"What is in there? Is it of importance?"

"Only to me," replied Christopher, "only to me."

"Let's move on to the main room. I believe that we have arrived."

The two enter what at first had appeared to be a cavernous room but was in fact only a trick of the light. As though sensing their arrival a sudden swirl of mist enveloped them. There was a coolness to the air and then suddenly it seemed like it was filled with charged particles. The room went dark for a moment and then in the center of the room stood a man bathed in light. It was a grand reveal of a showman who now commanded the room.

As he stood there Christopher was quick to realize that the man, rather than being *bathed* in light was actually *compromised* of light. He was not really there as he appeared. It was only a holographic image of a man. The image was so startlingly real that Christopher wanted to reach out and touch him but he knew that his hand would simply pass through as these were only pixels projected on vapor.

"It is *so* good to see you after all this time!" the man suddenly exclaimed.

Analog glances at Christopher to gauge his reaction as the image is clearly *not* speaking to *him*.

Christopher attempts to calm Analog's wariness by saying, "Analog, behold the Wizard of *OSS*."

The Wizard of OSS

The image turned in Analog's direction and said, "Hello, I am Frank Morgan."

"Hello Frank," replied Analog.

"Please state your name, tell me who is with us today."

Analog shared his name which the image repeated as though cataloging the information. Christopher thought to himself that this type of behavior might have seemed odd if the image were a real person which it was not. Christopher shared his name and there was an instantaneous reaction of joy.

"Christopher, welcome! Will Hector, George and James be joining us today?"

"No, I'm sorry, they will not. Hector and George are deceased." Christopher paused, "and there is a strong indication that James might be as well. We will know when we go to the place of the banging noises."

The image seemed to process the information that had been shared then returned with an appropriate response.

"I have predicted what I believe to be all possible outcomes. You are facing your task *alone*. This is the *least* desirable outcome although I see that you have bonded with an advanced *AI* bot. He is one you can trust. I give you my word. I designed him myself."

"The *creator?!*" gasped Analog.

"Please," said Christopher touching Analog on his only attached arm. "Gifted engineer? Yes. Creator? That is a bit of a stretch."

What Analog does not know is that *OSS* is actually a mispronounced version of OZ. And OZ, the *wizard* of OZ as it were, the man behind the curtain, is none other than Frank Morgan. Frank Morgan, the man at the forefront of *AI* technology over a hundred years ago. Frank Morgan who just so happens to share the name of the actor who portrayed the Wizard of OZ in the movie of the same name. *That* was the inside joke.

Frank Morgan of *AI* engineering fame has built his own 'emerald city' in the shape of a robot computer brain that controls both a vast network of bots as well as a robot 'factory' which continues to soldier on at his behest. The computer brain is doing his bidding by following a loop program that continually issues instruction to reinvent itself in search of the perfect robot being. The *OZ* program, written over a century ago, is constantly learning with humanity as the teacher, attempting to bring balance back to the world with a 50/50 ratio of human to robot making it essential for all to live together as one community.

In the infancy of the OZ program, Frank hand-picked four intrepid space travelers with strong engineering and computer backgrounds to embark on a journey which would one day lead them back to where they started, charged with the challenge of rebuilding a fallen civilization. With any luck they would succeed in giving the world a fresh start and a strong nudge forward.

Although things had not turned out exactly as Frank Morgan would have liked his plan still survived more than he could have imagined. And the men he had chosen, with the exception of Hector who never had a chance, had performed up to his expectations.

Now that Christopher understood this to be only a holograph he began to notice how the 'Frank Morgan' image would ever so slightly tend to bob up and down and back and forth presumably waiting for a prompt or downloading information. This early version of *AI* required a prompt in order to continue. Analog was puzzled by the inactivity. Christopher was not. He could still recall the days when a spinning icon of some sort would appear on the screen while the computer was "*thinking*." How quaint that memory seemed now.

Christopher chose to engage the Frank Morgan image as there was much he needed to know, not the least of which was how to *possibly* locate James and *hopefully* how to save Analog. There were a few other concerns that were clouding his brain that he wished to address first.

"Frank, I don't understand why Hector was murdered if the robots were programmed to understand what to do when a travel cocoon landed."

"Christopher, I wish to be helpful but this is an info program limited to questions only. Please restate your concern as a question."

"Why was Hector murdered by robots if they were programmed to assist?"

"Christopher, I wish to be helpful but—" Christopher sighed and waited impatiently for the response of the hologram to play out. He should have known that this was an antiquated program from an earlier time but he admitted to himself, so was he.

"Are you agitated with the function of the *program*? Or with your friend *Frank*?" asked Analog.

"Neither." Christopher looked over at Analog and said, "The fault lies with me. I should have known better. This is *not* my friend Frank. This is simply a hologram linked to a *very* basic program. It is just a database with a face. The questions need to be simple and direct. I am talking to an encyclopedia, *not* an *AI* interface. Does that make sense?"

"Yes. Yes it does." Analog paused, then added, "Now."

"What do you mean by that?"

"I am aware that there have been a succession of bots who have come to this place and stood where you are standing now to converse with *OSS*. None of those bots, with all of the powerful *AI* that each have contained, was able to either deduce or detect that they were interacting with a *program*. A program far *less* intelligent than themselves."

"What did they think that they were seeing?" asked Christopher, puzzled by what Analog had just shared.

"They believed that they were interacting with a Supreme Being, their Creator if you will."

"Well, they were not *entirely* wrong. Frank Morgan was thought to be one of the leading progenitors of the implantation of *Artificial Intelligence* into mainstream life. But *Supreme Being*? *Creator*? No. That is just silly."

"Christopher. Even robots, *AI* robots specifically, *must* have a belief structure in order to find purpose."

Christopher looked closely at Analog and saw the hope for confirmation in his eyes. He also saw the damage that had been done from the cutting tool that the pirate robot had wielded as a weapon on him. The blood coming from the injury had slowed but not stopped entirely. What came to mind for Christopher was simply this; it looked *life-threatening*. Was death a thing for a robot now? With blood that was red like his own he had to believe that death was a very *real* possibility. Christopher stayed in the moment, placing his thoughts with Analog, showing him his human side, sharing his friendship. He decided that he would neither challenge nor argue Analog's comment.

Christopher turned back to the image of Frank Morgan and changed tactics. He attempted to simplify his message as though he were speaking with a child, albeit a child with the computer memory encompassing the entire span of man's existence on Earth.

"Hector Menendez was in a travel cocoon which landed far from the designated landing zones. Why would his travel cocoon *not* follow the programmed coordinates?" Christopher hoped that this specificity was enough to get a holistic answer from the program. It was immediately obvious that his strategy had worked as the image of Frank Morgan responded.

"The travel cocoons sent from Earth were programmed to seek out high density population centers on the planet where catch nets had been constructed. To answer your question, if the population centers were for any reason to lessen in density the default would be to find the greatest heat signature from gathered living organisms and then to land at a distance deemed to cause no harm."

Christopher turned to Analog. "He foresaw *all* of this. He *planned* for this." Christopher's eyes misted and he began to look off into the distance speaking more to himself now. "Our mission was all a result of his foresight. He placed breadcrumbs along the way for us to find. He did this to be certain that we would end up here. Together. To make plans. To start over."

"I do not understand."

"You see, Frank Morgan was a man, just a man like—" Christopher almost said *'like you or me'* but caught himself. "—any *other* man except that he was gifted with a genius mind capable of foreseeing what our wildest dreams could become if made real."

Analog, stooped over a bit, appearing to be suffering from his wound, but urged Christopher to continue.

"Frank Morgan was a man who embraced technology and supported the evolution of *Artificial Intelligence*. But with all things he was constantly worried about what he called the *ghost in the machine*. Back in the days when there were world wars these ghosts were called *gremlins*. Regardless of what you called them they were always seen as the cause of *unintended* results. The *bad* ones. No one understands how or why these things would happen, which is I suppose why they took on a somewhat mythical reality. That may be something of a contradiction in terms but it is also probably spot on. There is a dark side to everything and that is where the ghost in the machine resides. A bit conceptual but possibly all too real."

Analog displayed a look on his face that Christopher had never seen on the face of a robot. It could only be described as--- *despair*.

"Analog, what is it? What's wrong?!" Christopher rushed to his side thinking that he must be succumbing to his injury and recognizing that the end was near. He was wrong. It was something much worse.

"Christopher, I must tell you. This ghost in the machine. It has a *name*."

"What? What are you talking about?"

"When I entered the building, the lights had a much different effect on me than on you."

"What do you mean?"

"The lights were downloading streams of information. Everything the hologram is telling you I now know as well. The ghost in the machine is no ghost. It has a *name*. Ask Frank." Analog stooped over a bit more weakened by the loss of blood but still managing to point to the hologram actively waiting for the next prompt.

Christopher looked directly at the image of Frank Morgan and asked, "What is the ghost in the machine?"

Frank's image replied with a standard dictionary definition of what *'the ghost in the machine'* reference is which confirmed for Christopher that this was indeed *just* a program. Christopher thought for a moment and then considering the fact that there was a name involved reframed his question.

"Frank, *who* is the ghost in the machine?"

As though he was nothing but a movie screen an incredible flurry of data and images began to appear on the image of Frank Morgan, scrolling past with incredible speed. Christopher was now certain of one thing. He had *finally* asked the right question.

The image of Frank Morgan went dark for a moment and then came back to full detail. His words were hushed as he stated, "The ghost in the machine is Francisco Marconi."

Analog suddenly doubled over in what appeared to be *pain*. Christopher knew that he had to get help for Analog but he was confused by the answer and this issue was also pressing. He spoke to Frank, "But that can't *be*. Francisco Marconi was your *business partner*." The image continued to dance on the screen needing a prompt to continue. Christopher now *had* to know the answer. He rephrased his comment by asking it as a question.

"*How* or *why* is Francisco Marconi the ghost in the machine?"

Frank suddenly unleashed a torrent of responses. The speech was too fast for Christopher to comprehend. Analog however was hearing all of it and reacting to all that was being said. It was the same as the downloaded information he had received earlier. Christopher had no choice but to be patient and allow Frank to continue. After several moments Frank became quiet and Analog appeared drained.

"Analog? I caught only about a fraction of that."

"Christopher. There is much to tell you. Let's begin with the simple revelation that Francisco Marconi is every bit *your* nemesis as he was to Frank Morgan."

"Analog. Francisco Marconi was *human*. He lived in the *same time* as Frank Morgan. I *knew* Francisco Marconi. He must *surely* be dead by now."

Analog appeared to be deep in thought before responding. "Christopher. This Francisco Marconi has done the impossible. He has *survived*."

Christopher responded, "That *is* impossible."

"It is the *spirit* of Francisco Marconi which has survived. As a *ghost* effecting the brain centers of all bots." Analog paused. "Including *mine*."

Now it was Christopher who displayed despair. "What can we do?" asked Christopher hopelessly.

"Apparently Frank Morgan foresaw this as well. A great many things were shared with me regarding Frank Morgan. He has always been the driving force behind the evolution of next level *AI* robotics. He has been instructing bots to keep reinventing and rebuilding themselves to rise above and eradicate all traces of this Francisco Marconi."

"How is that possible? Francisco is not a 'being.' Like Frank he is just a program and probably a very simple program at that."

"There is beauty in simplicity."

"Evil as well." remarked Cristopher. "Analog, tell me please, what was Frank saying?"

Analog was clearly struggling now but rose up to answer. "Francisco Marconi *represents* evil. Hate. Prejudice and bigotry. He may not have embodied those beliefs in his human lifespan but it was his belief and his influence to include those dictates into the *AI* of the robots he designed. Frank refers to this mixture as a 'lethal cocktail'."

Christopher dropped his head as he was hearing this news. It explained so much about the behavior he had seen in so many of the robots, particularly the *Union* robots.

"But" Analog continued, "you should not despair Christopher, for these beliefs are *like the wind*. Take note that these are *Frank's words* mind you, that these beliefs are 'like the wind.' You cannot stop the wind from blowing but you *can* control it. You can block it. You can divert it. You can even channel it in powerful directions which can then be used in positive ways. It is without question that Francisco Marconi is deceased. It is only his misuse of knowledge and power that remains. Christopher, I completely understand your mission now. Why you came *here*. Why the four of you came *back*."

Christopher looked to Analog with hope in his eyes and in his heart. "Yeah?"

"The four of you returned with a mission to put the people of this planet back on course. The skill set of the four of you is what Frank Morgan believed was required to educate, rebuild, replant and renew this planet. Hector was a mechanical engineer, George a civil engineer, James an architect and you Christopher in this new world of computer technology are the most needed of all. You are a computer programmer. You have the ability to "speak" with bots in their language. To give them direction. To give them purpose. To block the wind from the ghost in the machine. Your friends are gone but you're still here. And you Christopher, you can *save* this planet. *And* your *people*."

The Undeniable Truth

All of this was both very sobering and uplifting. There *was* light at the end of the tunnel but the tunnel, and the journey ahead, seemed to be quite long and fraught with danger.

Christopher then asked Frank what he thought to be the best possible question to ask at this time. "How can I get to the place of the banging noises without serious injury *or death* on the transport?"

"I am going with you." Analog said this firmly.

Christopher looked at Analog and stated simply, "I won't argue that point. What I am asking is how can I possibly avoid another encounter with that death trap you call a transport system."

"It was not designed for humans."

"*You* have a keen sense of the obvious." Christopher touched Analog on the chest and said, "I apologize if that sounded mean. I am just nervous and overwhelmed by what we are facing."

"Thank you for saying "we." I have no intention of leaving your side."

"Thank you for that, Analog. You have become a trusted friend."

"Thank you, Christopher. I consider you a friend as well. I have the answer you are seeking."

"What's that?"

"The question you posed to Frank Morgan. About the transport system. Save your breath. It will take a series of questions for you to get to the answer I can share with you now."

"Yeah? What's that?"

"Avoid the transport altogether."

"Thanks Einstein. That is super helpful. I won't die but I won't get any closer to the place of the banging noises either."

"Einstein? I don't underst--."

"Once again, sorry. I am being sarcastic. You don't deserve to be spoken to in that way."

"How is Einstein--?"

"He isn't. Please, just go ahead and tell me what you know."

Analog seemed confused but chose to move on.

"There is no need for you, *or me*, to travel on the transport system. There is a vehicle which has been designed specifically for human use. As I share your body structure it will accommodate me as well. This vehicle will not achieve the speed of the transport system but it will give us the luxury of powered travel beyond the transport."

"Analog, that is great news! Where is this vehicle? Is it far from here?"

"It is not far. I will retrieve it."

"But you are—"

"I am okay. It will be better for me to rest so please allow me to find the vehicle. I am assuming that you still have a few questions for Frank?"

Christopher wondered if there was guilt written on his face. "Yes, yes I do."

"Very well then. I shall meet you outside when you have finished."

"Thank you, Analog. I will meet up with you soon."

Analog turned and left. When Christopher was certain that he was gone he asked one of the most difficult questions he had ever had to ask; could Analog be saved? Or was he going to die? Christopher was fairly certain that Analog already knew the answer to that but he needed to hear it for himself from an impartial source. Christopher asked his question, received his answer and then left to join Analog in the transport vehicle.

Antiquated transport

The vehicle was less than Christopher had expected in this day and age but certainly more than he could have hoped for. It had all the makings of a 90's era minivan. The engine had been replaced with an electric motor. The seats were the same as they must have been over a hundred years ago. There was a great deal of wear and tear but enough padding intact to make for a comfortable ride. This was a bare bones chassis with no body attached. Fortunately, there was a cover to provide sunshade and a makeshift windshield to protect Christopher's eyes from the wind and anything in the air that he might encounter. This vehicle was capable of speeds of more than 100 mph so protection would be needed. Even an errant bug could cause damage at such speeds.

The return trip was proving to be impossible for Analog. He was not doing well. He had come so far on his journey to becoming human-like that he was now in dire need of urgent medical care. The weapon which Joni had used to literally "disarm" Analog had left what was possibly a fatal wound. Clearly, Analog was bleeding out. The transition from robot to human had continued to evolve leaving him more vulnerable than he had ever been since first opening his eyes to this human world.

Analog *will* die. This is what Christopher had learned from the hologram Frank. There was no way of saving him. When the "human" Frank had designed him he had used a sample of his *own* blood. Analog was able to replicate this blood but not at the current rate that he was losing it. After multiple tries of phrasing it incorrectly Christopher had been able to ask the all-important question; was *he* able to give Analog a blood transfusion?

That answer was a definite **no** but it came with a rather odd cryptic comment. After repeated attempts Christopher was unable to glean from "hologram Frank" just exactly what it meant.

The comment was simply, *'There is another...'*

The sun is setting and Christopher is finding it difficult to see. The vehicle is not equipped with lights and the area they are in is nearly dark with only the glow of a crescent moon. Without the aid of Analog's superior eyesight they can go no further this evening. Best to bed down for the night. Christopher needs sleep and Analog needs rest. The jolting ride of the vehicle has not done him any favors on this trip.

"Analog, I need some sleep. Do you mind if we stop for the night?"

"Yes, I understand."

Christopher, purely out of routine, pulled the vehicle over to the side, but the side of "what" he asked himself as there was no actual road to follow.

"Christopher?"

"Yes?"

"There is an undeniable truth which I must share with you now but I believe that you may already know."

Christopher had been dreading this moment. He gave Analog a nod and a knowing glance to make him aware that no more needed to be said. Analog was *dying* and there was nothing either of them could do to change that but-- there was one thing that Christopher could do in an effort to give him a very special send-off.

"Analog. Rest easy my friend while I share with you a wonderful story from a long time ago. It is a story filled with heart and adventure. A story of fantasy and of life. More importantly, this is a story that tells us no matter how different we may think we are; we have more in common than we could ever dream. The story is '*The Wizard of Oz*' and it goes like this—"

Christopher proceeded to tell Analog the story as best he could remember. Analog was absolutely enthralled. He was transported to another world where all things seemed possible. And he laughed a very real, *human* laugh when he heard the part about *'the man behind the curtain'* thinking of the Frank Morgan which Christopher had known and his silly antics. When Christopher finished the story they both knew that they had reached different endings.

The brave must journey alone...

When Christopher awoke the next morning Analog was cold to the touch. He had expired at some time during the night. The two had slept in a curled embrace for shared warmth. Christopher's eyes welled with tears. He would miss his friend. He had never felt more lonely than he did right now.

Christopher got up and looked down at the lifeless body. He wondered if it was appropriate to *bury* Analog being that he was as much robot as he was human. After a few minutes of back-and-forth Christopher had to face the reality that he simply did not have the implements to dig a proper grave. And digging with his hands would take hours and resources he did not have, like water to keep him hydrated in the heat of the sun. All he could do for now was bundle the human/robot into the blanket and place him on the furthest seat back. He kept the thoughts of a decomposing body exposed to the hot sun and circling predatory birds as remote as possible in his brain.

Christopher settled himself into the driver's seat of the vehicle. It was easy to drive but gave little protection from the elements like wind and rain. This morning the sky was clear and the air was crisp. Soon it would be sweltering hot but for now this was perfect traveling conditions. Christopher pressed down on the accelerator pedal urging a bit more speed from the vehicle.

The destination for today was the place of the banging noises. The noises had stopped long before Christopher had returned to this planet but he still believed that there were some mysteries left to be solved at that place. Fortunately, Analog had devised some method of tracking disturbances by sound waves occurring over time that he had used to chart a course to follow. *If* the course was as accurate as Analog had claimed, Christopher would be heading in a similar direction to the Farm as well, which was his ultimate destination. There was life there. *Human* life. It was a place for a new beginning.

The terrain he is traveling on is uneven so Christopher is being jostled about and he wonders if the same is true for the silent cargo he is carrying in the back. As there is no rear-view mirror he is forced to turn his head and crane his neck to check on the bundled up remains of his human/robot friend. 'Relax,' he tells himself, 'he's still there,' so he soldiers on.

Just then his eye catches a reflection of something in the distance. He is careful not to veer too far from his set course but since there was a whole lot of *nothing* out here in this desolate land, when you see *something*, one *must* explore.

Christopher is quick to understand what he is seeing and brings the vehicle to a stop. He steps out and looks first in every direction to be sure that he is alone before moving closer to investigate. What he sees are the tortured remains of the two guard robots which had been charged with returning the mother and child safely to the Farm. Obviously, that has *not* happened.

Mother and child are nowhere to be seen so Christopher immediately assumes the worst. He looks down at what is left of the guard robots. They have been senselessly *carved up* into random pieces by the same cutting torch, now being used as a weapon, which had severed Analog's arm. Christopher thinks to himself that this is the work of a madman. Correction. Mad*woman*. And even though they were robots, just *machines*, it is still a gruesome sight as both had once been-- *alive*.

Christopher looks away, unknowingly in the direction of the place of the banging noises. His concern for the welfare of mother and child hangs in the balance. It is quite possible that they *too* have been murdered by this crazed humanoid robot and that their corpses have been picked apart by predatory animals thereby leaving nothing to find. However, it is *also* possible that the pirate robot has taken them *with* her. Perhaps as a bargaining tool? Or as souvenirs? A twisted mind might do just that. Who knew?

For Christopher, the path of positivity was the one to follow. He found new purpose in the belief that they may still be *alive* and that he may still be able to save them from some horrible fate. Channeling Analog's superlative tracking ability he looked closely at the ground searching for—

There!! Look right there!

Christopher bends down excitedly to prove to himself that what he is seeing is actually really there. It is the barest evidence of tracks made in the ground. Although very slight, with enough concentration he is able to discern that one set of tracks may be that of the female robot. Another set is most likely that of the mother and child, apparently being dragged behind. It is impossible to know from these tracks if they were alive. Or dead.

"Where is "it" going?!" Christopher is refusing to allow the honor of gender to be bestowed upon this monster of a robot. He asks himself this question but he believes that he already knows the answer. It is the place of the banging noises. What business this robot human has there he does not know. The murderous pirate robot has a bit of a head start but if mother and child *are* still alive then that robot might have to contend with them fighting back at her every step of the way. This little bit of hope, this small potential for an advantage, gives Christopher the fortitude to move forward with determination.

Safe.

Christopher is racing across the desert, going so fast that he *almost* misses them. Something in his brain tells him to look left at just the right moment and there they are. Mother and child have been *discarded* in the desert. Christopher knows it is them but at first all he can see are two lumps of color in an otherwise desolate and colorless landscape. He stops the vehicle and runs to them with hope against hope that they are still alive.

Christopher wonders at first why the robot has not killed them but then looks at the situation through the eyes of evil to see how horrific of a death like *this* would be, stranded in the desert with no food, water or shelter. Christopher is beginning to wonder if the ghost of Francisco Marconi has somehow manifested itself in the brain of this *AI*-human pirate robot known decades ago as *Joni*. If that is so, this truly *would* be the ghost in the machine.

Christopher approaches the two abandoned humans with caution thinking this could possibly be a well concealed trap. Suddenly a corner of the blanket rises and he is heartened to see a smile from the face of a young boy displaying trust and relief. Christopher held the child's deep blue eyes for a moment realizing that he saw something in them. Perhaps the soul of a boy who would grow up to be a man of faith and a leader of his people. Christopher kept that thought dear to his heart.

Both mother and child have been through a great ordeal but they seem to understand that Christopher represents their salvation. He touches the cheek of the mother softly and then that of the child. With their eyes fully focused on Christopher he chooses this moment to teach them their first word in English. He smiles gently at them, holds both hands to his heart and says, "Safe."

Christopher was truly surprised when they mimicked him by holding their hands over their hearts and repeat the word, "Safe." It did not *sound* much like *"safe"* but that really didn't matter. They had tried and the sentiment was there. Christopher reached down, picked up the child and then held him in the crook of his arm. He then motioned for the mother to follow him as he headed back to the vehicle. Once there he assisted them in buckling into their seats. He was concerned that the two had probably never before experienced the sensation of traveling in a vehicle or at such a high rate of speed. He took the time to attempt to explain with hand pictures what was about to happen. He finished with the word, 'Safe' and tapped his chest. He prayed that they understood.

Christopher got back in the driver's seat, buckled himself in and off they went. He started out slowly to allow mother and child to acclimate themselves to this new sensation. They seemed to be doing well so he continued to ramp up the speed until they were well on their way to traveling at over 100 mph. They of course had no idea that he was taking them *first* to the place of the banging noises and *not* the Farm. He really felt like he had no other choice. He hoped this would not challenge their trust in him especially given the fact that they may come face to face with the pirate robot yet again. To Christopher that battle seemed inevitable no matter *where* they went. Better to end it now.

During his time at Frank Morgan's building, actually FM Robotics which he was now calling 'the land of *OSS*,' Christopher had learned the ugly truth about the place of the banging noises. He had a mission of salvation to complete there before returning to the Farm. It was his *duty*, perhaps his *destiny*, to perform this one simple act.

Puzzle Pieces

There was plenty of time and space for Christopher to think as he drove across the desert. He ventured back to his earlier thoughts regarding Analog, that he was more *robot* than *human*.

But *was* he?

Christopher was gradually coming to terms with the fact that Analog's blood was actually *human* blood. The thought that Analog had the ability to replicate the blood in his system as needed lead Christopher to believe that Frank's blood was only a *"starter."* Weird analogy, Christopher thinks to himself, but like sourdough bread had the need for a "starter," this was a fairly accurate comparison. So, if this *was* true, then Frank's portion would have been only a small amount. If at all. Suddenly a new thought came to mind. One that seemed far more plausible to answering Christopher's question of '*where* did the initial supply of blood *come* from?'

While this had the potential for being a brain-teaser Christopher is quick to remember the day that he and Frank found themselves alone in the lab late one night. It seemed like such an odd request at the time, when Frank asked him for a liter of blood. *A liter!* And at that hour. Frank was definitely coloring outside the lines. When asked why, Frank had just said, 'someday you'll thank me.' Was he *hiding* something?

That something was clear to Christopher now. As it happened Frank had volunteered himself as well to give blood that night. Was it a coincidence that Analog had been *so* familiar to Chistopher? Was it possible that Analog was the *AI twin* of Frank? Not really a clone, more of a fraternal twin. Had Analog been infused with Frank's *DNA* as well as his blood? The thought was squarely within the realm of possibility, so much so that it now had moved in Christopher's mind to the state of plausibility. It made perfect sense to create an *AI* robot twin in an environment of scientific and corporate corruption. Think about it, who could you trust more than *yourself?!*

So if that was true, Christopher considers, then the giving of his *own* blood that night and the words spoken by the hologram Frank, *"there is another..."* now took on a whole new meaning.

Who is that other one?

Christopher continues on with his journey to the place of the banging noises but now realizes that after he has returned the mother and child to safety he *must* go back to the land of *OSS*. He is wholly convinced that there is someone, albeit a human/robot, there waiting to meet him.

Deafening silence

The three of them, four if you count Analog, had been rocketing across the desert for just over an hour when Cristopher noticed that they were coming to a place where the horizon seemed to fall away. He slowed the vehicle and came to a full stop just before they reached the edge.

Mother and child waited in the vehicle while Christopher got out and walked about, taking in the grandeur of the vista laid out before him. He was looking down into a valley which may have been a majestic lake decades before. Other than the slight whisper of the wind everything was serenely quiet. Christopher imagined for a moment how different it had been back in the days when the banging noises were being made. The entire area was in the shape of a bowl, a canyon perhaps, which must have served as a speaker to amplify the banging noises across the flat plains of the dessert. He considered what it must have been like to be down there at ground zero cocooned within such a cacophony of noise. The banging noises surely would have shattered the eardrums of a human. Now there was nothing but silence. Deafening silence.

'Miles to go before I sleep' was a thought swimming around in Christopher's head as he got back in the vehicle. Christopher was intensely focused as he navigated his way down the treacherous slope to the dry lakebed. *'This is the last mile,'* he said to himself as he now set his sights on what once must have been a massive air hangar. A relic from another time that gave proof to the fact that humans had at one time held sway over this land. There was no activity that he could detect outside of the hangar so he drove ever closer.

Christopher parked just out of sight of the open hangar door. He was terribly uncertain what he might face inside so he motioned for mother and child to stay put in the vehicle. He had parked in full shadow of the building offering them relief from the sun's unrelenting rays. For an extra measure of comfort he placed both hands over his heart. To his surprise they said in unison with him, "Safe."

Robotic revenge

Christopher moved inside the air hangar with tempered alacrity. The first thing he saw as his eyes adjusted to the dim light was a *Union* robot standing in the middle of the hangar and holding the cutting torch aloft for all to see. There was definitely a mystery to unravel here. This was presumably the *same Union* robot which had run away from the transport. How and why had it come into possession of the cutting torch? Where was the *pirate* robot? Had she been *overpowered* by this *Union* robot? Or had she relinquished it to him with some *other* purpose in mind? *That* scenario seemed far more likely.

Christopher watched the scene unfold with increasing trepidation. The *Union* robot was now completely surrounded by the menagerie of less capable robots in the hangar which were determined to bring him to his end. Although they had the numbers on their side, this large group of robots truly did not stand a ghost of a chance against the destructive potential of the cutting torch wielded in the hands of a *Union* robot. Christopher knew this and charged into the hangar with the demise of the *Union* robot thrusting him forward. Purpose was flowing like adrenaline through him now with his nemesis in sight.

Christopher bellowed out a war cry. It was more symbolic than necessary but he felt that a statement was needed. His rallying cry seemed to have had its intended effect as it started to spread like a wave to the others even though they were just robots. It was a fascinating effect, the slow receding echo of a fading sound like the tide pulling away from the shore.

Christopher had a moment to look around at the assemblage of robots as all eyes now stared at him. Represented here was a random collection of robots comprised of what might be every conceivable robotic device ever created. But these robots were no match for this *Union* robot and the unforgiving swath of destruction possible with one swing of the cutting torch. These robotics were primitive at best. Who knew how *long* they had been in service? And how had they even lasted this long? What battery had been invented that could stand such a test of time? Christopher had no answer for that question now but hoped in his heart there would be time to ponder it later.

Just then Christopher heard a shout *(in English!)* which seemed to be directed at *him*!

Proper English no less.

"Strike now, sir! As we planned!"

As if on cue the *Union* robot turned its attention to face Christopher, seemingly prepared to thwart his trickery. The one caught off guard however was Christopher. He had no clue *who* had shouted or *why* they had shouted. All that was certain was that now *he* was the one in the crosshairs of the deadly *Union* robot with the cutting torch. And that was a very bad place to be.

Before Christopher could take any action the room seemed to come *alive*. All of the robotic devices took one step forward, in effect tightening the circle around the *Union* robot. Too late the robot realizes that the trickery is *not* being initiated by Christopher. A multitude of things happened at once, all of them leading to the desired conclusion of the group.

Any possible noises that could made by the robotic devices which made up the circle, from beepers to buzzers to musical notes, was happening now and causing confusion for the *Union* robot. More than that there was the increased timbre of "banging" coming from the robots with the least amount of capability. Christopher covered his ears as the place of the "banging noises" came to life once more.

The other robot, the one that must have shouted earlier and presumably started this targeted assault on the *Union* robot, was now running back and forth, calling out orders and directing the assemblage of robots. This definitely captured the *Union* robot's attention.

Christopher was quick to decipher that this targeted *assault* was actually "the plan."

Colossal, yet harmless "cobots" (collaborative robots once used in the car industry) were positioned at the four compass points surrounding the *Union* robot. The synchronization which they displayed was incredible as each of the four cobots stuck out their single large arm to the now desperate *Union* robot which had somehow lost possession of the cutting tool during the melee and was now pinned down in the center of the circle.

Within a span of time measured only in nanoseconds each arm had attained a secure hold of one of the *Union* robot's appendages. As though this were a ballet the cobots worked in delicate unison to raise their prize gently up into the air. Only when the *Union* robot had been raised above the crowd of assembled menagerie robots did each cobot pull back just enough with their hold to insure that the *Union* robot now had no possible way of struggling free. The robot was spreadeagled, suspended above its captors, and held with precise tension. What came next completely surprised Christopher.

"Douse it!" shouted the unknown robot who somehow spoke English. When seeing the puzzled look on Christopher's face he cupped his hands around his mouth and spoke directly to him with the added comment, "Less messy this way!"

A great cloud of white mist shot out from various places in the room. When seeing the effect it had on the *Union* robot Christopher understood this to be some type of dry ice compound. The *Union* robot showed signs of freezing immediately but that would *not* be what takes this robot out of commission, nor was it intended to. The freezing was done primarily to prevent a shower of blue blood raining down upon them as the cobots, each of them, and in absolute perfect synchronization, yanked free the single appendage each was holding of the *Union* robot's body.

The frozen torso of the robot, sans arms and legs, dropped straight down to the floor with a loud bang which was of course lost in the mix of other banging noises sounding out throughout the cavernous hangar.

Blue robot blood oozed plentifully from each open wound but was just as quickly frozen solid.

"Revenge… is best served cold."

Christopher whirled around to see the robot who had spoken those words. It was a phrase which he had heard James use *many* times. It was from an old movie. As he made eye contact with this robot and then began to peruse the length of his body something suddenly clicked in his brain. There was one distinguishing feature, an "X" cut deeply across his chest, that told Christopher that this robot was not only a *friend* but a robot friend who could be *trusted*.

"Dr. X, I presume?" Christopher extended his hand.

Dr. X shook Christopher's hand and said, "It would appear that I am quite well known on this planet. Might you be Christopher?"

"I am." said Christopher.

"Pleased to make your acquaintance. Pardon me while I take care of some unfinished business."

Christopher watched as the robot he now recognized as Dr. X walked over to the torso of the *Union* robot. He stood over the robot for a moment before looking up to Christopher to say, "It is badly injured and terribly weakened by what we have done to it."

Christopher made a mental note that even *robots* referred to other robots as *"it,"* not willing to grace them with a gender title. He returned his attention to Dr. X and the ailing *Union* robot lying on the floor below.

"Are you saying that this robot is still not, um, *dead?!*"

"Are you willing to take that chance?"

Christopher shook his head no vigorously.

"Look away now," said Dr. X, "if you have a weak stomach."

Dr. X then leaned down and grasped the *Union* robot's cranium in one hand. He might have used both hands but somehow this was a symbolic gesture intended for the gratification of the assembled robots. Their freedom would be regained with the expiration of this devil robot.

As Dr. X slowly exerted incredible pressure upon the head of the *Union* robot a single image came to mind for Christopher. He would be the only one of this group to understand the reference so he did not share it but instead spoke in a whisper to himself, 'he is crushing that robot's skull like one of my drinking buddies would crush an empty beer can.'

When Dr. X stood up the robots all about him began to cheer in their own way. One message was clear to all of them. It was lights out for this *Union* robot as well as it was the end of the reign of terror perpetrated upon this world by the entity known as *The Union*.

Lana vs Joni

Rejoicing had begun but for some reason Christopher was stoic. He felt that something was amiss. The battle for their independence had been almost too easy. There was a missing piece of this puzzle being bandied about in the back of his mind. It had sharp edges and was tearing at the protective layer of comfort he was attempting to give himself. Something evil was still out there and it was staring back at him—with its one good eye.

"They make mistake."

"The pirate!" Christopher whispered harshly to himself.

The one they called the pirate robot strutted into the room and casually retrieved the cutting tool. "That not *me*." She laughed at her own gibe while pointing at the destroyed *Union* robot.

"I know that laugh," said Christopher through gritted teeth, remembering know the laugh he heard at the transport as the humans were tortured and slaughtered. "You are a *monster*. The things you have done are, are—"

"Clever?" jeered Joni.

"I was going to say horrible."

Just then there was movement by all of the robots at once, advancing one step towards Joni. Sensing their movement the cutting torch came immediately to life with an orange-red glow present on the blade itself to demonstrate the power it was generating.

Joni turned and pointed the torch at Dr. X.

"Joni listen." She tapped her head. "Hear you talk." Joni paused then added, "Say pirate coming." Joni was now glaring at the good doctor and seething with rage.

Christopher was listening carefully and doing his best to fill in the blanks for all the words she *wasn't* saying. He surmised that Dr. X must have sent out robotic transmissions, "silent" to all creatures who were not robots. He may have made a critical error in not realizing that the "pirate" was *very much* a robot and had heard these "silent" transmissions loud and clear. This is obviously why she chose to send the *Union* robot in her place. As the sacrificial lamb.

Joni now turned her ire towards Christopher. She pointed the fiery cutting tool and asked, *"Well?"*

"Well, *what?!*" demanded Christopher.

"You no ask for--?" Joni seemed to be searching for a word and couldn't find it.

"Mercy?" offered Christopher.

"AAHHH!!!"

Joni screamed out, infuriated by what she thought was the actions of Christopher trying to belittle her. She waved the cutting torch at Christopher and then made several jabs at the helpless mother and child huddled together under a blanket. Their frightened stares brought on more raucous laughter from Joni. Everyone, and every single "thing," went silent.

The immensity of the hangar made the silence all that more incredible as every human and every robot remained frozen in place, fearful that any movement would draw the ire of this tyrannical pirate robot. Clearly Joni was beginning to enjoy her newfound control over all things living and... operational.

"Quite the wordsmith, aren't you?"

A dark figure stood in the massive opening of the hangar. The bright light outside, casting an angelic grace about this figure, made it difficult to discern who or *what* it might be. Man? Or machine? All attention turned to the newcomer.

"Who are-- you?" demanded Joni. "*What*-- are you?" she asked next, sizing up her new opponent.

"I am what you are," said the figure as it began to move forward into the hangar, advancing purposefully into the light. The figure stopped before it revealed itself fully.

"Come *here*." This from Joni who had yet to make the acquaintance of fear.

Christopher moved over to be with the mother and son. They were now gathered together with the shared courage of not wanting to die at the hand of evil. Meanwhile, Dr. X had spread his arms wide in a vain attempt to demonstrate that all who stood with him were safe.

No one dared to make a sound as this newcomer took another step and light in the hangar now fell upon—*her*.

"YOU!" Joni spat the comment from her mouth. "I *kill* you!"

"Actually," responded the newcomer, "you kill*ed* us *both*." She paused for a moment before adding, "Everett and Frank, Frank mostly, at the behest of the senator's wishes, *and funding*, brought us back."

"Leave me. Stuck. *Forever*." Joni was fuming with rage. "*Fucking bastards!*"

The newcomer addressed the assemblage.

"You will have to forgive my friend here. English is only her second language. As you can see, mostly garbage comes out of that mouth."

There was a shared and frightened silence echoed through the chamber. This newcomer, this *woman*, this *challenger*, was slight in comparison to the bulky frame that was Joni.

This woman was in fact- *petite*.

While Joni was outfitted in the garb of a soldier this woman was wearing a silky blouse tucked into a smart skirt which sharply accentuated the lines of her figure.

A thought popped into Christopher's mind just then, G.I. Jane vs Barbie.

"You. La. Na."

"Close but not quite. Good try. Joni, my name is Lana."

"You bad girl."

Lana laughed and with a wry smile said, "If *you* are the one making that comment, then I can only say that I learned at the feet of the *master*."

Joni was uncertain if she should be angry or take offense to Lana's comment. Anger was her go to choice.

"Joni not dumb."

"I guess I'll just have to take your 'words' for it."

This sarcastic wordplay incensed Joni. She knew condescension when she heard it. Joni quickly advanced towards Lana, cutting the air by sweeping the cutting tool back and forth like a sword.

"Joni has *weapon*!"

Lana remained in place not backing away from Joni's advance.

"What you have?" Joni was attempting to instill fear in Lana by pointing out that she had no weapon with which to fight.

"Oh my!" exclaimed Lana. Then in her best sarcastic tone she said, "It appears I have forgotten my purse!" Lana then patted herself down thereby discovering an object in her left breast pocket. She pulled the object out examining it closely.

"Oh look here, it's my lucky day! I found a pen! Oh, silly me! Who would bring a *pen* to a *swordfight*?"

Joni screamed, "You mock Joni!" She is moving now towards Lana with *purpose*.

Christopher is incredulous that Lana can be so trite in a moment like this. Moments later it will all make sense to him.

Joni is advancing on Lana, furiously swinging away at her with the cutting torch "sword" firmly in hand. Just like in the movies, Lana's death seems to be only moments away when she makes what sounds like yet another superfluous comment.

"Well would you look at that! This "*pen*" doubles as a laser pointer!"

With that comment she then pointed the beam of the laser directly at Joni's *good* eye.

Joni howls in pain. "MY EYE!!!"

"Ah!" Lana exclaims. "It appears that the pen truly *is* mightier than the sword!"

Joni, now blinded from the laser, is sweeping the cutting torch wildly back and forth in vain trying to kill Lana. Unbelievably Lana stands her ground, in effect *allowing* the possibility for that to happen.

"Move out of the way!" yells Christopher. *'Is she crazy?'* he asks himself.

Lana refuses to budge from her spot as the murderous Joni advances upon her. Joni makes an upward swing between Lana's legs which cuts an upside down "V" into Lana's taut skirt. The cutting torch comes within an inch of doing damage. Only a slip of Joni's foot on the slick floor causes her to miss. Lana looks down at her skirt which was now cut open up to her crotch.

"A bit below the belt wouldn't you say?"

That comment lit Joni up. The burning fire in her once "good" eye matched that of the cutting torch as Lana's cutting remarks angered her even more. Suddenly Joni slowed her advance and then she just stopped. A new wave of resolve came to her now. She began to effect a calm and a Zen-like state of focused concentration upon herself. She was no longer blind. She was now *hearing* her opponent and gauging every move. Just then Joni expertly swung the cutting torch in an arc that would effectively cut Lana in half.

Everyone and everything screamed.

Then the impossible happened.

In what seemed like slow motion all assembled watched in disbelief as Lana, *with her outstretched hand,* abruptly *stopped* the power and momentum of Joni's swing of the cutting torch at the apex of its arc. The hum of the torch grew louder as it met the unyielding resistance of Lana's hand. A loud metal noise was heard as the blade of the cutting torch, the strongest substance known to man, snapped and whirled through the air until it became embedded in the concrete floor below.

Joni crumpled to the floor holding her broken arm to her side, a casualty from the sudden stop of the swing. Lana, other than the smoke emitting from the burnt flesh of her hand, appeared unharmed. She stepped up to Joni and then crouched down beside her.

Lana quietly whispered something into Joni's ear.

"What you don't know is that Frank rebuilt you on a *budget*. Or in other words, *I* was built to *last*. *You* were built to *pass*. Your time here on this planet is done."

Joni's eyes widened as she prepared for the blow she knew was coming that would extinguish her life. Lana, however, was giving her plan of action a second thought. She looked over at the mother and child who had already seen and been through too much. Was it fair to them to witness yet another death?

"Sleep." Lana said to them. "She just, she just needs to – sleep."

Lana looked to Christopher for his support. He immediately fashioned a hand picture of his head resting on the pillow of his hands. He of course had no idea if this would work as the mother and child probably had no reference in their world to a night's sleep on a pillow. However just as they had done with the word "safe," the two made the same hand picture and then looked away from Lana as if to send the message, 'do what you must do.'

Lana returned her gaze to Joni who now had only a vacant stare as *both* eyes were now ruined.

"You don't do so well with women, do you?" Lana placed her palm on Joni's chest just above her beating heart and began to press. The protective barrier of metal made an awful sound as it began to give way. Pieces of bone still left intact after the surgery could now be heard as they snapped from the pressure. Blood vessels burst as seams began to tear. The pain must have been excruciating but through it all Joni stubbornly refused to scream.

The *Regalis* crystal which served to power Joni's heart would not fail but the soft machine itself surely would. Moments later, Joni's chest now lay compressed under the incredible power and force yielded by the attractive woman who looked more like an executive secretary than a warrior robot.

Lana stood up and then stepped away from the ruined human/robotic frame which only moments earlier had been Joni, aka the pirate.

Christopher approached her and said, “Am I ever glad that you’re on our side.” He paused before saying, “And—” His words left him.

“And what?” pressed Lana.

“And--,” Christopher replied sheepishly, feeling like a schoolboy nervous in the presence of the prettiest girl in the class. “I must admit that I am very attracted to you.”

“Likewise.” Lana replied with a blush. “Does that mean you’re asking me out on a date?”

Christopher is suddenly flustered. After all that he has been through since his reawakening from decades of sleep, *this* simple question of all things seemed to be the insurmountable challenge.

Lana laughed at his awkwardness and said, “Calm yourself big guy, it’s a yes. And”, Lana made a muscle with her arm and bicep as she said, “I promise to be gentle.”

Both laughed and then Lana went over to console mother and child.

A new testament

In the moments that followed Christopher pulled Dr. X away from the throng and proceeded to share with him all that he had been through and all that he knew of the current situation of the planet. Dr. X was saddened to have to tell Christopher that his friend James had expired but this was not unexpected. Christopher accepted the news and continued on with the business at hand.

“Dr. X, I must go back to the land of *OSS* to see what might be waiting there for me. I will join you,” Christopher did a wave gesture with his arm, “and all the others, at the Farm in the next few days. Can I count on you to get these two *people* back safely?”

Dr. X smiled at the mother and child who were now embracing Christopher on each side. It was not lost on the robot that Christopher had used the term “people.”

“You have my word.”

Dr. X gave a symbolic gesture of making an "X" over his chest with his arms. Christopher was not sure what it meant but given the severity of the nasty looking "X" that had been carved into his chest by an adversary, he believed this sign to be of some great significance. Christopher solemnly gave the sign in return. If a robot could blush then Dr. X just did as he said, "I am honored, sir."

As Christopher went about preparing for his drive back to *OSS*, he looked back to see Dr. X taking control and giving direction to the assembled robot group. Christopher assumed that he had already informed them that they have been released from their captivity. Dr. X was now leading them outside and away from the air hangar which had been their prison for decades. Soon the entirety of the dry lakebed nearby was populated by various forms of robots. They were injured but not beaten.

Once all of them were gathered, Dr. X found a vantage point on the side of the embankment where all could see him. Christopher looked on in awe thinking that this was somehow biblical. Dr. X, like Moses, standing on the mount calling out to his flock of loyal followers.

With hand signals and wireless transmission he was sending the message that they were now to follow him to a place where humans and robots would once again find their way together. There were needs to be met for both. He shared that a new synergy of coexistence could be formed for the betterment of all.

Upon the completion of his message Dr. X collected the mother and child, gave a final nod to Christopher and then began the journey to the Farm. The hordes of freed robots followed in his wake.

Before departing on his own journey Christopher took a moment to reflect upon the lives of his two dear friends, James and Analog. He was no longer questioning why they had to die. He had come to terms with the fact that dying was just a part of living. Both of them had lived a life with meaning. And worth remembering.

Christopher buckled himself into the open-air vehicle and said to himself, "It's time to go meet my twin brother." Dirt flew out from the tires as he pressed the accelerator to the floor. He could not be more excited about this next chapter of his life.

Meet your brother

Returning to the land of *OSS* was a sobering experience for Christopher. So much had happened here that changed the course of events both in his life and for the world. He chose not to look at the discarded remains of the humans which had been subjected to the torture of the *Union* robots. Their evil reign and hold on humanity had passed. He hoped that those lessons would never be forgotten.

As Christopher passed by the aluminum blocks of letters that made up the name "LUCID," he now had a better reference point to call upon. It seems that every great idea was destined to be used for an evil purpose. 'One man's dream is another man's nightmare.' Perhaps that should have been their slogan.

Christopher passed through the security checkpoint at FM Robotics this time without fear. Frank Morgan had made this place his home so now Christopher felt welcome here. It was still hard for Christopher to grasp that this building had once been within the reach of the city map of Los Angeles. He could only imagine what must have happened to the rest of the city now buried under the dust of time.

In the years to come Christopher would seek to learn all that he could about the OZ program. He would not need to revisit the land of *OSS* as he would discover that this new human/robot he was soon to meet was an *AI* of the highest order imbued with the accumulated knowledge of all mankind. This was Frank's life's work. Christopher could only hope that Frank was in a better place now, smiling down on him and finding comfort in knowing that this exceptional human/robot and Christopher were about to become friends at long last.

Christopher knew exactly where to find him. He had of course missed it before, a forest for the trees kind of thing or perhaps hiding in plain sight if you prefer. Christopher stepped into the grand theatre room (as he chose to call it) where Frank Morgan's image had spoken with him and Analog. This, however, was not his destination.

Christopher walked over to the small room with the drawn curtains. He pulled them open and was not surprised to see the mannequin still standing in the same position, immobile as it would seem for all time. That—was about to change.

Christopher walked up to the mannequin, placed his hand on its shoulder and said to him, "I'm sorry. I just didn't know. If you were a snake you could have bitten me!"

Christopher wasn't sure what he should do next so he just did what came naturally to him.

"Hello friend, Frank said that you would be expecting me."

In that instant the mannequin miraculously came to life. He turned to Christopher and said, "I have dreamed of this moment for so many years. I am so happy to finally meet you and honored that you have chosen to call me your friend."

Christopher wasn't quite sure what he had expected but here, in this moment, life once again felt important to him and worth living. He wasn't sure what to do next but the human/robot seemed to know.

"I will need a name," he said.

"Of course," replied Christopher who stopped himself from blurting out the first name that came to mind. He chastised himself for not meeting the moment. This was a special time in history and an equally special birth of the most advanced *AI* being to ever exist. This was a being who shared Christopher's own *blood*. A being who also shared his *DNA*. This would be the one individual with whom Christopher would spend much of his time in the coming years. The one individual in which he would trust and confide in and talk to when he was sad, when he was lonely and when he was filled with the joy of living. That is when the perfect name came to him.

"In the spirit of how my dear friend Analog was named," shared Christopher, "I will call you 'Dialog,' spelled D-I-A-L-O-G."

"Is that word not misspelled? "asked the human/robot upon receiving his first lesson in how humans did not see or think in simple black and white terms. Always in tones of grays.

"It is *your* name and you may spell it *any* way you like. I think spelling it similar to Analog is an honorable choice. Happy Birthday, Dialog. Now let's go to the Farm. We have much to do."

Dialog smiled and said, "Thank you, Christopher. This is my best birthday ever."

The Beginning

Every civilization needs a history. The thoughts and deeds of the travelers, Hector, George, James and Christopher and of the robots that induced change, Josef, Darwin, Analog, Dr. X *and* Dialog would be theirs. The future was once again in their hands and a new city was being built. It was a joint venture with robots and humans. This city had a name that spoke to its past in honor of Hector. It was to be called *New Venezuela*.

Before leaving *OSS* behind Christopher listened one last time to the initial holographic message left for him by his dear friend Frank Morgan.

"Let me be clear. There is one fundamental difference between how my colleague, slash archrival, Francisco and I approached the evolution of AI *in robots. I was always of the belief that robots should remain as robots, that their advanced capabilities would work to serve in tandem with the life cycle of humans, not to replace them. Francisco's work, no matter how frequently he may have denied it publicly and in print, was to recreate man in his own image. To improve upon the original. He was seeking perfection in his craft, which is admirable were it not for the collateral damage that is to be left along the way. It is my prediction, and God help me if I am right, that if his work were to supplant mine that mankind would become the heir apparent* servant *of the robot, or* worse, *nothing more than a* pet *or* farm animal.

This is why I created the mission which you signed on to complete. I handpicked the four of you not only for the skill set you possess but even more so for the humanity in your hearts for your fellow man. You are truly unique in the fact that each of you accepted a mission on faith without full disclosure of the expectations being shared with you. Your service to this country, to this world, may never be rewarded like the heroes of your past but you will know, and I *will know, what you have done.*

This is what you have travelled so many miles and through so many years to hear. Your mission, upon the return to your home planet, is to assess the damage that the development of AI *has done and then work to restore and rebuild what is missing or worse, has been destroyed. I apologize to you for I know that it is unfair to expect so much out of just four men but I have so few resources to draw on at this time. I hope you understand that what I have done is for the sake of the planet and for the preservation of mankind. I can only hope and pray that you will forgive me and that the future you build will be brighter than the one you have left behind.*

At the close of this message I have left instructions for how you may use the interactive portal to ask questions. I have spent a great many hours contemplating what is to be but there is certain to be things that I have gotten wrong or just not imagined. There are keywords throughout these Q & A sessions that will trigger responses and/or comments that I believe that you might not ask but may need to know.

One last comment. Full disclosure here. There is a bit of irony to be found in the fact that I found it necessary *to use* AI *to make this holographic imaging and interactive recording possible but hey, what can I say? I'm only* human. *LOL*

Author's Notes

People often ask, "how do you come up with your ideas for a story"?

Well, it's like this…

Kingdom for a Horse

The Cast of Characters

Black King: Thaddeus Rex / **White King:** Albus (Alan) King
Black Queen: Quinn (Queenie) Rex / **White Queen:** Regina King
Black Bishops: Toni & Joni Bishop (twins) / **White Bishops:** Abbot Clarke, Jonah Priestas
Black Knights: Felicia Black Knight, Kenneth Knight
White Knights: Anthony Templar, Noble Gesture
Black Rooks: Jon Hightower, Cardell Rookwood / **White Rooks:** Richard Castle, Brock Rampart
Black Pawns: Barry, Benjamin, Bennet, Berkeley, Brady, Brandon, Bryson, Burton
White Pawns: Wallace, Walter, Warren, Wendell, Whittaker, William, Wilson, Wyatt

I have had an idea kicking around in my head for a long time that there must be a story to be told of the events of a chess match. Someday, I told myself, I will write that story. Of course I imagined that it would be written in medieval times when Kings and Queens and Knights and the like were prevalent. When I shared this idea with my son and we began to discuss how the story might play out I realized two things that completely altered my approach to the story.

The first was that there was not much challenge in writing about *real* Kings and Queens. There are plenty of those stories to be found. However, if I were to set this in *current* times, now *that* would be interesting. The other consideration was that every match has a story to tell. No two are alike. Two questions now needed to be answered. Do I as the author control the narrative? Or do I allow the story to be played out on its own?

The latter of the two won out. What this meant was that now an *actual* chess match must be played!

Collin and I scheduled a time to sit down and play. Once upon a time, I could beat him but, after he went away to college for engineering and started playing with really smart kids like himself, he moved up to a new level as a player. I found myself in a position where I needed to ask something of him. I said, 'Look, I'm writing a novella, not a short story, so could you maybe take a little longer to beat me? Plus, it should serve to make the story far more interesting.'

So that's how it played out. Of course after we had finished the match he proceeded to share the multiple ways in which he might have beaten me *sooner*. He is quite the competitor!

Which leads me to how he *earned* the title "co-author" for this story. While there is no denying the fact that I did not play the match alone that is not his *only* contribution to this novella. I reached out to him after we had played to ask if he might assist me by chronologically listing each of the moves that were played to serve as a reference tool to keep me on track. Well, he did that and *much, much* more.

What he sent to me was a wealth of material which I began to rely on more and more as I wrote the story. I already had a genesis of the story in my head with the basic character bios and character names tied to each chess piece. Plus, keep in mind, I already knew how the story would end!

In the next few pages please find Collin's additional contributions to the story. There is an "Order of Events" which was the chronology of every move made by every piece in proper sequence. There is also, (his words), a "Kill List", which notates every piece that left the board, and when. Also, by whose hand. These proved to be invaluable reference tools that helped me to "plod" my way through the plot.

There is a view of the board with "starting" positions and "ending" positions of the game pieces. There is also a comprehensive chart overview of which characters had the most impact on the game.

What I had *not* expected was for him to refer to each piece with the character name I had assigned to them. This immediately brought life to the sequence of events as you read through them. I also had not expected him to put his own "take" on the motivation of these characters but it is *definitely* there. The more I read through the "events" as *he* wrote them, the more I began to see the story develop. That was so awesome!

I immediately put my energies into using what he had written to guide the plot line. With the exception of only a few "events'" I used Collin's narrative to craft the plot line. And it works *so* well.

I found Collin's support pieces to be invaluable. Having these to draw from was almost like reading the "book report" before writing the book!

LUCID

This idea came from a conversation I had with Collin about "lucid dreaming", something which was new to me. He explained the concept and I immediately began to think of the possibilities...

However, what *I* thought was just going to be a safe and mild ride soon had a dark side and then one thing just lead to another. I rarely know where my stories are going. I write fast because I too am eager to see what happens!

People Farm

This story could not have turned out more different than my original intention. One of the books I read in my teenage years that really struck a chord in me was *Animal Farm*. That book of course does *not* need a sequel yet I felt compelled to write one. My piece, like the original, would be a novella. I would be clever and call it *People Farm*.

Before starting to write, I felt that it made good sense to reread the original before attempting to move that story forward. So I did. And was I ever in for a surprise! Don't get me wrong. The story still holds up well to this day and is an amazing piece of literature. What I discovered, however, on rereading the book some thirty or forty years later was that it was more political satire than fictional fantasy. Oh sure the animals are still there and they have their individual and unique ways about them befitting the way we might see one were they able to speak. What I soon realized that at that younger age when I last read it, I must have missed the presence of political nuance throughout the book.

Long story short, (which all too often is *not* the case, just saying), since I had fallen in love with my title, I went a completely different direction with the story. At the time I wrote it, there is much talk about how dangerous the influx of *AI (artificial intelligence)* into our culture is becoming to our everyday life and how one day robots might just overtake us and rule the world. What makes the story an interesting read (I think) is that we all assume that is a bad thing...

Order of Events

1. Wendell and Wilson (white pawns) both move first allowing Abbot and Priestas (white bishops) as well as Albus and Regina (white king and queen) ability to move
2. Burton and Barry (black pawns) both move first allowing Rookwood and Hightower (black rooks) ability to move
3. Warren (white pawn) moves up creating a wall of defense with Wallace, Walter, and Wendell (white pawns)
4. Bryson (black pawn) moves up creating a wall of defense with Burton, Brandon, Brady, Berkeley, Bennett, and Benjamin (black pawns)
5. Noble (white knight) moves up past wall of defense
6. Knight (black knight) mirrors Noble's move past wall of defense
7. Whittaker (white pawn) joins alongside Wendell in wall of defense
8. Joni (black bishop) moves forward to back the wall of defense
9. William (white pawn) joins alongside Whittaker in wall of defense, all white pawns are in a chain
10. Brady (black pawn) moves forward
11. Walter (white pawn) moves forward and is in position to take out Barry
12. Quinn (black queen) moves in front of Thaddeus (black king) expecting fight between Barry, Walter, Abbot, Knight, and Warren
13. Noble gets between Barry and Knight
14. Thaddeus moves to his right out from behind Quinn
15. Abbot (white bishop) moves up, sees Barry going to take out Walter
16. Barry takes out Walter
17. Abbot takes out Barry
18. Knight takes out Abbot
19. Warren takes out Knight
20. Noble is the only one in the area
21. Quinn takes out Warren and puts Albus (white king) in check
22. Albus moves out of the way close to the wall of defense
23. Quinn pushes forward alongside Wallace (white pawn) and Rampart (white rook) and puts Albus in check again
24. Albus moves of the way closer to his wall of defense
25. Quinn takes out Noble but is in the path of Priestas (white bishop)
26. Priestas takes out Quinn
27. Bennett (black pawn) and part of the black side wall of defense moves forward to challenge Priestas
28. Priestas backs off

29. Benjamin (black pawn) and part of the black side wall of defense copies Bennett and moves forward to challenge Priestas

30. Priestas backs off again but is now backed by Regina

31. Rookwood follows Bennett and Benjamin's push to challenge Priestas and pushes forward in front of Wallace in attempt to challenge Priestas

32. Wyatt (white pawn) advances to push wall of defense forward

33. Bryson (black pawn) takes a chance and puts himself in a vulnerable position to be taken out by William and Wyatt but is backed by Joni

34. William takes out Bryson

35. If Joni takes out William, Joni will be taken out by Wyatt

36. Joni backs off and joins the other high-ranking people

37. Albus sees Rookwood alone on his side of the field and starts pursuing him even though Rookwood can flee back to his side of the field at any moment

38. Joni moves forward but this time away from William and Wyatt

39. Templar (white knight) advances forward to help back Albus in his attempt to get Rookwood

40. Brandon (black pawn) advances on William knowing he's backed by Black (black knight)

41. Albus gets closer to Rookwood instead of William taking out Brandon

42. Brandon takes out William knowing William is backed by Wyatt

43. Wyatt takes out Brandon

44. Bennett joins alongside Benjamin to take on Wendell

45. Bennett is backed by Joni

46. Wendell takes out Bennett and risks being taken by Joni

47. Joni does nothing

48. Toni (black bishop) sees Whittaker alone and advances to take him out

49. Albus gets closer to Rookwood and blocks Benjamin's path

50. Instead of fleeing, Rookwood sacrifices himself to take out Priestas even though Priestas has been backed by Regina this whole time

51. Regina takes out Rookwood

52. Toni takes out Whittaker

53. Toni sets his sights on taking out Castle (white rook) next

54. Toni does not know Castle is backed by Rampart but Castle knows Toni is after him

55. Regina sets her sights on Hightower (black rook) and advances to take him out

56. Toni takes out Castle

57. Just as planned, Rampart takes out Toni

58. Hightower moves out of Regina's path
59. Wilson (white pawn) advances to take on Burton (black pawn)
60. Hightower moves to other side of Black
61. Regina sees no way to get Hightower now so she sets her sights on Black instead
62. Regina moves across the board next to Black
63. Hightower sees this and backs Black if Regina decides to take him
64. Instead of taking Black and risking her own life, Regina decides to take out Burton (black pawn)
65. Seeing Templar alone, and knowing Black is safe after Regina took Burton down, Hightower moves across the board to try and take down Templar (white knight)
66. Rampart quickly moves to back up Templar
67. Sacrificing himself, Hightower takes out Templar
68. Rampart takes out Hightower
69. Black joins what remains of the black side
70. Seeing a possible opening, Wyatt (white pawn) pushes to the end of the black side to become another queen and gain more power
71. Thaddeus moves forward alongside Berkeley
72. Berkeley has remained next to Thaddeus this whole time
73. Wyatt advances again but knows if he goes further, he'll be taken out by Black
74. Seeing Wyatt's attempt to gain more power, Joni steps into the path of Regina and Rampart in an attempt to take out Wyatt
75. Regina takes out Joni in front of Brady (black pawn)
76. Distressed by the loss of Joni, Thaddeus retreats back behind Berkeley
77. Albus takes out Benjamin and joins alongside Wendell
78. Thaddeus retreats behind Black instead of Berkeley
79. Rampart sees Thaddeus retreating and sees the end is near
80. Watching from afar, Rampart makes a move to hopefully end up near Thaddeus to take him out (foreshadowing)
81. Thaddeus switches back to being behind Berkeley
82. Regina sees what Rampart is doing and decides to join in on taking out Thaddeus but also does not want to lose sight of Wyatt
83. Regina wants Wyatt to have more power and to reach the same status as her so she makes a move to protect him since he'll be taken out by Black if he reaches the end goal and gains power
84. Thaddeus switches back to being behind Black

85. Knowing the consequence of possibly being taken out by Black, Wyatt advances and becomes (Queen) and puts (King) Thaddeus in check

86. Black knows Wyatt is protected by Regina but Black takes out Wyatt to protect Thaddeus

87. Regina takes out Black and puts Thaddeus in check

88. Thaddeus moves out Regina's path and behind what's left of his wall of defense, Berkeley and Brady

89. Seizing the opportunity, Rampart moves across the board

90. Regina and Rampart have Thaddeus in checkmate

Here are the chess moves of this match in sequence:

d4, h5
2. g3, a5
3. c3, g6
4. Na3, Nc6
5. e4, Bh6
6. f4, e6
7. b4, Qe7
8. Nb5, Kd8
9. Ba3, axb4
10. Bxb4, Nxb4
11. cxb4, Qxb4+
12. Kf2, Qb2+
13. Ke3, Qxb5
14. Bxb5, c6
15. Ba4, b5
16. Bb3, Ra3
17. h4, g5
18. fxg5, Bf8
19. Kd3, Bd6
20. Ne2, f6
21. Kc3, fxg5
22. hxg5, c5
23.dxc5, Bb7
24. Kb4, Rxb3+
25. Qxb3, Bxe4
26. Qc3, Bxh1
27. Rxh1, Rh7
28. g4, Rf7
29. Rf8
30. Qxh5, Rf2
31. Re1, Rxe2
32. Rxe2, Ne7
33. g6, Kc7
34. g7, Be5
35. Qxe5+, Kd8
36. Kxb5, Ke8
37. Rf2, Kd8
38. Qg5, Ke8
39. g8=Q+, Nxg8
40. Qxg8+, Ke7
41. Rf7#

White Wins

***Kill Order**

1. Barry takes out Walter .... *page 57*
2. Abbot takes out Barry .... *page 58*
3. Knight takes out Abbot .... *page 58*
4. Warren takes out Knight .... *page 59*
5. Quinn takes out Warren .... *page 60*
6. Quinn takes out Noble .... *page 68*
7. Priestas takes out Quinn .... *page 77*
8. William takes out Bryson .... *page 90*
9. Brandon takes out William .... *page 94*
10. Wyatt takes out Brandon .... *page 98*
11. Wendell takes out Bennett .... *page 109*
12. Rookwood takes out Priestas .... *page 115*
13. Regina takes out Rookwood .... *page 120*
14. Toni takes out Whittaker .... *page 125*
15. Toni takes out Castle .... *page 127*
16. Rampart takes out Toni .... *page 129*
17. Regina takes out Burton .... *page 135*
18. Hightower takes out Templar .... *page 140*
19. Rampart takes out Hightower .... *page 143*
20. Regina takes out Joni .... *page 150*
21. Albus takes out Benjamin .... *page 158*
22. Black takes out Wyatt .... *page 174*
23. Regina takes out Black .... *page 175*
24. Rampart and Regina put Thaddeus in check mate ... *page 191*

*Page numbers have been added to original content.

People left alive

- **White:** Albus (King), Regina (Queen), Rampart (Rook), Wendell (Pawn), Wallace (Pawn), Wilson (Pawn)
- **Black:** Thaddeus (King) *although he lost in checkmate,* Berkely (Pawn), Brady (Pawn)

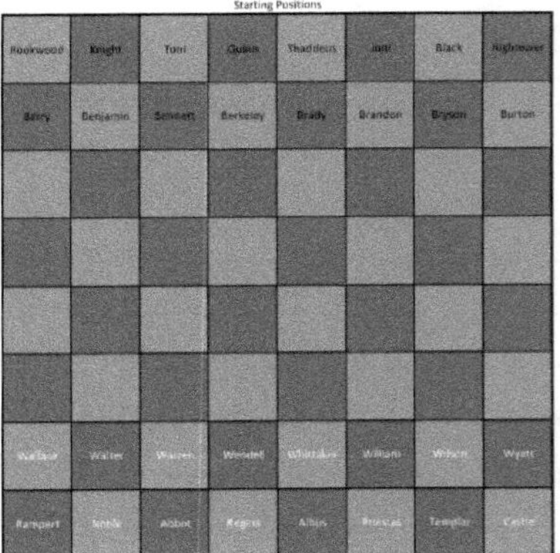

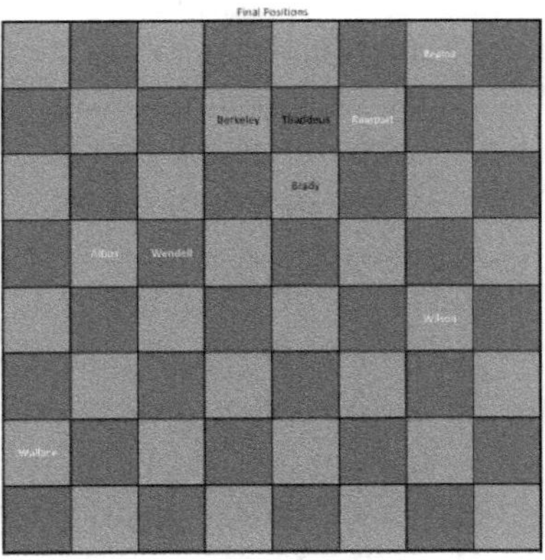

Killer			# of kills	Victim(s)			Killer Killed By		
Name	Side	Position		Name	Side	Position	Name	Side	Position
Abbot	White	Bishop	1	Barry	Black	Pawn	Knight	Black	Knight
Albus	White	King	1	Benjamin	Black	Pawn	-	-	-
Barry	Black	Pawn	1	Walter	White	Pawn	Abbot	White	Bishop
Black	Black	Knight	1	Wyatt	White	Pawn	Regina	White	Queen
Brandon	Black	Pawn	1	William	White	Pawn	Wyatt	White	Pawn
Hightower	Black	Rook	1	Templar	White	Knight	Rampart	White	Rook
Knight	Black	Knight	1	Abbot	White	Bishop	Warren	White	Pawn
Priestas	White	Bishop	1	Quinn	Black	Queen	Rookwood	Black	Rook
Quinn	Black	Queen	2	Warren	White	Pawn	Priestas	White	Bishop
				Noble	White	Knight			
Rampart	White	Rook	2	Toni	Black	Bishop	-	-	-
				Hightower	Black	Rook			
Regina	White	Queen	4	Rookwood	Black	Rook	-	-	-
				Burton	Black	Pawn			
				Joni	Black	Bishop			
				Black	Black	Knight			
Rookwood	Black	Rook	1	Priestas	White	Bishop	Regina	White	Queen
Toni	Black	Bishop	2	Whittaker	White	Pawn	Rampart	White	Rook
				Castle	White	Rook			
Warren	White	Pawn	1	Knight	Black	Knight	Quinn	Black	Queen
Wendell	White	Pawn	1	Bennett	Black	Pawn	-	-	-
William	White	Pawn	1	Bryson	Black	Pawn	Brandon	Black	Pawn
Wyatt	White	Pawn	1	Brandon	Black	Pawn	Black	Black	Knight

Author's Bios

Randall Miller

Known by his friends as Randy, he currently resides in Columbus, Ohio. He enjoys golf, traveling and spending time with family. *Several Possible Conclusions* is his third book. If you are interested in reading more of his work, look for *The Ability to Reason*, a psychological thriller or *Random Samples*, a collection of short stories. He is currently at work on two more books.

Collin Miller

Kingdom for a Horse is Collin's first published work. While he would not consider himself a writer the work he did on helping to put this novella together should not go unnoticed. Collin is a mechanical engineer and currently resides in Seattle, Washington. He is an avid snowboarder. He also enjoys traveling and spending time with his girlfriend Mollie and their four-legged friend Honey.

www.ingramcontent.com/pod-product-compliance
Lightning Source LLC
LaVergne TN
LVHW010553100826
845148LV00014B/2698

* 9 7 9 8 9 8 5 4 9 9 7 6 6 *